THE HIDDEN FALLING

THE HIDDEN OF VROHKARIA

BOOK ONE

KELLY COVE

Cover Design by Incognito Designs

Edited by Kalynn Trammel

Proofread by Magnolia Author Services

Map by @Saumyasvision/Inkarnate

SERIES WARNING

This series is only suitable for those 18+ and contains matters that can be triggering. This is a dark fantasy romance. The world is not kind, nor can be its people, or the main male character. He's an alpha-hole. This is an enemies to lovers story. This series is rough going, but they will have their HEA.... eventually.

For those that would like to go in blind, skip this page. If you have any triggers read the following below. Please note – More may be added with every book.

This series contains, but is not limited to the following below either on page/memories/flashbacks or references. Abuse including child abuse, child sexual assault, murder, graphic violence, torture, death, child death, rape, explicit sex, kidnapping, dubious consent. Harm of the Main female character by the Main male character (Whipping). If you have a specific trigger that is not listed here and would like to check if it is in this book, please feel free to contact me by email at Kellycoveauthor@gmail.com

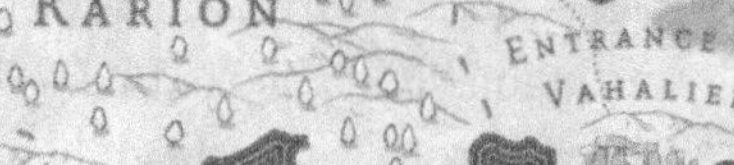
THE DRYLANDS
WOLVORN CASTLE
VOKHEIM KEEP
ALISEON
KARION
ENTRANCE TO VAHALIEL
WITCHES REST

LEGEND
ROUTES
PACK LINES
KEEP
VILLAGE
RUINS
CASTLE

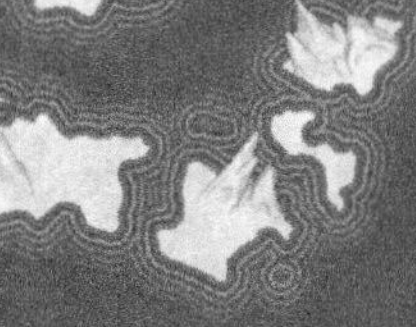

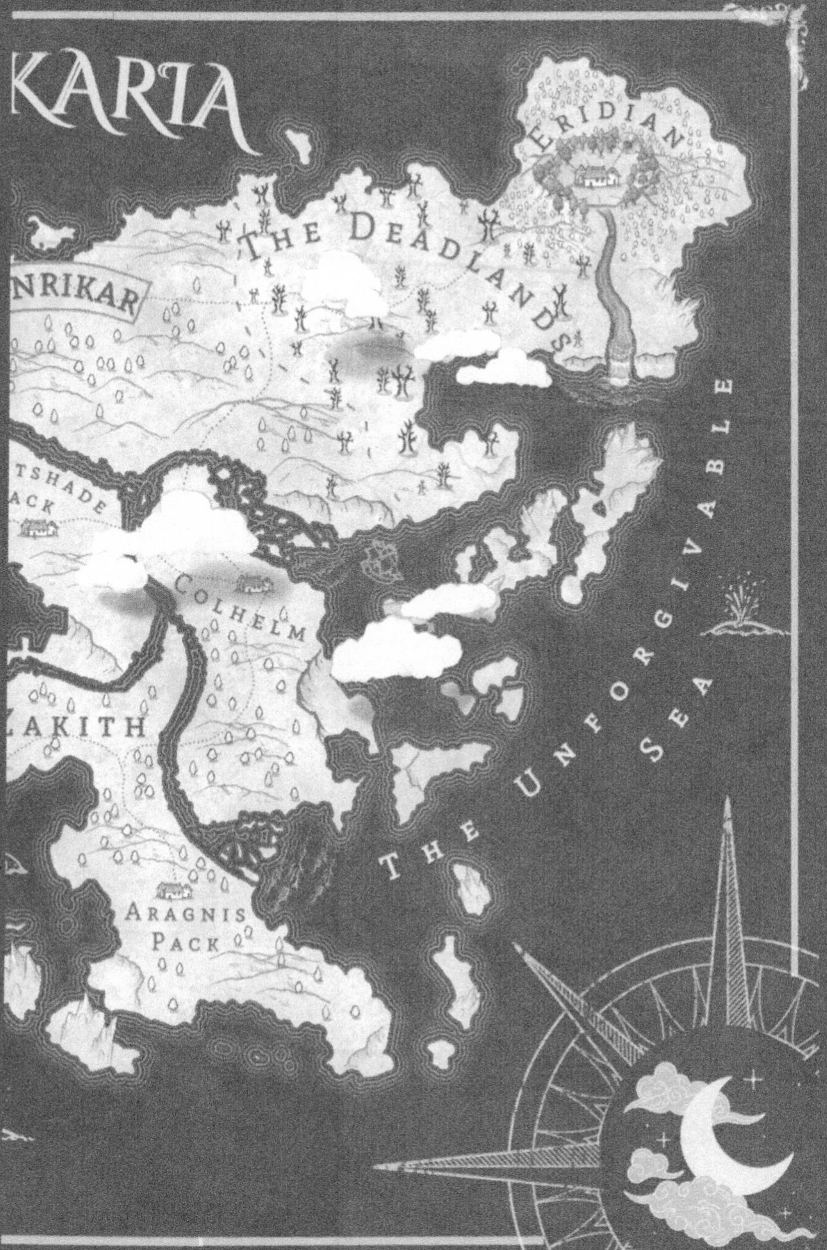

KARIA

ERIDIAN

THE DEADLANDS

NRIKAR

TSHADE
ACK

COLHELM

AKITH

ARAGNIS
PACK

THE UNFORGIVABLE
SEA

For those that raise their hand to the moon
and watch it shine between their fingers.

PROLOGUE

"You can't do this!" the woman screamed, horror written all over her bloodied face. She tried to pull free from the chains wrapped around her wrists. They were attached at the top of two pillars on either side of her, holding her arms stretched wide and dangling her above the ground.

"We already have, Catherine," the man said at the edge of the rounded stone platform beneath her, a smirk upon his face. "This has been planned for some time now. After disposing of the problem that arose, it was easy to guide you where we needed you to be."

"W-what?" Catherine asked, shocked as she trembled from exhaustion and pain. Blood dripped down her wrists where the chains dug into her skin, the steady flow painting splashes of color on the gray stone below her.

"Well... you see, Derrik was getting too close to finding out things he shouldn't. He had to be dealt with swiftly in order for us to proceed with the ritual. A hunting accident was the perfect way to go about it, wouldn't you say?" A slow, satisfied smile spread across his face as he watched the woman jerk in despair.

"No! No, no, no. How could you?" Catherine sobbed, tears dripping down her face. "He did everything for this pack. For his family!" she screamed. "You were his closest friend. He helped you when you needed it, helped you become who you are. And this is how you repay him? Repay us?"

"Yes, well… his sacrifice was needed, as is yours," the man scoffed. He stepped up onto the raised circular stone platform as ancient writing began to glow along its edges. "Don't worry, my dear, it will soon be over."

Catherine frantically tried to free herself from the chains, wrenching her body from side to side and kicking her legs out as the man came closer.

He pulled a blackened blade from beneath his cloak as the hooded figures surrounding the edges of the platform began to chant the language of the old. Catherine's eyes widened as she realized what this was, what was about to happen.

"You have no idea what you are doing," Catherine whispered. "You will plague these lands with creatures that are not meant to be. Creatures that should stay below and never surface. You cannot undo this. Think this through. The lives of so many will be lost over time," Catherine begged, her eyes pleading with his dark stare.

"Not for you to worry, my dear. I think I can handle a few pesky creatures that come out of the below, especially with what you are about to give me." The man laughed, floating up to her so they were now face to face.

The chanting grew louder, the ancient writing glowed brighter with an ominous mix of violet and black, pulsing to the same rhythm as Catherine's heartbeat. The hooded figures raised their arms above their heads, swirls of red extending from their fingertips, flowing toward where Catherine hung.

The man looked over Catherine's face and raised a hand to cup her cheek, almost lovingly. "You were always supposed to choose me, you know," the man murmured. Catherine's eyes hardened at his words, disgust written on her face. "If you had, perhaps this wouldn't have happened, and I would have waited for your replacement instead."

"Don't you dare touch–"

A blade to the throat cut Catherine off, a small whimper escaping her as the man's sadistic smile widened. "Don't worry, I won't be touching anyone anytime soon. I have things I am required to prepare for."

Catherine's body was slowly being drained of energy, exhaustion weighing her down while grief blurred her mind. The feeling of helplessness and what she was about to lose sparked the last of her saddened soul to cry out, moving her lips as if Zahariss herself was speaking.

Catherine's delicate markings begin to appear on her face, curving around from above her eyebrows, trailing around her eyes and down below her cheekbones. The man watched in confusion and awe. He had never seen these markings in person, only read about them in historical texts.

"I curse those who commit wrongs against me and mine," Catherine said in a voice that was not her own. "I curse those who steal what is not freely given to feel pain and suffering over time. I curse these lands until their last days. His hounds will hunt and gather and kill all who did an injustice against the line!" Catherine screamed as a pale colored light shot out of her markings, flying toward the night sky as her life slowly began to fade from her eyes.

"No!" the man roared, his blade slicing through the air and straight through her neck in one swift motion. Blood poured out onto her chest, dripping down her naked body onto the stone below. Her lifeblood began seeping into the lines of the glowing runes, turning their color red.

"Did it work? What's happening?" a deep voice said beneath the cloak he wore, rushing to step onto the platform.

The ground beneath them began to tremble as the man still hovered before the now lifeless woman, her skin taking on a bluish tint. The markings were gone from her delicate face, leaving bloodstained skin the man had wanted for his own.

The platform began to crack beneath him. He looked down as swirls of black smoke flowed toward him almost angrily. He inhaled sharply as the smoke made contact with his skin, breathing through the prickles of pain as he accepted the power of old into his body.

"I suppose we will await the next moon cycle to see if the ritual worked," he replied to the cloaked figure as he looked around the grassy clearing. He breathed deeply, a cruel smile curving his lips as power rushed through him. "Either way, this is a new beginning."

ONE

RHEA

I lean back against the deck railings, relishing another sip of my warm coffee before breathing in the early morning air. Dew and the smell of spring flowers tickle my senses as I tilt my head back toward the rising sun, letting the heat caress my face in a loving touch as I ask the Gods for strength that today will go without a hitch.

I can hear people milling around in front of me, getting ready for the day ahead. Their quiet chatter reaches my ears, but no one approaches me. Not yet. Everyone knows not to unless it is an emergency. If I don't have at least one cup of coffee in me before the day starts, you're more than likely to get your head bitten off. I am one of those people, unfortunately, but it is what it is.

I slow my breathing and try to center myself, willing a calmness I never feel when I'm preparing to pick up someone new to bring back to Eridian. We've been preparing for her arrival since the news came a week ago, and even though it's business as usual for us now, it feels like a shadow clouds my mind this morning.

It happens occasionally, this off feeling, but recently it has been more frequent, and I don't know what to think about that. I even went and spoke to Solvier about it, but he just brushed it off and assured me everything was fine.

I don't feel fine.

I sigh, putting my mug down beside my feet and pulling my ashy-blond hair into a ponytail. The shorter front ends fall lightly into my face, tickling my skin as I walk down the steps of my deck.

I make my way leisurely along the dirt path toward the center of Eridian to the gathering, where most of the pack congregates for meetings or meals. It's a circular clearing between scattered trees with benches that we had hand carved to sit on, and a sunken fire pit in the middle where we cook our meals. With its flattened dirt floor and easy access, we turned it into a place where the pack could gather and just enjoy each other's company.

The path from my home declines a little as I walk. I listen to the birds chirping their morning songs and a few scurries of rabbits in the distance, just enjoying the calmness of the morning.

In the nine years since we've been here, I've never gotten tired of it. The sight, the smells, the feel of this place. It's all precious to me, this life we have made for ourselves.

Our home isn't lavish by any means. It's rugged, but clean, with many cabins and only the necessities we need to survive, but we make it a place where we can safely be and live freely.

The Eridian Forest is truly a beautiful place to live, with flowing rivers and waterfalls cascading down the cliffs that surround us, encasing us within their safety. The life that flows through here energizes me. The rare flowers that only bloom twice a year make you feel awed just by looking at them, knowing not many get to witness them as they glow under the night sky. It never gets old. When you're gifted by its presence, the forest feels like it has a life of its own in ways no one could ever explain. I suppose that may have something to do with Solvier. He always seems to be everywhere at once, though he does protect us after all.

As secluded as we are down in the valley, without his protection we would be overrun by creatures. The ring of lilk trees surrounding our home keeps any unwanted visitors out. But if you go out of that ring, you lose that protection and must fend for yourself in the surrounding Forest.

There are not many dangerous creatures roaming around, but some come from The Deadlands at the top of the smaller cliffs west of us. This is where the rogures come from when they decided to grace us with their presence. They stalk down the slopes in search of prey inside the forest, including us if we don't get to them first.

Rogures are never on their own and only have one thought in their mind, kill. They're beast-like hounds, skin gray and weathered and falling from their body in rotting lumps. Their two sets of teeth make for a nasty bite, but the black, venomous foam dripping from their mouths is the real killer. No one knows where these hounds originally came from, only that they keep coming from somewhere, and they're not slowing down, growing in numbers with every moon cycle.

Edward likes to keep me updated on Vrohkaria's current status with them, amongst other things. Keeping me informed on what's going on outside of Eridian, even if I don't plan on venturing out from here or beyond The Deadlands for any other purpose than to collect someone.

A squeal of laughter draws my attention, and I turn my head to the side, smiling slightly at the sight of some of our pups playing tag while running rings around their moms. It's a heartwarming sight considering what some of these kids have been through. It makes all our hard work worthwhile to see them laughing and their parents' smiling faces as they watch them. It strengthens my need to go get the girl we are about to collect, so she too will be surrounded by this goodness.

Edward's scouts have reported that over the last few days, her beatings and abuse have been getting worse. No one wants to risk waiting any longer, not when Edward knows he can get her out of there and bring her here before irreversible damage is done. Physically anyway. Mentally, that's something else.

I pick up my pace, walking through the blooming scattered trees, pressing a hand to them in thanks for sheltering us. I spot Josie and Danny at the center of the gathering next to the fire pit. Josie has a bucket in her hand, waving her free arm wildly at Danny. I huff at the ridiculousness of the couple arguing over who will go to the river to collect fresh water for the large pot in the fire pit.

"I've fetched it for the last three days. Three, Danny! How is that fair?" Josie growls, her free arm still flailing around.

"I do it all the time. It's doing great things for that gorgeous ass of yours anyway. Why are you complaining?" he asks, looking at her ass as his mud-colored eyes darken with heat.

I roll my eyes. They are always at each other's throats, but it is more out of sexual frustration than anything else. He's clearly in the doghouse again.

I stride forward, making my way through the hand-made wooden benches toward them. "Danny, just fetch the water. Stop getting her all worked up just because she won't suck your dick. It's your own fault," I tell him, stopping in front of them and putting my hands on my hips.

Danny's eyes snap to mine, oblivious to my approach with his focus on Josie's… assets. He makes a small sound, biting his lip to suppress a smile that I know would be there if he didn't.

"Sorry, Rhea," he mutters, clearly not sorry one bit. He grabs two buckets off the ground and gives Josie a wet kiss on the lips before he walks off in the direction of the river just inside the forest.

"Gods, he's so annoying," Josie whines once Danny is out

of hearing distance. "I should stick one of those buckets on his head and hope it gets stuck." I snicker as she bumps her shoulder against mine, giggling.

Such a simple gesture, yet it took me a long time to handle being touched without assuming it would come at a price. Eleven years later, I still have moments where I flinch at the slightest contact if I'm caught unaware. But they're rare now. Josie has taught me a lot over the years with her acts of affection and surprise touches. I can now touch and receive others' touch without breaking out in a sweat or triggering my fight or flight instincts. All my pack members know I don't like to be touched much, and are wary of doing so for any length of time, making me love them even more for their thoughtfulness.

It's nice to be at a point where I can feel others' affection and gratitude the way wolves are supposed to. I just prefer it in small doses, so I'm not too overwhelmed.

It's strange for a wolf shifter to dislike being touched. This is how we wolves interact with each other most of the time, and it's needed for our wolf side. But my pack knows, more than most, that everyone here has been through some shit. They respect that I'm different and don't pry into things, which I'm grateful for.

Josie looks over at me, her chestnut hair swishing around her face with the movement, with an understanding that only very few could.

Josie and Danny were some of the first people to come to Eridian years ago, and she's been there for me ever since. She hugged me as soon as she saw me, crying her gratitude that we helped them as I stood stock still at the contact. She knew immediately something wasn't quite right, and luckily, I didn't put her on her ass for it. That's when she began to help me with my issues. Despite her being only five feet two inches tall, she has claws when needed if her maternal side comes out.

"You know you won't hold out any longer. You might as well give in now so we can all have a peaceful dinner," I tell her, nodding in the direction Danny went.

"Yeah, I suppose you're right," she says with a sigh. "If he wasn't my mate, I would have his balls by now and wear them as a bracelet." I snort.

Josie had been with Danny for years before they came here. They're each other's chosen mate and have been inseparable since they first laid eyes on each other. She told me once they had an instant connection, and they couldn't do anything but nurture it. I'm happy she has someone who loves her with everything he has. I don't think that kind of love happens often, especially with chosen mates rather than bloodmates.

I've resigned myself to the fact that I won't have a love like theirs someday, not even a slither of it. I'm okay with that, though. I don't want a mate, I don't think I could be what a mate would need me to be. Though sometimes I think if things were different, if my life had taken a different path, I might want a family of my own. A life filled with laughter and love and someone that's mine. Just mine.

I shake off the thought and shove it down. *"Josh, get everyone needed here at the gathering for our final discussion before we head out,"* I order through our blood link.

"On it," he replies instantly, probably already rounding them up as we speak.

A blood link enables you to speak to another person directly through your mind. It's a very personal connection and usually only exchanged with those closest to you. We can choose who we speak to, either separately or all at once if you have more than one link like I do. It's established through an exchange of blood, then a symbol representing the link is tattooed into your skin using that blood.

It comes in handy most of the time. Other times, it's

annoying, like when you just sit down for the day and get told there's a problem you need to get back up off your ass to deal with.

"You're going out today, right?" Josie asks, bringing my attention back to her as she picks up a log to throw into the sunken fire pit.

"Yeah, I just asked Josh to gather everyone." Looking around through the trees toward the cabins, I can already see a few members of today's outing making their way toward me.

"Okay, I'll let you get on," she says, giving me a quick squeeze before heading off in the same direction her mate went. I snicker, knowing they won't be back for a while.

I take a seat on one of the benches behind me and wait for everyone to arrive. I stare up at the opening in the trees above me. The blue hue of the sky is full of different shades, making me think of my own ice-blue eyes and my family.

I'm proud of where Josh, Kade, and I are at this point in our lives. Although lately, I do feel like Kade has been distancing himself from the pack, or more to the point, distancing himself from me. I know it's more to do with his wolf emerging five months ago when he turned eighteen, but it seems like he's spending more time in his wolf form than human these days, and it's worrying me.

It's always a difficult time when we first get our wolf, having to learn control and adapt to the enhanced senses we acquire. But he's had his wolf for a while now, and with no sign of Kade returning to two legs any time soon, I really need to talk to him.

I sigh, bringing my head back down, and notice how low the stock of wood is getting in the center. I make a mental note to bring more down from the storage shed later today. We self-sustain as much as possible out here, which is a lot. We go hunting in the surrounding forest for our food and fish in the river south of here. If we want anything we can't get down here in the valley, Edward will send most of what we need through a pair of teleworkers stones that transport goods between the connected two. It's not often that we need to use it, but it's there for when it is needed.

We are quite happy with what we have. It's peaceful, quiet, and most importantly, safe.

A simple way of life.

TWO

Rhea

"Alpha," the blond male addresses, dipping his head respectfully as he comes to stand in front of me. I roll my eyes and kick my leg out toward him, wondering if now is an appropriate time to kick his ass.

He knows how I feel about him using that title, even though I am Alpha of Eridian.

His light gray eyes twinkle as he looks at me, knowing full well he's annoying the shit out of me. I know he's just trying to ease my mind about going into The Deadlands. He knows me better than anyone else. But seriously, only Josh would irritate me on a day when we have important things to do.

I look him over and see he's ready to go, dressed in dark combat gear with blades sheathed at his hips and his dark-blond hair in the usual bun, keeping it out of his face. The rest of the guys behind him are dressed in camouflage, waiting for my instructions to set off.

I stand up, tightening my ponytail and blowing out a breath. It's time to put our plan into action. I just hope Edward's help is at the meeting point with our girl, and hopefully alone. Sometimes we get stuck waiting for them to arrive if they've been delayed by the creatures dwelling in The Deadlands. Other times, it's a battle for us to get to them. Either way, we will know when we get there.

"We went over the plan last night, so we know what we need to do, but let's go over it one last time. Axel and Finn, you're staying where we port in to keep it clear for when we need to port back home. Josh, Taylor, Seb, you're with me to collect Sarah. Colten and Hudson, you've got our backs and keep an eye out for any trouble. Any questions?" I ask, looking at each of them.

"I doubt there will be any problems, but stay sharp and alert. There has been more activity in The Deadlands than usual," Taylor, the male that trained us all, tells us. They nod in acknowledgement, a seriousness coming over their faces.

Taylor is a six-foot one, coffee haired, amber eyed powerhouse that moves fast and strikes hard when needed. He's trained us to be the best fighters we can be and expects nothing in return. I'm thankful he came here. We barely even knew how to hold a blade until he came along.

My gaze moves to Josh as I pinch my bottom lip between my fingers. "Is everything in place for while we're gone?" Leaving Eridian always makes me nervous. It's my responsibility to ensure everyone's safety. I know they're in good hands and that they'll be well protected, but with the news of more rogures being seen throughout Vrohkaria, and having more activity than normal in The Deadlands, my mind whirls over every single security measure we have in place.

"Everything is set and prepared," Josh replies, shaking his head slightly as he adds, "Kade is still out hunting."

From the look on his face, Josh is clearly fed up with Kade being out all the time just as much as I am. I sigh. Kade's battle for dominance with his wolf, Axis, is not going well. It's been nearly three days since he shifted and went into the forest surrounding our home.

With Kade being new to having his wolf, he's struggling to separate himself from Axis. We all go through it when we get our wolves. You're expected to be out of control for a year or longer, but sometimes the battle for dominance is lost, and the wolf takes over. If that happens, you lose control of yourself completely until you either win and gain control back, or someone else controls you. Kade's wolf is strong, and I fear that him spending more time in the forest than at home is not helping him gain the hold he needs to take control of his wolf.

I might need to speak to Solvier to see if he can offer any advice on how to help him. Either way, Kade is about to have pissed off Josh on his ass. But even more unfortunate for him, when we catch him, he'll have to deal with me first.

"Okay, let's get going then. I want to be back in time for dinner, guys. In and out," I say as cheerfully as I can muster. With the pack's safety and Kade plaguing my mind, along with the look Josh threw my way, it's safe to say my cheerfulness falls flat.

We walk out of the gathering heading west, cutting in between the cabins and into the forest. We're quiet as we walk, lost in our own thoughts as we prepare to enter The Deadlands. It's always dangerous, but this is what we do.

Sticks snap under our feet, the sound echoing along the wind with the melody of the birds. The tree branches sway gently above us, casting flashes of light onto the rich ground. It doesn't take long before we come to a stop in front of the lilk trees that circle our home, separating us from the thick dense forest beyond it. I look up, admiring the pastel pink and orange petals flowing to their own dance in the breeze. The scent of sweetness and earth hits my senses, and I breathe deep, allowing it to calm me.

The others are silent as they wait for me, knowing this is my usual routine before I leave. I move forward, pressing a hand to the ivory bark, feeling the smooth wood beneath my palm. Closing my eyes, I send a silent thank you to them for protecting me and my family. My pack. For giving us a safe haven to just be and live and have a chance to find some sort of peace. My eyes spring open when I feel a slight tingle on my palm, a subtle acknowledgement of my feelings being conveyed. I smile, rubbing my thumb over the bark, just once, before I drop my hand and step back.

"All good?" an amused voice asks. I turn to the right, looking slightly up at the owner of the male voice.

"Of course, just giving my thanks." I grin at Sebastian, knowing he's the most impatient out of us all. He's also the tallest, which makes me feel like a squirrel standing next to him. Do squirrels climb into the lilk trees? I've never seen one.

"Earth to Rhea." He snaps his fingers in front of my face, and I blink up at him. "Do you have to do this every time we venture away from home?" He wiggles his dark eyebrows at me. "I can think of a better way to pass the time."

I shrug, ignoring his last statement and my internal question about squirrels, focusing on his tawny eyes. "I don't want Eridian to think I'm ungrateful, it's not a big deal. Anyway, Solvier always said the land appreciates it."

"Solvier," Hudson mutters, and I look over at him. "I've not seen him once in all the years I've been here. He's a goddamn ghost."

"No, he's not," Colten snickers, coming to stand next to him and elbowing him in the side. "He's just picky about who he thinks is worthy of his time."

"You little shit," Hudson growls, grabbing the younger man by the shoulder. No doubt ready for another round of 'who taps out first.'

"Alright, alright," I say, coming between them and putting my hands on their chests. "You guys can beat each other to a pulp later, after we've returned safe and sound."

"Let's get going. We don't want to be in The Deadlands when

the sun goes down," Taylor says, walking through the lilk trees and out of the protective circle.

I follow, feeling a rush of magic flow over me as I step through the invisible barrier and into the unprotected forest. It feels like cobwebs being removed from my body in one smooth glide, pulling me at the last second before it finally releases. I freaked out the first time I felt it, but now, I embrace the feeling when I exit and enter our home.

We walk a meter apart from each other and stay alert to our surroundings. The forest of Eridian can be just as dangerous as The Deadlands. The last thing we need is a bulcar or a family of bora to come for us, or worse yet, a pack of rogures.

Thankfully, we haven't seen any rogures for some time now.

We walk for a while, remaining silent and communicating with our eyes and hand signals. The only person with us here that I have a blood link with is Josh, so we communicate internally anything we see, then let the others know.

Taylor stays slightly in front of the rest of us. He was out here last night to pave a quiet path to the base of the cliffs, so we let him guide us, trusting him to get us there. His steps are light and soft on the ground, missing sticks and leaves to ensure he doesn't make a sound. We follow his lead.

We don't usually stay this quiet when we're in the forest, but we do not want any unexpected attacks slowing us down when we have somewhere we need to be. Especially since we don't know what will be waiting for us when we port into The Deadlands. We can't risk delaying our arrival.

Coming up to the forest tree line, we pause, staying hidden within the trees. Scanning the start of the barren earth before me, I look up to search the top of the cliffs that surround Eridian, encasing us in its valley. The path toward the top is steep and uneven, with many jagged surfaces that could cut you in two. With no signs of any danger, we head for the base and begin our ascent. It takes a little over an hour to climb to the top. With our wolves helping us from within, we managed to gain only superficial cuts.

Heaving myself over the top, I stand and look ahead. A shiver runs down my spine at seeing the top of the dark, dead trees that decay but never crumble. Twisted and thin, the branches intertwine around each other, always connecting to the other trees around it. The trunks of the trees are deeply rooted into the dry earth. No one knows how deep down they go, and I've never seen one uprooted or toppled over in all these years. Mind you, I don't go into The Deadlands unless I have to.

Taylor takes out the port stone from his pack. Small and square, that little gray stone is powerful enough to travel all of us to the location we set. He looks over at us, checking to see if we're ready to go. At our nods, we step forward. I put my hand on his shoulder, and the others come around us to do the same. As long as you are connected to the stone by touching it directly or touching a person connected to it, you can port with them to the same location.

A buzzing sensation fills my ears and I close my eyes as a breeze-like caress touches me, but that soon turns into the feeling of being compressed, making the air leave my lungs in a rush. It only lasts a few seconds, but it's always extremely uncomfortable.

I open my eyes when the feeling disappears and quickly move my hand from Taylor to grab the blade at my hip. We all stand back-to-back, looking throughout The Deadlands, opening our senses to any unexpected creatures that may be lurking nearby.

The ground is dry, the darkened earth littered with broken sticks and stones that we try to avoid as we move around slowly, checking for danger. The small clearing we ported into shows no signs of any life form aside from us, and I relax my hold on the blade.

I turn and see Taylor give the port stone to Axel for safekeeping. He pockets it and takes up a defensive stance. Port stones can only port you twice before the power inside runs out, and it either needs to recharge or be thrown out.

Finn steps up beside Axel, keeping an eye on our surroundings, as the rest of us start to move forward to meet with Edward's help and the girl. The others stay back, protecting the area to make sure we can reach them when we are ready to go home. Hudson and Colten trail behind us, keeping a reasonable distance to protect our backs, as Josh, Taylor, Seb and I keep moving forward on silent feet.

The Deadlands are eerie, dark and gloomy, with enough space between the trees for us to pass through easily. You can't see the sky here. Even with the dark twisted branches having no leaves or flowers, they intertwine so tightly together above our heads that they leave no space for light to filter in between. The enhanced vision from our wolves and the greenish glow of the weeping liquid from the trees are the only reasons we can see in here.

A cloaked figure appears in the distance after we've walked a little while, holding a limp form at their side next to a large rock. We slow instinctively as we approach, the blade in my hand twitching as I clench my fingers tighter around it. The hooded figure turns our way as we get closer and bows their head subtly in recognition. They look back down to the form they are holding, shaking them slightly until I hear a small, soft groan.

"Sarah, help is here. Wake up now," the male voice urges, standing her up as best he can.

Sarah. This is the girl we came to save. I feel the group relax, and I look at Taylor with a nod. He stays still with Sebastian as Josh and I walk the distance left between us and them.

The man is still struggling to hold the girl upright when I move forward slowly and look down at her face, eyeing the male for any sudden movements. Delicate but bruised, Sarah looks to be in her early twenties.

Sheathing my blade at my hip, I reach a hand out to grab her arm gently, helping the male steady her on her feet. She whimpers quietly before opening her eyes slightly. Bloodshot eyes meet mine, and then widen as I feel her body tense beneath my hand.

"You're okay," I whisper gently, stroking my thumb on her arm. "Edward sent me." Tears fill her eyes, and she visibly relaxes, taking a breath and releasing it slowly.

Until her eyes land on Josh.

She screams, thrashing in the male's arms, freeing herself from our grips and staggering back on weak legs. "Stay away," she orders shakily, putting a hand out in front of her as she steps backward. Her dark hair is a mess of curls around her face as her panicked eyes flutter around from left to right.

"We're not going to hurt you," I tell her calmly, showing my hands in a gesture that is the 'I'm harmless' signal. *"Josh, stay back,"* I say down the link.

I could sense him creeping forward to the right of me, trying to get around the back of her without her noticing. But she does, her eyes constantly tracking his every move.

"She's going to bolt, Rhea," he murmurs back to me.

The Deadlands are no place for Sarah to run around blindly and alone.

"Sarah, Edward sent us to bring you to our home, in Eridian. We have been waiting for you to arrive here so we can take you there. You trust Edward, yes? Edward trusts us. We only want to help."

She looks at me and then back at Josh, until finally her eyes meet the male who brought her here. "D-did you set me up?"

Sarah trembles while she backs away further from us. "You said you would take me to someone who would help me."

"No, of course not. They are here to help," the male assures her.

"Then why is he here?" She points a trembling finger at Josh. "You told me a female ran the settlement. If that was true, he wouldn't be here."

"I came to ensure you and my Alpha get back home safely," Josh tells her, looking her over with a curiosity I hadn't seen from him before. "I won't hurt you."

"We must go, Sarah, it's not safe to be still for too long in The Deadlands. I run the settlement, it's our home. Josh and some others came with me to keep us all safe and bring us back. The Deadlands are dangerous. This is for your safety as well as ours."

She looks at all of us, shaking her head and continuing to back away. The cloaked male removes his hood, walking toward her as his light eyes plead with her to listen. "It's alright, Sarah–"

Snap.

My head flies to the left where I spot a shadow moving through the trees. The darkness of the forest makes it impossible for me to see clearly what it is, but something is there.

I hear another snap, then a growl.

I stay still, breathing slowly as I carefully reach for the blade at my hip. I flick my eyes over the trees, scanning them to try and determine where the creature is. I move my left foot, turning my body at a snail's pace so I can face whatever it is head on.

"Josh, you're going to have to grab Sarah when this thing comes at us. Take her and go to Axel and Finn. The guys will help you," I order him as I prepare myself.

"I'll grab her, don't worry. Just be careful," he replies through the link, shifting slightly to get ready to run and grab Sarah by any means necessary.

I sense the male to my right, thankfully he is staying as still as us, knowing there is danger. I caught a glance of his face when he removed his hood. The dark, three dots within the upside down triangle in the center of forehead stood out against his pale skin, letting me know he's an omega. Which means by nature, he's not a fighter.

A deep, long growl sounds before me as the creature suddenly lunges out from between the trees. Its scaly skin is dark as night, and it's coming straight for me.

Sarah screams, the shrill sound echoing around the space before I head for the creature.

We collide, slamming against each other and falling to the ground in a tangle of limbs. The bora lands on top of me, and I bring my blade up, striking deep in its shoulder. The bora shrieks, its jaw gaping open with the sound. Sharp, pointed teeth come for my face, and I move to the side, barely escaping them. I elbow the temple on its narrowed face, stunning it, while I lift my hips and buck it off of me, dragging the blade down its shoulder as it falls to the side. I roll away, coming to a stand. I steady my stance and bend my knees slightly, ready for the next attack as it gets to its feet and shakes its head. Blood pours from its shoulder, and it's limping from the injury made when my blade sliced down its leg. Its head lowers and a menacing growl passes through its mouth. I growl right back.

The bora looks young. The sharp jagged spikes on its tail are smaller than a fully mature bora. With the realization that it's just a babe, I have to wonder where the mother is.

I glance around quickly and realize that the others have got away and are headed back to Axel and Finn.

The bora lunges again, its strong hind legs making it a powerful one. I turn my body at the last second to avoid being hit. I bring my blade up, slicing along its side as it rushes past me. I spin to see it land on the ground, its legs folding underneath itself from its injuries. The young bora gets unsteadily to its feet and lifts its head back, letting out a screeching wail.

I cringe, covering my ears with my hands while stepping back to create more distance between us. The sound stops suddenly, and the bora's bone-colored eyes stare at me, waiting. Growls erupt around me, and I freeze. Shit. Its mother and family were closer than I realized.

Time to go. Now!

I pivot and run at full speed straight ahead, dashing through the dead trees and jumping over large rocks. I check my surroundings as I run, making sure the boras are all still behind me. The last thing I need is for them to ambush me from all sides. A ragged branch slices deep across the top of my arm and I hiss at the sharp pain, feeling blood trickle down. I keep going, not needing to look behind me to know they're gaining on me. I can hear their panting breaths and growls getting closer.

Damn, they're fast.

"We're ready to port. Where are you?" Josh asks me down the link.

"Oh, you know, just having a little race with a family of bora," I snark at him, trying to concentrate on not falling on my ass.

"Rhea, I don't think now is the time to get cute." Cute? The cheeky fucker. *"Are you coming to where we are to port, or do you want us to come for you?"*

I push forward. *"Have you got Sarah?"*

"Yes, and the omega. Sarah passed out after a little chase, and I grabbed her. She's fine. It will probably be easier to get her to Eridian while she's unconscious anyway."

"Okay, I'll be there shortly," I tell him. *"Get ready to port straight away."*

Sprinting in between a narrow gap in the middle of two trees, I make a wide turn to loop back on myself. Heavy breathing reaches my ears from behind me, a second before a mouth is about to clamp onto my ankle. I spin around, sending my foot out with the turn and colliding with the side of the mouth that's trying to bite me.

The momentum sends me crashing against a tree, the rough bark digging into my hands as I stop myself from face planting it. Ignoring the pain, I push myself off, and carry on looping back around toward Josh.

Still hearing the sounds of the bora chasing after me, I pull in some extra speed from my wolf, allowing me to soar across the dry, forest floor. My wolf is resistant at first, but an extra nudge from me has her releasing some of her strength into me.

Rounding another cluster of dead trees, I see Josh and the guys waiting for me, all touching one another, ready to port. My breathing comes in fast pants, and my legs feel like a newborn deer as I sprint directly to them.

An older bora suddenly jumps through the trees ahead of me from the side, its spiked tail high, ready to meet me head on. I curl my hand around the hilt of my blade so it's pointing toward the ground, ready to defend myself. A flash of steel catches my eye as it flies in front of me. I follow its path as it hits its target, right in the side of the bora's head. It comes to a sudden halt, sliding across the ground in front of me. Dead. I'm glad Seb has good aim.

As I leap over the dead bora, I see the orbs of its essence start to float upwards from its body, heading toward the thick tree branches above, casting a warm white glow.

"Hurry, Rhea!" Taylor demands, bringing my focus to him as he looks behind me. The rest of the family of bora come into sight, charging straight for us.

I sprint the last few steps and reach for the hand Taylor holds out for me. Once our hands connect, and I hear the shattering wails of the bora, grieving the loss of one of their own, as we port out of The Deadlands to safety.

THREE

Rhea

We arrive at the bottom of the cliff within seconds, the bora's wails still ringing in my ears, tearing at my soul. Although the bora would have ripped me to shreds and the young one had attacked me first, it was still a living, breathing creature with a family it was only trying to protect.

Taylor lets go of my hand, noticing the blood from where the bark dug into my palm. He turns his own hand over, looking at the red there, then looks to the top of my arm, scrutinizing the wound.

"I'm fine," I reassure him with a small smile. "Just a scratch."

I look over at Josh who cradles a still unconscious Sarah in his arms. He looks down at her, examining her face before looking up to the top of the cliffs. Blowing out a breath, I follow his gaze and listen for any sign the creatures are above us. We ported quite far into The Deadlands, so I don't think the bora would know where we are, but it's always safest to make sure. With no sound reaching us, we're confident nothing has followed our trail and start toward home.

"Alex? You and Finn stay here a little longer to make sure we are not being followed." He nods and turns to set up a post with Finn, both of them effortlessly shifting into their wolf.

Taylor walks next to me, constantly scanning the forest as he shoves the now useless port stone into his pocket. I see him looking at the wound on my arm again subtly, but I don't call him out on it. He trains us to the best of his ability to keep us safe, so he takes it personally when one of us gets injured.

Shame we can't protect ourselves from trees though.

"What was that young bora doing on its own anyway?" Colten muses aloud behind me. "That young they don't leave their family to pee on their own, never mind wander so far away."

I was wondering the same thing. It's so out of the norm. I can't imagine why it did that, or why the rest of its family didn't notice sooner. They are notorious for protecting their young.

"Maybe something spooked it," Hudson suggests. It would make sense, but what could have spooked only one bora? A family of bora can be up to twenty large. They are ruthless together and have no sense of self preservation when protecting their family, making them dangerous. Most times it's better to run than take them all on.

A throat clears, bringing my attention to the omega male. The hood of his cloak is still down, making his dark hair hang loosely to his jaw. He looks me in the eyes briefly before dropping his gaze to the floor. "We have been in The Deadlands for hours, and it has been restless. Edward told me there wouldn't be an issue, but we fled from many creatures and barely had any time to stop and catch our breaths. It wasn't as safe as what Edward told me that area would be."

Looking at him closely, I see the tiredness in his eyes, the exhausted slump of his shoulders I didn't notice before. "I'm sorry you've had a hard time. Activity has been increasing in The Deadlands, and it's worrying."

The Deadlands has its fair share of deadly creatures. They aren't usually this aggressive or sighted as close to the edge of the cliffs as they have been these last couple of weeks. I have people checking the perimeter weekly to see if any creatures are trying to come down into the valley. Thankfully, they haven't.

A couple of years ago, several families of bora came down the cliffs from The Deadlands. The bora and the creatures of the Eridian massacred each other over the span of thirteen days. It disturbed the animals we hunt, and food was scarce for a while. We also worried they would manage to get through the protective barrier around Eridian. While the lilk trees' invisible barrier stops strong magic from being used inside its circle and creatures from passing through, if a lot of creatures try to pass through at once, the barrier can weaken enough for them to slip inside.

I breathe out heavily, remembering the last time some of the creatures got through. We lost some good people that day. And that's why I now have someone checking the cliffs and The Deadlands regularly. If we see any creatures getting too close, we try to divert them or regrettably, put them down if we cannot change their course.

Since starting the patrols, we haven't had any incidents like that again.

"What's your name?" I ask the omega, shaking off my memories as we walk. The only reason I'm bringing him to Eridian is because Edward trusts him enough to escort Sarah to us, and he needs rest before he travels again.

"Ellian," he says, tipping his head down in a show of respect.

"Well, Ellian, we will take you to our home and give it a few days for things to settle. We will get you back to where you need to be, after some rest," I smile, reassuring him.

He gives me a gentle smile back before averting his eyes. "I have no doubt."

Taylor makes a grunting sound, and I look at him out of the corner of my eye. Lifting an eyebrow in question, he shakes his head and continues forward. I guess he's not happy with us bringing Ellian back with us. But Edward always chooses those who do not live close to The Deadlands or the home where they pick people up to bring to us. Ellian will need rest before he will be able to port to another location from The Deadlands and spend days traveling again to his distant home.

Making our way through the forest silently, I sneak glances at a still unconscious Sarah in Josh's arms. She doesn't even twitch as we walk, and Josh doesn't seem bothered by the added weight, walking as if he's not holding another person. She must not weigh much at all. We will remedy that in time.

Finally reaching the lilk trees, we cross the sightless barrier into Eridian. I sag in relief, pressing my palm to the tree as I pass. We all made it back, safe and alive. We head straight for the healer's cabin, Josh plowing forward in his haste to get Sarah there, his brows scrunched in worry. The oak wood cabin is to the left of the gathering, central to the other cabins around it. We reach it soon enough, and Anna opens the door for Josh to pass through as he nears the door.

"I'll take Ellian to one of the spare cabins," Taylor says. He motions for the omega to follow him as Ellian looks around our home with wide eyes. I don't blame him, others did the same thing when they first came here.

Seb winks at me, sauntering off toward the gathering, whistling as he goes. He's probably going to find any leftovers. He eats like a bottomless pit.

"Hope all goes well with Sarah, Rhea. Come find me later?" Colten calls out. I turn to catch him wiggling his eyebrows at me, which earns him a slap on the back of the head from Hudson.

"Come on, pup, leave them to it." Hudson grabs his arm, moving him along. "Leave the flirting to Sebastian."

"Stop calling me pup," Colten growls, trying and failing to get his arm free.

"Stop acting like one then," Hudson chastises.

"I didn't do anything!" They continue to bicker as they walk off, and I turn, heading inside the cabin.

I walk down the narrow hallway and to the first room on the right. Herbs and medicines assault my senses as I walk into the room and see Sarah laid out on the bed. The white sheets are a stark contrast to her dark hair fanned around her head on the pillow.

Anna flutters about, grabbing supplies while she barks out orders. "Take off her cloak and any other clothes. I need to see her injuries after I get some fluids in her. Grab some warm water and towels as well."

I go to do her bidding as I watch Josh out of the corner of my eye. He removes the pin on her cloak that keeps it together before slowly moving the material to either side. He sucks in a sharp breath, his nostrils flaring as he takes in her small camisole top that is covered in blood.

I knew I smelled blood in The Deadlands, and I'm sure he smelled while he was carrying her, but seeing it is much different.

He looks up at me, his gray eyes filled with pain, and I know without words what he needs me to do. I go over to him, giving his hand a squeeze as he clears his throat and moves away from the bed. I take over, slowly cutting and peeling away her bloodied clothes as he goes to grab water and towels.

Anna comes to stop next to Sarah, gathering her red curls in a bun atop her head to keep it out of her face. Looking down at her, she shakes her head, sadness in her eyes as she glances at the bloody clothes I put to the side.

Josh comes over with towels and water in a bowl, setting them down on the table next to the bed. Anna takes out a clean sponge from the cabinet above the table and dips it into the water. Wringing some of the water out, she brings the sponge to Sarah's slightly parted lips. Squeezing gently, she pushes the sponge slightly into her mouth, so the water trickles down her throat.

I grab a sheet while Anna works and cover Sarah's body from the waist down. My eyes land on the deep slash across her abdomen, blood oozing from the jagged stitches that had been put there carelessly. By Ellian or Sarah herself, I don't know.

Josh stands back, still as a statue to give Anna room to work while I help her clean up Sarah, assessing the injuries on her body as we uncover them. Most are deep and infected, which takes a lot for a shifter. She must have been unable to shift to heal herself to prevent infection, and I dread to think what they did to stop that from happening.

I refuse to acknowledge the thought right now.

Sarah groans softly as we roll her to the side so Anna can see her back. I shush her gently as Anna stills, flicking her blue eyes up to mine briefly, before prodding at Sarah's back. I peek over to see what she's doing and cringe at the sight.

Letters have been carved into Sarah's skin, making crude lines along the whole of her back. They're weeping and raw, the skin around them puffy and red from infection. My heart pangs at the pain she has gone through, the pain she is still in. My whole body itches at the thought.

Anna grabs a bowl of salve. It's made with plants that we collect from the Eridian Forest, making sure we always pick the ones aged to get the most from its healing properties. She grabs a yellow fettle leaf, thick and wide, and lathers the brown colored salve onto it with a spoon. She places the leaf, salve side down, onto one of the wounds on Sarah's back, then continues the process until her back is covered completely. We wrap a bandage like cloth around her to keep the leaves in place, securing it with knots as gently as we can.

"Ease her onto her back, please?" Anna whispers.

I do as I'm asked, gently rolling Sarah onto her back and

taking a peek at her face. Her mouth twitches as if she can feel the pain, her brows furrowing as her breathing picks up a little before settling again. She can't escape this, even in her sleep, and the thought saddens me.

We get to work on the slash across her abdomen, picking out the old stitches and adding salve into the cut as Josh watches on silently. Anna starts stitching the wound closed. I watch her hands move through the process with precision, always amazed by her speed.

Flicking my eyes to Josh to see how he's holding up, I see him watching Anna's movements intently, his eyes never leaving her hands as she works.

He hates seeing anyone in this state, hates feeling helpless. It brings back memories we both try to forget from a long time ago, when I was on the ground and Josh didn't know what to do. It's not something we want to relive, but we can't turn our back on helping others in need because of our past. I refuse to.

Sarah starts to stir as I'm cleaning her hands with a damp cloth, trying to get the dirt and blood from the sides of her broken fingernails. She whimpers, and I see Josh's leg twitch out of the corner of my eye. Focusing on Sarah, I see her eyelids flutter and then she opens them slowly, blinking a few times. Her fingers twitch in my hand and she looks toward me, a crinkle in her brow. Her eyes go wide next, her breathing increasing and her gaze flies around the room until it lands on Josh.

"It's okay, Sarah," I tell her soothingly, running my thumb over the back of her hand.

She ignores me, moving to sit up and wincing at the sudden movement. Josh takes a step forward, but stops when she releases a long, piercing shriek. She hops off the bed clumsily, causing me to move back to give her some space as she backs away into the corner of the room. She grabs the closest thing to her, a small sharp blade that is amongst other equipment that we use to cut through skin. Holding it up and pointing it at each of us, she warns us without a word. I have no doubt she would use it in her desperation, but I can't let her take it that far.

"Josh, please leave the cabin, I'll update you later," I tell him down the link, my eyes moving from Sarah to him.

He looks over at Sarah and clenches his jaw. Taking a deep breath, he looks down to the floor before he nods once. Heading toward the door, he closes it gently behind him without looking back.

Sarah relaxes slightly when she hears the door close, but she still aims the blade at me and Anna.

"Why don't you put that down and hop back into bed?" Anna asks, gathering the sheet off the bed and holding it out toward her.

She looks at the sheet confused before noticing her naked body and jolts. Red tinges her cheeks, and she steps forward slowly, grabbing the sheet with a shaky hand and wrapping it around herself.

"You're safe here, sweetheart. We promise you that," Anna murmurs gently to her.

She looks at Anna. Her lips tremble, and her eyes fill with tears. The blade in her shaky hand clatters to the floor, and she follows it, exhaustion winning over her will to stay standing.

I dart forward, wrapping my arms around her as gently as I can, and guide her back onto the bed. When she's settled, I pull a chair from across the room and take a seat next to her, grabbing her hand softly before I bring my eyes to hers.

"I know you're scared. I know you're hurt. But please, let us help you. Edward sent you here because he trusts me. He sends all manner of people here who need some help, and we make sure whoever he sends gets that help," I assure her, rubbing circles on the back of her hand.

She nods at me, her breathing now steady and calm. My body

relaxes with relief. It won't be an easy road for her to walk, but we will be here to do everything we can to help her along the way.

I clear my throat and extend my free hand. "Hi, I'm Rhea, Alpha of Eridian. I would like you to tell me what you can. It doesn't have to be everything at once, but I would like to know who did this to you, and anything else you are willing to share at the moment. If you don't want to tell me anything, that's not a problem. We can take our time."

Tears spill over her eyes, and she takes a deep breath. She shakes my hand and then brings the sheet closer to her body, wanting some form of protection.

Then, she opens her mouth and speaks.

FOUR

Darius

"What do you mean go into The Deadlands?" I ask Charles, tilting my head and wondering if he's lost his fucking mind.

I move my eyes to Leo, my second in command, and see his brows furrowed in confusion, just like mine. His blue eyes briefly meet my green ones before he settles back into his seat next to me, returning his gaze to Lord Higher Charles while he waits for his reply.

"It's just like I said, Darius," he sighs. "A member of the Nightshade pack has been taken, and Alpha Christopher asked for my help a few days ago. A sighting was brought to my attention this morning by my scouts after our regular meeting. I showed them a drawing of Christopher's missing pack member for them to keep an eye out, and a female matching the woman's description was seen with another person going into The Deadlands two nights ago. My scouts saw her side profile, and are adamant it was the same woman in this sketch. Who else could it be? No one willingly goes into The Deadlands."

"They can't tell if it's the girl just from looking at the side of her face," I scoff.

"No," he agrees. "However, they said the person with her was half dragging her into the forest."

"And they didn't think to check if there was a problem?" I ask. Some fucking scouts they are.

"Of course not. I don't pay them to intervene with nonsense." He huffs, shaking his dark head before he continues. "I sent more scouts to search the area to see if they could track a scent. There was no trace because of the heavy rain we have been experiencing. I need you and the Elites to go into The Deadlands to find this woman to see if she is, in fact, the missing Nightshade member."

"We don't deal with missing people." I eye him where he sits behind his desk. "We take out creatures, manage power spikes and search for a way to stop the rogures." I lean back in the chair, spreading my legs, already done with this conversation. Why would he even help the Alpha? "Packs usually deal with their problems internally, so who is this girl for them to ask for outside help?"

Even as Elites, we are a pack. We know how pack structure works. Things like this are dealt with internally and handled quietly. To ask for outside help is very unusual. For Lord Higher Charles to ask for *our* help with this, even more so.

"She is set to be mated." He steeples his hands atop his desk in front of him, dark eyes boring into mine with determination.

"Have her mate look for her. This matter doesn't affect us at all. It doesn't affect you."

"It does affect me," Charles says in a hard tone, and I raise an eyebrow at him. Leo shifts uncomfortably in his seat next to me, not liking the Higher's tone any more than I do. "Alpha Christopher is an important ally to us. We have had an alliance with him for over fifty years. He has personally come here to ask for assistance, and I assured him I would help in any way I can."

"You could get anyone to search for her. Why the Elites? We are needed elsewhere for more important issues. The rogures are an important issue." I'm not letting this go until he tells me. Something is up, and I want to know.

We Elites mainly hunt creatures causing havoc across

Vrohkaria. When we get a power spike hit from the Highers' witches after they scry the lands, we go and investigate. It could be that a spell was cast by someone to bless the land or heal a large number of wounded, or it could be a spike of power from a creature that has no business running amok in a village. If we're not hunting creatures, we're actively searching for a way to stop the rogures that are plaguing Vrohkaria.

We don't search for missing women.

"We are on a time limit. You are the best of the best. If anyone can find her, it is the Elites." He keeps his stare on me, and I stare right back, not giving him a word until he tells me why it is so important. He lets out a heavy sigh. "She is from a good line and due for an arranged mating four months from now," he finally concedes, shocking me into silence.

"An arranged mating?" Leo asks before I can. "We don't have arranged matings anymore. It's been proven that the mated pair struggle with fertility. There hasn't been one in hundreds of years."

"We know of the complications it can bring, however, this arrangement gains the Nightshade pack a new ally in the Aragnis pack, and therefore, the Highers. The other Highers and I have agreed to accept the arranged mating that was proposed. We have also agreed to allow others to go ahead with arrangements if their application is approved by us. We are also looking to offer other pairings to our current alliances," Charles tells me, sitting up straighter. "The people are beginning to question our authority, causing riots because we are the most unaffected by the rogures. These matings will bring hope to the people and help regain faith that their Highers are doing this for them. That I am doing this for them. This is greatly beneficial to us all, especially with the rogures slowly, but surely, reaching all Vrohkaria and closing in on Fenrikar. Food sources are getting lesser, materials thinner and villages torn apart."

He's not telling me anything I don't already know. I travel all over Vrohkaria for weeks on end, visiting different territories. I see all this firsthand. Mothers cradling children who were killed by rogures, villages destroyed, people fighting over food, murders over materials, and it's just getting worse. Especially with the rogures numbers growing. He's lying about one thing though, food is not as scarce as it seems to be as he has it stored here within the castle.

"It's time to unite us all across Vrohkaria and bring in more alliances. We have had eight sightings of rogure packs in Fenrikar this month alone, and each time they are creeping closer to the surrounding homes of Wolvorn Castle. We need to come together and be rid of them once and for all," he growls, slamming his palms on his desk.

"We kill off any rogures we see. We hunt them, and more keep coming. We need to find the original source, but our scouting missions have come up empty. We have no idea where they're coming from, or how many there are. We keep searching but come back with nothing. We have been trying to get rid of them for years. Gaining more alliances and approving arranged matings won't change that," I state, and Leo nods his head in agreement.

"It is done, and I need you to find the girl." His tone leaves no room for argument. It is a done deal in his eyes.

I grind my teeth and look around the obnoxious office. We sit in the center of the room, a window at his back overlooks the courtyard. Lord Higher Charles has a taste for the expensive and rare. His thousand-year-old, hand carved, white wood desk is made from wood as rare as finding a Phoenix. His high back, you guessed it, white, wood chair is embedded with terbium that has been magically turned solid around the edges of the silk, padded seat. The chandelier above us is translucent ore, one of only twenty made, and let's not forget his blue crystal tumblers to go with his extensive, expensive liquor collection, just to name a few items. How do I know all this? The first time I stepped into this room after my father passed, he bored me to near self-mutilation by telling me about the rarity of every single object.

Even his door has a spell on it so that no one can gain entry. Charles doesn't like anybody touching his things without permission. None of this will matter, though, if we don't find a way to deal with the rogures.

The rogures appeared about twenty-one years ago, seemingly out of nowhere and started creating havoc throughout Vrohkaria, and *only* Vrohkaria. The rogures are mindless, bloodthirsty creatures that look like large, deformed hounds, with rotting gray skin dripping from their bodies and a double set of sharp, pointed teeth. They kill anything and everything apart from others like them.

No one knows how the rogures came to be. Some say it was a spell gone wrong by the blood witches, while others say the fae put a curse upon Vrohkaria for selfish reasons. Others still think the demons want to see us suffer for their own amusement. The most recent theory is the Gods are punishing us for taking advantage of the land they gave us and not giving back to it.

No matter what may have caused it, we have tried and failed countless times to get rid of them or figure out where they come from. And they keep coming back in greater numbers. We have had the most powerful witches cast every known spell to try and eradicate the beasts from Vrohkaria. But all we manage is cutting down a few with no real end in sight.

"With this new alliance between the Nightshade and the Aragnis pack, and with many more coming in the future, the result will only be beneficial to us all. We'll be gaining more numbers while also gaining peace among territories. We will be able to send out search parties much more efficiently, and do so without trespassing on other territories in the process. Of course, we are still in conversations with other packs to search their lands, as well as the witches in the southwest woods. After all these years, they still refuse to form any kind of alliance with us. But with some added pressure and the knowledge that our alliances are growing, the witches will come around." A dark look spreads across Charles's face before his expression returns neutral. "There is the pesky problem of The Deadlands being included in the area we haven't searched yet, and you could do so while looking for the girl."

"We haven't searched that land for a reason. The creatures living there can be deadly, and not many are up to the task. We also haven't searched there because we haven't witnessed any rogures coming from the area. There is no reason to risk lives unnecessarily. We don't have the numbers behind us to kill the rogures roaming the lands and search for a way to stop them, while also continuing to hunt other creatures that become a problem. I don't see why you and some of the other Highers can't go in there yourselves to look for the missing woman."

"You can also search for rogure dens while you're in there," he adds. "You know the other Highers and I are needed here to ensure the laws of Vrohkaria are upheld. We are extremely busy with day-to-day meetings and going over reports while also attending trials. And we now have the added workload of reading through proposals for arranged matings and packs coming and going from the Castle that we need to cater to. These potential matings are very important if we are to have any way of getting rid of the rogures. We don't just sit in our offices and do nothing, you know this."

I do know this, but surely if this woman is important enough that he asked for us, it would take importance over anything else. Charles is the most powerful Higher out of all seven. With his wolf strong and magic powerful, it is why he is *Lord* Higher over Vrohkaria. The crest that hangs from his neck proves it. So why do the Elites have to go if he's not willing to? I don't give a fuck about this woman. She is of no interest to me.

"So let me get this straight," I start, leaning forward in my chair. "You want some of my Elites to search for this missing woman while also searching for rogure dens in The Deadlands?" I shake my head. "It's a suicide mission."

"Not just any Elites, I want you to go. You can of course take whoever you want, and I will supply people to take over whatever Elite business you have while you are away," he offers.

"Even with me, it's still potential suicide. You know most of the creatures that are in there, but not all of them. No one does. Never mind if we do cross any rogures. The woman is probably already dead, as well as the person who took her, and I'm not losing any of my Elites, trainees or otherwise, for a dead-end mission," I growl.

He leans back in his chair, smirking at me. If he wasn't my father's best friend and unrelated uncle to me for all my life, his face would have a few broken bones by now.

"You are strong enough to handle it. The Higher's authority over Vrohkaria is currently being questioned, especially here in Fenrikar. We are accused of not doing enough against the rogures or having caused the problem, which is preposterous. The more time passes, the more they think we are unfit to rule. The people will come banging on our doors as they assume they are a better fit to rule the lands. I have made great progress, and peace has settled in the lands since I became Lord Higher many years ago. This plague of creatures is destroying whatever is in its path and disrupting the peace I have worked so hard to maintain. Alliances need to be made, and the rogures need to be killed. I won't take no for an answer, Darius. Or are you ready to be a Higher and show your worth like your father wanted?" he asks, sliding a sketch of a woman toward me on his desk, and

I give him a dirty look. "Or do you need more…persuading."

I hold back a growl. It is a low blow mentioning my father and his persuasive methods.

He could force me to become a Higher, and there is nothing I can do about it, regardless of being Elite. Before my father died, he nominated me to become one. That nomination remains and can be called upon at any time. If I refuse, the Highers will call upon the oath my father made on my behalf, and force me to take a seat amongst them while using my men to make me bend. I have too much to do before he calls upon that nomination. He's backed me into a corner, and he fucking knows it. So, what choice do I have? Become a Higher or do as he's ordered.

"Fine," I state reluctantly, grabbing the sketch off his desk. "I will go, and you can keep the word Higher and my name out of your mouth." Getting up in one smooth motion and pocketing the sketch, I walk to the office door with Leo following behind me.

Charles's voice makes me pause as I reach for the door handle. "Keep me updated on your progress, son. You have four months. This alliance is extremely important. It will help us all and put the people's minds at ease."

I say nothing, opening the door and walking out, Leo following at my back.

I grit my teeth in frustration, walking with measured steps down the winding hallways toward the entrance hall before reaching the castle doors. Hemsworth, the castle attendant, opens the doors when he sees me, nodding his head respectfully. I pass without saying a word.

"Why did you agree?" Leo asks, catching up to walk beside me when we are further into the castle courtyard, passing sellers and their goods. "You could have said no."

"No, Leo, I couldn't. You know I promised my father I would help Charles in whatever he needed when I became Alpha of the

Elites, and he would also use you to get what he wants. It's either helping him or becoming a Higher myself. He has the power to make it happen. The laws state that he can induct me whenever he wants, and there is nothing I can do about it. I need to get rid of the rogures before they destroy us all and avenge my family for what they did to them. If I have to find this fucking woman to achieve that, I will," I grunt, walking quickly through the courtyard, ignoring everyone staring around us.

It isn't hard to move easily through the people considering they give the Elites a wide berth. They know what we could do, what we are capable of, even though all we do is protect them. But they still fear us.

There's a crowd forming around some men that are shouting about the Highers not protecting them against the rogures, and how it's strange that these creatures never attack the castle. The Highers' guards soon appear and push through the listening crowd, most likely to arrest them and take them to the cells beneath the castle to await sentencing for their slander.

"I know, brother," Leo replies, his tone low as he watches a guard tackle a male to the ground. "But to send you there for a girl who is probably already dead is fucked. We did our rite of passage in The Deadlands, and we barely made it out alive. That was what, nearly twenty-five years ago? Imagine how bad it is now."

"I know, but we had to go deep in The Deadlands for that. I doubt we will go deep enough for the more deadly creatures to give us much trouble. We will find her body, somehow, and get back home."

"Let's hope so. We could take some trainees as an exercise, if they volunteer," Leo muses, cocking his head in thought.

"I'll think about it, it might be a good lesson for them if we aren't going to go that deep. I'll talk to everyone when we get back," I tell him, making way toward the castle gates to head back to Vokheim keep.

My men aren't going to be happy with the news, but ultimately, Charles is the leader of Vrohkaria and what he says goes. To refuse him would cause more problems that we don't need right now.

FIVE

Rhea

Throwing wood in the fire pit, I stand up straight and wipe the sweat from my brow. I've been working around the settlement all morning, doing chores and dealing with squabbles amongst some of the members.

We don't get them often, but they do happen every now and again. It doesn't help that some of the females are going into heat soon. It's hard to balance the added workload on top of our usual daily work, especially with tensions running so high.

I've made sure we separated the male and females, so they work at opposite ends of the Eridian, and we rotate when needed so they are near each other as little as possible. The males won't be shifting into wolves until the females' heats are over, unless they are far out in the forest and well away from the large three story cabin that we allocate the females to during their heat. If they choose a male to help them during that time, they go to their own cabin.

The males are also running high on testosterone, and with the number of people who will be otherwise occupied for a few days, we have to pick up the slack of those not around to help keep our home running.

With the last log placed into the pit for tonight's dinner, I sit down on the ground, my back to the wooden bench behind me. I take out the small blade that I've had with me since I left my old pack. I trace my fingers over the hilt, feeling the carved words *'we bleed wolf'* in my family's language beneath my fingertips.

Grabbing a broken piece of wood that was left on the ground, I begin to cut into it. I started doing this years ago, randomly, not really sure what I was doing at all. My first carving was of a wolf that took me many tries and several weeks to complete. I've been carving for years now. I'm not great at it, but that's not the point of why I do it.

The motion of my hands moving with practiced ease as I carve at the wood calms me. The methodical movement helps me to process my thoughts when I have a lot on my mind. It has become a ritual of sorts.

After sending Ellian back to his home with a port stone, my focus has been concentrating on Sarah. She's still recuperating in the healer's cabin, slowly recovering from her injuries even after two moon cycles. They're healing well, but they will definitely scar as they have been left untreated for too long. If she would have been able to shift when she was injured she would have been fine, but her body has been changed without her permission, and she will have to learn to live with the physical scars as a reminder of what she went through. She will eventually learn that those scars show her strength, but it does take time, and that amount of time differs from person to person.

Once Sarah told me her story about how she ended up the way she was and who did that to her, she retreated into her own mind, staying very quiet. I don't pressure her to speak, to tell me what she's thinking, sometimes speaking to our demons is the only way we can process things.

Her injuries weren't just external. Anna examined her after our talk, and she was torn in places no woman should ever be. It was clear she had been raped. Many times. Sarah told me they gave her some kind of drug that paralyzes your body, but you're awake and completely aware of what's going on around you.

She could see, hear, and feel what they were doing to her, and all she could do was lie there and hope it was over soon.

I shake my head as fury coats my skin. I take a deep breath to calm myself, shaving the wood into a rounded shape at the top with a little too much force. It's hard to hold onto anger with no real release. It's draining when all you want is to unleash it on the person responsible, but the situation makes it so you can't. The kind of anger that you're terrified to finally let out, dreading the outcome after holding it in for so long.

If I let out that anger, it wouldn't just affect me. If I followed my instincts to tear apart all the people responsible for the suffering of my pack members, it would affect them all, and I can't do that to them. Edward mostly sends wolves that need to escape a life of abuse to Eridian. I can't just throw our home away, our safety, for revenge, and I can't let others do that either. They would know we have a settlement somewhere, and we need to remain hidden. That's why once you're in Eridian to stay, you're in, and you don't leave. Apart from myself and my closest pack members who I trust when we venture out into The Deadlands.

If anyone left after they lived in Eridian, they could risk the whole settlement and the people that live here.

I can't risk that.

When you create a new pack, you have to declare it to the Highers, those that rule over Vrohkaria, and get permission to claim a territory. And since we are hiding out here, we haven't told them. That's another reason no one can leave. Because if they find us, we will all be punished for breaking the law of the lands, many times over.

Especially me.

The people we save understand this before they agree to come here. Edward informs them, and it's up to them if they want to come to this safe haven and agree to the terms. I don't know how Edward finds people in need or even manages to speak with them, but it doesn't matter as long as we can continue to help those in need and they arrive here safely.

We've grown in numbers over the years, our home slowly expanding every time someone new joins us. I was worried when we first started out if there would be enough food for us, if we'd be able to house anyone and build a life here. But everyone pitches in. Whether it's collecting water, harvesting vegetables in the gardens or chopping wood. We have certain people who are skilled at hunting that go out and find food, and there is enough prey around for us that we don't have to kill unnecessarily. We are never greedy and don't take more than the land offers. That's important to us.

Blowing the shavings off my lap, I reposition my hand and start at the bottom of the wood, carving lines out for the legs and slowly adding in tiny details as I go.

Pack members come and go from the gathering, dropping things off and refilling the large pot with water to put on the fire later to cook. They don't talk to me as I continue chipping at the wood, knowing I'm not in the mood for conversation if I'm carving, my mind being elsewhere.

I wonder if Sarah talked to anybody while she was being abused. She didn't mention that she had, only that she was down there for what felt like a really long time. At least a full season. She must have been lonely on her own, with only her own mind for company. I can relate to that more than she knows.

I had hoped when she mentioned they gave her drugs that she wouldn't remember most of it. I'm not sure how much she remembers, but she does remember some of it. After talking with Anna and going through her medical journals, we came to the same conclusion that it had to be the dassil flower that was given to keep her helpless. The symptoms match what she described had happened to her.

What I don't understand is why someone would go out of their way to get the flower. It grows in The Drylands, west of Fenrikar, deep inside caves in damp places. The Drylands are mostly barren and scarce of any plant or animal life. It's why no one travels or lives out there. Why would her pack go through all that effort to get the flower to drug Sarah?

Sick fucks.

Apart from what had happened to her, she hadn't told me any names, just that her pack did this, and she needed to get out. I won't force her to tell me anymore, just like I won't force her to shift to heal. It would help her, but she has been forced to do things she didn't want to for a while now, and I won't add to the list of people who did that to her. My worry is that it's been nearly two months, and even though there has been improvement physically, mentally, nothing has changed much. She hasn't even left the cabin and if any males go near her, she loses it.

I need to at least try to persuade her to get some fresh air, I muse to myself as I finish the details on my newest carving, blowing any excess shavings from the now carved wood. I put my knife back into my boot and look at my handy work with a small smile. It's jagged in places and the small designs I tried to carve have small chips here and there, but I know Kade will like it anyway.

My wolf mentally stretches inside me, peeking her eyes open at the thought of Kade. She treats him more than just pack. To her, he's her pup. Just how I see him. I raised him from when he was seven, and even though he is my aunt's son, he's more than just a cousin to me. It wasn't easy raising him at first, so many struggles and doubts, but I soon got into the swing of things, and I wouldn't change it for the world. Mostly everything I do, I do for him.

"The perimeter has been checked, and the Eridian is calm," Josh

says through the link, and I tilt my head back, watching the sun high in the sky.

"That's great, all good at the cliffside?" I ask him.

"Yeah, no problems, and no sign of any bora or other creatures."

"It's been long enough since we went into The Deadlands. I don't think the bora know where we went. Call off checking it every night," I tell him, thankful we've had no trouble following us after we got Sarah.

There is a pause before he asks. *"How is she?"*

I don't need to ask who he's on about, he's been asking every day. *"As well as expected, I'm going to try and get her out for a bit, some fresh air will do her some good I think."*

"Hmmm, maybe," he says hesitantly.

I stretch my legs out in front of me. *"Is the cabin prepared for the females?"*

"Yes. They keep hounding me for things. I don't know why they do this to me every time," he sighs, and I can picture him dragging his hands down his face.

Whenever the females go into heat, syncing up together as women do, they always pester him for things to go in the cabin, or they ask him to help them through it every time. He never joins them though.

"Oh, come on Joshy, you love the women's attention." I chuckle.

"For fuck's sake. Here comes the fucking Joshy," he growls. *"Are you purposely trying to annoy me?"*

"Me?" I fake gasp. *"Never."*

He mumbles something down the link that sounded a lot like 'fuck off' but can't be sure. *"Are you done for the day? I still haven't got a hold of Kade yet,"* he says, and I sigh in resignation. Me and the kid really need to have a talk, but it's like I can't get through to him lately.

"I've got some work to do in the office for a little bit and then I'm going for a run. Are you all good for a few hours?"

"Don't worry, I can handle the pack. Let me know when you're back."

"Yes, Dad," I snark back. His chuckles bounce down the link while I pocket my newest carving and move my ass back to my cabin.

SIX

Rhea

I sit on the edge of the water, watching the water flowing down over the edges of the large, circular opening above that mirrors the size of the pool below. The moonlight shines down on the water, making it glisten like a thousand tiny stars are stroking the surface, rippling in a wave of color with the splashes. Small blue-green wisps float around the edges, gliding through the air between the few lilk trees that are inside here, playing with each other in a dance only known to them. Some are as small as the palm of my hand, while a few others are bigger. I gaze at their smoke-like power trailing behind them as they fly before the essence of that power disappears behind them into nothing.

I love being in the cave I have claimed for myself, my own hidden paradise. It's peaceful listening as the water flows down in soft crashes and the soothing swish of the wisps by my ear when they get close and fly past. They don't bother me when they swirl around or hover nearby. I take comfort in their gentleness. They know when I come here, I'm respectful and mean no harm. Mostly, this is the only place you can see them, apart from the few times out in the forest.

The first time I found this place a couple of years ago, it was by accident. We hadn't been this far north in the Eridian Forest, and I was curious, so I went off on my own. I reached the cliffside and was about to move on when I saw an opening within the rock. When I went inside and followed the tunnel, I never expected it to lead to a hidden cave with its natural light flowing from the opening above, or for it to contain lilk trees standing strong and healthy. It was majestic, and one of the most beautiful things I had ever seen.

The moment you first come across pure beauty, it never leaves you. You just stop and stare and take every little detail in. Then you tuck it safely away in your memories for all time, cherishing it. The moment I first saw this cave was one of those times.

Not many people know of this place, and the few who do, don't come here often as they know I've claimed it as my own. Well, with the wisps. But I'm very territorial over it as wolves are when something belongs to them. I've made a home away from home here, with some tables at the sides and a few chairs. My carvings are displayed in crevices that act as shelves in the rock walls, proud, precious, and in clear view. I even have some bedding if I want to spend the night here, which I do when I can.

I close my eyes and give a gentle touch to my wolf, stroking her across her head and then down her nose in my mind. She doesn't let me do this as often as she should, but spending this time together here calms her as much as it does me. She loves it here, feeling more content than she ever has. I have a feeling it's because we are hidden away but not trapped, the opening above makes it feel like we are out in the open. She needs her alone time to refresh, even if she is still a grumpy wolf. Apart from Kade, Josh, and a few others, she simply tolerates everyone else. She wants to be a part of the pack, but also to be on her own or just with her family. It is a predicament sometimes.

She hasn't come out for fourteen years, no matter how hard I try to encourage it. I received her, and then lost her to the safety my body offers. She lost her freedom, and I lost my wolf in the physical sense. She's still there inside me, I can still feel her emotions and she gives me a boost when she's in a giving mood, albeit reluctantly, but with a nudge from me she will if it's absolutely necessary. I miss her though, even though I only had her completely for a short time. It wasn't a pleasant experience, but being able to go wolf is what makes you well, wolf.

Without being able to shift, I feel like I don't belong… anywhere.

"What am I going to do with you, Runa?" I say aloud, my voice echoing around the space slightly as I feel her move beneath my skin.

I don't even know what she looks like. I can't see her clearly in my mind, just feel that she is there. The one time she did come out, I was too busy keeping alive rather than taking a look at my paws.

I lay back, feeling the rich earth beneath my fingertips as I watch the wisps fly over me, chasing one another. I sometimes pretend they are the essence of the ones we've lost, staying close to home. Many have died over the years, especially when we first started accepting people. It was rough with only a few of us having to try and learn to survive out here. We made a lot of mistakes.

I made a lot of mistakes.

I became obsessed for a little while with our safety, hunting on my own, keeping members inside the settlements and refusing to allow them to leave the protection circle the lilk trees provide. The ones we lost were either buried on the farthest edge of Eridian or lost them to the creature that killed them. I still feel guilt from their deaths, amongst other things. It wasn't until Taylor and a few others joined that we trained to protect ourselves properly. He taught us a lot about safety precautions and how to hunt correctly. You could say we owe him our lives, because we really were in bad shape when he arrived. We lived out of crude shelters and ate scraps, barely getting by. He saved us all, and since then, we have saved many and none. Unless they lost themselves, walking to the end of the valley and jumping into the Unforgivable Sea.

Solvier protects us within the circle of lilk trees as best as he can, but he cannot protect us from our inner demons.

I hear movement to the left of me, and I turn my head just as Kade steps into the cave, looking around until he spots me. He gives me a small smile and walks over to me slowly, almost hesitantly.

He's gone from a snot-nosed kid to a six-foot tall eighteen-year-old made of pure muscle. His golden blond hair has gotten thicker on the top since the last time I saw him, and his blue eyes, a slightly different shade than mine, look tired.

I sit up as he plops down next to me, both of us watching as the water hits the sides of the pool and splashes some unsuspecting bugs. Runa comes closer to the surface as we sit in silence, lost in our own thoughts. He's distanced himself from me, still spending more time as a wolf than human. He just brushes me off when I ask about it and says he's fine, but I know something is bothering him. I usually wait it out until he tells me, but my patience is running thin. I'm worried. I even went looking for Solvier again, to see if he had any words of wisdom, but he's been nowhere to be found lately. He does this every so often, but I could really do with some advice on how to handle this.

"You okay?" I ask Kade softly, leaning my head on his shoulder. I pick at the end of my shorts, twirling some loose thread around my finger as I wait for his reply and make a mental reminder to ask Edward to send more material to make some new clothes.

"Yeah, I'm good, Rhea," he says with a sigh, bringing his head to rest on top of mine.

A few wisps fly past us, and I watch as Kade lifts up a

hand. One of the smaller wisp flies down, circling his hand and hovering above his palm like it's perching there. I giggle as he wiggles his fingers, and the wisp bounces like it affects his position. It doesn't, but it amuses me anyway.

"Where have you been? I've not seen you in a few days," I whisper, trying not to disturb the playful wisp.

"Here and there." He shrugs, jostling my head. "Done a lot of hunting and roaming, getting used to all the new smells around Eridian."

He's been doing that for weeks now. "No trouble?"

"Nothing I can't handle," he replies vaguely.

I lift my head off his shoulder to look at him, but he just stares at the wisp, not giving me his eyes. After a tense silence, he turns to look at me with a troubled gaze and a grim look on his face which makes me immediately alert.

"What is it?" I whisper, knowing I'm not going to like what he is about to tell me.

He hesitates for a few seconds while grinding his teeth, before finally telling me. "I spotted a few rogures this morning. Don't worry though, I took care of them," he rushes to add when he sees my eyes widen at his mention of rogures.

I shoot to my feet in one move, my panicked eyes looking down at him. "What do you mean you took care of them?" I shout, horrified at what he's telling me. The wisp flies off with the others, darting behind the trees at my raised voice. I would feel bad for scaring them off, but I'm too preoccupied with my panic. "How many were there?"

"Three, and I handled it, so it's not a problem," he says as he stands to his full height, towering over my five-foot six frame.

"Not a problem," I repeat. "Not a fucking problem. What in the Gods' names were you thinking?" I growl, poking him in his chest. "Have you lost your damn mind?"

"I said I took care of it, and I did," he states, throwing his hands up in the air and glaring at me. "I got rid of the problem, there was no more. Why are you making a big deal out of it?"

"Kade." I pinch the bridge of my nose, willing myself to stay calm. Runa bristles beneath my skin, not liking that he had been in danger either. "You could have been fucking killed, does that even matter to you? And why am I just hearing about this now?" I demand. I'm panicking. I panic for him, panic for the pack and why we had an unexpected visit from some rogures. Were there more around? Are they on their way here now?

"Josh," I bark down the link. *"Do a perimeter check. Now! Three rogures have been in Eridian, they're dead but there may be more."*

"Shit. On it, I'll update you," he rushes out, not asking how or why. I have no doubt he heard the slight fear in my voice. It wasn't fear for me, but fear for everyone else.

I look back to Kade as he speaks. "They were northwest from here at the cliffside. I'm fine. I only got a few scratches, and they're all healed," he tells me, as if it's no big deal that he decided to take on three fucking rogures on his own. I look him over, seeing no visible injuries which calms me somewhat. "And I've only just come back," he continues. "That's why you haven't heard about it until now. It happened not too long ago. I was already out this way when I caught your scent. So here I am."

"You took on three rogures on your own, as a new wolf. You didn't retreat and call on me or Josh through the link, you just decided to come back home like everything is fine. You're telling me you see absolutely nothing wrong with that?" I question in disbelief, shaking my head at him.

Did he suddenly lose his head when he got his wolf?

He lifts a shoulder and tucks his hands into his front pockets or his cargo pants like he doesn't have a care in the world.

Like he didn't just play with his life.

I explode.

"There could have been more of them, Kade! Shit, there might even be. They travel in large packs, you *know* this. You're lucky you're even standing here," I shout, forcing myself not to strangle the kid for his stupidity. "You're an eighteen-year-old who only got his wolf five months ago," I grit out, barely resisting a snarl toward him. "You have no idea how to control your instincts. You should have called for me or Josh down the link. You should have come back to the settlement, and we would have taken care of it. You can't just endanger your life like that. You can't–"

"I can, and I did!" he roars, losing his nonchalant attitude and stunning me into silence with his outburst. He continues as he starts to pace, "I saw them, and I took care of them." He breathes heavily, fists clenching and unclenching. "I ripped them to shreds and tore out their throats until there was nothing left of them but blood and guts. I did what I should have done years ago!"

Confused, I stare at him as he paces back and forth, wondering what he's talking about. What does him tearing rogures apart and putting himself in danger have to do with anything years ago?

Then it hits me, and my face instantly falls.

Shit.

"Carzan," I say gently, speaking the male term of endearment of our family language as I walk toward him. Stepping in his way to make him stop his pacing, I bring my hands up to his face to make him look at me, but he shakes his head and squeezes his eyes shut, refusing my silent request. "Look at me, please," I plead with him, stroking my thumbs over his cheekbones.

He inhales deeply before opening his eyes for me. What I see there breaks my heart for him all over again. So much pain and torment reside in those blue eyes of his, and I wish I could take it all away from him. I wish I could heal these wounds he carries on his young heart. I hear Runa whimper inside my head, affected by his pain as well.

"There was *nothing* you could have done," I choke out, and his face twists at my words. "You were a *child,* Kade, just as Cassie was. The blame is on me and me alone." He opens his mouth to speak, but I cut him off with a shake of my head. "I was responsible for you both, and I failed. Me, Kade. I am forever sorry, and I know sorry doesn't make it any better." I inhale a sharp breath and blink back tears at the pain. I will never forgive myself for not protecting them both. "Her death is on my shoulders, not yours. You did everything a thirteen-year-old boy could have done. It was not. Your. Fault," I whisper the last words, bringing his forehead down to mine, hoping he hears me. Feels the sincerity in my voice.

He breathes in a shuddered breath, then brings his arms around me, hugging me close. My hands drop from his cheeks when he rests his head on top of mine. "It hurts," he says in a guttural tone that has more tears stinging the back of my eyes. "My wolf, he feels the loss of her. He wants something he can't have. Can never have. I don't know what I'm supposed to do, Rhea." His shoulders shake while he burrows his face in the crook of my neck, clinging to me tightly.

I wrap my arms around him, holding him as I feel his tears coat my skin. I'd never even thought about what it would do to both him and his wolf when he got him. I'd seen his and Cassie's bond from the first moment they met, not long after we left our old pack. They were enamored with each other. He was so sweet and protective of her, and she adored and followed him everywhere.

One night, one moment, changed all of that. Leaving heartbreak and grief behind.

I hate that it's my fault that he's feeling this way, that I failed to protect what was most precious to him. He and his wolf are hurting so much, and there is nothing I can do to ease it for them. How didn't I realize that until now?

"I am always here for you, always. Whenever you need me, I'm here," I whisper hoarsely, trying to keep myself together for him. "I pray to Zahariss and Cazier that time will help your heart, Carzan."

More tears wet my neck as he takes a few deep breaths and tightens his hold on me. "Arbiel cana," he says, so heartbreakingly that a lone tear falls silently down my cheek.

"Arbiel cana," I repeat, bringing a hand up to stroke the back of his head to comfort him. The same way I have always done since he was just seven years old.

I hold him to me as I look toward my newest carving over his shoulder. It's a younger version of Kade with a bright smile on his face. So innocent and free, full of life and love.

Before life happened and rogures took his mate from him.

SEVEN

Rhea

I groan as the sound of tapping wakes me up from my much needed sleep. It was late by the time I got back last night, with Kade and I spending hours upon hours talking before we eventually headed back home.

Josh reported back that there were no signs of any other rogures in the area once he came across the ones Kade had killed. What was left of them anyway. It's extremely strange that only three rogures came down from The Deadlands, but I'm thankful regardless that there aren't anymore.

The tapping continues. Whatever it is making that sound has a death wish, one I am more than happy to fulfill. With a growl, I open an eye and peek toward the window on my left. A small, familiar winged creature stares at me through the glass, its dark eyes never leaving mine, as it continues to tap its beak against the window. I huff and rub my eyes, sighing at the thought of getting out of bed. I pull the covers back, yawning as my feet touch the wood floor.

I shuffle toward the window, grumbling with each step until I reach it. It's then I notice the moon still high in the night sky, telling me it's far too early to be getting out of bed. I look back toward the winged creature, and notice the leather strap tied around his neck with a small package attached to the end of it. Unlatching the lock from the bottom of the window, I lift the glass. The cool night breeze caresses my bare skin in the places my night shirt doesn't cover, causing goosebumps to form across my body. I reach out a hand and stroke Illium on the top of his head and underneath his black beak as he caws at me under my attention.

"Sorry, little guy," I coo. "I don't have a midnight snack for you. Why don't you head down to the gathering on your way out, there might be something there for you," I tell him as he caws again softly, nuzzling my hand with his head. I reach for the back of his neck and untie the leather strap, scratching there lightly to ease the muscle.

Croneians are small but clever creatures that are extremely loyal to those they have chosen. As dark as night with midnight blue tipped wings, they are easily hidden as they fly through the night sky. Illium has been flying here for years at Edward's request, sending little packages and messages when he can or when needed. But he's never sent him here in the middle of the night, usually the start of it.

"Thank you, Illium," I murmur, giving him another quick stroke before watching him take off to the sky once again, remaining unseen.

I examine the small package in my hand and move to sit on my bed. With a flick of my wrist, lanterns softly light my room in a warm glow as I get comfy and cross my legs. I remove the leather strap around the package and open the cloth material gently. A rolled-up letter falls out along with a lightweight, dark crystal that I haven't seen before. I pick it up, running my thumb over its smooth edges as it fits in the palm of my hand. A mix of blue and yellow flashes inside the stone, and I feel the gentle thrum of power within it.

Curious as to what Edward has sent me, I undo the string around the letter and roll it open. I recognize Edward's writing straight away from the curve of certain letters, and I can't help the small smile that graces my face. It's been a very long time since I last saw him, and I have missed seeing his face and the stories he tells me about my parents.

Edward is one of the Highers of Vrohkaria, living in Fenrikar at Wolvorn castle with the other Highers. We met each other about two years after I left my pack by accident. I was trying to get food for Josh, Kade, Cassie, and I from a little village he visited that day. He saw me browsing the foods they had and noticed I hadn't bought anything, even though he could probably tell by my thin frame that I wanted to. How could I buy food when I had nothing to buy it with? I wasn't used to the world, and I didn't know how things worked.

I decided it was too quiet to try and steal some food and to come back a little later when it was busier. He followed me out of the village and toward some small woods when I rounded on him, dull blade in hand. I needed to get him to move on and stop following me so I could get back to the others. I didn't know what he wanted, but it wasn't the first time I had to defend myself against someone who wanted to try their luck with me.

He stared at me for a long time, and I stared right back, refusing to let up until he either went away or I had to make him. He took a deep breath like he was trying to smell me, and his eyes widened and started to water slightly. I was confused by his reaction as I stood there, stunned, watching a tear roll down his tanned face. After a moment, he whispered one name, one name that changed everything and nothing at all. It was then that Edward would tell me about my parents and about Eridian. About how I would be safe, and no one would find me. How he thought I was dead.

I was nervous, he was a stranger and a Higher. How could I trust him? He told me many things I didn't know, but made some things make sense, explaining why my life was the way it was. By the time he finished talking, we were both sitting on the ground, surrounded by nothing but the trees and the earth beneath us. I thought about everything he had said to me, and I knew I didn't really have a choice but to trust him. We were starving out here, Josh and I had no home and two kids to take care of. So, I told him. I told him some of my life and who I was with, and he didn't bat an eye, though his face was solemn. He told me if he had known, he would have come to get me, that I never should have had the life I had lived and that he was sorry he couldn't protect me.

But it was just words, and it was too late to change the past. He asked me to meet him back where we sat later that night, and he would get us all to Eridian. Feeling like I had no choice, I spoke to Josh, and we came to the same decision to wait for him to return to take us to this Eridian place.

Edward kept his word and ported us to Eridian, where we would live from then on. He couldn't stay with us, but he said he would help us whenever he could. He had to go back to the castle, and his important day to day duties as a Higher meant he couldn't be away for long the rare times he did visit. After months of us living in Eridian and trying to make a life for ourselves, Edward started sending people to us who also needed a place to start a new life. It's been this way ever since.

And I wouldn't change any of it.

The smile on my face vanishes as I begin to read Edward's letter, and I sit up straighter, reading through his words again and again. My hands tremble, shaking the paper and making the words blur as my breathing picks up. Pure dread overcomes me, and with a muttered 'fuck,' I jump off the bed and head over to my dresser against the wall. I grab some pants and shove my legs into them with one hand, the letter still clutched tightly in the other while I get dressed as fast as I can.

Pants on, I rush out of my bedroom, grabbing the crystal off the bed as I go. My feet slap against the dark wood flooring with my steps, passing Kade's door before I rush down the stairs, holding the banister as I take two steps at a time. I round the bottom and aim for the back of the cabin to the door on the right. Pushing down the handle and opening the door, I walk around my desk and flop down in my chair, putting the crystal and the letter down on the desk amongst my things.

"I need you in the office. Now," I rush out down the link, running my hands through my hair, snagging the tangles but not bothered by the slight pain.

I lean back and grip the armrests of my chair as I wait, looking around the room to try and calm my breathing. My office is simple. A dark wood desk and three chairs, two rows of bookcases filled to the brim with books on the walls to my right, stopping at the floor to ceiling window. To my left, there are two seating benches with small homemade cushions and a small table in the middle of them. There are shelves placed around the room, full of keepsakes I have from Kade and pack members.

My walls are light wood, the same as the rest of my cabin, and framed pictures the pups have drawn for me hang on them. I even had some that Kade did when he was younger, losing interest as he grew older. The bookshelf at my back is for the pack. They contain small information folders on each of my pack members. It's how I keep track of who is here, and what, if any, issues they may have with certain things. It also has details on what females want to go through the heat alone or with help from males, amongst other information about what jobs they would like to do and their skill set. Only a few are allowed access to them, including the pack member. We don't hide what I have written about them. It's their information, they are entitled to see it. There are no secrets.

Unless those secrets are dangerous for others to know.

I grab a pen off my desk, twirling it in my hand to try and shift my thoughts and not let panic set in. Sweat beads at the back of my neck, making my hair stick to it, and I feel Runa twitching inside me, sensing my unease.

They can't find Eridian, they just can't, and more than that, they can't find Sarah. She's been through too much shit to be dragged back to the nightmare she has ran from. No, fuck that. Not happening.

I hear the front door open and close quickly before I hear footsteps rushing my way. In the next second, Josh is standing in the doorway to my office, looking disheveled. His jeans are undone, hanging off his hips, his dark-blond hair is out of his usual man bun, and he's carrying a black t-shirt in his hand, leaving his defined muscles and tattoos on display. His gray eyes find me in the dark instantly, and he lets out a sigh of relief at seeing me unharmed.

"I'm not dying, Josh. You could have at least done your jeans up." I force a chuckle, but it trails off at the glare on his face.

Now I'm the one sighing as I open the top drawer in my desk and take out a hair tie to put my hair up in a ponytail, tossing him an extra one. I wave my hand and the lanterns around the room come alight as Josh closes the door behind him. I wait until he gets himself reasonably decent before sliding the letter across the desk toward him. He picks it up and flicks his eyes to mine quickly before he takes a seat in one of the chairs across from me.

I sit in silence and watch his reaction to the letter while I pick up the small crystal, tossing it in the air and catching it again. His brows furrow, then his eyes widen and snap up to mine, probably thinking the same as I am. I nod wordlessly. He looks back at the letter and continues reading, his eyes moving rapidly as he reads the words. After a few minutes when I'm sure he has read it multiple times, just like I have, he finally speaks.

"What the fuck," he mutters. He keeps looking at me and then back to the letter like it might change before he finally puts it back on my desk.

"They cannot take Sarah or find Eridian, Josh. They just can't," I stress, looking out my window at the forest that continues on until it reaches the surrounding cliffs. I can just make out the dead trees resting atop of them, never changing, never moving. "We have worked too hard and too long for our home here, to find some sense of peace and safety. If they find it, I don't know what we will do. We've never been in a situation of potentially being discovered." I bite my lip as I think. "We could fight, but if Edward is correct in that letter, we aren't strong enough to face who's coming. We could evacuate, but where would we go? We can't stay in Eridian if they find us, but this is the safest place for us in Vrohkaria. We can't even go into another region without a letter of free passage, and the lands are more dangerous to roam than ever. We could be lucky enough that they don't find us, but what if they come across Solvier in the forest? Would they send more people if there aren't enough to capture or kill him? They wouldn't just see him and leave, and they would definitely find us then. It would just be a matter of time."

I get up and walk toward my window, resting my head on the cool glass and closing my eyes against the onslaught of so many emotions running through me. Fear. Panic. Stress. Worry. Dread. They rush through so quickly that it isn't until a hand lands on my shoulder from the side that I realize I'm struggling to get air in my lungs.

"Breathe, Rhea," Josh says calmly. I listen to him taking deep breaths in, and then exhaling slowly. I stay still, focusing on his breathing until I'm mirroring him and getting some much needed air into my lungs.

When my breathing calms, he moves to stand behind me, leaning down to rest his head on my shoulder and look out toward the forest. He takes my left hand in his, rubbing his thumb over the back in small circles, comforting me. We're both silent while I continue to breathe deeply, squeezing his hand in mine as I lift my head off the glass and relax back against him.

"I don't know what will come or will happen," he tells me as gently as he can. "We'll figure it out, we always do, don't we?" I nod my head. "You won't let them get to Eridian, and if they do, you will do everything you can to keep the pack safe, no matter what. You won't roll over, and neither will the rest of us. I know you're scared about what it would mean if they found this place. So am I. But I will be with you through it all, together like always, as a family," he vows, giving my cheek a nudge with his, rubbing against it gently. I feel Runa directly at my cheek beneath my skin, feeling the contact for herself. "I follow you by choice, not pack, you know that."

He brings his right forearm up in front of me from my side, and I look down at the design he has covering his skin there. It's the same one Kade and I also have on our forearms, with only small differences in the designs that we put there ourselves. We all have a few blank spaces left so we can add to the design when we choose.

I trace his forearm with a finger, following the ancient writing, lines and swirls before moving over the marking of the blood link that rests above the blank center, pressing down slightly on it and feeling the tingle in my mind at the connection. I continue downward until I reach his wrist where the runes of our Gods are, the symbols for Zahariss and Cazier intertwining with each other. One full circle at the bottom, one outlined above, slightly overlapping each other with a crescent moon inside each. The tattoos are a sacred marking of my family, given to those who are deemed worthy of their chosen people. We also have other markings that can be given to those in your inner circle. The differences don't diminish the value of such marks upon your skin, they just mean different things to different people.

Seeing the markings so clear in front of me, to look upon what I could lose, gives me the determination to calm my panic and clear my thoughts. I have had much fear in my life, and I won't let it rule me. The cost would be too high.

"We fight," I tell Josh, with steel in my voice. "Protect the pack at all costs. Protect Kade no matter the cost."

I feel him hesitate before he nods his agreement as we look out toward the forest, lost in thoughts of what may come. I won't let our home fall into the hands of the Highers, and I won't let them take any of my pack members back to where they escaped from. We have a home here, and I won't let them take it.

Even if the cost is myself.

EIGHT

RHEA

I turn, giving Josh a quick peck on the cheek and move back toward my desk. Josh leaves without another word, his aura pulsing beneath the surface of his skin as he tries to control his emotions to gather everyone.

I pick up the letter and small crystal off my desk, then crouch down to the bottom drawer. Biting the end of my finger until blood swells to the surface, I place my bloodied finger onto the drawer. I watch as the red liquid soaks into the wood, whispering under my breath as dark runes appear, then change to a pale green. I move my finger away and open the drawer, putting the letter and crystal inside, nestled safely amongst the other important items I have in there.

That done, I stand and head back for the stairs again, closing my office door behind me. I slow my walk as I near the top of the stairs, passing Kade's bedroom door quietly on the landing and listening for any movement inside. Only the sound of his soft snores reaches my ears, letting me know he's still asleep.

That kid sleeps so deeply sometimes. It makes me wonder what keeps him sleeping so soundly when we have hearing like ours.

Moving on to enter my bedroom, I grab the things I need from my dresser and head for my bathroom, flicking my wrist until the room is bathed in light. White units and shelving greet me with splashes of green from my towels and a few plants I have in here. Apart from that, it's all white and dark wood. I open the shower door and turn the knob, letting the water heat up as I place my clothes down next to the sink. Glancing up at myself in the white framed mirror, I let out a defeated sigh at myself.

My lightly tanned skin looks pale, my ice-blue eyes tired, and my ashy-blond hair definitely needs a wash, looking like an animal made its home there while I slept.

I look a fucking mess.

Walking in the shower and going about my normal routine, then change into some dark leather pants and t-shirt. I add a blade to the holder at my hip from my stash in the bedroom and call it a day. Padding barefoot back down the stairs to the open plan kitchen and dining room, the countertops gleam with their light color as I make my way to the liquid of life.

I grab a clean mug and make a coffee before hopping up on the counter and looking at the large dining room table in front of me. Josh, Taylor, Kade, and I made it when Kade mentioned he wanted to eat together with just us and a few others sometimes. Not being able to get what he said out of my mind, we made it happen for him, just like my parents made theirs. We have had many meals together at this table. It even still has Kade and Cassie's little carvings they made together on the top where they sat next to each other, giggling and smiling at secrets only they knew.

He hasn't sat down in that seat since she died.

Swinging my legs back and forth, I wonder if I can find and warn Solvier after I speak with the pack. He can go for days on end without being seen, but I doubt I even have the time to try and find him. If he doesn't want to be found, he won't be. It's as simple as that, but he always seems to disappear when I need to talk to him.

Edward's letter said the search party for Sarah set out over two months ago, and he only found out about it yesterday morning, which has me the most worried. Why was he excluded from the decision to send the Elites into The Deadlands? Edward taught me all about Vrohkaria, its laws and how the Highers ruled over it. He also taught me how the Highers work together. So for an important decision like this to be made, all the Highers would need to be present to cast a vote to approve or deny the task, with the Lord Higher getting the last vote. Yet, Edward wasn't present. He wasn't even told.

The Elites carry out important and deadly tasks across Vrohkaria. For some of the strongest members of the Elite to venture into The Deadlands and be away from their work for this long is unnerving. Why is Sarah so important? She never told me who she was, and I wouldn't pressure her to tell me, but what do they want with her? Her pack abused her, starved her, drugged her, and chained her. But they want her back, for what? So they can continue doing it?

"Fuck that, and fuck them," I growl aloud in the open space.

If the Elites knew where they were going, they could reach us in about thirty-three days on foot. No one knows of Eridian apart from the pack and Edward, even Ellian would have been spelled to forget when he met up with Edward after porting out of here. Those spells are hard to come by though, so they are only used by Edward when it's absolutely needed. So unfortunately, if the Elites found this place, we couldn't just spell them all and send them on their way like nothing happened.

We do have one witch in our pack, Anna, but she isn't strong enough for a spell like that. It takes days for her to recharge one port stone, which from my knowledge, is basic magic. But she doesn't work with the type of energy that's needed for recharging them, so it's a blessing she can even do it at all.

My legs swing faster as I think over the best way to deal

with the Elites. They could be dead already, torn apart by the creatures of The Deadlands, but unless we find evidence of that, we have to assume they are still on the hunt for Sarah. We have the element of surprise. We could track them down and redirect them, or maybe I could bait some creatures and let them deal with them. But in doing so I would be seen, and if one or more Elites somehow survive, they would go back and inform the Highers, causing them to rain disaster upon Eridian.

The other issue I have is Sarah. If they manage to get to Eridian, I need to hide her. She refuses to leave the cabin, and if I just drag her out of there kicking and screaming, I fear it would just worsen the situation. Her progress is small, but it's there. She sometimes gives me a small smile when I visit, and she doesn't fight Anna when checking over her injuries anymore, which are healing slowly due to the dassil flower being in her body for so long. I don't want to do anything that will stop her progress in its tracks or make it worse.

I've never had to deal with something like this before. Sure, I have dealt with pack matters, keeping us safe from the creatures that surround us, but we have never been threatened by people coming here. Never mind the goddamn Elites, who Edward told me a long time ago are the most feared warriors in all of Vrohkaria. They are trained since they are young to hunt and kill the most dangerous of creatures, for fuck's sake. They are the Highers weapons, and effective weapons they are.

I shiver at the image of them coming into Eridian, grabbing women and children and dragging them before the Highers for leaving their packs without permission. For keeping a child from their mother or father. The laws of Vrohkaria are bullshit, and so are the pack laws.

I exhale a breath that sounds more like a growl and throw my mug into the sink, watching as it smashes into pieces with disinterest. Sarah is obviously important to her pack. But how?

Edward never gives in-depth details on the people he sends here, just their name and sex along with a time to go and get them. Sometimes, it's not even that. All that matters is that they are innocent. If they pull their weight around the settlement when they're able to and aren't a threat, we don't care who they are or where they're from. We have a hierarchy in place to keep the peace, but we are all equals here in our daily lives. Sure, it's not the norm for packs, but we are not the norm to begin with. Whoever Sarah is, she is important enough in her pack for the Highers to send the Elites to collect her.

Which means we're in deep shit.

I look across from me to the grandfather clock on the back wall behind my dining table. The ticking noise is the only sound in the room as my thoughts race, and I squeeze the edge of the counter in my hands as I focus on it. Edward has given me many books over the years, and when I came across a grandfather clock in my reading, I fell in love. We can't just go into a nearby town and buy one, so I made it, just like we make most things in Eridian. I chose a lighter wood from the trees that grow near Lovers Falls, using it for the whole body, and a darker wood for the side panels. The clear glass has dried petals in between them from the lilk trees, adding some color to it. It took a long time to create the clock. It's beautiful, and one of my most treasured creations.

But time is something we can't control. We can't get it back. Whenever I look at the clock, I remind myself that time in my past is gone, and I can only go forward, like the hands of the clock.

Seeing it's nearing six thirty in the morning, I look out my window to the morning light shining down on the tops of the trees and realize it's time to get moving. The pack are definitely not expecting what I'm about to tell them this morning. It will be a shock for sure. It sure as the Gods was for me.

"Kade," I call, thankful the link is open between us.

A pause, and then he groans. *"Whaaat?"*

"Emergency meeting at the gathering. Get dressed and head there as soon as possible,"

"Huh? What?" he says, panicking already, and I haven't even told him anything yet.

"Just come, and I'll explain." I hear him stumbling out of bed upstairs and a curse flying from his mouth after a bang. No doubt he ran into something in his haste.

"Josh, get everyone together at the gathering. It's time." I hop down from the counter and walk toward the door, stopping briefly to put on my well-worn boots, tying the laces extra tight. I grab my knife from the entry table and shove it inside my right boot, being extra careful not to nick myself with it. Checking my weapons and titbits that I always carry, I make my way to the meeting with the pack.

Walking between the scattered trees that surround the gathering, I see most of the pack members are already seated on the benches or on the floor, looking half asleep and confused. I hate that I'm about to tell them something that will cause panic, but I promised to always be honest if it affected them, and I will always keep that promise. I keep my face blank as I approach the circle, my steps even as I walk to my usual bench and take a seat. I don't speak, I just sit in silence and wait for everyone to arrive. The pack stops talking when I continue to sit there, looking toward me to begin as a few shuffle nervously in their seats or shush their pups.

Josh eventually arrives with a few others, Kade and Taylor among them. They all take a seat as Josh comes and stands next to me, always the protector even though I'm perfectly safe here. He gives me a subtle nod, letting me know everyone is here and folds his arms as he scans over the crowd.

I stand and everyone's attention stays on me, showing me the respect I've earned by protecting them and giving them a life here in Eridian. I look each member in the eyes briefly, showing that I see them and giving my unvoiced thanks that they came without question. I look at Josie who sits next to Danny, her eyes full of worry and apprehension. I have never called a pack meeting at this time of day in all the years I've been here, she knows something's up. I tighten my ponytail.

With nothing left to wait for, I open my mouth and tell them. "I was informed in the early hours of this morning that an unknown number of Elites are currently in The Deadlands," I state bluntly, seeing no point beating around the thorny bush.

"The Elites?" Kade questions, rubbing his jaw. I nod my confirmation at him. "What are they in The Deadlands for?" Pack members look from him to me, waiting for my answer.

"They have been requested by the Highers to search for a missing woman from another pack," I say, cracking my knuckles to ease some of my growing tension as all eyes immediately fly to the healer's cabin.

"To state the obvious, yes, it's Sarah they are searching for," I confirm. "But she is not the only one here who has gone from their pack or home without requesting it and getting it approved by the Highers. We all have good reasons for being here, but in the eyes of the Highers, we broke the law and are still breaking it by living here. I don't know the location of the Elites in The Deadlands, or if they are dead or alive. But we have to assume that as of right now, they could find Eridian at any moment," I finish, crossing my arms over my chest and taking a deep, subtle breath.

Panic. My pack goes into an instant panic.

A few members get to their feet, looking around with wide eyes as if the Elites are hiding in wait behind a tree. Some start shouting, some crying, and some hold their children close. A younger male knocks over a bucket of water trying to leave the gathering, to where I have no idea, but Taylor grabs him by the back of his shirt and sits his ass down, giving him a stare that would make most people shit themselves. The male doesn't try to leave again.

I rub my temples and look over at Josie. Danny's holding her close as if someone is already trying to rip her away from him. Seeing their fear and hearing their panic sets me on edge. Runa growls inside me, pacing from all the noise. My eyes slide to Kade's, his face slightly pale from the news, and I clench my hands. I never want him to be scared of anything, but he knows what could happen if the Highers get hold of Eridian. Of us, specifically.

He doesn't know all the details about our pack, about his years before we left. I asked Edward to use a memory stone on him to hide the memories of his time there. He doesn't know I did that, but I couldn't see him suffer any longer. What he does know is that our old pack is a danger to us, and if a situation ever arises where he is near them, he runs.

"Alpha?" Katy cries to the left of me, and I turn to look at her. She's holding her son, Oscar, tightly in her lap. "I-I can't go back. Don't let them take me b-back, p-please!" she sobs, tears flowing down her face and into her three-year-old son's dark hair, the same color as hers. I can see her shaking from here, and her green-brown eyes hold so much terror in them that I feel it straight to my soul.

Katy has come far in the seven months she has been here with us, and she's just now coming out of her shell and starting to integrate properly in the pack. I refuse to let anyone take my pack away without a fight. I just don't know if I can win.

"Calm down," I command, and she does instantly, sniffling and wiping at her cheeks. "I will not let anyone take you away from your home, do you hear me? They will not take you back to where you came from," I growl deep at her, at all of them.

Runa joins me, the feeling of protection we have for our pack flowing through us. She might only tolerate most of them, but they are hers to tolerate and she will protect them with me.

Most of the members start to whimper and turn their heads to the side, exposing their necks to me. It takes me a second to realize that I dropped my hold on my dominance, letting my aura flow freely from me.

All Alpha wolves have an aura of dominance that we can control, letting it flow freely or stay locked up tight. Being in a pack with more abused members than not, all the Alpha wolves here keep our aura low for the sake of their comfort. Dominance scares most of our members, and we don't want to scare them anymore than they were, or still are.

I mentally stroke Runa, sending calm to her to help gather myself and regain control. The last thing we need is for the pack to be in any more distress right now.

"Sorry," I say to them, dipping my head down briefly. "We all need to settle. Katy, Oscar senses your unrest. Be calm for him," I tell her gently, using a voice I wouldn't have thought was possible for me right now. I stretch my neck from side to side before I continue, looking out over everyone. "Your safety, all of you, is my top priority. I will not let the Elites report any of you back to the Highers. I will not let them remove you, and I will not leave you unprotected here," I vow. They relax slightly after hearing my words, sitting up a little straighter knowing I will do everything within my power to keep them safe.

"The good thing is, right now the Elites aren't near us. They're still in The Deadlands. Either as bora food or alive and lost. We can work with that. I will take a team with me to The Deadlands to handle the situation. All I need from those left behind is to be alert, to be brave and wait for me." I pause, making sure they hear what I have to say next. "If it has been too long and I haven't returned, I leave Alpha duties to Kade.

He will do right by you."

I know Kade has been unpredictable lately with his wolf, but he will look after the pack in a way I know everyone will be happy with, and he will keep them safe. They trust him. He is my Heir to Eridian, and even though he's young, I've trained him for years to be a leader. I look over at Kade, but he keeps his eyes straight ahead, refusing to look at me. Despite his feelings, he sits there like an immovable force in front of the pack, strong and sure.

I smile to myself at the man he's becoming. I need to accept that he's not a kid anymore, and I can't wrap him up in cotton leaves to keep him safe. He will face danger again throughout his life, but I can try and control what danger that is.

And I'm determined for the Elites to not be one of them.

NINE

RHEA

The pack shuffles out one by one after being dismissed, touching me briefly before they leave in a show of strength and support. Runa settles at their touch, happy they have calmed down and are trusting us to take care of the problem.

Josie comes up to me last with Danny, her eyes red around the edges from holding back tears of fear for me, for us all. This could be the last time we ever see each other. I grab her and pull her close, breathing her in as wildflowers fill my senses, her favorite scent. A soft cry escapes her, and I rub soothing circles on her back, shushing her gently. Danny puts his hand on her shoulder, squeezing tenderly and prying her away from me. We stare at each other, so many unspoken words passing between us. Not a single sound escapes us, but knowing exactly what we are saying.

Come back to us.

"Be safe," Josie whispers, her voice trembling with the words. I nod, unable to speak over the lump in my throat, to tell her that I will be when we both know I can't promise that.

Danny guides her away from the gathering, their steps slow as they walk. When they reach the edge of the trees, Josie looks back at me one more time, sadness flooding her eyes before she turns and disappears from sight. They will probably go back to their cabin and hold each other tight tonight, like they are the only ones in the world. A sharp pain goes through me at that thought. Would I ever have that? Would I ever have someone to hold me tight and look at me like I was their world? Would I ever let anyone? Would I even have the chance?

Colten sighs and throws himself onto a bench heavily, pulling me out of my depressing thoughts. "Well, how screwed are we?" he asks.

"Col," Hudson snaps at him, glaring so hard at the younger male you would expect him to drop dead any second. Taylor and Sebastian come closer to where we are standing, checking around us for any listening ears.

Colten shrugs, looking down and picking at his pants. "What?" he replies, unbothered. "We're fucked unless by some miracle they don't find us here. If they have a task, they see it through. My father was exactly like that. He would become obsessed and be gone for weeks and weeks at a time until he completed what he set out to do. They are called the Elites for a reason. They are the best at what they do. With a reputation like theirs, most people usually stay out of their way. They may live in Vrohkaria, but they are a class of their own. Even the Highers are wary of them."

This isn't news based on what Edward has told me, or from what I have read in the texts on Vrohkaria's history. The Elites have been around for hundreds of years, created by the first council of Highers after the King and Queen died. But hearing it come out so seriously from Colten sends a shiver down my spine. He knows firsthand what an Elite is like.

"I know their reputation, well some of it, but they bleed like anyone else. Elite or not, we have to protect the pack at all costs." I look at each of my closest pack members, and they nod in agreement, knowing we have to do whatever it takes. Kade stays silent, still refusing to look at me.

"Sarah is still not in any fit state to move," Josh interjects, steering the conversion away from the Elites and tilting his head in the direction of the healer's cabin. "If the Elites do get into Eridian, she can't be moved. She wouldn't be able to handle it." My eyebrows raise at him in surprise. How does he know what she could or couldn't handle? He's not seen her since the day she arrived many weeks ago.

I pinch my lip with my fingers, wondering what the best thing would be to do. If we had to move her, she would need to be sedated, it would be too risky otherwise. Although, being drugged and waking up in a different place again wouldn't be good for her mental state. But it's better than having to return with the Elites if it came down to that.

"I think it's best if we leave her where she is for now," I offer, and Josh's shoulders relax. His chest rises with a deep breath before letting it out slowly. *Interesting.* I set my eyes back to Taylor as I ask, "How many trap stones do we have?"

Taylor tilts his head, his amber eyes focusing as he thinks. "Eight," he finally says. "We also have a few slow ones."

"Hmmm," I contemplate, reaching down and pulling my knife from my boot and twirling it in my hand. I copy the moves that Sebastian is doing with his own blade since the pack members left. He notices me watching him after a few moments and his tawny eyes flash in amusement before executing more difficult movements. "Asshole," I grumble when I can't keep up with him. He chuckles, throwing me a wink, then flips the blade around and launches it in the poor, unsuspecting tree across from him.

"What are you thinking?" Hudson inquires, pulling my stare away from a smug faced Seb.

I put my knife back in my boot and place my hands on my hips before turning to Hudson. "I'm thinking that the best way to deal with the Elites if they are alive, which is highly likely, is using the creatures of The Deadlands against them. If we can lead a lot of the creatures to where they are without being seen, they will be overrun and left with only two options. Die or retreat." I don't want anyone to die, but if it's between them or my pack, I'll choose my pack every single time.

"I agree." Taylor nods. "If it works, they won't know anyone is living out here, and they will have to conclude that Sarah has also died."

"I think it could work," Colten chimes in, standing up and stretching while Hudson, Josh and Seb nod in agreement. Kade doesn't respond.

"There is one problem though," Taylor says, his eyes holding mine. "If they die, won't more Elites or the Highers come looking for them?"

Well, shit. I didn't think of that. I groan out loud. "So we have to send them back, and make them give up the search." I nod, resigned, knowing this is going to be more difficult than just having them die. If we fail, we are more than likely not coming home. "Edward can't help us either. He doesn't know where the Elites are specifically, and he isn't even supposed to know they were sent to The Deadlands. We're on our own with this."

I know if Edward could help us, he would. He has risked his life many times over the years in helping people come here, in helping us. If the Highers found out about what he was doing, he would be sentenced to death. He's broken too many laws. Repeatedly.

I've always felt like Edward was our safety net. And now to have that suddenly gone, we are free falling with nothing to catch us. It's scary having to face a problem as serious as this ourselves when we have never faced something like this before. The outcome will affect every single member of the pack in ways that are yet to be seen.

I look at my friends, the people I'm closest to, memorizing their faces as they do the same. The air changes with a sense of helplessness that I try really hard not to feel. This might be the last time I see them in our home, and a lump forms in my throat. I cough roughly to cover up the sob that wants to escape, causing the guys to look away from me and pretend they hadn't noticed that show of vulnerability.

Sebastian flips a new blade aggressively, his jaw tight. Taylor stands extremely still, staring hard at the floor like it has all the answers. Colten rubs the back of his neck, looking up into the sky, and Hudson stares at Colten with a look of determination in his blue eyes. Josh still looks at me, his stare on the side of my face roaming over my features. And I… I look at Kade. His sharp jawline, strong nose, high cheekbones, his hair blowing gently in the breeze. I memorize every detail down to the tattoo on his right forearm, the blood link proudly displayed in between the lines and swirls.

He got his tattoos just hours before his eighteenth birthday as part of a sacred ritual my family completes before they get their wolf. It is a blessing upon oneself, a show of faith in our Gods, a show of respect to his wolf, and a show of loyalty to his family. That night is a precious memory I hold close to my heart, thankful I was able to be there for that monumental moment in his life and to be included in marking him permanently. I'm truly proud I can call him family.

Right now, though, he isn't happy with my decision for him to stay here. I know he will gladly step up and be whatever the pack needs him to be, but he believes he should be going with us. He doesn't have to speak for me to know this, I just know him well enough to gauge his thoughts.

"Tell Finn, Axel, and Eliza to go wolf when we leave, Josh. It might take a little bit for Kade to get his head on straight after we leave."

Josh nods subtly at my request, not saying a word as he looks at the man we have brought up together. He walks over to Kade and plonks down next to him, both sitting in silence as I watch. They got into so many arguments when Kade was younger. He was always an act first, think later kind of kid, not realizing the dangers around him. Josh would constantly lecture him about looking where he's going, or to think before he decided to chase a rabbit down a narrow hole and get himself stuck. But seeing them sitting side by side, their body language says it all. All three of us formed a bond because of our old pack, and it's unbreakable. I wished for a long time that we had a good life in our old place, that we were surrounded by our families, that we were loved and taken care of. I don't wish that anymore. My home is here, my people are here. I wouldn't change my past because it meant I ended up here with my chosen family.

Josh nudges Kade's shoulder, a small smile on his face. "Come on, Carzan, it's not all bad. You're really needed here to keep the pack safe. We're not just shoving you out the way. You need to keep things running smoothly and help anyone who needs it. We trust you with this."

"I can help you out there," Kade grounds out. "I have my wolf now, another person is another chance of making the Elites leave."

"It's also another person that we could lose," I explain, eyeing him warily. "You are about to stand in for me, Kade, you are the only one who can while we are not here. You have to put pack needs before your own. They will be looking to you to reassure and guide them. I have taught you everything I do here. I have been since you were eleven. It is important you step up now and put your feelings aside. I have no doubt you will be what they need, whether it's for a few days, weeks, or permanently." I gulp over the last word, hating it is a possibility, but knowing we can't hide from it. We can't ignore that we may not come back.

The Deadlands are more dangerous the further inside you go.

We could run into all sorts of creatures and be killed off before we even have a chance.

Kade shakes his head, fists clenching on his knees as he still refuses to look at me. "You expect me to just let you leave me here while you go out to possibly die? We are always together."

"I know we are." I walk forward and sit down next to him, taking his clenched fist in my hand. I pry his fingers open and link ours together. I don't like this any more than he does. The possibility of never seeing his face again will tear me up if I think about it too much. But the alternative is just not an option.

"I'm not saying you are not capable of helping, I wouldn't have put you in charge if I thought otherwise. We don't know what we are getting ourselves into when we leave. We are going in blind. I need someone here who can take care of the pack, especially the pups. They love you and have missed you a lot since you have been going out for longer lately." I give his hand a gentle squeeze. "I don't like leaving you behind any more than you do, but it's the right decision. You know this is the way to proceed. Emotions cannot sway these decisions that are made for the pack." For you, I add to myself. I whisper down the link to him. *"Please understand."*

He lets out a small snarl and then blows out a breath. Finally, he looks at me, his eyes sad but sure in the decision he has made. He nods, and accepts that he's staying here, pulling me into a hug. I lean into him in relief and look at Josh over his shoulder. Josh gives me a small smile and wraps his arms around us both, pulling us close. We sit there holding each other close for a few precious, quiet moments, breathing each other in while our wolves rub up against the others below the surface of our skin. Until Seb decides to open his mouth.

"Do I get to join in, or is it limited to three?" he drawls. Before I can open my mouth to tear him a new asshole, we're being jumped on. The breath I took to verbally rip him to shreds turns into a squeal when I feel the weight of him on my back.

The next thing I know, the rest of the guys are there adding to the pile and squishing us until we fall off the bench and onto the dirt floor. I laugh as I pinch someone's side and they let out a high pitch squeal that makes me snort. Oh, that is some good bribery material I could use for later. I flick my eyes forward to see Josh pulling someone's hair, Kade squashed beneath us all eating dirt, and Hudson with someone in his armpit. Gods help them.

"Tap out! I tap out!" comes a muffled voice from somewhere as the sound of someone gagging hits my ears. I shove Seb, the squealer, off my back, but not before getting in a cheeky nipple pinch and rolling off of Kade. He looks like he's barely breathing after the weight of us on top of him. Taylor stands next to us, arms folded, but I see the amusement in his eyes. Still chuckling, I sit up and look over to see Colten on all fours gagging.

Well, at this point I think it's safe to say it was Colten that was in Hudson's armpit. To make it worse, Hudson is shirtless. The poor guy will be picking hair out of his teeth for a few hours.

"You." *Heave*. "Dirty." *Heave*. "Bastard," Colten manages to choke out while shooting Hudson a dirty look. Hudson just smirks back at him. Meanwhile Sebastian is on the floor, crying with laughter that is just too damn contagious for me not to join in. I fall back on the ground, laughing along with them all at Colten's expense. He's a good sport though, and eventually joins in with us, spitting out the odd hair.

"I'm surrounded by idiots," Kade chuckles, wiping dirt off his face and looking up at the clear blue sky trying to catch his breath. I join him, looking at the cloudless sky. The weather is warm with a slight breeze, the trees swaying along with it. Such a pretty, peaceful day for such dreadful news.

"Yeah, but we're your idiots," I reply with a fake smile on

my face, breathing in the scent of my pack, grass, and flowers. Spring is my favorite season. I hope I'll get to see it again if all goes to plan.

Either way, Kade will still be able to continue to see it, if it's the last thing I do. Emotion clogs my throat, and my eyes burn, but I won't let it overrule me. Not now. I need to be clear headed for the unknown that we are about to face.

"Arbiel Cana." It's a whisper, but it comes out strong. It's a vow and a statement all at once.

TEN

Darius

"I'm sure Charles has lost his mind. What in the Gods was he thinking of sending us here?" Leo grumbles from behind me. "We've been in this fucking dead place for weeks now. It's never ending." I grunt in agreement. It always seems never ending inside The Deadlands.

In the history of the Elites, no one has ever traveled this deep into The Deadlands, not even for our rite of passage at age twelve. Those that did end up in its depths and never came back out again, falling to the creatures that stalk this land.

We don't know how many creatures actually live in The Deadlands, but I've read about many in texts and seen enough sketches to know they shouldn't be fucked with. Two of our Elite trainees have already been injured from running into a couple of gresins, and I don't think they will survive another attack.

Gresins are tall, skinny creatures with thin, pale green skin, clawed hands, and long tusks curving out of their cheeks that they use to strike if you're close enough. They're strong, despite their skinny frames, and they managed to claw one of my trainees through the stomach and pierce another through the leg. They fell behind as we moved through the dead trees, and the gresins thought them easy targets.

We took the creatures down before they did any more

damage, but now we have two injured in the center of our group, slowing us down when we should be picking up the pace. I made them shift to their wolves to heal faster. It hurt them to do it, but it benefits us all in the long run. They shouldn't have lagged behind if they didn't want to be thought of as a snack. I shake my head to myself at their stupidity. If they really thought being at the back kept them safe, then they have learned their first lesson out here the hard way.

We haven't seen any more gresins since. We've run into quite a few other creatures while we've been here, but the gresins have been the worst so far. We can take care of ourselves easily, but having Elite trainees here is a different story. Having to fight while defending dumbasses that can barely hold a blade right splits your concentration.

We all thought it would be a good training experience for any trainees who volunteered to come with us. I bet they're regretting that decision now, because I sure fucking am.

They should have stayed at Vokheim.

"Charles wasn't thinking, brother," Damian eventually grouches to Leo. "I've been on some shit tasks, but even I have to admit that this takes the cake and the frosting on top. How many creatures have we come across since entering this land? And we haven't found any sign of this woman or whoever took her in here." He kicks a stone off the ground. "They're probably dead, gobbled up by Gods knows what. There is no way they survived here," he concludes next to me as he snaps a branch from a nearby tree, stripping the dead bark with his fingers in frustration.

"They're definitely dead," Zaide grunts next to me, the scowl on his face showing his displeasure about being here. I have to admit, even I'm getting sick of being here. Weeks and weeks and we've not come across any other living person.

I stay silent, not bothering to add to the conversation.

We carry on wading around dead trees, broken branches cracking beneath our feet as we move. The only sliver of light we have in here is the greenish glow coming from the oozing liquid that seeps from the blackened trees. I don't even know what it is, but I'm not touching that shit. It started appearing about three days ago and I have a feeling it's because of how deep we are now.

With all of this and added complaints from Leo and some of the trainees, I'm close to chopping someone's hand off to really give them something to complain about.

We walk for another few hours, the time stone I have helping to keep track of the time and days for us. There is no other way to tell in here with the branches covering up the view of the sky. We arrive at a small clearing between the trees with a pool of slush-like water off to the right. It's still as the night with glimmering mushrooms growing sparingly around it.

"Set up camp," I order my men, and everyone drops their gear beside them and starts unpacking their necessities. Furs are placed on the ground, water skins set out to be refilled, and dried foods passed around. Maize, an Elite witch, starts putting protection crystals around us in a wide circle to keep unwanted visitors at bay as we rest. She touches each one as she places them onto the ground, and their clear color changes to azure, letting us know they're activated. The light coming from them is bright enough to light our resting place, which is helpful.

I drop my own pack and lean against a tree that isn't oozing light, watching my team rummage around and make their resting place for the night. The two that are injured curl up near the center, feeling sorry for themselves. Strange noises hit my ears. They sound like whispered shrieks flowing near us, but there is no breeze to carry it. I tilt my head to try and decipher it, acknowledging that it's the same sound I've heard every time we have stopped to camp. We haven't met the creature it comes from yet, unable to pin it down and remove the potential threat, though I think we may meet it soon.

I scan our surroundings through the trees, keeping my team safe as they work. Leo huffs near the center of our made-up camp and lies flat on his back, looking at the twisted branches above. His legs bend before he puts his arms behind his head, relaxing like he isn't inside a deadly land that could kill him in his sleep. I shake my head at him and look at Zaide as he approaches. He leans against the tree next to me, blades hidden in his scabbard as he watches the others.

"Do you feel anything?" he asks.

I focus on my senses and shake my head. "Nothing different than usual." Apart from sensing the odd small power spike every now and again, there is an ominous feeling since entering this place. It's like something is calling to me, and I can't stop it. Or refuse it.

"How long are we going to keep going?" he asks. "This whole rescue mission is pointless." Shifting his weight with his eyes still on our pack, he waits for my answer.

"I'm not sure. We still have over two months until Charles's deadline. But I agree with you, she has to be dead, and I doubt we will even find a body now." I run a hand down my face. "We haven't come across one single piece of evidence of anyone even entering here, or any rogures. I don't know what Charles expected us to find, but we sure as shit aren't finding it." I keep my eyes on the trees, watching for any movement. "We will keep going until the deadline then port back. If we go back too early, he will be on our asses."

"Sure," he mumbles in response. He doesn't offer anything else, but I know he will stick with me until I leave.

I take out the square, white time stone from my pocket. The lines on the stone are black, followed by shorter lines in-between. Seeing the glow of one line near the top, I know it's late into the night. "Get some rest, we're covering more ground tomorrow." I hear a few sighs and grumbles from the pack, but I ignore them. If they didn't want to put in the effort, they shouldn't have become Elite. Lazy bastards.

You don't get to hold the title of Elite until you can prove you have what it fucking takes, and moaning about hard work will get your ass kicked out and sent home. Being an Elite is simple. You strive to be the best and put in the effort, or you don't. There is no in between.

Maize saunters over to me, hips swaying in her barely there shorts. A few of the males stare at her ass as she comes to a stop a foot away from me. She's pretty and acts innocent, but she has a nasty streak that she seems to think no one knows about. Dark hair, light eyes, big tits, and an ass most trip over, she has no issue using her assets to get what she wants.

"The crystals are done. Is there anything else you would like me to do, Alpha?" Her voice is smoky and seductive, most men would be drooling by now with the added look of lust in her eyes. I'm not most men. I used her mouth a few times a long time ago, but stopped as soon as she talked about feelings. Clearly, I picked the wrong woman to satisfy my needs. I don't want feelings. I just want to fuck when I need a release.

"That's all I need," I say dismissively, running a hand through my dark hair as I turn to look back out through the trees. She stays in front of me for a few moments while I ignore her presence. Eventually, she huffs under her breath and walks away.

Leo cackles on the ground, witnessing me brush off her advances, and I shoot him a glare. The little fuck knows how much her pestering makes me want to snap her neck.

Much more lately with this restlessness within me.

I would be pushed to do it too if the Highers wouldn't drag me to another seat and make me become one of them. Maize might be in my pack, an Elite, but I have no doubt that the

Highers have her in their pockets and on their cocks. Another reason I stopped using her mouth.

I sit down, banishing the thought, and pick out some dried meat from my rucksack, taking a strip and chewing the hard texture. It tastes like shit, but it's our only source of food out here. We only have clean water because Maize duplicates our water sacks, and even those are dwindling.

Eating the last of my food, I rest my arms on the top of my knees, getting as comfortable as I can for the first watch. Zaide moves toward the center of our makeshift camp, kicking Leo's leg as he passes and Leo howls like he's lost a limb. He must have pissed Zaide off with his complaining earlier.

I close my eyes and listen to the even breathing of everyone as they sleep, letting my senses go wide.

Nothing, not even a twinge of movement.

Just that small hum of power somewhere in the distance.

I wake at the sound of shuffling, and my eyes snap open. Looking around the camp, I see no one moving, not so much as a twitch. My eyes slide to Damian who is on the last watch. He gives me a confused look at my sudden movement, then straightens when he sees me tilt my head, knowing I'm trying to pinpoint where a sound came from. It's soft, barely there, but I hear it.

A scrape of dried dirt. A slight snapping of branches.

I get to my feet slowly, my blade already in hand as I edge toward the right side of the camp. Damian slowly follows, his steps quiet behind me, knowing I need to concentrate. Stopping as I reach the protection crystals, my brows knit together as the sound comes and goes. I look over at Damian and nod my head in the direction of the others, a silent command to wake them. He rushes off quietly, and I look back through the trees, my eyes narrowing. Nothing is moving, but the air feels thick and heavy, yet somehow warm as I grip my blade tighter in my hand.

I let my senses flow free and feel *something* up ahead in front of me. I sense the rest of the Elites getting to their feet, alert and wary at being woken up suddenly. I glance over my shoulder at Max and Rilo, the two injured trainees who are still in their wolf forms. Their ears perk to listen, but they are still a little sluggish on their feet. My eyes land on Zaide next, his curved, twin blades in hand as he focuses past me while remaining in a defensive position in front of the others. Leo notches an arrow to his longbow, aiming just past my left shoulder, covering me while my eyes are elsewhere. Jerrod takes the back, his body at an angle so he can see us all and holds his twin blade axe in his grip.

My eyes roam over the trees before narrowing at a spot in front of me, feeling eyes on us. On me. I shift my feet slightly apart and straighten my back to prepare for whatever is coming.

The air is tense. The dark of the forest is suffocating while we wait for the creature to show itself. And when it does, I will rip its spine out and hang it in the trees as a warning for any others that try to attack us.

The shuffling sound comes again, but it's closer this time, and I let out a deep warning growl as my lips peel back, my face twisted into a snarl as my wolf nears the surface. A choked, wet gurgle suddenly comes from behind us, and my head snaps its way as it grabs my attention. Near the dark pool of water, a woman has her serrated teeth in the neck of one of my men, its eyes rolling in pleasure as it sinks its teeth deeper into its prey. Weston's eyes lock with mine, terror and pain filling them. I can do nothing but watch as she rips out his flesh, blood spraying the ground as she consumes it. He wouldn't have survived a bite like that, no matter what I did. He was dead the moment she clamped her teeth into him.

My body tenses as his body goes limp, eyes dimming, but she doesn't relent, making sure no one can take her meal away from her. Snarling in rage, I turn toward the creature, furious that she even got in our protection circle. The Elites back away from the pool of water, never taking their eyes off her, knowing this predator just became our prey.

Leo's blue eyes flick to hers briefly before he returns his attention to the disturbance at my back, covering me. I don't know what type of creature she is, but she chose her own death by killing one of my Elites and having the nerve to come into our camp.

Her sunken, dark eyes hold mine, still chewing the flesh of my male as I stalk toward her. She shuffles back into the pool, the water coming up to her ankles, and I dart forward, grabbing her jaw and squeeze tightly. She lets go of Weston, his body falling in a heap at our feet as she scratches at my arm. A pained sound leaves her, but I pay it no mind, looking into her eyes and letting her see what she has awoken inside.

She stills with what she sees. Her arms fall limply to her side, and her eyes are full of terror. I bring my blade up slowly and put it to the center of her forehead, keeping a tight grip on her jaw so she stays still. Pushing the blade slowly into her pale, wrinkled skin, I let her feel the burn of pain as I sink it to her skull. She's shrieking now, fighting me with renewed effort, but it doesn't matter.

Her life was forfeit the second she came into my camp. Her end will be painful for killing one of mine.

My grip tightens on the blade, and I twist, relishing in her high pitch squealing before I force it forward to the hilt.

Then she's silent, just like everyone else.

ELEVEN

RHEA

We crouch behind the dead trees, using strips of cloth to plug the glowing fluid leaking from them. We make sure to keep the luicium off of us as we do so to remain in complete darkness, using the shadows to our advantage as we watch the Elites sleep in their temporary camp at a distance. A brown-haired male keeps watch, scanning the trees surrounding them, but not noticing we are here.

After days and days of searching, I thought we'd lucked out and they had either left or were headed in the wrong direction. But when Taylor scouted ahead of us to check if it was safe to rest for the night, he came back and told us that he had found them. We packed our things up quickly and stalked through the trees toward them, silent as the air in the forest and set up to observe them, trying to find any weaknesses.

I shuffle on my knees somewhat, trying to ease the ache there when I see a dark-haired male suddenly snap his eyes open. I freeze mid move, my heart pounding with my knee slightly lifted off the hardened ground. He then tilts his head and gets to his feet in a silent, fluid motion, and my eyes track every move. That shouldn't have been possible for a man his size, but he did it with the ease of an experienced warrior. He's tall, probably taller than any other male I have come across, and he keeps getting taller as he heads closer toward us. I feel the others tense around me at his movements, none of us moving a muscle as we watch him. He's in all black, his t-shirt seemingly attached to his body like a second skin, outlining his muscular figure and defined muscles. Tattoos peek from the collar, gliding up his neck a little, and I look over them curiously before I glance at the ones slithering down his arms and stopping at the crease of his elbows.

As I gently lower my knee back down on the ground, my thigh burning from the effort, I stop breathing as I feel his eyes land directly in our direction. His weighted gaze is heavy as it seems to stay on me. I drag my eyes down from his arms hesitantly and look at the dark blade in his hand, slightly curved and wicked. I absentmindedly lick my dry lips. He bends his knees a little, and my eyes fly back up to his face, unable to resist any longer. The pounding of my pulse increases as I realize he knows something is here, watching them.

My limbs become frozen when I see fury in his gaze. It feels like he's crawling inside me, like I'm some sort of prey about to be slaughtered by the predator before us. Runa growls at my thoughts and gives me a harsh nudge under my skin. She doesn't like us being thought of as prey. We are far more than that.

My lungs expand before I let out a long breath, shaking off the feeling and moving my eyes to the male beside him. It's the same male who was on watch. He's slightly smaller than the dark-haired male, but he's also looking in our direction, features tight as he scans the shadows. He suddenly wanders off to the center of the camp, waking the rest of the sleeping bodies. Quickly after, a blond male is aiming an arrow our way, eyes hard and clear. Another male with twin blades stands, getting into an offensive position in the center, ready to face the threat head on, while a huge guy with an axe moves further back.

The tall male, who is still staring at me, releases a low,

threatening growl, causing the small hairs on my body to stand to attention. My body warms, and tingles spread across my arm at the sound, my heart missing a beat before starting up once again. My brows furrow at my reaction to the deep and violent sound while Runa perks her head up inside of me, ears forward as she listens. Another sound suddenly reaches my ears, and the warmth that held my body turns ice cold. The dark-haired male turns to look behind him, and I lean to the right, hands gripping the dead bark of the tree to hold me as I follow his gaze. I nearly gasp out loud at the sight.

A pale, ghastly figure of a woman has her teeth sunk into someone's neck, blood dripping down the man's front as she digs her teeth in harder. A fucking water hag. Shit. I exchange a quick, worried glance with Josh, who's hiding behind the tree next to me, before looking back to the creature. The water hag suddenly tears her teeth away from the man, and I swallow a couple of times. Seeing the lumpy, bloodied flesh hanging from her mouth is not something I enjoy. My vision starts to blur at the sight, my heart kicking up a notch while my breaths start to come out in small, fast pants.

"Rhea, you're being too loud!" Josh calls out down the link, but my head is hazy, like I'm listening underwater.

I close my eyes and will myself to calm down, to stave off the dizziness that I'm feeling. It's not like I haven't seen something like this before. I have seen dead bodies and gruesome injuries. But seeing it so suddenly combined with the look on the man's face as she tore at his neck was enough to set off a reaction I can't control. His look of pure, unadulterated terror, knowing he has no chance at surviving an injury like that. It's hard to witness.

A soft, cloud-like touch presses down on the top of my head, the feeling causing me to grimace at the painful stabs to my scalp. Barely there fingers soothe the pain and then trace along my forehead, down to my cheek, and the dizziness starts to fade away. The ghost-like caress feels wrong but welcoming at the same time as my breathing evens out.

A hand touches my shoulder, and I jolt. My eyes spring open and my mind clears as I look into Josh's worried, gray eyes as he crouches next to me. *"I've been trying to get through to you. You shut down the link,"* he tells me anxiously, squeezing my shoulder lightly.

I shut down the link? I didn't even feel it.

My brows furrow in thought. How did the link shut down and I didn't know it? When your link shuts down, it's like an empty space inside your head. An endless void, waiting to be filled by the presence of the one who owns the space there. It's uncomfortable and unnerving. It's why I don't understand how Kade can be so unaffected by it when he shuts us out.

I shake my head. *"I didn't know I closed it,"* I reply. Lifting my hand to my forehead and trailing my fingers down my cheek, I still feel a slight tingle where something touched me. What the fuck was that?

I ignore it and Josh's curious stare and look back out toward the camp. The man the water hag has in her clutch slumps forward, but she doesn't let him drop to the floor. She holds him closely, keeping her prey with her. The tall, dark-haired male stalks toward her, sure and steady, and I lean forward, wanting to see what he will do. His hand flies out, gripping her jaw tightly, not a single sign of worry in his posture as she drops the dead guy and claws at his hand to try and get him to release her. I watch on, fixated as she stills completely with her horrified gaze locked on the man before her. The male brings his curved, black blade slowly to her forehead, and then starts to press forward through her gray skin. He pauses the blade as she starts shrieking, the sound echoing her pain from the weapon lodged in her flesh. Her shrieks are so loud it's like she's right next to us, and I shove my hands over my ears to try and block it out. I see everyone else do the same apart from the dark-haired male and some other men in the camp who are eagerly watching on as we are.

After a few short moments, he plunges the blade through her skull, the sound of her shrieking instantly stopping and replaced with the sound of bone splitting. It echoes around the now silent night as I remove my hands from my ears. He pulls the blade back out in one upward move, slicing her head open and darkened blood spills over him and the ground. The water hag stays upright for a few moments, unseeing eyes staring ahead, until she falls back, landing in the pool of water with a splash. We don't move, watching on as the male stares at her, cocking his head to the side in a pure animalistic move. It's like he's not sure if he's done with her yet.

The forest seems to freeze. My shoulders tense, and my breath is trapped in my lungs, waiting to see if her shrieking has roused any other creatures of The Deadlands. A few moments pass without any sounds of movement, and I slump in relief. I look around to the rest of the people in their camp and see all their focus is on the male, except for the blond guy still aiming his bow our way.

This is it. This is our chance while they are distracted, if we can remain unnoticed by the archer.

"Josh, Taylor said he can get some bora here fast, right?" He nods his confirmation. *"I don't think those crystals will hold up against a large family of bora. Let's stick to the original plan."*

He waves subtly to get Taylor's attention who's leaning behind a tree with Seb to the right of us. Josh signals to him that it's time to put our plan in place, and his eyes harden before he nods. Taylor looks around the edge of the tree to the camp briefly before he quietly slips away deeper into the forest, grabbing Hudson and Colten on the way. Seb takes the place

Taylor left, crouching low and taking out a few stones from his pack as quietly as possible before putting the pack behind a tree.

Quiet murmuring comes from the camp, and I watch as some people move toward the dead, male body on the floor, sadness etched on their faces. I feel bad using the death of a man to my advantage, but I can't pass up this opportunity. I lift my hand and sign for us to start our task, backing away from where I was hiding to gain a good distance from the protection crystals.

We meet at a tree further back and pass out the stones quickly before we part ways again. As quietly as possible, I sneak around their camp on the edges of their visibility and hearing, placing the dark, violet stones on the ground. Avoiding broken branches as I go to keep silent, I continue around knowing Josh and Seb are doing the same thing until eventually, we create a circle around them. Just like they did with their protection crystals.

As I round the camp at a safe distance, I keep a watchful eye on them. The dark-haired male is still standing where I last saw him, and the archer is still aiming where we were, so I know we have moved undetected. I spot Josh a little distance ahead of me, placing his stone down gently.

"This is the last one I have. Seb is waiting for Taylor, Hudson, and Colten to come back. It won't be long now." He runs a hand over his hair, careful not to dislodge his bun as he leans against the tree closest to him, his eyes focused on the Elites.

I crouch low and hold the stone just slightly off the ground, ready to put it down when it's time. Taylor has spent a lot longer in this forest than any of us, so he knows how to track bora down quickly. He also knows how to piss them off, and with Hudson and Colten helping, I think pissed off will be an understatement for the bora.

Still watching the camp as they now carry the dead man to the center, we wait, muscles tense and ready for the bora to come and for us to get at a safe distance away from what's about to happen.

Closing my eyes, I will myself to not feel guilt for what I'm about to do, but I know it will be of no use. I place my free hand on the ground, waiting for the slight tremble that I know will come. It's not long before the rumbling of the surface tickles my palm, a slight warning, and my eyes flare open. I move my head slightly to the right across the camp, anxious for the first sign of the bora. The trembling intensifies, and the Elites look down at the ground confused, while the red-haired man lowers himself to one knee and puts a palm to the floor. My heart thrashes in my chest as he shoots to his feet, unsheathing his weapon, and looks toward the trees. The others become aware that something is wrong and gather for the incoming attack, the two wolves taking up a defensive position in the middle, but it's too late.

Dozens of bora shoot through the darkness, running straight for them. Black as night, teeth bared and spiked tails high, they are furious. The camp gathers to arms, weapons at the ready. The protection crystals glow brighter as the bora clash into an unseen barrier. They let out a series of yelps and whines, falling to the ground, but soon snarling, going back for a second round. A shimmer of azure appears, surrounding the camp with slight ripples flowing through it like water. The bora don't let up, attacking the barrier with teeth, tails and claws, trying to get to them. When the ripples become larger, I place the stone to the ground, and it reacts, giving off a dark violet glow. I see the dim light of the others that have been placed on the ground reacting, letting me know it's ready.

I shuffle back and hide behind a tree, Josh following me as the glowing stones brighten. A line of purple light escapes from the stone I put down, shooting to the next one on its left, and then it continues going round, connecting the stones together before finally reaching my stone again. All the stones now pulse with a dark, violet light, signifying the ring is now complete and working. I ease away from the glowing light, aiming to get to a safe distance to not be seen. My steps speed up a little, ready to sprint to the meet up location we set before we came here to wait out the bora.

I'm just about to start running at a full sprint when I check over my shoulder to see how the barrier is holding up. But my steps falter and my eyes widen before I reach out for the closest tree to save myself from falling over my own feet.

But the tree won't save me from the furious, dark-haired male looking directly at me.

TWELVE

RHEA

Murderous eyes hold mine as I'm frozen to this spot. I can't look away, entrapped by his stare as all sounds fade away. No bora snarling, no shouts from the people in the camp, just…silence as we watch each other. The strange hold he has on me breaks as his eyes track down to the ground, finding the glowing violet ring that surrounds them outside of the protection crystals. Looking behind him quickly at the bora, his eyes slowly come back to mine, and my fingers dig into the rough tree bark. Runa paces inside of me as my knees tremble and sweat dampens my lower back. A high pitch sound fills my ears as I realize what this means.

He's seen me. No one could see us. They would know we were out here and wonder why. They would start asking questions that we cannot answer. We couldn't be seen, and I just failed. I fucking failed. How did he even know I was here? I was careful, and he was distracted by the bora. I was sure of it. Yet the dark-haired male is looking directly at me.

He pays no mind to the bora family attacking the protection barrier around them, uncaring that they will eventually bring it down. He's confident enough in his Elite's skills that they just seem like pests. Even if there was a slight chance that the bora might kill themselves attacking the barrier or be killed by the Elites, the Elites couldn't leave anyway. The trap stones we placed won't let anyone leave the ring for a full day, but anyone can enter. Now that they know it isn't just the bora out here with them, this changes things.

Josh suddenly appears next to me, and my panic escalates further. He takes in my features, looking over my body for injuries. His light brows draw together when he sees I'm fine, but then he takes my hand from the tree, slowly prying my fingers from the bark and bringing it up to his face to inspect. Seeing the blood on my hand, he looks over my bloody fingers and sees where the bark broke through the skin from how hard I was digging into the tree. He looks from the tree back to my fingers, then pauses when he finally looks at my face. Following my gaze, he eventually sees what I'm staring at, and he sucks in a shocked breath as his grip on my hand tightens.

Josh holds my hand as the male watches us, his stare moving to where our skin touches. His lips start to move, and the guy with brown hair, the one who was on watch while the camp slept, walks over to him before looking in our direction in shock. They speak, their faces tense until the other male's face becomes confused. His eyes widen a little as the black-haired male continues talking to him. The tall male points to the violet glow the trap stones are giving off, and the brown-haired guy's face turns hard, and then he's glaring at us.

Now it's my turn to grip Josh's hand tightly. We watch them watch us, apprehension washing over me. What the fuck should we do now? We can't run back to the location we agreed to meet up with the others. If the Elite's somehow manage to send a message back to the Highers, they will know what direction to aim themselves in to follow us. They can't survive now. We have to stay here and make sure the bora finish them off. The guys will come and find us sooner or later, hopefully out of sight, and we can make a new plan.

The bora start to renew their efforts, and the men give me one last look before they turn their backs on us. Their protection barrier forms more ripples, letting everyone know that it will come down any second now. I turn my body to face them fully, no point in hiding now that we've been seen. Josh stands at my side, still holding my hand, and we share a look before we take stock of the bora. Some are dead on the floor, their essence floating from them high up into the curved branches that cover our head. Others are twitching where they stand, still whimpering from the pain the barrier causes them every time they hit it. The shrieks of the ones attacking get louder, their growls more aggressive in their frustration at being held back from their prey.

I look further right and see the largest one walk away from the barrier, and then turn back toward it. Its large, narrow face dips low as its spiked tail moves straight and far back while its eyes remain intent on the barrier. It lets out a growling howl, and the other bora joining in as the sound pierces the air. This is the head of the family. The large bora charges forward and the others follow suit, aiming for the barrier as one. They hit it hard and fast, the ripples expand larger than before, becoming more widespread as the bora attack. The large, head bora brings his spiked tail high and whips it through the air to crash into the barrier one more time. The barrier stills.

Everyone stills.

And then it breaks.

The bora charge forward to attack, their excited snarls sounding around us, but the Elites are ready. An arrow flies through the air and lands in the middle of a bora's chest, killing it instantly as it pierces its heart. The Elite with red, plaited hair styled down the center of his head swings his axe up high before coming back down on another bora, a pain filled howl following the action. Two bora charge at the wolves in the center of the camp as they bash through other Elites, and all I see is teeth tearing into flesh, claws scraping across bellies and bloodied fur on the ground. I watch on, not in anticipation, but in dread. I planned for the bora to be here knowing there would be death, and their deaths are on me.

This is for the best, I tell myself. *There is no other way.*

Twin blades flash in a twirl of violence as another dark-haired male slashes through the bora, aiming for their head near their temples and moving with ease, quickly charging from one to the next. The head bora is tearing apart another man on the floor, his arm dangling from its mouth. The bora drops it and goes back for more. I swallow hard and block it out, looking for the tall, dark-haired male.

I find him in the center of it all, that black blade of his moving so fast that three creatures are dead on the floor in no time. I watch as he turns, slicing the blade through the air into the mouth of another and then his free hand comes down to the back of its neck to hold it still. His blade hand tips down, making the end of his weapon pop out of the bora's head through the roof of its mouth. My lip's part at the strength and practiced ease he has at killing them, at how quick and precise he is with his movements.

A wolf's cry shouts out in the air, and I slide my eyes toward the sound as a bora tears out the wolf's throat, blood spraying across the ground as more move in on it.

This is utter carnage. A slaughter.

I look down, tearing my gaze away. Even though I know it had to be done, to protect my pack, to protect Kade, I'm the cause of these deaths. Shame fills me at the thought.

The fighting continues for a while. Josh still holds my hand as I continue looking at the ground, waiting for it to be over so we can confirm that the Elites are dead, and go home to tell the pack that we are safe again.

Eventually the sounds of growls, cries and shrieks stop, and I finally will myself to look up at the mess left behind. I suck in a breath as I see bodies, man, wolf and bora alike, littering the ground. It shimmers with red from the massacre in the glow of the trap stones. My eyes scan over them, taking in the mangled shapes and disfigured features, forcing myself to see what I have done, and also face the realization of what I failed to do. I know what I will find before I lift my eyes off the ground. I can feel their stares aimed our way, burning holes into my face. I steel myself, spine straight, my head held high and face carefully blank as I look at the Elites left alive. There are more than I expected. I take in their tense stances, hard eyes and furious expressions as I examine them.

These are the Elites. This is the reputation they hold. Fearless. Brutal. Merciless. Covered in blood and flesh from the creatures they slayed, they truly look formidable.

The tall, dark-haired male looks over my shoulder, his nostrils flaring before his hard eyes come back to mine, and I suppress showing any emotion on my face. I know what he sees. I heard them coming in the direction they came from, it would be pointless to try and hide. I feel Taylor, Sebastian, Hudson, and Colten at my back, a silent strength as Runa nudges my skin as if to greet them. They would have assessed the situation and decided their best option was to stand with me and Josh. The Elites are trapped so there is no need to hide.

"Well, how do you think we should play this?" I ask the guys quietly. "They saw me and now they have seen us all. They can't have the opportunity to find Eridian or tell the Highers they have seen us here. We have a day before the stones lose their power."

"We could always get more bora, or another creature?" Josh suggests, releasing my hand to shove them in his pockets. "Gresin maybe?"

I stretch my fingers out, feeling the blood flow coming back into my hand. "I don't think that will work. We already used the element of surprise. They won't be caught off guard again. You saw how quickly they just destroyed an entire family of bora. It won't work unless we get a lot of them, and that was the closest family near here, and gresins are too dangerous."

"We can wear them down. Go inside the ring and tire them out?" Taylor voices. "I could find some more creatures and bring them back here later when they are exhausted."

My hand grips the strap around my waist where my blade is kept. "It seems our only option at the moment–"

I cut myself off as the dark-haired male suddenly moves forward, staring at the violet ring that circles them past the now useless protection crystals. The toes of his boots stop just before he touches the ring, looking down at it. The barrier blocks any further steps forward, and his brows draw together as he speaks to the other Elites. We're still too far away to hear them, but the lines on his face give away the tension as he talks to them. More Elites walk over to the larger male, every so often glancing our way while others, including a female, tend to injuries.

"Let's go," I murmur, bracing myself as I walk forward toward them. They stop talking at our approach, watching our every move and looking over our weapons. We stop fifteen paces away. I grip the hilt of my blade, ready to attack them inside the stones we placed when a dark-blond male speaks up.

"Who the fuck are you?" He aims the question at Josh, folding his arms over his muscular chest. Josh stays silent. "Did you set the bora on our camp and put down these stones?" He nods at the dark violet glow surrounding them.

The dark-haired female, who must have finished treating injuries, comes up from behind them with a snarl on her face, looking at us as if we're a disease. I pay her no attention and look at the silent, tall male who is still watching me, silently observing. I wonder if he's the leader of this team. Every member seems to look to him for direction.

The red-haired male speaks next in a low voice, capturing my attention. "Did you enjoy getting our people killed? Have some fun watching them get slaughtered?" With his axe still in hand, he twirls it, most likely wanting to throw it at us. I hold back a scoff at his words. Of course, I didn't enjoy it. I never wanted any of this, but here we are. Shitshow central. I have no doubt they have done worse things. Who are they to judge when they go around killing things all over Vrohkaria?

We keep at a distance, not saying a word as they get increasingly agitated with our silence. There is no point prolonging this, and we didn't come closer to have a chat.I take a light-colored stone from the small pouch I have attached to the strap at my hips, rubbing my thumb over the rune engraved into it to activate it. Sensing movement behind me, I know the guys are getting ready to attack on my command. We have no choice.

The Elites watch us with murder in their eyes, but there is nothing they can do to stop what's about to happen. They're trapped inside the stones with no way out, only able to defend until the trap stones deplete. But by that time, we will have worn them down and taken them out. If we are careful, we are not up to their standards.

Raising my hand I bring my arm back high over my head, ready to throw it down at their feet through the barrier. As soon as the stone lands it will activate, slowing the movements of whatever is within a certain radius.

I shift my right foot further back to get more force into my throw. I'm about to let the stone loose when the dark-haired male crouches and places his hand onto the violet barrier. Pausing, I watch as it shimmers, blinking violet and translucent and then to my utter horror, it breaks entirely. The trap stones explode one by one into tiny pieces around them until the glow they held disappears.

I stumble back in shock, and the guys move with me. That's impossible. No one can break through trap stones. They take years to make with the highest magic, powerful enough to hold most creatures. Edward had given me them from his collection that he had collected over the years. Now eight of them are gone, just like that, and they didn't even work when we needed them to.

The guys tense behind me, not expecting what just happened as we slowly shuffle back, keeping our eyes on the Elites in front of us. We're outnumbered, the trap stones broke, and they are looking at us like they want to rip us apart. We can't fight them and win. We can't take them all on and survive. The black-haired male comes directly for me, his gaze never leaving mine and ignoring the males around me. I do the only thing I can think of.

Throwing the stone at their feet, I grab Josh's hand, turn, and then push the other guys to move and run.

The plan has changed once again, and I'm not sure how we will survive it.

THIRTEEN

RHEA

We sprint, our wolves giving us the extra boost we need to be able to move as fast as possible. Dodging between the dead trees and hitting the hardened earth with heavy steps, we power forward. I can hear them pursuing us, and it feels like their breath is against the back of my neck, itching for its pound of flesh. We have to leave. We have to get away, regroup and come back with another plan.

We just need to lose them first.

Breathing heavily, I squeeze between a narrow gap in the trees, hearing the whizz of air before an arrow lands into the bark where I just passed. Shit. If I hadn't moved at that moment, it would have pierced my shoulder. I look to my right at Hudson and Colten, who are keeping a steady pace with me, and then to my left at Josh, Sebastian, and Taylor. We're running like mice all together. There are more of them, all aiming in the same direction, and they will catch us eventually.

"We need to split up," I pant. "There are six of us and at least eighteen of them, we don't stand a chance like this." They could probably take two if not more of us at the same time. Taylor may be able to keep on par with one of them, but it's not looking good for the rest of us. We've fought creatures, not warriors like this. I don't think our sparing is up to their standards.

Taylor ducks under a branch as we plow forward. "I hate to

admit it, but I agree. Splitting up is the best option. The port stone is with our packs we stashed back in their direction. One of us could try to go back and get it."

"It's too risky for that," Hudson breathes, going around a tree and coming back next to me. "They would notice straight away if one of us goes in a different direction."

The howls of wolves echoes through the air. "Shit," I hiss, jumping over an exposed root. "Let's just split up. We'll meet up at the second location near the end of The Deadlands," I whisper, not wanting to risk the Elites overhearing about our meet up location.

They nod in agreement and our pace picks up. Colten's pants snag on a large tree root sticking out of the ground, nearly making him stumble until Hudson grabs him and hauls him along. I notice him glancing down quickly at the blood now staining Colten's pants, before dragging him in front, pushing him in another direction to the right. Looking back over his shoulder, Hudson takes off in a different direction, narrowly avoiding another arrow that whizzes past us.

"Go," I urge Josh, his reluctance to leave me evident in his eyes and making me feel on edge. I nod, letting him know it's okay, and he squeezes my hand briefly before going ahead. Sebastian gives me a concerned look as he leaves with Taylor, who gives me a small nod of his head.

I blow out a breath and take a quick glance over my shoulder. I spot the ones who turned wolf, and I nudge Runa for some added strength. She gives it to me without a second thought, knowing we really fucking need it as the howls of the Elite wolves shake my bones. My legs move faster, and my arms move at my sides as I travel through the trees, listening for anything that may be in front of me while trying to hear the Elites from behind. There are fewer footsteps behind me now, meaning they have also split up to follow the others. It might have been better for my guys to also go wolf, but it's hard to fit through the narrow gaps between the trees in wolf form.

I just hope they can get away. We know this forest better than the Elites. We have been its neighbor for years now. I know the Elites come here as part of their rite of passage, and we avoid The Deadlands when it happens once a year, but they don't come in as deep as we do. We have been to many different locations within The Deadlands to bring people back with us to Eridian, so we have a slight advantage.

I keep a steady pace, winding between trees and easing into the darkness. I can still hear the rushed footsteps behind me, but I'm gaining ground slowly, using small gaps to my advantage. No more arrows come my way, thankfully. They probably can't take a clear shot at me. So, with that thought in mind, I press on, determined to lose them and meet up with the others.

I've been running for what feels like hours. My legs tremble, my breaths come out short and quick, and I know exhaustion is setting in. The others are on my mind. Did they get to the location? Are they safe? Did they get caught? My thoughts whirl around inside my head, going back and forth between worry and determination to get to them, but my body is slowing, and my muscles are aching. Runa stopped lending me some of her strength a little while ago, her reserves also running low, and I feel every sore part of my body.

I leap over a rock, landing in boggy water, and I instantly pause to listen. I hear no footsteps or wolves snarling behind me. In fact, I hear nothing at all. I wade through the sludge like water, keeping my senses alert. It's disgusting, but it will cover my scent. The area of water is long, almost like a river, but with no flow. When something slithers across my lower leg, I move faster, not wanting to know what the fuck it was that touched me. Water splashes up at me with my hurried movements, causing more noise than I should allow.

The further I go into the water, the deeper it gets, coming up to my waist now. Goosebumps travel across my body as the cold seeps into my bones. I keep my arms above the surface, blade in hand as I continue on. I stop every now and then to listen, making sure I'm still alone, not wanting to be caught by surprise. It's eerie, not a sound can be heard apart from the splashes the water makes as I wade through it.

I heave myself up when I reach the end, gripping a large rock for purchase. I lean on it and catch my breath, teeth chattering, then look down at my boots with a grimace. They're covered in algae-like strings that are bleeding black fluid. I shake my feet one at a time, trying to get the damn things off of me and failing miserably. Giving up, I inhale quickly before straightening and walk on. I shouldn't be too far from our backup location now, and the thought gives me a little nudge to speed up my steps. The squelch on my boots is the only sound I hear as they hit the ground, the area having much more space to move with the trees growing more sparingly here. My blade hangs loosely in my hand at my side as my vision wavers a little, trees begin to double, and I shake my head to try and clear it. I need to rest, desperately.

"You okay? I haven't heard from you in a while," I call out to Josh through the link, and get nothing in return. Again. I pause and check the link, feeling it's still open, so why isn't he responding to me?

I continue moving, the glow of luicium sap helping light the way as I pass a large, dead tree with a hollowed space underneath, like its own little hidden cave. I immediately know where I am.

This is the last landmark before I reach the location, it shouldn't be long now. I breathe a sigh of relief, my shoulders slumping with the thought of being able to rest, even just for a little while. I round the large tree, eager to get to the safe place when a voice stops me in my tracks. It's deep, clear, and speaks from behind me.

"Found you, little wolf." My eyes go wide, the blade in my hand shaky as I whirl around and see the tall male standing about ten steps away from me. Runa raises her head at the sound of the voice, rising on exhausted legs.

I blink rapidly as my shoulders tighten, staring at the Elite with my heart now in my throat. His head tilts just slightly as he looks at me, his dark hair resting on his eyebrows. His lime-green eyes bore into my ice blue ones with furious intent. When he takes a step forward, I take one back. Something I haven't done in a long time. I lift my hand with the blade, holding it tightly and pointing it in his direction. He keeps stalking forward, and I keep backing up. He's taller than me, broader, and I know he can easily overpower me, especially in my exhausted state. My eyes roam over his form, to his bare hands that twitch at his side as he pays no attention to the weapon in my own hand. His gaze never strays from mine when I look back up at him, and their intensity makes me swallow roughly. How am I going to get out of this?

A few steps away, he darts forward suddenly, and I drop to the ground in a crouch on instinct, slashing my blade through the air and aiming for his thigh. He shifts to avoid the strike, and I roll to the side and stand as quick as I can. Knees bent slightly, right foot back, I'm ready for him to come at me again. I blow pieces of hair that have fallen on my face as we face each other, and he tracks the strands, watching until it relaxes back onto my skin. Then he assesses me, sliding his hard eyes to the blade in my hand and lifting an eyebrow at me. It's like he didn't expect the move I just made, but also finds it amusing. I glower.

He comes at me once more, strong, bare hands attempting to grab at me while I slice at him, and he dodges my every move. Sweat gathers on my forehead, and my limbs weaken and shake the longer we go on. We go back and forth, but I know he's holding back, playing with me, taunting me. I saw what he's capable of when he was cutting up the bora, this is child's play to him, and the thought pisses me off. I let out a growl in anger, renewing my efforts to either kill him, or survive long enough to escape him.

He pauses for just a second at my growl, and I manage to cut him on the side of his bare forearm, blood instantly coming to the surface. I back off as he tries to counter, aiming a kick at my midsection that I avoid before he suddenly stills. He looks down at the wound I created on his arm with furrowed brows, as if he either didn't realize I cut him, or he can't believe I did. When he's finished examining the split flesh, he glares up at me slowly, and lets out a snarl that rattles my bones. Even Runa backs up within me at the sound, and even more so when he takes out his wicked, curved, black blade from the sheath at his waist. Twisting it around his hand with ease, he once again starts to stalk toward me.

I think playtime is over, and I know I won't survive it.

I can't fight him and win this. I fight creatures, not people with brains and muscles. Never mind a Gods damn Elite! I feel my chest start to cave in, throat tightening at the thought that this is it. He's going to kill me, find Eridian and everyone hiding inside it. He's going to take them all back to the Highers and take the pups away from their mothers. Then he's going to take Kade, and the Highers will force him to go to our old pack.

My vision blurs again, my breaths coming in ragged puffs of air as my hands shake. I feel as though I'm watching him in slow motion as my death awaits me. He's getting nearer and nearer, but I can't move, I can't get enough air into my lungs as he brings his blade up with a wicked smile on his face. I feel numb, I can't feel my body. Not my legs, not my arms, not even the beating of my own heart. He says something with a sneer on his face, but I can't hear it. I can't hear anything anymore.

My face begins to tingle, and it causes a jolt to move through my body. The touch is cold, but I feel it. I feel something other than terror, other than numbness and panic and the fist wrapping around my heart. A trail of coldness travels to my temples, remaining there for a second as I watch the male bring his blade up to my throat. I jostle, and the end nicks my skin, making me hiss as I feel the warmth of my blood against my neck as it flows down. Down, down, down, until it stops at the beginning of my t-shirt, soaking into the material. The male watches as it flows with disinterest before grabbing the collar and hauling me up off my feet. The cold touch moves and prods my cheek, hard, and that's when I finally move, bringing my own blade up to defend myself, but he suddenly throws me to the side.

My body flies through the air before I hit the ground, a sound of pain leaving me as I roll. Tiny stones and twigs scrape my exposed skin until I eventually crash against a tree. My body thrums in pain as it fully wakes from its numb state, and I gather myself onto my knees, groaning at the movement. I lift my blurry vision toward the male, wondering if he's coming straight for me or if I have time to grab the blade I dropped. But instead, I have to blink a few times to register what I see.

I watch as a head rolls off a water hag's body, landing half in and half out of the boggy water I just went through. I didn't even know the water hag was there. The male looks at the head with distaste before kicking it, sending it through the air like he just did to me. I hear a splash as it lands in the water further in the distance. No essence comes out of her dead body at his feet, she wasn't worthy enough to dance with the land. No, she will rot with the below instead.

I stumble my way to my feet, my hand touching my boot for a split second before I rise. My body begins to shake as it finally reaches its limit. The male looks over the boggy water one last time before bringing his piercing gaze back to mine and prowls toward me. I let out a warning growl to stay back, but he doesn't falter. I raise my arm when he's close enough and I let him latch his hand around my throat. He kicks my legs out from under me, and we both go tumbling to the ground. He straddles my thighs, his full weight pressing down on me as his face hovers an inch above mine. I grunt, gritting my teeth as I let loose a hiss of pain as I glare at the asshole pinning me to the floor.

My pulse speeds up, and his fingers around my throat twitch in response, feeling the thumping of my heart for himself. He's unconcerned about the blade I have at his neck, the one I took from my boot just before he grabbed me. I placed it at his throat as we hit the ground. I press it into his skin, ready to end his life, but his free hand curls around my wrist, trapping it in his grip to stop the blade from going any further. I bring my other hand up, digging my short nails into his arm, trying to push forward with no success.

We once again stare at each other, and I breathe heavily while he examines my face, my eyes, my nose and cheekbones, before trailing his gaze down to my throat in his grasp. He pauses for a moment. His green eyes flare, probably at the sight of my blood on his palm, before meeting my eyes once more. I breathe in the heavy scent of him: cedarwood, damp earth, and a power that I want more of. I can't look away from the brightness of his eyes, or from the way they are so focused, so intently locked on mine. It's like he can't look away either.

I lift my hips, lightly growling at the effort to dislodge

him, but he's like a boulder. Completely unmovable. His hand tightens on my throat, a warning not to move as his jaw ticks, and his eyes narrow on mine.

"You broke the laws of the land, little wolf." His murmur is low and deadly, full predator as I squirm beneath him.

I speak for the first time, croaking out my reply, but still strong. "That's not my name."

He squeezes my wrist. "It is now."

I glare. "And I broke no laws."

His eyes darken. "You sent creatures to murder my Elites. You are as guilty as them. Murder is against the law."

"The Deadlands are not under Vrohkaria law." I take small, steady breaths through the tightening grip on my throat before continuing. "There are no laws here, but you are trespassing."

"Trespassing? The Deadlands are unclaimed but still under Vrohkaria's rule. It does not belong to you," he growls, eyes still hard and the brightest green I have ever seen. The light of the luicium sap makes them glow, captivating me in their depths. They remind me of fresh grass peeking through the snow's surface after a long winter. They're mesmerizing, and I couldn't deny the asshole had been graced with a beautiful image, in a rugged kind of way.

He's pure alpha.

His dark, messy hair hangs loosely, the front locks ending just above his eyes. A thin, white scar runs across the middle of his nose, slightly longer on the right side than the left. A steel sharp jawline with a little scruff on it brings my attention to his lips, which are currently set into a hard line. Add this to all his hard muscles and power in a body that moves like he weighs nothing... He is dangerous in a wholly different way than just his skills as an Elite.

"How do you know this land doesn't belong to me and is not claimed?" I question as he twists my wrist and slams it into the ground next to my head, forcing a whimper from me as I clutch the blade tighter, refusing to let go.

"You are nothing, little wolf, that's why The Deadlands don't belong to you," he hisses at me, watching me closely. "Your dominance is as low as an omega's. You might move like some amateur warrior, but the fact that you're as fragile as a newborn pup still remains. It will be easy to break you for murdering my Elites. It will be slow. I'll take my time until you're a mess of tears, blood and piss, begging to be put out of your pathetic, little life," he says vehemently, a shine to his eyes at the thought. I force my face to go blank, to ignore the words he just said and the vision he just put inside my head. "Your crimes will be paid for in your blood after I've taken you to the Highers, but before that, you're going to tell me what the fuck you are doing in The Deadlands, and you are going to–"

He's thrown off of me, a blur of dark, gray fur colliding with him from the side. I blink rapidly before turning my head to follow him, choking on my first full breath of air now that his hand around my throat is gone. A wolf growls menacingly, and my head snaps up, my heart thrashing wildly within me. I stare at the wolf, shaking my head to clear it, because what I see cannot be possible.

Blood flows down from the side of its neck, landing on the darkened earth and a shocked breath escapes me. My widening eyes move to where the asshole male stands, a cruel smirk on his face as he looks at the wolf with deadly intent. I watch on, my body shaking as he holds up his black blade, watching as the blood drips down the metal and over the hilt.

Blood that came from the wolf.

Blood that came from Kade.

FOURTEEN

RHEA

Blade in hand, I rise to my feet as fast as I can, ignoring the pain flooding my body, ignoring everything as I rush forward on shaky legs and stand between Kade and the male. Tremors run through me as I open my arms to block this asshole from going for Kade again, the small weapon in my hand hopeless. But he will not get to him. I breathe heavily as the dark-haired male watches me closely, looking at me and then to the wolf.

"Kade! What the fuck are you doing here?" I shout down the link. *"Leave now and go home quickly. Please,"* Iplead, but it doesn't reach him. There is nothing but silence. He has completely shut down the link.

I keep my eyes on the male, who watches on in confusion, before I peek over my shoulder at Kade. I grunt and grip the blade tighter, swallowing down the nausea that rises. His normally blue eyes are darker, bleeding to silver from the edges of his irises, and his pupils are larger. Kade isn't in charge right now, Axis is.

Fuck!

No, no, no. *"Josh, I need your help,"* I rush out down his link, but still I get no reply. I bite my lip to stop the sound of panic that wants to leave me and look into Axis's eyes, trying to find any hint of Kade in there. But there's nothing. Kade isn't in there. Gods, what am I supposed to do?

The sound of boots moving on the ground has my head snapping back to the male as he steps closer, and I swear my heart stops. "No!" I cry. "Don't." I loathe the way my voice cracks as I speak, and Runa begins to move restlessly within me, a whimper leaving her at my distress.

The male pauses, titling his head as his eyes find their way to the wildly beating pulse in my neck. They slide to Kade and then back to me, a snarl leaving him. He turns his blade so he's holding it with the metal running along the outside of his forearm and comes closer. I lift my hand, throwing my small blade toward him as I back up closer to Kade. He easily deflects it, hitting it away with his own weapon, and I brace for him to come at me. From blade or hands, I ready myself for more pain, determined not to let him near the wolf at my back.

A savage growl comes from behind me. Just as I turn toward the wolf, he charges toward the male, knocking me to the ground as he barges past. "No!" I scream, watching as they crash into each other. I scramble to get back to my feet, but my legs refuse to cooperate. "Stop!"

The male hits Kade in the side of the head with his fist, knocking him to the left momentarily, but Kade goes for him again, rabid sounds leaving him as I watch on in terror. I dig my fingers into the dry earth beneath my hands as the male keeps knocking the wolf back every time he gets close. He's toying with him, like he did me, and Kade just keeps going back for more. Every blow he receives adds another injury to his body. He won't stop, he won't let up. He's acting like a crazed beast whose only desire is to tear the male into pieces. Blood pours from different places on his body where he's been hit and cut as the ground turns wet beneath them. Kade's dark, gray fur is even darker from all the blood.

Kade tries to tear into the males' arm after he's been flung back again, but the male slices across his shoulder, making him yelp in pain. I will my body to move and rush forward toward him, managing to grab the slick fur on his back to try and get him to stop, but he just pushes his body hard into me, forcing me to let go. I'm knocked into a tree, and I hiss as the rough bark slices into my arm and the side of my face. I bring my hand up and feel blood seeping from the cuts.

"Kade," I whimper, pain radiating through my chest as he continues, my soul screaming at the savage growls tearing out of him. "Please… please stop," I beg. Tears sting the back of my eyes at the sight of him so out of control. My vision blurs as I push off the tree, my movements sluggish and slow as I stagger toward him. It feels like the forest is closing in around me, the dark, twisted branches wrapping around my heart and squeezing until they pierce it, making me bleed out. "Carzan, enough," I plead, my breathing erratic as my knees give out. I land hard on the unforgiving ground, and my knees burn with pain. "Please!" I scream at him, the raw sound tearing from my throat. He has to stop, he's losing too much blood. He's going to get himself killed.

He. Has. To. Stop.

The male snaps his head toward the sound of my scream, looking at me on my knees, and then to the tears in my eyes. He grunts and looks away as Kade attacks him again, but this time, he grabs Kade by the scruff of the neck and pins him to the floor on his stomach, his knees straddling the wolf on either side. He did it so effortlessly, handling the five-foot wolf with ease.

"Shift," the male demands of Kade, while the wolf's cold stare is aimed at me. Kade bites at air around him, saliva dripping from his mouth and onto the ground. The male puts his free hand on the back of his head and forces it down. "Shift, now," he orders in a deep growl, the dominance radiating from him far superior to Kade's young wolf.

Unable to resist the order, Kade's pupils start to shrink, the bleeding silver around his irises pull back, and his dark blue eyes start to lighten to his normal shade. His body convulses. Bones start to move, fur starts receding into skin, and his teeth shorten. It doesn't take long for a male to appear where the wolf once was beneath the dark-haired male. Panting for breath, Kade's fingers dig into the ground, his face twisted in pain from his injuries and being commanded to change against his will. I sit up on my knees and take in Kade's bloody and bruised body as the fight drains from him, and he slumps into the ground.

"Now, why don't we start with you answering some questions," the male aims my way. "Who the fuck are you, and what are you doing in The Deadlands?"

I stay silent, biting on the inside of my lower lip as I wonder how to answer him, how to get Kade away from him. He stares at me, waiting for me to respond. When I take too long, he grabs a fistful of Kade's hair and snaps his head back, exposing his neck. I jolt when his blade comes up and presses against his throat, and my fingers curl, digging into my palms. I swallow hard. The male presses the blade into his skin a little more, and Kade's eyes fly to mine.

I find exhaustion, defiance and an apology in his blue orbs, telling me everything that he can't say. I bring my shaky hands to rest on the top of my thighs, clenching them into the soggy material of my pants as I try to reach him through the link, but it's still not open.

"Hmmm, do you need some more motivation?" A cruel smirk slides on the male's face, and in the next moment, Elites are coming out from within the trees, dragging my pack members with them.

My eyes widen slightly before I force my face to go carefully blank at the sight. I don't look at them, choosing to keep my focus on the male who is obviously in charge. I see another dark-haired male dragging Josh forward out the corner of my eye, forcing him to his knees to the right of me. I glance in his direction and notice his hands are tied behind his back with rope that glows, cutting into his skin. I grind my teeth.

"It's okay," Josh tries to reassure me, his link finally open. *"If we can find an opening, get Kade and run toward–"* The link suddenly shuts down, and my eyes look to Josh as his face twists in pain. What's going on?

"It's rude to have a private conversation. If you have anything to say, you can answer my questions," the asshole murmurs, and my eyes go back to him. How did he know we were talking? He wrenches Kade's head back further, causing a cry of pain to slip from his lips. My insides revolt at the sound, and I can't contain the warning growl that slips free. Runa bristles at what the male is doing to her pup, and the leader looks from Kade to me, confirming he has the advantage here. "Well?" he demands.

My eyes flash as Runa forces herself through my eyes, and I reel her back in. We can't win here. There are too few of us, those that are here are tied up, and I'm completely exhausted. I also can't risk Kade. Nothing is worth risking Kade. Reluctantly I grit out, "My name is Rhea. We live in The Deadlands."

"Rhea," he tests my name with distaste, and I suppress a shiver. "What do you mean you live in The Deadlands? Nothing can live here, it's uninhabitable. It has been for all of time. Don't fucking lie to me."

"I'm not," I rush out, my gaze going to Kade. His form slumping little, causing the blade to slice his skin. I close my eyes briefly. "There is an area where we live that is full of life," I answer quickly as I panic seeing the blood that seeps from Kade's throat. I tell him anything to let him go.

"You're full of shit, nothing like that is in here," he growls. Moving the blade from Kade's neck, he aims it to the back of his shoulder, the tip pressing down through his t-shirt and against his skin. "Did someone send you to try and kill us? You must be fucking stupid to try."

"No, no one sent us to kill you," I answer. It's the truth. We weren't told to kill them, that was our decision. "I'm not lying. The Deadlands are our home." He pauses, looking at me to continue. Fuck "I... if I come with you to the Highers, will you let them go? I was the one who set the trap stones, and I caused the bora to come for you." I ignore the Elites' hard stares on my face at my confession. "I knew what they would do when they found you. Some of your men died, and that's on me and me alone."

He lets out a mocking laugh. "You think you can bargain with me? In your current position? Oh, little wolf. You are all going to pay for the deaths of my trainees."

My brows furrow. "Your trainees?"

"I'm the Alpha of the Elites," he says casually, and my face pales. He's not just the leader of this team... he's the fucking Alpha. I start to tremble. "The men that were killed were my trainees. How do you feel about cutting short lives that should have long lived?" he sneers, and the men around him growl in response.

I look down, unable to look at the loathing in his eyes. I did what I had to do, what I felt like I had to do to protect my pack. We were backed into a corner. I acted with what I thought was the only option. They wouldn't have stopped looking for Sarah as they are relentless at their tasks. They have gotten this deep into the forest and survived. It was only a matter of time before they stood atop the cliffs looking down at Eridian. Now, all that we had done didn't matter in the slightest. I killed people, young people, for nothing. Because now we are in the grasp of the Alpha of the Elites, the Highers' most fierce weapon, and I have no idea the outcome. I failed. I failed them all.

Forgive me, Zahariss.

"Nothing to say?" he asks, his voice condescending. I shake my head, still looking down, trying to not let the guilt drown me, trying not to let the situation suffocate me. Shove it down Rhea. "Pathetic," he spits, and I can't help my slight flinch at his words.

"Pathetic, can't even get your wolf to come out. How you were born is a fucking miracle! You should have been strangled as soon as you came out of your whore of a mother's cunt! Aww… are you crying? Poor pathetic little girl. Do you want mommy? Well, mom–"

"Rhea!" Josh shouts, and I blink, looking up toward him. His eyes are wild as he struggles against the male holding him, trying to stand to get to me as the others do the same. I shake my head and press my knuckles into my eyes, shaking off the memory.

It has been a long time since I was sucked into a memory like that.

I clear my throat and drop my hands back to my thighs. "I'm okay," I whisper to Josh. I then look to the Alpha and say, "I accept sole responsibility for what I did to your Elites.I accept your decision, but leave the rest out of it."

"Why are you accepting sole responsibility when all of you were involved?" he questions me, brow raised.

"I'm the Alpha of this pack," I state, as I nod to my members. My spine straightens, and my chin lifts at the declaration. I'm proud to be called Alpha of Eridian. It's an honor.

"A female Alpha with no mate?" His face shows his surprise for a split second at my nod before he controls his reaction. There are not many females that run packs on their own anymore. There is usually an Alpha male and female that run a pack together. "So, this isn't your mate?" He nods his head toward Josh, and the question surprises me.

"No." I shake my head. "I have no mate."

"And this is your pack?" I nod again. "Is this *all* your pack?" I hesitate, and he picks up on it. He looks thoughtful for a second, looking toward the dark, blond-haired male who has Colten on his knees in front of him. The blond male looks at the rest of the Elites, especially their injured who are a little further back. I follow his line of sight and see the woman from earlier cleaning some of the injured men's wounds.

"Maize," the blond calls, and the woman looks toward him. "How many injured, and how badly?"

"Six injured, three badly. They may not make the night even with shifting. I suspect one has a broken rib in his lung. He needs a healer, Leo, if he stands a chance at living," she replies coldly, looking directly at me.

The Alpha's face hardens again, and I look at Kade and all the blood he's losing. His eyes are drooping as he takes slow, raspy breaths and pure fear sets in. It's the only reason for what I say next. "I can take your injured to a healer," I force out in a rush, and my guys look at me in shocked surprise. They then look in the direction of Kade. Worry soon shines in their eyes. Josh struggles again, eyes on Kade as he tries to get to him, but the other dark-haired male holds him steady. I have no choice but to do what I'm about to do. Kade needs help, and there is only one person who can help him right now. "I can take you to a healer," I say louder when no one speaks, demanding their attention. I feel all eyes on me as I continue. "I will take you if you vow no more harm comes to him." I point at Kade. "Or my pack. Or anyone at our home," I add.

Everyone is silent as my words set in. I failed the mission, and now I'm inviting the Elites to our home. The home I was trying to keep them so very far away from that I was willing to kill for it. Have killed for it. But I must get Kade help. He won't be able to shift for hours yet. It would put too much strain on his body, and if the Elite Alpha forces him to shift back now in his weakened state, he might not make it. And that is not an option.

I put my pack before everything… everything but Kade. I will figure something out if he agrees to go to Eridian. But Kade is my priority now.

Finally, the Alpha speaks to me. "I could just torture the pup until you tell me where your home is."

"You could," I whisper, my voice steady despite the thought of him doing that making me want to throw up. "But he is innocent. He had nothing to do with this. He was just trying to protect me. He wasn't even supposed to be here."

"My trainees that died were innocent," he spits, nostrils flaring as he glares at me.

"I know," I agree with a nod. "You can do whatever you see fit with me, and I will take you to the healer." He stares at me, and I stare back, letting him see the truth of my words. If he has to take me back to the Highers, then so be it. But Eridian and the lives there will stay secret. If I can't do it, then Solvier will make sure there is a way to do it. I just need time.

He searches my face for a few moments before looking toward his injured, then looking back at me, "How long will it take to get my men to a healer?"

"I have a port stone in my pack I left behind." I nod in the direction we came from. "If we don't collect it and go on foot, it will take days, depending how fast we move."

"We have a port stone. We will use that," he decides. "Damian, grab the stone and gather everyone together," he orders the brown-haired male that was on watch in their camp. "Leo, Zaide, round up the assholes that attacked us." The blond male in front of Colten grabs him by the arms and hauls him up roughly, causing Hudson to growl where he's on his knees next to him. The other dark-haired male, Zaide, does the same to Josh while Sebastian and Taylor grumble as they are pulled to their feet. I snarl at their rough handling of my pack, unable to help myself while they just smirk at me. Unconcerned. Just wait, assholes.

The Alpha stands, causing me to look in his direction as he sheaths his blade. He bends and picks up a barely conscious Kade and throws him over his shoulder. Not seeming to care about the blood dripping on his clothes he moves over to the side and picks my knife off the ground. Walking over to me, his face lethal as he brings his free hand down and grips my ponytail. Tightening his hold on my hair, he snaps my head back while I glare up at him.

He growls down at me. "If you try anything stupid, I will slit the pup's throat and make you watch. Is that clear?"

"Yes, it's clear," I grit out, ignoring the pain in my scalp. His chuckle is dark and low as he puts my knife back in my boot. "To see you play later."

"Darius, everyone is ready," calls the blonde male, Leo.

Darius, a name to put to the Alpha asshole.

He pulls me up by my hair, my head still tilted back at an awkward angle as his face hovers close to mine. "You fucked up, in more ways than you know." He drags me over by my hair to where everyone is huddled together, ready to port. He stops when Damian hands him a stone. He puts his back to everyone and looks down at me. "Hold the port stone and set the location."

He passes me the stone while still holding my hair tightly, but allows my head to straighten. Everyone is still touching, and the red, plaited mohawk guy stands next to Darius, flicking his eyes to me before placing a hand on his shoulder. I close my eyes and feel the tingling in my palm as I visualize where I want to port in. I would usually port to the base of the cliffs, but time is of the essence with Kade, so just inside the Eridian Forest will do. The one good thing with porting there, is that they still don't know where it is. They could store the location in another port stone, but they don't know exactly where it is from there toward our home, and that's an advantage I won't ignore. They also don't know you can't use magic inside Eridian's barrier, so they can't communicate with others about the location, giving me an opportunity to think about how the fuck I'm going to get them to keep it a secret.

Or try and kill them, again.

"It's ready," I tell Darius as my eyes open, and I hand the stone back.

"Then it's time to port," he says, staring down at me. "Let's see where you live, little wolf."

FIFTEEN

RHEA

We arrive inside Eridian Forest, and I blink a few times, adjusting to the now bright area and breathing in the comforting, sweet smell of home. The sun is high in the sky, so I know it's around noon, which means most of the pack members are at the gathering eating their lunch. Maybe it's not such a bad thing. With everyone being in one place they will all see the Elites arrive, so they won't accidentally stumble upon one and get the shock of their life.

The Elites look around the forest, shock on their faces at seeing the lush of life in the healthy trees, shrubbery and berries growing around the area. A bird squawks in the distance, and they look up as one, following its path as it glides through the air and zooms past the cliffs at their backs.

"What the fuck?" Damian asks, looking toward the top of the cliffs that he can see peeking through the trees.

I shrug, looking at Darius, who still has a hold of my hair. His grip tightens for a second before he releases it. He scans the area before looking back at me, confusion evident in his eyes. "Welcome to our home," I say overly sweet, the sarcasm in my words as loud as a screeching rull in mating season. Just like the bird they all watched disappear behind the cliffs.

Darius's eyes darken. "Watch your mouth, Rhea, unless you want me to shut it for you." I go to open my mouth again, but a small groan from Kade pulls my attention to him.

I move forward instantly, Darius watching my every move as I lift a hand to Kade's bloody face, gently moving his blond hair out of his eyes. He sighs at my touch, feeling me and Runa there before I step back and nod my head in the direction we need to go. There is no point in hiding my worry for Kade. He's already seen him as my weakness, so I won't deny myself by holding it back.

We walk at a brisk pace, heading straight for Eridian and to Anna with my heart in my throat. The bleeding has slowed from Kade's body, but he's not out of danger yet. My feet slow when we are just a few meters away from the lilk trees that surround Eridian, and apprehension flows through me. Am I doing the right thing bringing them here? I don't have much choice, but I know my pack won't react well to our visitors.

I breathe in the scent of the blossoms on the trees, their colors turning darker with spring about to end. Letting their sweet scent welcome me home, I turn and face Darius. "I need you to keep your dominance low when we pass through these trees." He opens his mouth to speak, but I cut him off. "It's important, and I'll explain later, but we need to get the injured guys looked at as fast as possible. And to do that, you need to keep your auras of dominance as low as possible." I clear my throat. "We can use a spare cabin as the healer's is not large enough for this many injured." Darius and the Elites just stare at me, not saying a word, and I snap at them all. "Do you understand?"

Darius gives me a furious look, but I don't give a shit. Here, I'm the Alpha, not them, and this is what needs to be done to go forward. We continue to stare at each other, my blue eyes to his green, until he reluctantly nods at me. I feel Darius and the Elites' auras shrink down to a low simmer and relief fills me. I let out a quiet sigh as I nod back. Hopefully, this will help when they meet my pack.

We move on, and Darius slides up next to me as I look at him out of the corner of my eye. I watch him take in the lilk trees ahead, their blossoms gently falling to the ground, and then to a few cabins he can see through them. His face is set with a stern look while his eyes travel everywhere, focused and alert. He's suspicious, and I can understand that. This has been under their noses since forever, and they never knew. No one did.

We trail through the lilk trees, my hand gliding over the closest one as we pass, and I see Darius shiver as he feels the invisible barrier. His head snaps my way, and I shrug, hiding my smirk behind my hand and not bothering to explain it. I hear some murmurs of his Elites behind us as they walk through, but I continue forward, readying myself to head to a larger cabin to the left that sits below mine. All is quiet as we enter Eridian, the cabins empty, the circular shape of our settlement all but abandoned until we near the gathering at the center.

I see heads turn our way through the scattered trees that surround it, and murmurs of excitement reach me as they see I'm home. Then they see the Elites, and their alarmed voices hit me. Mothers start grabbing their pups to hold them close, others cower and let out cries as some of the more unaffected members move to stand in front of them protectively. I raise a hand in greeting and give them a small smile, trying to reassure them while ignoring Darius's muttered 'what the fuck' next to me.

"Josh, can you go on ahead and let Anna know we have injured that need tending to and get her to the spare cabin?" I ask him. I also need him to get Anna away from the healers cabin and to keep Sarah quiet. She can't be found. Zaide, the short dark-haired male who is behind him, looks at Darius for the okay, and I growl at him, my patience running thin. "Do you want our help or not?"

"Untie him and the others," Darius grunts, looking at my

pack at the gathering curiously. "They are no threat to us, not here," he tells them with the confidence of an asshole that he most certainly is. Zaide nods, untying Josh's hands while the rest follow, releasing my pack members from their binds. Once released, Josh rubs at his wrist and gives Zaide a dirty look before going on ahead to the healer's cabin.

"You can put the injured there." I point to where the large, worn cabin is ahead of us on the left. "I need to talk to my pack, quickly," I say to Darius, and turn to walk toward the gathering. I'm hauled back with a rough grip on my arm, causing my eyes to snap to Darius's while the rest of my pack release warning growls, which he ignores.

"Damian, grab the pup and take him to the cabin with the others. I'll follow shortly," he orders, not looking away from me. I watch as he slides Kade off his shoulder and hands him to Damian like a piece of meat, causing my hackles to rise. He ignores my death stare and addresses the other Elites. "Check the perimeter and around where we came in. We wouldn't want any more surprises today, now would we?" he says, giving me a hard look.

"Taylor, Seb, go with them, please. I can't have cavemen messing up our home and scaring unsuspecting bugs," I grunt, ignoring Darius's last words as I jerk out of his grip and continue walking forward. Hudson and Colten come with me while Darius follows at my back.

I have a babysitter. Fucking fabulous.

As I near my pack, their expressions vary from terror to anger. I give them a small smile, to let them know that all is well, even though it's far from it. Josie comes barreling forward, her chestnut hair flying around her as she slips out of Danny's arms and crashes into me, giving me a tight hug. I hold in the cry of pain as her body connects with mine, not wanting to show weakness in front of my pack.

"Are you okay?" she whispers, a tremble in her voice. Pulling back from me and looking me over, she notices the dried blood on my exposed skin, especially down my neck, and her eyes widen. "Kade went to–"

"I know, and I'm fine. Don't worry," I tell her. "Come, everyone sit," I say loudly, getting everyone's attention. Once they're all seated, albeit reluctantly with the tall Alpha at my back, I walk into the gathering, but stay at the edges of the benches. Darius positions himself next to me, arms folded with a hard look on his face that makes me want to smack him. I clear my throat instead. "We ran into some trouble. The Elites will be staying with us until their injured men are healed from a bora attack," I announce. It's not a lie. They did get attacked by the bora. I just left out that I was the cause of it, but I suspect they know as I feel Darius tense beside me. "They are no threat to the pack. This is their Alpha, Darius." I nod toward him. "His Elites will not cause any problems and will respect boundaries, won't they?"

Darius looks over the faces of my pack who freeze at the mention of who they are. Darius's face is carefully blank, but he must sense all is not right here. He's the Alpha of the Elites. He'll be able to pick up on the fear they are giving off. He must see the horror on their faces, hear their quiet cries and notice their bowed heads. It has my blood boiling that his presence is doing this to them, but I only have myself to blame for it.

He nods once before he speaks. "We will be leaving once our injured Elites are healed, and I have spoken with your… Alpha on some business that needs taking care of," he assures them. He was reluctant to agree with what I told them, but he did. He also could have just let loose his dominance that he has bottled up. They would kneel to the ground and expose their necks in a heartbeat. I'm curious to know why he didn't just do that considering he wants to slowly tear my head from my body.

Small mercies for now, I guess, until he decides to drag them from their homes and take their children from them.

It wouldn't be the first time the Elites have done just that.

I address my pack. "Things will run as normal here. If anyone needs to change their schedule, let me know after I have finished in the spare cabin where the injured are being looked at. Those that can't continue after lunch with their daily tasks are free to go back to their cabins. I'll come check on you later, okay?" I ask them. They nod hesitantly, mothers still holding their children close. I look at Hudson standing close to Colten, nodding my head subtly to the pack, and he nods back without hesitation. They will stay with them and make sure they're okay as they can be.

I give my pack a nod and turn on my heel, heading toward the cabin, desperate to get to Kade with Darius practically up my ass. I slow my walk until he steps up beside me, and I hold my breath as I pass Anna's cabin, listening for any sounds of Sarah inside. But thankfully, all is quiet. I feel his stare on me after a few paces, and I look over at him, raising my brow in question.

He looks back over his shoulder at my pack still at the gathering, and then back to me. "What are they so scared of?" he demands. "What are you doing to them? Threatening to kill them if they don't fall in line?"

The fuck?

I halt in my tracks, fury coating my skin. "What am I doing to them?" I speak slowly, testing the words. He can't be serious. "Are you fucking kidding me?" I whisper hiss at him. I get close to him, standing toe to toe. "You fucking idiot. It's you they are scared of. You and every Elite who walked in here." I poke his chest, furious at him for insinuating that I'm hurting them, threatening them. I'm too exhausted for this shit. "We have never had anyone come here, never mind a group of Gods damn

Elites. Don't you fucking dare accuse me of doing something to scare them when you don't know shit!" I fume at him before stepping back and stomping toward the cabin where Kade is. Strong footsteps reach my ears, and I'm spun around by my shoulder to face a furious Darius. "Would you stop manhandling me?"

He ignores me, getting low in my face. "You killed some of my Elite trainees. You tried to kill us all. That's who you fucking are, little wolf. A murderous bitch. So, tell me what the fuck you are doing to them. Now."

I practically vibrate with his words. I am a murderer. I have killed to keep my pack alive. Killed to keep Kade alive. Killed to keep myself alive. Do I feel guilty for killing some of my own people? Yes, but not all. Some deserved to be sent to the dark one below, to be tormented for all of time. But innocents? I feel the crushing weight of it down to my soul. I feel their deaths like they are attached to me, haunting me. But I had no choice, and did the only thing I thought I could to protect my family. I have to remember that.

I must.

I look up to the sky and close my eyes, letting the heat of the sun warm my exhausted body. To ask Zahariss for strength and forgiveness. My eyes are still closed as I speak. "I did kill some of your trainees," I agree. "I did what I felt I had to. Whether you believe me or not is your problem. I can't change what I did, but the reason behind it is the truth." I open my eyes and see him watching me, watching my every reaction to my own words. "I am sorry it came down to that, but I can't say I'm sorry for doing it." I shake my head and mutter under my breath. "Too much is at risk." I walk more quickly to get to Kade, he's my priority right now. Not entertaining the Alpha's questions.

"What the fuck do you mean too much is at risk?" Shit.

"I will answer your questions after I have seen the injured. Just drop it for now. There are more important things to do than stay out here and argue with you.' I wave my hand as if I can bat all his questions away. He wants answers, and he will get them. Maybe just not the correct ones.

We come up to the cabin, trailing up the worn steps and entering. The open plan living and kitchen area has been turned into a makeshift workspace for Anna. Pallets have been put on the floor, furs and clean sheets over them as she goes from man to man to assess their injuries. She spies me as I enter, briefly looking over my shoulder at my babysitter before barking out orders for people to hand her things, not letting any of this overwhelm her. Even though I know that she is internally freaking the fuck out.

Josh stands near Kade at the far right of the room where he lies unconscious, his naked body half covered with a sheet, and I rush over, landing on my knees beside him. I ignore the looks I'm getting and lift a shaky hand to Kade's face, stroking his cheekbone and shaking my head down at him.

"You stupid boy," I whisper, my feelings caught between worry and anger. He should have been safe. He should have been at home, not in The Deadlands. That wasn't part of the plan.

I look up at Josh briefly, wanting an update as I look over Kade. He's covered in blood and dirt, but I can still see the cuts and bruises over his body. The cut on his neck isn't bleeding anymore, and the gash at his temple and shoulder already has some salve over it, the brown substance thick against it. The other gashes on his body are bare of the healing salve, left to heal on their own.

I suspect we don't have a lot to go around with us not normally having to treat this many at once.

"Anna says he will be fine," Josh starts. "She stopped the bleeding from his wounds before it became dangerous, and I gave him some blood for a little boost to replace some of what he lost. He's mostly exhausted and will need to rest for a few days. She doesn't want him to go wolf until then; with him being forced to shift before, it drained the last of his energy." He runs a hand down his face, his exhaustion showing with the strain around his eyes. "He's also dehydrated, has deep muscle damage to his shoulder, and more cuts and bruises that will hurt for a bit, but are not a problem. She told me to keep giving him water through the sponge." He nods at the bowl of water next to him on a small table before whispering, "He never should have been in the fucking Deadlands. What in the Gods was he thinking?"

"I don't know." I grab the bowl, taking the sponge out and squeezing lightly before bringing it to Kade's lips and letting the water flow into his mouth slowly. "I'll speak with him when he wakes, let's move him back to my cabin after he's rested for a bit longer. I want him to be in his own room."

"Give me a knife," I hear Darius demand, and my head whips around at the harsh sound. Anna passes him a blade, and he crouches down next to one of his Elites, placing the tip at the side of his ribs. "Get something to soak the blood." Anna grabs a cloth and holds it below where the knife is, and I get up and walk over to get a closer look.

The man is pale, breaths coming in wet exhales. I watch as Darius slides the blade down the man's skin, blood instantly rushes to the surface and Anna collects it in the cloth she holds below. Darius then takes the knife back to the middle of his cut and pushes in deeper in a straight line. He doesn't stop until he's almost at the hilt before pulling it back out slowly.

"Swap with me," Anna says as Darius drops the knife and takes over holding the cloth. Anna crouches down next to the man and puts her hand over the wound, her eyes squeezing shut for a moment before opening again. She looks at me briefly, asking for permission, and I chew my lip, shuffling on my knees.

I look around the room at the number of Elites in here with us and then look at the man's slowing breaths before nodding. If someone else dies, I don't think Darius will listen to anything I say. I'm more likely to get a knife to the stomach.

I watch Anna close her eyes, her face scrunched in concentration as everyone watches on in silence, confusion written on all their faces. After a few seconds, she pulls back her hand slowly, a rope of blood following her out of the wound. I rush and grab a bowl off the side before coming to sit next to her. Her eyes open, and she guides the blood into the bowl I'm holding, careful not to spill any. I hear the Elites inhale sharp breaths at the sight of Anna using blood magic and internally cringe, not looking at Darius even though his gaze is on me. This will be another conversation he will want to have, I'm sure. She repeats this process again and again until the man's breaths become clearer, and no more blood is left to remove from his lungs.

"All done," Anna pants, sweat beading on her brow as she lifts her red hair off the back of her neck and fans herself. "I'll put the broken rib back in place that is piercing his lung. I'll have to remove blood from his lung again as I'm doing it and hope I can get it done the first time. He can't shift until his broken rib is back in the correct place, otherwise the shift will move that rib straight through his lung. If it goes in any further," she trails off, shaking her head. "I don't think I will be able to repair the damage. I'll assess his state once the rib is back in place and determine if he's healthy enough to shift afterward. He has a nasty gash on his leg that will need stitching and his wrist needs to be checked out." She gets up and moves to wash her hands in the sink in the kitchen before coming back to me. "He will live if this all goes smoothly," she tells me and Darius. Then to everyone else in the room she says. "Now, will you all leave while I work? I need quiet to concentrate. There are too many of you in here to do that, and I have many others to tend to."

I give Anna a small smile before I look back over to Kade one last time. Josh walks next to me as we leave the cabin, exhaustion hitting me hard now as my adrenaline fades with Kade out of danger. I lean my head on Josh's shoulder as he rubs his chin on my head, sighing through the ache in my bones. I'm just closing my eyes when my babysitter speaks from behind us.

"Time for answers," he growls, and I grunt. I just want to curl up in bed and sleep for a week.

I want to pretend none of this happened and I don't have Elites crawling all over my home, breathing down my neck while I try and figure out how I'm going to answer him.

Because he can't know it all, but I have to give him something.

SIXTEEN

RHEA

I sit in my office chair, gulping down coffee as Darius leans against the wall by my door, glaring at me. We have been in this sort of standoff for a few minutes now and my mood is already sour. I've had a shower and put some salve on the cuts I had gotten from The Deadlands to help the healing process, but I can't do anything to help the aches throughout my body. I would rather be sleeping as my exhaustion is already over its limit, but here I am, getting ready to answer the questions I said I would answer. Kind of.

Josh is with me, as well as Taylor, Sebastian, Hudson, and Colten. They all stand near me around my desk, Josh the closest to me as always. Zaide and Damian stand while Leo relaxes back in the chair across from me instead, his blond hair brushed away from his face as he watches us all.

I have no doubt his relaxed pose is just a facade though.

I sigh, putting my mug down on my desk before leaning back in my chair and folding my arms. I really don't want to do this now, but it's far better than them harassing my pack. "Go ahead, ask," I say in a bored tone, waving a hand at them to start even though I'm dreading their questions.

"How long have you all been here?" Leo asks in front of me, looking around my office and out toward the window. I knew they would be curious about our home, but I didn't think they would ask that right away.

"We were born here," I lie, my face set into a neutral mask.

"That's not possible," Darius adds, shaking his head. "In the history of the Elites, we have been to every place in Vrohkaria. This wasn't here, there is no way this has been here all this time. We would know."

"How would you know?" I question him with a lift to my shoulders. "We are deep in The Deadlands. It's always been here, you just haven't ever come across it." I don't know this for sure, but Solvier told me he has always been here, and he's hundreds and hundreds of years old.

"We would know," Darius assures me, and I suppress an eye roll. "The Elites have access to all Vrohkaria's history from the Highers. They are the keepers of knowledge. Their records would have shown this place existed, so I call bullshit." He pins me with a hard, green glare, not backing down. Well, neither am I.

"I don't know what to tell you." I shrug. "We have always been here on our own. Away from everything in Vrohkaria and any civilization. We self-sustain and live peacefully."

"If you live peacefully, why is everyone so scared then?" Darius questions, coming forward to stand in front of my desk next to Leo, glaring down at me.

I tap my forearm where my arms are crossed and think about how to answer him. If we lived here all our lives, why are they so scared? Shit, I didn't think this through. "They had some… issues not too long ago."

"What issues?" he presses, and I grind my teeth and look out of my window.

I don't want to go into this, and it's not my place to tell them either, but I have to give them something. "Look," I start, before turning my head toward him and the other Elites. "I won't betray their confidence by telling you their personal experiences.

What I *will* tell you is that some shit happened and big scary men, well… scare them, okay? It happened, and it's done, but mentally not all are one hundred percent healed from it. They get by the best they can and live peacefully here. However, since I brought you all here, it's causing issues for them, and I will have to figure out the best way to deal with that. I asked you to keep your dominance low to try and not frighten them as much. As you could see before at the gathering, it didn't do much, but their reaction would have been worse if you had just let your aura loose."

"Is that why your aura is like an Omega's? You give off barely any dominance," Damian says, as he walks over to my bookshelves and starts looking at the books I've collected over the years.

"That's the whole point," I state, blowing out a breath and trying to ignore that he's touching my things. "Omegas are non-threatening. They are kind and gentle, so we have always kept our dominance as low as possible to make the pack feel safe."

"So, what you're saying is something happened here, and since then you all keep your dominance down so the rest of the pack feels safe?" Darius says slowly, eyeing me to find a crack in my facade.

I nod, my face still blank even though I feel like he isn't buying my half-truths. But what does he expect? I just spill all of our secrets? Not a chance. I need to find a way to keep this place hidden, to stop him from telling the Highers. But I honestly have no idea how. He's going to take me back to the Highers one way or another, and I'll accept that if I can reason with him to let the others stay here and Eridian's existence be kept secret.

"You know you have already broken the law by murdering some of my Elite trainees, and injuring others." Darius's stare becomes cold. "You have also broken the law by not declaring your home and pack to the Highers. When my injured are healed, you will come back with me, face sentencing and your punishment will be in my hands. But before that." He cuts off the protests of the guys at my back, waving a hand at Leo.

Leo pulls out something from the pack he has on the floor. It looks like just a small piece of crumpled paper in his hand, that is until he flattens it out, puts it on my desk, and turns it over. I keep my face from giving any reaction as he slides it toward me and my heart stalls in my chest as I look it over. Dark, shoulder length hair, toffee eyes, a bright smile and delicate face. I force my brows to furrow as I look it over in confusion.

"Who is this?" I ask Leo, whose eyes haven't left mine.

"This is the reason we are in The Deadlands in the first place." He taps the picture. "A woman matching her description was seen entering The Deadlands with another person. She was taken from her pack, and we have been tasked with getting her back."

Rescuing her from her pack is more accurate. "How long ago was she seen coming into The Deadlands?"

"Just over two months ago," Darius informs me. So they have been searching for her pretty much since we brought her here, and they still haven't given up. Great.

I chew the inside of my bottom lip. "You guys haven't seen her?" I ask. At the shake of their heads, I continue. "Anyone that enters The Deadlands is as good as dead." At Darius's flat look, I scoff at him. "Apart from the Elites, clearly. But anyone else would last a few days at best. There is no way she is alive and out there somewhere."

Darius tilts his head. "She isn't here?"

"No." I swallow. "Why would she be? No one has been here and we haven't seen another person in the forest apart from you guys and creatures. How would this woman get here if you guys didn't even know it existed?" He looks me over, and I hold my breath. My ice blue eyes clash with his light green ones, neither giving anything away and neither backing down as we look for weaknesses. I don't know if he believes me, but I know he definitely doesn't trust us.

A knock comes to my office door before it swings open. Anna stops in her tracks when she sees us all in here before straightening her shoulders and looking at me. "Everyone is stable, but they will need to take a few weeks' rest before any traveling is recommended," she tells us, and I know she was reluctant to give us that information considering we don't want them here. "Especially Jase," she continues. "His rib is back in place, but his lung will take time to heal and shifting is not an option right now, for him or anyone else. They are too exhausted for the change. Kade is ready to move upstairs to his room. I gave him something extra for the pain to help him sleep, so he should be out until tomorrow morning." Anger floods Darius's face like thunder by the time she has finished talking.

"Thanks, Anna. Rest up and head to the gathering." I look toward my windows before looking back at her. "Dinner will be soon." She nods and leaves as quickly as she came, passing the Elite with the plaited mohawk as she goes. He follows her, no doubt keeping an eye on her.

I'm glad Kade is ready to be moved to his room though. I want him close at the moment.

"She's a blood witch, isn't she?" Zaide states, the first time he's spoken since he's entered my office. His voice is quiet, but still strong. He's the type of male who only speaks when needed.

I lean forward on my desk and clasp my hands together. "She is a blood witch," I confirm, and they inhale sharply, all apart from Darius who looks at me with a curious expression.

"I knew she wasn't a wolf, but I didn't expect a blood witch," Damian spits, finally coming over to us and leaving my bookshelves alone. "You're harboring a dangerous being in your pack, Rhea. All blood witches are to be killed on sight."

"That blood witch saved your men," Josh growls from my right, coming around to the side of my desk.

"And whose fault is that?" Damian fires back, getting closer to Josh until they are almost touching. "You caused those injuries."

Josh gets in his face, their height evenly matched. "And we saved the injured. If the others hadn't died, she would have saved them too."

"We have a right to kill her. She is not allowed to be left alive!"

I stand so fast my chair crashes into the bookshelf behind me. Everyone turns to face me as I growl at Damian, "You will not touch her. I will rip you to shreds before you even touch a hair on her head!" I feel Runa in my eyes, and my pupils dilate as a tingling sensation creeps up my neck as my anger builds.

Hudson comes up behind me and puts a hand on my shoulder. I sensed it was coming, but I still flinch anyway. The tingling stops, fading away instantly, and I manage to get myself under control.

"No one will touch her, Rhea," Hudson tells me gently, while Sebastian, Colten, and Taylor grunt in agreement. "They are in our territory, not theirs. Vrohkaria law doesn't apply here."

"He's right," Taylor adds. "They can't kill her."

Darius takes a hold of Damian's arm and guides him back. "The Highers rule over Vrohkaria," Darius tells me, his eyes roaming over my form.

"As I've already said, The Deadlands are not claimed by them." I shake my head and move closer to Josh at the edge of my desk. "If you want justice for the men that have been killed, I agree to go to the Highers with you without a fight."

"Milal–" Josh starts, but I cut him off.

"I will go, willingly, but I want something in return." I keep my shoulders straight and head held high as I tell them, acting like going to the Highers is no big deal, when internally, I'm scared shitless. Edward told me to avoid them at all costs, and his reasons are understandable after what they did. So I agreed, of course I agreed. But if it saves my pack, I will go to them.

"Leave us," Darius orders. When no one moves, he lets loose a dominating growl that almost sends me to my knees in submission. The windows rattle, the floor shakes, and I'm stuck between awe and fear at the power that one growl holds. But I stay standing, even as the rest of the people in this room show slight signs of submission. I would be doing the same if I was a normal wolf, but normal I am not. And I don't think he is either.

I eye Darius as my guys reluctantly shuffle out of the room at my nod, the rest of the Elites following them while Darius and I are locked on each other.

I've never been more captivated looking into another's eyes as I have his.

As soon as he hears the door click, he rounds the side of the desk and stops in front of me. I hold my ground and lift my head to look at him, trying not to hold his scent in my lungs. A second later, his hand wraps around my throat and I'm shoved back into the wall next to the bookcase. A sound of surprise escapes me as my eyes widen, not expecting the move, and then they lower as I bare my teeth at him.

I will not cower.

"Who are you?" he demands, and my brows furrow.

"I already told you."

"Why don't I believe that?" His thumb runs along the side of my neck, the touch gentle compared to the way he's firmly holding my throat.

"I will go to the Highers," I tell him again, ignoring his question. "If you–"

"I find it amusing that you think you can bargain with me," he laughs at me mockingly. Lowering his face, until his nose touches mine, as he looks directly into my eyes as I struggle for breath under his grip. My hands grab his bare wrist, trying to release his hold on me. When that doesn't work, I lift my knee, aiming between his legs, but he moves, closing the little distance between us and pinning my hips to the wall with the tops of his thighs. "You are in no position to tell me what you will do, little wolf. You will pay for the deaths of my men, either from the Highers' orders or from me alone. But never doubt that you will be coming back with me whether you're willing or not."

"I know that," I choke out. "But leave the rest of Eridian alone. Tell no one of this place."

"Eridian?" He tilts his head, his eyes still holding mine, and I swear I see them start to bleed black at the edges of his irises before going back to normal.

What was that?

"It's what we call our home and the forest surrounding it," I say in a rush as he eases his hold just enough for me to get more air in to speak. His fingers stay on my pulse, monitoring it as it beats widely. "There is no reason to tell the Highers about this place. We broke no laws."

"This place needs to be recorded as there is life here. The Highers demand that all such places in Vrohkaria are known. It doesn't matter that they haven't claimed this as their territory. They never had to because it's always been known as uninhabitable. It was pointless until now."

I lick my dry lips and his eyes drop there for a second before looking back into my eyes again. "You can't tell them," I stress. "There is no point. What would it accomplish?"

"It would accomplish putting that look on your face again."

"What look?" I stammer, trying to keep my face blank and failing.

"The look of pure terror that you had when I had the pup in my grasp. Why are you so adamant that you don't want the Highers to know of this place?" he questions, then swings me around by the throat and slams me onto the desk on my back, my legs dangling either side of him as he looms over me. "What are you hiding, little wolf?"

I growl at the position he's put me in. I try to get my feet up to push him off of me, but he's just too big. He's immovable, and I'm exhausted. He lets out a low chuckle as he brings his free hand up to take both of my wrists and hold them above my head in his grip. He feels the pulse at my neck again, digging his thumb in as it beats rapidly beneath his touch.

"Get off me, asshole!" I arch my back, wriggling to get him off me. When my efforts do nothing but exhaust me more, I slump back onto the desk and close my eyes, trying to breathe through the feeling of helplessness. Helplessness I swore to myself I would never let myself feel again.

"Are you ready to give me some real answers?" he murmurs, and I feel his breath on my cheek, so close, but not touching.

Why is he so close? And why do I want to wrap his scent around me like a second coat?

"I answered all your questions. I killed some of your men, I get it." My eyes open and look him dead in the eye as I tell him my truth. "But believe me, I had *no* choice."

His eyes roam my face like they did in The Deadlands. "Why?" he demands, his hold on my wrists and throat tightening for a second.

"You have seen my pack. They're scared of outsiders. If you told the Highers, they would demand that we all go and declare we live here. They couldn't go through being surrounded by powerful Alphas. They couldn't cope with it, they are already frightened. To be forced to go to the capital of Vrohkaria to be surrounded by strangers?" I shake my head. "They wouldn't survive it," I whisper, my throat tightening at the thought. "I will fight anyone and anything every step of the way to stop that from happening. If I lose at the end, then I lose, but my pack will be safe. Kade will be safe."

I'm out of my depth here. He needs to understand he can't take them back, but how do I do that without telling them we take them from packs for their safety?

The Elites belong to the Highers, and you never trust a Higher. Unless you're Edward.

"The pup?" He scoffs. "You so easily give away your weakness. I could force you to do whatever I wanted just by holding a blade to his throat. I should do that anyway for him attacking me."

"You already know Kade is a weakness, so what's the point in denying it? And give him a break. He's just got his wolf, and he's going through a lot."

"Everyone goes through a rough time when they get their wolf. It's the natural process."

"It's more than that with Kade, he's hurting and so is his wolf." I sigh and look at my ceiling. "He lost someone important to him, and his wolf is mourning." I can feel him watching me, trying to sense if I'm lying, but I'm not. I need him to understand the struggle Kade has so he won't punish him.

He finally speaks after a tense silence. "You will come to the Highers with me after my men are healed. I will decide when we get there if I tell them about Eridian." I freeze, my eyes snapping to him. There's a chance he won't tell them? It can't be that easy. "But it looks like you're stuck with us Elites for a few weeks while my injured heal." His slow smirk is cruel as he tells me. "We will continue to look for this woman in the forest while here. You better set up rooms in this cabin for my closest men. I won't be letting you out of my sight, little wolf."

He digs his thumb into my pulse one more time before he

stands straight, staring down at me. His gaze tracks over me, not missing a single inch of my body, and my cheeks heat. He grunts, giving me a last look before he walks out of my office. I lay still, breathing through frustrated breaths and resisting the urge to touch my throat. It still feels like his hand is wrapped around it.

Our simple life isn't so simple anymore.

And if Darius finds out I lied? We're all going to suffer for it.

SEVENTEEN

RHEA

Morning light peers through my window, casting colors into the room that bounce off some of the objects I have in here. Sleep didn't come easily last night. Between worrying over having strangers in my house and keeping my ears open for any sign of Kade waking, I've only had a few solid hours at best.

I stretch and get my ass up, knowing there is absolutely no point in staying in bed. Grabbing a t-shirt and shorts, I take a quick shower. I get dressed and leave my room, shutting my door behind me and listening for any sounds in the cabin before knocking on Kade's door. A snore answers from the other side, letting me know he's still sleeping, so I pad downstairs to the kitchen.

I round the banister and nearly halt in my tracks at the sight of Darius sitting at my dining table. He's bent down, lacing up his boots, and I try not to look at the way his muscles flex in his arms. When did I suddenly become someone who notices these things? I ignore him and head to the kitchen.

"Morning, little wolf," Darius practically purrs, and I shiver at the sound. Why did his voice have to sound like that? Deep and low, like a caress on my skin. I mumble under my breath and ignore him, but he doesn't appreciate that. The way he's at my back not a few seconds later, practically breathing down my neck, clearly gives that away. "I said, morning, little wolf."

"It's morning? Shit. I didn't even realize, I thought it was midday you know, with the sun just rising," I snark out, moving to grab a pan. Filling it with water, I put it on the stove and set the flame.

"Not a morning person I see," he says, and I feel a touch on the top of my head, causing me to freeze a second. Why is he touching me?

"I wonder what gave that away," I mutter, moving away from him and grabbing a mug before filling it with some coffee granules and the now hot water. Moving around Darius, I head for the table and take a seat. Darius follows me and sits back down across from me, watching me. I ignore him and pretend he's not there while I drink the elixir of life and look out the window.

"Why don't our stones work here?" he asks suddenly, and I nearly jump out of my skin at him breaking the silence.

"Eridian is protected. We mostly can't use magic inside the settlement, whether from objects or ourselves. Unless it's powerful enough and the land lets you. We can't go to our wolf forms either unless you are in the forest."

Out of the corner of my eye, he slouches back in his seat, his dark t-shirt pulling tight across his chest. "Unless the land lets you?"

I roll my eyes and finally let them go to him. We lock eyes and heat starts to spread at my chest. "Yes, the land. It's living and breathing, just like you and me. It chooses what can be used and what can't." I take a sip and watch him acknowledge what I've said.

"It sounds like you live in the way our ancestors did hundreds of years ago, when the old ones were around." I shrug because we do live like that here. They would be wise to start too. "What does it let you use then, this… land?" He rolls his green eyes, and I can tell he thinks I'm being ridiculous.

"That's not for me to decide," I tell him, and hear a door opening from upstairs and then hard footsteps coming down the stairs. "I can't tell you what it deems worthy." A throat clears, and I turn my head toward it as Kade comes into the dining room, scowling at Darius.

I check him over. He's only wearing dark pants, which lets me get a look at his injuries on his bare torso that are healing, thankfully. He looks a little pale and tired, but otherwise okay. He comes over to me and rubs his cheek against mine before heading into the kitchen. I grab his arm before he gets far, and he huffs back at me. He humors me as I stand and run my fingers around the wound on his shoulder that's been stitched up before looking at his throat and temple closely. The wounds have closed nicely, and apart from some redness, they're healing well.

"I'm okay, Rhea," he whispers softly, and I look into his blue eyes, a shade different from mine, as he gives me a small smile.

"Go grab some food and we'll talk, okay?" He nods, and I squeeze his arm before I drop it and let him go.

I return to my seat, shifting uncomfortably as Darius looks between me and Kade with far too much interest. "I'm sending Elites out to search The Deadlands. Since we can't use our stones as they have been drained of their magic, what is the best way to keep track of locations there?"

"I can send Taylor with you, he knows The Deadlands better than any of us and can make sure your men don't get lost. I also need you to make sure anyone staying behind keeps their distance from my pack members and make sure they keep their aura low. If they need to speak to them, do it with care and at least with a good amount of space between them. If any of us see your Elites crossing the line, we will act. You can understand that, right?"

He nods, his eyes bouncing between mine before he stands. "Although, I don't know why you are Alpha of this pack," he starts. "I understand that when the need arises, you need to take care of things. You have my permission to do so if the circumstances call for it, and only then." He places his hands on the table and leans forward, bringing his face closer to mine. "But don't try anything you shouldn't, little wolf. You are already in deep shit, and you won't like the extra consequences." He stands and walks away without another word, the front door closing behind him as he leaves.

Well, that was interesting.

I reach out to Josh, our links now, thankfully, open again. *"Send Taylor with the Elites that are going into The Deadlands. I'm sure Taylor will know how to navigate them around without them being able to track exactly where we are. You can stop by when you're done if you want."*

"Got it. Is Kade awake?" he replies.

"He sure is."

"Good," he says, and the link closes as Kade sits down next to me, still not sitting in his usual seat where he used to sit with Cassie. I nudge his shoulder before drinking my coffee again.

He eats his mountain of food in silence, and he gets down to the last of his fruit on his plate before I ask him, "Are you done?"

He nods, putting a gooseberry in his mouth before pushing his plate away from him. "I am now," he exhales, patting his stomach.

"Good." I put my mug down and grab his ear, pulling him toward me. "Now you can explain why the fuck you were in The Deadlands," I growl, dragging him up out of his seat and toward my office.

"Ow, ow, ow, shit, Rhea, that hurts," he whines as I pull him with me.

"You're lucky I'm only trying to rip your ear from your head and not kicking your ass all over Eridian. Plus, you won't miss an ear, it's not like you listen anyway." I open my office door and bring him with me, shoving him down in the chair at my desk. With him sitting, I start to pace.

Kade rubs at his ear, watching me with a scowl on his face. "Rhea–"

"No. No, Kade. Don't you Rhea me, you little shit. Do you have a death wish?!" I shout. "Was it not enough that you decided to risk your life with rogures before we left? You had to come into The Deadlands where you could have died?"

"It wasn't like that," he protests, but I'm not ready to hear it.

I tug at my hair before shoving it into a knot on top of my head. "It was like that, Kade. You know how dangerous it is out there, and you knew what we were doing," I hiss at him. "You knew you were putting yourself in danger by going in there. And not only that…" I point at him as the front door opens. "You put our pack at risk. I put you in charge because I trusted you to look after them. But instead, you left them alone and vulnerable, and went searching blindly in The Deadlands for who? Me? The fucking Elites?"

Josh enters the office and spots the shitbag in the chair, seeing Kade's eyes burning as he looks at me. "Ah." That's all Josh says, before moving to sit down near the windows.

Kade says nothing, just continues to stare at me, his lips pressed in a hard line as I fume. I fling my hands out. "Answer me!" I demand.

He sighs, running a hand through his hair before he stands. He winces slightly, trying to not show it, but I see it. I instantly feel guilty for doing this right now. But fuck, he nearly died. What he did was reckless, stupid and so damn irresponsible.

Kade shoves his hands into his pockets. "I know you probably think my decision to go to The Deadlands was impulsive, but we had a vote."

"A vote?" Josh repeats, his brows raising.

"Yeah." Kade nods. "You had been gone for days. We were all

getting worried. Josie suggested maybe a few of us go and look for you guys. I didn't like it, but the rest of the pack agreed. It was either I go alone or some were likely to sneak out to go find you, regardless of whether I told them not to. I picked what I thought was the best option in a shit situation," he sighs, looking down at his bare feet.

Well, that changes things. It's Josie's ass I will beat next. Why would she even suggest this to him and the rest of the pack?

"That's really fucking stupid," Josh mumbles, and I nod. "Looks like Wrath Rhea is going to be aimed at someone."

I point at him. "Hey! I can aim it at you if you want." I hate that nickname.

"I would do it again," Kade pipes up, and I look at him.

I sigh, the fight going out of me. "I understand what you did and why. If this was any other situation I would be on your side. But Kade, the situation is dire, and there is too much at stake. Whether you like it or not, me and the guys going out was to prevent them from coming here, but yours and the pack's decision sealed that fate when you nearly bled to death." My voice hitches at the memory, and Kade steps closer to me, pulling me into his body and holding me tight. "I suppose it doesn't matter now, but you have to look at the pros and cons before heading into an unknown situation. You have to be sure it's what has to be done. You can never put yourself in danger like that again."

"I know, I'm sorry," he mumbles into my hair. "I messed up."

I shake my head against his chest. "I'm sorry, too." For shouting at him when he's hurting. For bringing the Elites here and putting him in danger. For fucking failing.

"Come on, Carzan," Josh says. "I still need to chew your ass out, but we will leave Rhea here and do it somewhere else." Kade grumbles as he lets me go and sulks out the room, Josh on his heels. I close my eyes and just breathe.

Good fucking morning to me.

EIGHTEEN

RHEA

Rhea

"Any idea how we're going to get the Elites to keep Eridian a secret?" I ask the guys quietly. Darius said he would think about keeping Eridian quiet, but we need something solid, not a maybe.

We watch the Elites spar with each other in front of us. We are just outside the lilk trees in the forest and a good distance away from them so they can't hear us. Some Elites are in wolf form, some not. I drag the elk we hunted for dinner closer to me, my bloody hands leaving red prints on its legs.

"I have no idea, Milal. But I'm not about to let you go to the Highers either way." Josh steps up beside me and watches the Elites intently, tracing their moves.

Two wolves attack each other, their paws swiping and teeth biting. I watch on in rapt attention. They are so well trained, we look like puppies compared to them.

"We could kill them," Colten muses, bringing my attention to him. "Poison?"

Hudson shakes his head. "They would smell it a mile off. They are highly trained. It won't be that easy."

"I could slit their throats in their sleep,' Sebastian says, twirling his favorite knife in his hands, eager to throw it as usual.

"I doubt you could get close enough without them knowing you're there." I sigh, watching as Darius steps up to two Elites and guides them through a defensive move. His face is set into a mask of authority, his stance unyielding as he asks them to go through the move again and again.

Maize steps up to him, disrupting their drills and that mask breaks into annoyance. She waves her hands around wildly, and Leo walks over, listening to what she's saying.

I haven't seen much of Maize since the Elites came here a few days ago. She mostly sticks with the other members of the Elites or goes off on her own. The witch seems to have an eye for Darius though. It shouldn't bother me, there is no reason for it to.

But every time her eyes are on him, I kind of want to pluck them out.

Leo shakes his head and walks over to Zaide, leaving her with Darius and starts throwing a series of punches. Maize starts pointing toward the barrier, and I bristle. The fuck is she talking about?

Darius starts to wave her off, but freezes when his eyes land on me just outside of the lilk trees.

Maize continues to talk to him, but his attention is solely on me, on the blood that covers me from the hunt, and I see his eyes flash. His body turns and takes a step toward me, but Maize grabs his arm to halt him. He pauses and turns his head to her, making her hand drop from his skin. I can barely hear the growl he releases toward her, but it has an effect because she storms off, head bent low.

He turns back, and with purposeful strides, walks toward me. He passes sparring Elites, not concerned with being accidently hit or caught in between anyone. His steps eat up the distance between us until he's a few feet away from me. His eyes roam over my body, paying extra attention to the areas covered in blood, before looking down at the elk.

My body tingles under his attention, and my brows furrow at my reaction.

"Hungry?" he asks, and I lift my eyes to him.

"Dinner for the pack," I reply, refusing to let the heat I feel at his perusal redden my cheeks. "She was an older elk, unable to breed any longer. She didn't have much time left, so she was a good choice today."

His brows pull together. "You hunted her because she's old? Why not go for the younger, healthier one?"

"Then we would take out a young, healthy, and still fertile female that can reproduce and keep their numbers reasonable. We can then still hunt elk without worrying about their population decreasing." Taylor answers him for me, his amber eyes glancing around the Elites at Darius's back.

"You only hunt ones that are not as able as others?" Darius asks, his brows furrowing, and I can't understand why this confuses him at all.

"Not all the time, but mostly. And we only hunt to eat, not to just chase or kill." I shrug, wiping my hand on my shorts to try and get more blood off. Darius follows the movement, and I pause at the look in his eyes.

"Alpha," a male greets. Darius and I both turn our heads at the title as Axel and Finn walk toward me. "All is well around the cliffs. No sign of anything close by. It's fairly quiet."

"Okay, good," I tell him. "Rest up. Is Ben still out?"

"Yeah," Axel says. "He wanted to go for a run." He looks toward the Elites sparring with interest before clearing his throat and looking at Darius. "Would you mind if some of us spar with you?" I choke on my own saliva at his words, and Josh pats my back as I bend over slightly and cough.

A growl sounds in front of me, but then cuts off as my eyes spring up to Darius in surprise. His eyes are on Josh, his look screaming danger before his expression clears, and he looks at Axel.

"I don't see why you or anyone else can't spar with them. Though it may be better if you spar with some of the trainees," Darius suggests.

Oh, he woke up and chose violence, I see. "They have experience," I say proudly. Sure, we're not exactly at their level, but were scrappy fuckers when we fight. Plus, Taylor has taught us everything we know and he was trained somewhat.

"Darius," Leo calls, clearly eavesdropping, and we look toward him. "Let them play. It will be fun." The fucker smirks, his blue eyes dancing in amusement, and my blood boils.

I straighten and walk around Darius, dropping the legs of the elk and heading directly for Leo. He examines me curiously, and the Elites around us slow their movements as they watch on. I feel the weighted gaze of Darius at my back, but I refuse to turn and meet his eyes. I have something to do first.

Leo shoves his hands in the pockets of his combat pants, his stance relaxed at my approach. He smiles when I'm two steps away from him, head tilted in amusement. "Wanna play–" My fist flies, aiming for his jaw, and it lands, forcing his head to whip to the side. His body follows as I sweep my leg, taking his feet right out from under him, and he lands with a hard thud on the ground. "Fuck," he grunts, looking up at me in shock.

The Elites suck in sharp breaths around me and laughter rings out from behind as Colten loses it, cheering me on. I smirk. "Play?" I tap my finger to my chin. "I don't think playing is the right word for me putting you on your ass."

"What the fuck just happened?" Leo asks as he stands, brushing the dirt off his pants.

"You got your ass handed to you." Damian cackles. "That's

what happened."

"Shut the fuck up," Leo growls at him before he starts toward me. I'm just about to uppercut the cocky shit, knowing I need to be quick, but he's on his ass again before either he or I can blink.

Darius towers over him, features set in stone as he looks down at him. "You got put on your ass because you underestimated your opponent. You can stay down a little longer for that trainee mistake."

Darius turns toward me, but I'm already walking off. "Axel, why don't you ask some others if they would like to join you in sparring with the Elites. I'm sure it would be good for those that are okay with that." He nods before he walks off with Finn.

I bend down when I reach the guys and grab the elk's legs, pulling it along the ground behind me. As we walk toward the barrier, something pulls on the elk. I turn with a growl, a snarl on my lips at someone touching my kill.

Darius lifts a brow at me, yanking on the elk, but I don't let go. "Give it up, little wolf. I'm carrying it so you can change quicker."

"Why?" I wonder.

He pauses for a moment, his grip tightening on the elk as his eyes darken. "Because the sight of you covered in blood makes me want to hunt you."

I swallow at his words, at the thought of hunting me in a way that makes the Alpha in me want to rise to the challenge. I let go, wanting to get away from him and the way he has my body reacting in a way I'm not sure I understand.

He picks the elk up easily and flings it over his shoulder like it weighs nothing when I struggled to drag it. We stare at each other, and the world narrows down to the two of us and nothing else. No one can penetrate this bubble we've created a few times now, and no one can stop it, not even us. Runa comes to my eyes, watching him intently as confusion stirs inside me at the way he commands my attention and focus.

I feel my guys are near me. I know the Elites are too. But it's as if their presence is muted, like whispers at the edges of my being, and the only solid form is the one in front of me. He's a force of his own, taking up all the oxygen around us and demanding my eyes to be on him at all times or else I'll suffocate for the failure to do so. But I don't think this feeling is one sided. He looks at me like he's trying to figure me out, trying to understand what he's seeing just like I am.

I don't think either of us know the answer.

He steps forward while I'm rooted to my spot, my head the only part of my body moving as I tilt it back, unable to look away from his eyes. His gaze drifts over my features again. Moving over my eyes, my cheekbones, my temples, my nose, until his gaze slides down to the side of my neck, before finally moving and landing on my lips. The air around us thickens and heats spreads through my body when his scent hits me. My lips part, and his head lowers, getting closer and closer. His mouth is a breath away from touching mine, and I don't think I breathe. He skims his lips against my cheek, barely touching my skin, before he whispers against my ear. I shiver.

"Keep looking at me like that, Rhea, and I'll show you how I hunt and devour my prey." He moves around me, the world coming back into focus as I stand there, sucking in air and wondering what the fuck just happened. Again.

"Gods," Sebastian breathes. "You two giving each other fuck me now looks? That's a disaster waiting to happen." My mouth drops open at his words. "A hot disaster, but a disaster all the same.

"There were no fuck me looks," I object as I clear my throat and turn to head home.

"There kinda was," Josh says, and I shoot him a look of

betrayal. He shrugs. "Just remember he's the enemy."

"How could I ever forget," I mutter. He's enemy number one, even more so with the way I react to him. He holds Eridian in his palms, and I have to find a way to make nice with him, or kill him, to keep Eridian hidden.

Now, I just need to ignore the fact that when he looks at me, I feel something I don't think I have ever felt so strongly before.

Desire.

And that is a hard fucking no.

NINETEEN

DARIUS

"Any news on the sighting of the woman?" I ask Leo. We're on the deck of Rhea's cabin, leaning against the wall while Leo sits on the top step, arms dangling between his legs while we both look out over Eridian.

From here we can see the main housing cabins surrounding us, and the place at the center that Rhea calls the gathering, where I first saw the pack. We've been here for over a week now. Taylor, Zaide, and Damian have been taking some of the men with them to search The Deadlands, making sure the Elites are safe. The only way they can get back here is on foot since our port stones have been drained of magic since entering through the invisible barrier, so we have to be careful they don't get lost.

I still don't understand how the barrier around Eridian drained those stones. I haven't come across a barrier like that apart from when the Highers' witches get together to create one, and that's only possible if the witches rank at a high level. The Highers have the strongest witches in Vrohkaria, except for the ones that live in the southwest woods with their coven. But they refused to bend to the Highers' will and law, and they still don't cooperate now. So how did Eridian get its barrier? From those witches?

"Nothing. Nothing at all," Leo grumbles, finally answering me. "This whole search and rescue is fucking pointless. We were never going to find her in the first place, or rogures."

"I agree, but it's either I become a Higher or this, and I need to get rid of the rogures before I commit to anything. The lands across Vrohkaria are going to shit with no end in sight, and the people are fighting amongst themselves then pointing fingers at who they think is to blame. If we can't find a solution, there will be nothing left by the time the rogures destroy everything." I couldn't give a fuck about becoming a Higher. It was something my father wanted me to be, and at the time, I agreed. But things change. The lands fucking changed. "We are the Elites, we are supposed to protect Vrohkaria, and we haven't managed to do that."

The taste of failure is bitter and leaves anger in its wake. The Elites' purpose is to protect, and we can't even do that.

"We can only do so much, Darius. You can't shoulder the full responsibility of the rogures on your own." He sighs, scanning the area and watching Rhea's pack get on with their daily chores.

"I swore I would get justice for my family, and I will. Nothing will get in the way of that." We've had this same conversation many times before. Leo tells me I'm taking on too much, and I reply that it's my responsibility as the Alpha of the Elites. It only leaves us both pissed. I shake my head and watch the people mulling about, changing the direction of the conversation. "There is something not right about this place, and I can't figure it out." Eridian shouldn't exist. No record or map shows life in The Deadlands throughout the history of Vrohkaria. Eridian is an anomaly, and not knowing how it came to be angers me.

"I know, it's definitely not normal," Leo says. "But if you can't figure it out, we have no chance of doing so." We watch the pack give my men a wide berth as they move around the center, scurrying off with their pups as soon as one comes in sight. Jerrod looks in the direction a mother and son ran, pausing as he watches the now empty space before carrying on. "Why do they act like that? It's like they have never seen another person."

"I don't know, and I don't believe the bullshit Rhea told me either." The lies that come from that woman's mouth just show the type of wolf she is.

She has tells when she lies, and over the past week, I've figured them out. She's naive to think she can hide from the Alpha of the Elites.

He scoffs. "You would have to be a fool to believe what comes out of her mouth."

I nod. I don't believe half the shit she said to me in her office that day. I think she knows it as well, but what is she hiding that she can't just say? What's the problem with declaring to the Highers where they live? It doesn't make sense. They could even live a better life than they are now. It isn't a shit hole here, but it isn't anything that's considered as standard in the lands either. Even the way the pack is structured and works is strange.

"It's time to start asking more questions. She thinks I've dropped it by leaving it alone for a few days. She should have realized that I've just been observing. She has no idea that the men have been reporting back to me daily." Stupid wolf. She thinks she's safe in her own home. She will soon understand nowhere is safe for her anymore. Not from me. I have her scent. Earth and rainwater, with hints of a wildness that I can't pinpoint where I have scented it before. Either way, I can track her anywhere if she is close enough, and my wolf likes the thought of that.

"Want me to come with you?" Leo stands and shakes out his arms, still observing Rhea's pack.

"No. Go and wait for the men at the bottom of the cliffs where they left yesterday," I tell him. "They will be back soon."

I'll admit, I'm still shocked at what I saw when we went atop the cliffs where The Deadlands are. The cliffs encase an odd rectangular valley below, that is what they call Eridian, that protects the life that flows through it. Tall, healthy trees grow in the valley, and there are two different sized lakes with the bluest water I have ever seen. There are strange birds and some unusual animals that live there. Further along, there is an opening that looks like water spilling over the edge toward the Unforgivable Sea, the only opening in the valley.

There are waterfalls coming out of the cliff sides that surround Eridian, and when you look toward the center of the valley, there's a ring of what I now know are lilk trees, their colors vibrant amongst the normal greens of the other trees. That's the protection circle that surrounds Eridian. Everything about this place is unnatural. I refuse to believe this has been here all this time.

I walk down the steps of Rhea's home, our temporary resting place, and make my way down the dirt path. Leo goes off to the right toward the forest outside the barrier, heading to the cliffs. There are some creatures and animals in the forest, but nothing like in The Deadlands, so he has nothing to worry about. I continue forward, then veer off to the left when I pick up Rhea's scent, a beacon to my wolf who stirs in excitement.

He likes being near the little wolf, when all I want to do is strangle the life out of her, but maybe do it while I'm inside of her. I shove that thought away. Whether they were trainees or not, the fact is that the little wolf killed some of them and even dared to try and kill all of us. That can't be forgotten, no matter how I forget about everything and anything when I look into her eyes.

Those fucking eyes.

I continue on, eventually coming up to the lilk trees. I study them as I pass through the invisible barrier, feeling a caress against my soul that I always feel when crossing it. My wolf, Drax, practically fucking purrs at the feeling, contentment oozing from him, and I growl within myself at him. I pick up speed, heading into the forest and opening my senses around me. Nothing in particular reaches me as I track down the little wolf, only the usual sounds of animals skittering about.

It isn't long until I hear her footsteps up ahead, quiet, but not quiet enough to hide from me. I stalk through the trees, excitement running through me at seeing the spark in her eyes when she sees me. I don't think she even knows she does it, but she does. Her reaction to me intrigues me like no other, and my reaction to her makes me want to kick my own ass.

From the first moment I saw her in The Deadlands, everything within me wanted to hunt her. To get to her. Her eyes were wide, lips parted, chest heaving, and I wanted nothing more than to pin her to the ground and watch her eyes go wide for a different reason.

Drax was also riding me hard. He wanted to tear out of my skin and run to her, and it took a lot of my control to get him under wraps.

Our reaction to her isn't normal.

I follow the sounds of her steps, light and delicate, until eventually I see her up ahead, her hand on one of the trees with her eyes closed. I stop and watch her closely. The steady breaths she takes, the stance she is in, and the round curve of her ass in her shorts as she stands still. I tilt my head.

What the fuck is she doing?

I stalk forward, silent and sure, until I'm at her back and feel the heat of her body soaking into mine. I lean forward slowly until my lips are next to her ear. I see her still, her breath hitching, and it causes me to smirk, knowing she feels my presence. "What are you doing, little wolf?" I murmur, my bottom lip touching her ear as they move.

She spins, and I move my head back while she glares up at me, her ice-blue eyes so full of anger it gets me hard. I want to see tears in them again. I want to see them shine like the clearest glass as they water. I want it.

I *crave* it.

Fuck.

She crosses her arms over her chest, and my eyes flick down on their own accord. Her breasts strain against her dark t-shirt, rising softly with her breaths, and I can't help but imagine how they would feel in my hands. How they would look with my teeth marks on them. I clench my jaw and will my cock to go down.

This attraction I have to her is going to end up being a pain in my ass.

I drag my eyes away and up, slowly looking over her throat and pausing before coming back to her eyes. She scoffs at my perusal, giving me a hard look before turning and walking away from me. I chuckle under my breath. Doesn't she know never to turn her back on a predator?

And I'm not just any predator.

Catching up to her in a few short steps, I place my hand in between her shoulder blades and shove her forward against the nearest tree. She makes a small sound that I ignore while I keep her pinned there. I like her helplessness under my touch. "I wasn't done talking," I say, my voice low. I dip down so I can see her eyes from the side while she spits curses at me.

"You asshole! Get off of me!"

"Now where is the fun in that? Are you going to be a good little wolf and have some manners?" I ask her, smirking at the tiny growls she makes.

Adorable.

I find *nothing* adorable.

I growl to myself.

"You're talking to me about manners?" She brings her head back, trying to hit me, and I bring my free hand to her ponytail, wrapping my hands in the strands and then wrenching her head back.

I look down into her seething eyes and smirk. "Are you going to be good?" She says nothing, so I tug on her hair more and press her more firmly into the tree.

The breath wooshes out of her as we lock eyes, and I get lost in their depths. Her pupils start to dilate, and I know her wolf is watching me from within her. I let Drax come to my own eyes, showing both of them that I'm not fucking around.

Finally, after a tense moment, she slumps forward. I shake her head a little, wanting words. "Yes," she grits out between clenched teeth. I release her, watching as she straightens her clothes. Anger pours off her in waves that makes me run my tongue over my teeth in anticipation of how she will react.

I may tower over her with my six four frame, but she's a little fighter.

I examine her tattoo that I saw when we first encountered each other with interest. It's on her right forearm and the language is old, so extremely old that I can't make out what it says, but the runes on her wrist I recognize. They symbolize the old wolf Gods, Zahariss and Cazier. "Why do you have the old Gods on you?" I nod at her arm when her eyes meet mine in question.

She brings her hand up to touch it, and she shrugs. "Why wouldn't I? We are wolves, are we not?" She scuffles a booted foot in the dirt.

"There are different kinds of wolves, and no one follows the old Gods anymore. They follow the Highers rule. You're what? Late twenties, and you follow the old Gods?" I tilt my head at her. "That doesn't make any sense."

"Twenty-eight, and I've always followed them. The whole pack does. We give our blessings to them for the life we have here and the food they provide us. They are the land we walk upon after all. They also gave us our wolves, so why wouldn't we give thanks to them and honor them?"

"The legends state they had gone mad, especially the male, Cazier. Between Zahariss and him, the lands started to rot with their madness, and they disappeared, leaving us with no explanation. Why would anyone want to honor Gods that were out of control and abandoned us?" I walk deeper into the forest before looking over my shoulder when she doesn't follow. I look from her to the spot next to me, my meaning very clear. She huffs before stepping beside me, keeping some distance between us. So I immediately close that distance, not letting her get what she wants.

"You're ridiculous," she mumbles under her breath before answering me. "I don't know about them abandoning us, but they have given us the gift of our wolves. How can we not honor them for that and all they have created?" she says, trying again to move away, but giving up when I again move closer. "Legend does state that Cazier did go a little mad because he couldn't be with his mate, and Zahariss wasn't doing well without him. He lived in the below while she lived on the lands. It was pretty much impossible for them to even be next to each other for long periods of time. She walked above, and he traced her footsteps below. They were so close to each other, but never touching. I feel sad for them and the life they led. Wouldn't you go a bit mad being separated from your mate? Not being able to go to them?"

"I don't know, and I don't particularly care either. Having a mate is of no concern to me, especially if it turns you mad." I lift a shoulder. I don't care for or want a mate. Having your life intertwined with someone else's without your control? Fuck no.

"Do we actually agree on something? I'm shocked." I believe her on this. Her eyes are wide as she looks at me, and her brows scrunch together as if she truly can't believe we agree on something.

I grunt and move on. "So you follow the old Gods because they gave you your wolf?"

She nods. "I do, and so do my pack. The Gods may not be here with us, but they are here in everything we see and touch." She runs her hand on the leaf of a bush as we pass. "Do you not feel it?" she asks, and I give her a look. "You're missing out. Though I guess it's all blood and guts with you being an Elite and all."

"We are Elites. We do what we must." I tell her, ignoring the way she side-eyes me. "Did you know we would be in The Deadlands?"

Her eyebrows raise at my question, and I continue to watch her as we walk. She shakes her head slowly. "It was a chance meeting, and we acted. How would we have any idea you were in there? We had been in The Deadlands for a few days to collect Luicium." At my confusion she adds. "The glowing liquid from some of the dead trees. We put it in jars and use them as light in places around Eridian. Anyway, we were just in the same place at the same time, that's all."

She's lying. I can tell by the way she avoids my eyes when she's done talking, pretending to watch the ground while she walks, and the way her fingers twitch at her sides while she speaks.

What are you hiding, little wolf?

"What do you know of rogures?" I ask, instead of calling her out on her bullshit. For now. Being out here, I would be surprised if she knew how the rest of Vrohkaria suffers while she stays with her pack in their own little oasis. The thought quickly angers me.

"I know of them," she says slowly. "We have had some come here into the forest. We got rid of them, but the sightings have increased over the last year." She shakes her head and stops to look at me. Bright, innocent eyes hold mine. "Where did they even come from?"

"No one knows. That's another reason we are in The Deadlands. We're looking for rogure dens as well as this missing woman. We have no idea where they came from and neither do the Highers." She looks away. "I've been taking my Elites all over Vrohkaria to different parts of the lands to try and find their original den or find a way to stop them. All we know is that they are plaguing the lands, killing and mauling anything in their sight with no sign of slowing down.

"I hate them," she mutters. "They destroy everything." Sadness flashes across her face quickly before it's gone. "I can tell you I haven't seen any dens in The Deadlands in all the years I've lived here though."

"All the years you've lived here? I thought you have always been here?" I question, looking at her dead in the eyes.

"I have." She waves her hand at me. "I just meant since I've been alive."

Hmm. "What about your parents? Have they seen any dens before? Where are they anyway?"

"The only family I have left is the one I choose," she says coldly, all emotion gone from her face, and my brows furrow. "No one alive in Eridian has seen any rogure dens. We are thorough in checking our perimeter for them. Many years back, a pack of them came into the valley and killed many of us. Since then, we have taken no chances. Some appeared a few months ago, but there were only a few of them, their pack small. We don't know where they came from, and we haven't seen any since."

We stop, and I fold my arms over my chest, ignoring the way her gaze moves to my arms. "I'm surprised they have even been this deep into The Deadlands. We never see any come out of there, and you clearly don't see many come in here. How nice it must be to stay away from the lands that are being plagued by them. Living your life out here peacefully while others suffer and die."

"You think we don't suffer?" she hisses at me, eyes narrowed as her anger takes over, and mine rises to the challenge. "You don't know the fucking meaning!"

I scoff at her, looking her over like the unimportant bitch she is. "So, you think you can be attacked here a few times by rogures and think that's suffering?" My hand whips out, and I grab her by the jaw, digging my fingers into her skin. She winces, but otherwise doesn't make a single sound. That just pisses me off more. "Do you hear babes being ripped from their mothers' arms? Mauled alive while their mother tries and fails to save them? Do you hear the screams of people running for their lives, only to be hunted down and ripped apart?" I shake her chin. "You live here in your own little paradise, peacefully passing the fucking time while the whole of Vrohkaria is out there suffering every fucking day! Do you know the number of people that could have been saved if you had declared to the Highers where you fucking live!"

I growl at her before raising my other hand pushing her chest. She falls to the floor, landing on her ass as I tower over her. "What—"

"Many could have been saved and been brought here if you weren't such a selfish bitch, keeping Eridian to yourself," I cut her off, and hurt flashes through her eyes at my words. good. "Hundreds could have lived here happily instead of rotting in the ground. More deaths are on your soul it seems than just my trainees." Her hands clench at her sides. "When we leave here, I'll be taking you to the Highers, and you will tell them about this place. You will stand there, in front of them all and the public who join, and you will tell them how you kept a safe haven hidden from everyone when you could have helped your own people!"

Helped my fucking family.

Her eyes flash up at me, her jaw clenched, but she doesn't utter a single word. I look at her in disgust and turn my back on her before I kill her too soon. I walk away from her while Drax nudges me to go back, but he can fuck off. The more I think about her not declaring this place to the Highers, the more I want to tear the whole fucking valley apart. The number of people that could have lived here, that could have been kept safe inside the barrier while we try to search for a way to stop the rogures… It would be invaluable, and she just kept it to herself. Not caring about the rest of Vrohkaria wasting away and dying. It's people like her that are the fucking problem. Selfish, self-important and only looking out for themselves while leaving the rest of us to rot. She will soon be in shock when we get back home. Her whole life is about to change.

Eridian is soon going to be overrun by people, and there is not a damn thing she can do about it but sit back and watch her home be taken over.

All the while, she will be left in my hands to be dealt with as punishment for murdering my men.

TWENTY

RHEA

"Fucking asshole," I mutter as I get to my feet and stomp after him. We don't suffer? Every member of my pack has suffered one way or another. He can see it clearly in some of their faces, for fuck's sake. All I have ever done is help other people survive, my family included, and he calls me selfish! The audacity of this overgrown babysitter. He can go fuck himself if he thinks the Highers are getting their grubby hands on Eridian.

I won't tell them shit.

I pick up speed, growling beneath my breath and clenching my fists at my sides as I follow in the direction he went. I finally spot him up ahead a good distance away, his broad shoulders tense with every heavy step he takes.

I look down at the forest floor and pick up a small rock, tossing it in the air a few times and feeling the rough edges before I take my aim. I bring my arm back and power it forward with an extra boost from Runa. I watch as it soars through the air, flying perfectly to hit its target. Yes! Sebastian teaching me how to throw knives at targets on the trees has really paid off.

I'm so busy basking in my smugness at hitting Darius between his shoulder blades, the same spot he pinned me by to the tree earlier, that I don't actually notice how still he's gone. It's only when I see him turn his head slowly to the right, that I realize that's the only part of his body moving. There's not a twitch of his fingers or the rise and fall of his shoulders, like he's not even breathing.

I may have just made a wrong move.

I bite the inside of my lower lip as he turns slowly, so slowly, until he's eventually facing me. He looks down toward the forest floor, to where the stone now rests and tilts his head at it in an animalistic way. His dark hair hangs just above his eyes. I freeze at the way he looks at it, and a stillness surrounds us. My heart rate picks up, my palms start to sweat, and when he finally lifts his head to look at me, my eyes widen, a gasp leaving me as I look into his eyes. His pure black eyes where the whites should be. His larger green pupils glow as he stares straight back at me with an intensity I feel down to my soul. I take a small step back at the sight of him, the shock of him, but he follows, taking a step toward me.

I pause, and he stops.

Darius's wolf watches my every move, head still tilted, body still tense, ready and waiting to get to its prey. His nostrils flare, and then he releases a deep, low growl that pins me in place. My body shivers at the sound, and Runa looks out of my eyes, watching him with me. She whines softly, and looks over at the male that is now releasing dominance freely, no longer holding it back. Runa bristles as it hits us and tries to get me to release ours, but that would be poking the very angry wolf, and I do not want to do that right now. We may be strong, but Darius and his wolf are also pure Alpha, pure power. To be able to hold and control the change, but still work as one together completely… His eyes confirm it, and there is only one explanation as to why he can do that. One I don't want to even think about right now as I face an extremely furious male.

I stay as still as possible, watching him watch me as his scent drifts toward me stronger than ever. Cedarwood, damp earth that comes with the aftermath of a thunderstorm, and power.

Pure fucking power that wants me to kneel before him and bow in his presence. My legs begin to shake, but I lock them, refusing to bend.

He takes slow, measured steps toward me, stalking me like a hunter would his prey. His muscular body moves with intense precision, his steps silent even as I feel the ground tremble with every step he takes toward me. The trees nearby vibrate with the power he's giving off, and I swallow, unsure what to do here. My body trembles as Runa keeps fighting me to release my hold on my dominance that I refuse to let loose, and I have only one instinctual thing left on my mind.

Run.

So, I do.

I spin and take off, forcing Runa to give me some strength because we sure as fuck are going to need it. We can't compete against the Alpha at our backs, I know it and so does she. Yet with the need to flee, another thought niggles at the back of my mind. This isn't just us running to get away, but a need to assess the male behind us.

A strange urge to see if he is worthy.

If he can catch me.

I jump over small boulders and exposed tree roots, not even daring to look behind me as I dart through the trees and duck under branches. I hear Darius growl behind me, shaking the very air, but this time it's not in anger, it's in… approval. My brows furrow at the unusual sound, but I continue on, ignoring how that particular sound lights me up from within.

I'm fast, and I know this forest well. It's my home. I've been nearly everywhere in here, and that's the advantage I'll need. I aim for one of the rivers up ahead. If I can cross it and duck under the water quickly, it will hide my scent when I get to the other side, giving me more of a chance to lose him and leave him to calm down.

Throwing a rock at him was childish for sure, but the bastard deserved it. His words hurt, and assuming we haven't suffered made my blood boil, so I threw a stone. I don't think he appreciated that. I grimace, but keep my senses open, only hearing the movement of animals ahead of me scurrying away at my approach. But I feel nothing behind me. Did I lose him? I hear the sound of rushing water up ahead and move my legs faster, spotting the river just in the distance. I check over my shoulder, seeing nothing but trees, and I blow out a breath. I think I actually lost him, but I'll still go through the river to the other side. He will catch up to me eventually, but he'll have to find me first.

I glide around a huge tree and aim for the water. I hit it with a splash, feeling its coolness seeping into my skin. With it being so deep inside the forest, it doesn't get much sunlight to warm it up, but at least it's not freezing. I wade through it as fast as I can, making as little noise as possible. Reaching halfway, the water is up to my waist now, I'm just about to duck under when I'm collided with and forced under. I open my mouth on a scream, but all I get is a lungful of liquid. I thrash in the arms that surround me, my feet kicking out, trying to dislodge him. I'm running out of air, my lungs constricting, and I start to wriggle more fiercely when I'm suddenly brought to the surface. I hack up water, spluttering and taking in deep breaths of air as I thrash to get away from the male at my back. I don't get far as arms are banded around my chest tightly, my own pinned at my sides as I continue to twist in the asshole's arms, my legs pushing off the riverbed to try and aid me.

I bring a hand up and grip his forearm, my short nails clawing at the skin until his nose presses against the side of my neck, just below my ear. I still at his touch. At the place where he shouldn't be touching me.

My heart slams against my chest, and there is no way he

doesn't feel it with the arm banded across me. His growl is a low rumble, pressing his nose further into my skin, and I can't hold back the tiny sound that escapes me. He pulls me more firmly against him, drawing me closer, and I feel hardness digging into my lower back. My stomach drops and my nipples tighten at the feel of him, the heat of him, the scent of him. I pant as he brings a hand up, stroking my side leisurely until he slowly wraps a hand around the front of my throat and tilts my head to the side, exposing more of my neck to him as he speaks against my skin.

"You shouldn't have run, little wolf," he rumbles in a low husky voice. "It excites me." He nips my flesh, and my body flushes at his attention.

"You were angry," I pant, unconsciously tilting my head further as his teeth travel up my neck, biting me softly. My eyes close as his hold on my throat tightens, his arm moving from my chest further down to hold my hip.

I'm not panicking at his hold on me. I'm not flinching away from his touch like I would have with others. Through the slow haze that's clouding my mind, I realize that I have not once ever flinched away from him.

He spins me suddenly, using the hand that's still on my neck to guide me as I face him. He takes his hand off my hip and grabs me under my chin, adding pressure until I look up into his eyes. My lids slowly open, the feeling like I'm floating at his nearness consuming me as I try to clear my mind. His eyes are a little dimmer now, the white of his eyes only showing black that's bleeding at the edges. Although his wolf may have pulled back slightly, one prominent thing still has me entranced as I look in his half-lidded eyes.

The heat in them.

They're burning, threatening to eat me alive and devour me in the ashes that he will leave in his wake.

He pulls me closer by my throat, a soft sound spilling from my lips as my hands land on his solid chest. "I am angry," he says in a low tone. "But then you had to run from me. You know as well as I do how we wolves like the chase, the hunt, the challenge. And I always catch what I'm hunting, Rhea, you should know that from when I caught you in The Deadlands." He dips his head lower, so close to me that I see flecks of silver dancing in his pupils, looking like tiny shards of exploded glass. "Now, I'm not just angry, I'm excited." He growls, gripping my throat tighter, and Runa growls back before I can stop the sound escaping. He pauses, his eyes dropping to my lips before looking back up at me.

His body tenses at the look in my eyes, his thumb rubbing smoothly over my pulse and his brows form a line. He makes a frustrated sound at the back of his throat until he closes the distance between us, a breath away from my lips.

"Fuck you and fuck those eyes of yours," he growls before he capture me in a brutal kiss. I let out a squeak of surprise, my fingers digging into his chest as I keep my eyes wide open, just like him. His eyes darken, and his lips press firmer on mine before he bites my lower lip in reprimand when I don't kiss him back. I'm too stunned to do anything, to understand what the fuck is happening. He pulls away, his heated eyes take in my startled ones, both of us panting heavily and sharing each other's breaths as we stare at each other. "Open for me," he demands in a low tone. When I say nothing, he grabs and pulls my ponytail, holding me still. His mouth comes back to mine once more, squeezing my throat in warning to do what he says.

Unable to resist, I do, even though I have no idea what I'm doing, but he doesn't seem to care.

My eyes close and a small moan escapes me as I relent to his demanding mouth as it moves with mine. I kiss him back, unsure but fiercely, my hands traveling up his chest to the back of his head. I grip his hair tightly in my fists, pulling him closer. Needing him closer.

He makes a sound of approval into my mouth, and the sound goes straight to my clit, causing wetness to pool between my thighs. His grip on my hair and throat tighten simultaneously, no doubt smelling my arousal that he caused, and that just excites me further. His hand moves away from my throat to my jaw and squeezes until my lips part for him. He invades my mouth, our tongues tangling in a battle for dominance, and I whimper at the feel of him, the taste of him. I want to bathe in him as his scent wraps around me.

I rock my hips forward, feeling his hardness pressing into my stomach, making me feel delirious with want. Need. I feel him turning us and walking me backward, the cool water splashing against my heated skin as we move. My nipples rub against his chest through our wet clothing, and I release a long, low moan, wondering what it would feel like skin to skin. He lets go of my jaw and bends slightly, moving his forearm beneath my ass and lifts me up against him. I wrap my legs around his waist, feeling his cock against my center as I bring my arms around his neck. He releases my lips and trails open mouth kisses down the side of my neck while I move my hips, rubbing my pussy against him through our clothes. My back hits a hard surface, but I pay it no mind, feeling my body thrum with pleasure as I rock into him. His lips attack my collarbone, his hand squeezing my ass helping me move into him, guiding my body how he wants it as he tastes my skin. Why does this feel so good?

He grunts against my shoulder, moving me faster, his grip on my ass bruising with every rock of my body. "You smell so good, little wolf." The gravel in his voice has pleasure thrumming through me. "You want to come, don't you?"

"Yes," I moan, and scrape my nails down the back of his neck, making him groan against me. He lifts his head and captures my mouth, devouring it as our tongues taste each other, and I feel my orgasm creeping closer. "Darius."

His chuckle is deep as tiny sounds escape me as the tightness in me builds higher and higher as he grinds his cock against me, hitting my clit with just the right amount of pressure. His free hand roams over the swell of my breast, squeezing and roaming before he pinches my nipple through the fabric of my t-shirt, I suck in a sharp breath.

"Fuck," he breathes against my mouth before everything tightens at the slight pain, at the pleasure I haven't felt this strongly before flooding through me. I arch into him as my orgasm hits me hard and fast. My lips part as I moan, loud and long, and Darius groans low at the sound as my pussy contracts, my legs twitching around his hips.

He holds me close as my orgasm fades, my body slumping against him. We stay like that as I come back to myself, mouths not moving against each other, just touching as I catch my breath. I peel my eyes open, not realizing I closed them, and his eyes hold me captive, the desire in them sending butterflies into my stomach as his fingers twitch against my ass. When my breathing is under control, I hum at the satisfied feeling in my body, relishing in this new state, and then almost stop breathing, my body locking up around him.

What the fuck did I just do? How did that even happen?

I jolt and lean back away from him, moving my eyes away from his as I drop my hands from around his neck and loosen my legs from his waist. He removes his hand from my chest and around my ass and drops me slowly to the floor, saying nothing, but making me feel every inch of his body on the way down. I feel his eyes still on me, but I continue to look away as I move past him to the river, wading through the cool water and dipping low until it's up to my neck. His stare caresses my back, but I don't speak and neither does he, my mind whirling with what I just did. The shame of it.

I just got off on dry humping Darius, the Alpha of the Elites, the man who can tear my world apart as soon as he gets back to the Highers, while he pinned me against a fucking tree.

What. The. Actual. Fuck.

When I feel the cold of the water settle into my bones, I stand and walk back over to Darius where he hasn't moved. I stop a few feet from him, shivering, and not in the way he just made my body feel. I stare at the ground, my hands moving to my hips wondering what in the Gods I'm supposed to say.

My mind is a mess of confusion and disbelief. Even though we didn't even get naked and have sex, I still held on to him like I never wanted to let go, and he definitely kept me there, gripping me just as tightly. I put myself in a position of vulnerability, and I never do that. I let it get too far, even if I encouraged it, even if he started it by running. I shouldn't have even let him kiss me. I should have kicked him in the balls and told him to fuck off. But I didn't. I've given myself orgasms before, that's nothing new. I've only had one other person be intimate with me sexually, and it was a one-time thing. Fuck, I've never kissed anyone before until him, never been that close to another person like that. How he made me feel, how I relented to him and pulled him closer, needing him closer. I've never felt that way before, never felt that need.

I shake my head. Insanity.

I'm still running through the whole situation in my mind when he speaks. "What's wrong, Rhea?" he says mockingly, and I stiffen at the cruel sound of his voice. "Never come before?"

"I'm not some naive, virgin girl," I snap, bringing my head up just in time to see his eyes flash black. "But what the fuck just happened?"

"If you're not a virgin, then you know you ground your pussy on my cock until you came. How you make these little whimpering sounds when I pulled you close–"

"Stop being an asshole!" I cut him off, glaring at him. This is serious and he couldn't give a fuck. He shrugs and crosses his arms, my eyes following how the wet material stretches across his body, and I can't help as my eyes lower to see the outline of his abs. I flick my eyes back up to him quickly, but the smirk on the mouth that just devoured mine tells me I was caught checking him out.

"You ran from me. I was already angry and then you had to go and run." He tilts his head, his wet hair sticking to his face. "I've been in The Deadlands for months, I haven't fucked since before then. The hunt excites me, excites my wolf." His gaze trails my body as I stand there, wet and flushed. "You were there, and your body begged for release, so I gave you one. You're lucky I restrained myself enough that I didn't bend you over and fuck you until you had to crawl back home. Remember that the next time you try to run from me."

"Lucky?" I scoff, trying to ignore how coldly he is recalling what just happened. "What makes you think I would let you fuck me?" He runs his tongue over his lips, and I'll be damned if I lower my eyes and watch.

"I would fuck you, Rhea, and you would welcome me into your tight little body, begging me for more like a greedy slut." I flinch at his words before I can stop myself, and his smirk is slow, vicious. "However, it depends if I want my cock in a hole that has probably had so many, because I don't just put it in anyone. Your body may be tight, but your pussy?" He tilts his head. "That's questionable."

With those last words, he turns and walks off without a care in the world while I struggle to keep the prickle of tears from my eyes.

That hurt. His assumption about who's been inside my body, of how many people I would just let that close to me without care. That's not me, I don't let anyone touch me like that.

Yet here I am, pissed and slightly confused at being aroused by the thought that he could have fucked me against that tree, and I would have let him in that moment. I don't even know him. He's the enemy.

I scrub my hands down my face and sit in the dirt, cold and wet, wondering if I need to go to Anna for a checkup. It's just the stress of these last few weeks, finding the Elites while searching The Deadlands, Kade being distant, and now having strangers in my home.

The reason I'm acting strange is because of that.

That's all it was, and that's all it needs to be.

Ghostly fingers start stroking along my shoulder to my neck, and I reach a hand up absentmindedly, putting my palm against it. Unexpected warmth touches me, and I close my eyes, feeling reassurance wash over me while a tingling sensation starts in my chest. When it crawls upward and reaches my cheeks, I open my eyes and will the feeling to stay. Runa whines inside me, and I mentally scratch behind her ears, letting her know I'm here. The tingling feeling finally goes, and I lean back on my hands and open the link. Determined to ignore what just happened.

"Everyone at dinner?" I ask Josh, hoping my voice sounds normal.

"Yeah, they're just waiting on you. Kade is there too," Josh replies.

My brows rise in surprise. I didn't expect him to be there. Kade's been pretty much keeping to himself unless he's with Sam, and he should still be resting and taking it easy. *"I'll be there soon."*

I jump to my feet, my eyes lifting to the glow of the wisps as they play in the trees and head home for a change of clothes and a shower. I can't exactly walk into the gathering with the smell of Darius on me, feeling the results of my orgasm in my panties with each step I take. That would definitely cause some questions I'm not sure how to answer and more problems I do not need.

And I don't need to keep thinking about the asshole who just left me after he gave me something I never knew was possible for me.

TWENTY ONE

Rhea

I sneak through the back door of my cabin, closing it behind me slowly while I listen for any sounds inside. Hearing nothing, I rush down the hallway and around the banister to head for my bedroom. I get three steps up the stairs before I halt at the amused voice aimed my way.

"I didn't think you would have to sneak into your own home," Josh says suddenly, and I turn slowly toward him.

Shit.

"I didn't want to be bothered,' I tell him tentatively as I shuffle toward the living area. I see him sitting on the sofa, flicking through the pages of the book he's reading.

"I can smell him on you, you know." I cringe and move from foot to foot where I stand. He sighs and looks up at me, taking in my wet clothes and my disheveled hair. "I didn't see that coming," he says, continuing to look me over.

I blush and roll my eyes before walking forward and taking a seat on the chair across from him. "Yeah, well," I mumble. "I didn't either." I pick at my fingernails.

He shakes his head. "I also didn't see you letting anyone near you like that either, and though I'm glad you finally have, I hate the person you decided to do that with."

"We didn't fuck," I blurt out, and then clear my throat at the confused look on his face. "We just sort of… grinded a bit." I groan and rub my eyes.

Please ground. Swallow me.

I won't lie to Josh. He's my brother without the same blood. But shit, I didn't want to have this conversation right now, or, you know, ever. But I also know he won't let it drop. He loves and cares for me, and I know he just doesn't want to see me hurt. So if talking about what happened with Darius will ease his mind then that's what I'll do then forget it ever happened.

"Oh," he trails off, looking like he's about to piss himself from holding the laugh that I know wants to escape at my expense. I scowl at him, and that does it. He drops his book, and his head falls back as he laughs into the silence around us. I pick up a pillow and throw it at him.

"Josh," I groan.

"Okay… just give… just give me a second," he breathes. I cross my arms and scowl in his direction, waiting until he finally calms down. He sees the look on my face when he's done and straightens, his face serious. "Did he hurt you?"

"What? No, he didn't hurt me," I tell him softly at his concern, and he relaxes. Sure, he didn't hurt me physically, but his words did a little dent on me. Asshole.

"This isn't a good idea, you know. You and Darius." He pulls his knees up and rests his arms on them. "For starters, you guys practically hate each other. Not to mention he's the Alpha of the Elites, who do the Highers bidding."

"I know." I sigh and tip my head to rest on the back of the chair. "I don't know how it even happened, Josh. He was saying all kinds of shit, and then I threw a stone at him when he was walking off and–"

"Wait, you threw a stone at him?" Josh cuts me off, amusement written on his face.

"Yes. I threw a pissing stone at him. Then he went all human wolf and shit, and I ran and he chased me. Then we were in the river, and then I was against a tree rubbing myself over him like the green on grass."

Silence. Absolute silence.

I bring my head up slowly and look at Josh who appears as shocked as I felt. He shifts a little and clears his throat. "Well, shit, Rhea." I nod. Shit indeed. "That's quite the escalation."

"Yeah, it really is." I shake my head. "Now it's going to be awkward, and he probably won't take me seriously because of what happened, but nothing has changed. He needs to leave and keep his mouth shut, because after watching him and the Elites since they arrived, there is no way we can kill them." I hesitate. "I… I also don't think I can handle more deaths on my hands," I say quietly, looking down at my lap.

"You shouldn't feel guilty, Milal. You did what you had to do to survive. We all did," he says gently, and I shake my head.

"I just feel like there could have been a different way, some other route we could have taken. They were just trainees, Josh." My voice cracks. "Dammit, they had families."

Josh gets to his feet as soon as the first tear escapes and travels down my face. The dam finally bursts within me, and I can't hold back any more as another tear streams down my face. Josh sits next to me, pulling me to his side. I bury my face in his shoulder, soaking in his comfort as he wraps his arms tightly around me. My emotions flow free, and I cry for the lives that I took. For the trainees that had full lives ahead of them. Lives that I robbed them of. I try not to let the guilt and sadness consume me, but it's so hard.

"Shh, Rhea, it's okay. I'm here," Josh soothes, rubbing my back.

He is here, he's always here. I honestly don't think I would have gotten this far without him. He saved my life all those years ago and has done so many times since then. Always with me, always supporting me and loving me. I wrap my arms around him and hold him closer. I'm so grateful for him.

He's seen me at my worst, at the top of the cliffs at Lovers Falls when I wanted the Unforgivable Sea to take me in its grasp and never let me go. To let me have peace.

Only Josh and Kade held me back from those waters, and now my pack does too. But the stain on my soul, the dark mass that will forever be there for the things I've done, even if it was to ensure we survived, robs me of the will to breathe at times.

Josh lets me cry on him until my sobs turn to sniffles, constantly rubbing soothing hands up and down my back. He's one of only two people that have seen my tears like this, who have seen me exposed and breaking down. I can't trust anyone else with them. I get myself under control and lift my head to look at him. He lifts a hand and wipes my cheeks, his eyes full of concern. "Okay now?"

I nod, and he relaxes. I lean back, taking his hand in mine and squeezing lightly. "Much better now."

"Just be careful, okay?" he says after a while of us sitting in silence, just enjoying being near each other. Runa definitely doesn't mind the closeness with Josh, feeling his wolf where our arms touch.

"Hmm?" I ask.

"With Darius. I've seen the way he watches you. Just be careful." I know he does. He's a stalker as well as a babysitter.

"I will," I say, smiling softly, ignoring what he said about Darius. Then I let loose a bigger smile when I ask, "So, how's Sarah doing?" He shifts uncomfortably. Well, well, well.

"She's doing good, really good actually. Anna says her healing is coming along great, and I'm keeping her up to date with everything that's happening like you asked me to. She's okay, scared obviously, but not scared enough to retreat into herself fully."

"That great news, Josh." And it is, Sarah has come so far

with her recovery, especially with letting Josh near her. "When the Elites leave, hopefully she has enough courage to venture outside. I'm sure you will be there to help her." I nudge my shoulder with his.

His cheeks redden, and he pushes me away from him as he stands. I hold back a laugh. "Go shower, you stink. I'll meet you at the gathering." He turns to leave, but stops at my words.

"Will you keep an eye on Maize? I saw her lurking through the forest on the way back here. I haven't seen her around much, and I don't know what she was doing there. But I just thought it was strange."

"Yeah, I'll let the others know about it. Now go, hurry before you miss dinner." He shoos me away, and I stand and head for the stairs. Time to scrub the Darius off of me.

Yet as I stand in the shower, about to rid myself of his scent, I hesitate more than I should have.

TWENTY TWO

Rhea

After a quick shower and a change of clothes, I make my way down to the gathering. My steps are slow, and I crack my knuckles as I follow the dirt path. The Elites haven't once been to the gathering at dinnertime since they arrived. They eat in their cabin, and Darius and his closest men eat in my home. Which I make sure to avoid. Breakfast is enough, especially after the nightmares of my past have come back to haunt me in my sleep.

I'm not comfortable leaving them alone in my home, but they can't get into my office without knowing the spell to open the door, and my office is where they might find anything useful. With that in mind, I avoid them in my home as much as I can.

Nervous about going to dinner, I pinch my lip between my fingers. It's not like anyone will know what I did, but shame still fills me. The Elites are a threat to us, and I just grinded on one until I came. Even after a long shower, after I scrubbed Darius's scent off of me, I still don't know what came over me. It doesn't help that Runa just let it happen either, basking in his attention when he caught us. She fucking hates people, yet she practically rolls over for a belly scratch from Darius. The traitor.

I shake my hands out when I reach the first trees that scarcely surround the gathering and straighten my spine. My face gives nothing away as I approach my pack, smiling at those who call out to me in greeting, acting like everything is absolutely fine. Which it's fucking not, not in the slightest.

Taking a seat on my usual bench, I nudge Kade's shoulder gently, mindful of his injuries. He turns and looks at me, a sad smile on his face before turning back to the sunken fire pit in the middle, the glow of the flame caressing his face. I bring my hand up and rub the back of his neck, reassuring him and letting him know I'm there. I know he feels he let me and the pack down, but he needs to move on and learn from it. It just may take a little time with the way he stews over things.

I ripped the entire pack a new set of assholes, especially Josie, for voting for Kade to go to The Deadlands and completely disregarding my orders. I told them all that nothing can be done now and that they were safe, regardless of the Elite now being here. They're still extremely wary of them wandering around our home, but they're not outright crying and running away anymore. That's something at least.

Josie walks over to me, a smile on her face as she presses her cheek to mine in greeting. She hands me a plate with strips of meat and vegetables, and the smell makes my mouth water. I see extra meat, and I know it's her way of apologizing to me again for pressuring Kade. "Thanks," I tell her as she walks back over to Danny and sits down.

I may still be more upset with her because of how close we are, but as she and Danny hold each other's eyes for a moment, jealousy rises in me. I don't want a mate, and I know I'm not capable of what they have, but it still doesn't stop me from wishing for it deep down sometimes.

A family to call my own. Someone who is solely mine, and I'm theirs. Just like Josie and Danny are to each other. Their love is strong and true, with a pureness that cannot be replicated.

Shaking my head at myself, I watch the pack continue to

hand out food for everyone, the smaller plates being handed out for the pups first after me. I don't know what's wrong with me lately. Everything just feels off, and I'm desiring things I haven't wanted before, at least not as strong as it is now.

I spot Katy and Oscar across from me, huddled together, but otherwise looking okay. Taylor stands with Sebastian, plates in hand and Seb lifts his plate in greeting, giving me a wink. I roll my eyes at his usual flirty self. Hudson and Colten sit close together on the bench further to my left. Hudson looks annoyed while Colten looks bored, resting his head on the back of the bench with his hands behind his head. They're always bickering about something, but it seems more often lately.

A blur of motion has my head turning as Sam runs over to us, her smile shy as she looks at Kade. "Hey," she whispers, tucking a piece of hair behind her ear.

Kade ruffles her light brown hair, and she scowls up at him as he grins at her. "Hey, winglet."

"Kade," she whines. "Stop calling me that."

He laughs, and my heart warms at the sound I don't hear often anymore. "Never. Go on to your mom and eat." He spins her by her shoulder and nudges her toward her mom, Sybill. She scowls at him over her shoulder as she goes, and I chuckle at the pout that forms.

She's shy around most people, but Kade is an exception. "She likes you," I say to him, and he just shrugs at me, watching as Sam takes her seat on the ground at her mom's legs and starts to eat.

Josh appears at my side and sits to my right with a plate of his own piled high with food, giving my shoulder a little squeeze. "Damn, have you not eaten today?" I ask him, looking at the amount of food on his plate. He moves the plate in front of me and passes it to Kade and my mouth drops open at him. "Where in all of Vrohkaria are you putting all that?"

Kade smirks and goes to dive in when I slap his hand away. "What?"

"I want to bless the food tonight. We haven't done it in a while," I inform him, and he sits back and waits for me to continue. I clear my throat, about to start the blessing, when movement catches my eye over the fire in front of me.

I suck in a breath as Darius, Leo, Damian, Zaide, Maize, and Jerrod walk into the gathering. My pack is silent and shuffle in their places at their arrival. But no one panics or screams thankfully. My pack looks toward me, and I pass Josh my plate of food, standing awkwardly as I address my pack. "They are our guests," I tell my pack, loud enough for all of them to hear. "There are plates on the table near the pot, grab whatever food you would like," I say to the Elites swiftly and take my seat again, plate back in hand.

They walk to the center, some of my pack getting up and moving to sit away from them. Their wary eyes tracking their movements. The Elites know what is going on around them, but they don't appear bothered by it. It's like they don't care that my pack is scared of them at all. I watch Darius under my lashes as he picks up a plate and takes a selection of meats and vegetables from the low wooden tables in front of the fire pit. He looks at the recently vacated benches and takes a seat, the rest of the Elites joining him. Maize is the last to grab her food, her light eyes looking toward Kade every now and again in a way that sets me on edge. I wait until everyone has gotten their food and just before they start eating, I start the blessing.

I bow my head slightly and close my eyes. Blocking the Elites' watchful eyes on me, I say our prayer. "The earth is my witness, of the blood that's been spilt. The moon is my eyes, that food will not wilt. The human is my mind, as I honor this feast. The wolf is my protector, as I safely eat. Zahariss."

"Zahariss," my pack echoes the name of our female wolf

goddess as I open my eyes, and they start to eat their food.

Feeling an intense gaze on me, I look up and see Darius staring at me over the flames of the fire. His face has an eerie glow as his stare bores into mine, and I shift in my seat, feeling a warming sensation in my chest. He has a look of confusion on his face, and I guess it's because he has never heard the Goddess' blessing before. No one follows the old Gods anymore, so I'm not surprised.

I break eye contact with him and take strips of meat off my plate and start to eat. The dinner is quiet, much quieter than the liveliness we usually have. I lean back on the bench, not feeling very hungry anymore, and watch my pack. Worry for them is at the forefront of my mind, wondering how I can get them to relax. I know the threat that Darius will take me to the Highers and expose our home is still there. If that happens, once they find out the truth, the Highers will take my pack members back where they originally came from. But they won't hurt them now, not physically. They have nothing to gain from it. Apart from maybe getting to me.

"Alpha," a small voice calls as most of us are finishing our food, and I look toward Samantha, sitting with some other pups.

"What's up, Sam?" I ask her, leaning forward to put my plate on the floor, and Kade looks at her with a confused look on his face.

"Can you tell us the story of the Canaric wolves again?" She fiddles with her fingers, her hair covering her face as she looks toward the ground. She is still far more nervous than a thirteen-year-old should be when speaking up and having attention on her that's not from Kade. If I ever saw her father, I would happily put him in the ground.

I get up and walk toward where she's sitting on the ground, her mom sitting on the bench behind her. I lower myself down and sit cross legged across from her, giving her a smile as I put a hand atop her head and stroke down her hair.

"Of course, I will." I slide up next to her and put my arm around her, holding her close as I look into the fire, aware of everyone's attention on me. I won't refuse her though, even with the Elites here. "Thousands and thousands of years ago, a man and a woman loved each other very much, but they couldn't be together. Their families demanded that they had to mate other people of their fathers' choosing. The man and the woman knew this, but they were too madly in love, and wanted to run away together. It took many months of planning until they finally had a plan set in stone. All they had to do was wait until a situation arose where they could sneak off, away from prying eyes.

"During the wait, the woman fell pregnant with her lover's babe. They became more desperate than ever to escape their packs, so they could live and love freely. To be mated and be a family. She hid her pregnancy from everyone, using tonics to hide how her scent changed, especially from her family. Only her beloved knew. Luck was on their side when the woman was around six months pregnant. The mate of the King of Vrohkaria, who the people loved dearly, had just birthed a son. The lands were full of celebrations, and the king invited all of Vrohkaria to join them a week later to celebrate and welcome their new son at the castle in Fenrikar.

"A week went by, and on the night of the celebration, the man and woman planned to sneak out and run away together. It was the perfect time as everyone would be too busy celebrating. So, they went to the castle and waited for the right moment." Even though most of my pack have heard this and many other stories before, they still hang on to every word, their focus entirely on me. "As the night went on and it was getting closer to the time they had agreed to leave, the woman couldn't find the man. Panicked, she searched many rooms of the castle until she decided he must have gone to their meeting place to wait for her. Convinced, she made her way through the castle, but she came across something she never wished she had. That she wished wasn't true.

"The love of her life was with another woman in the hall that led outside to the gardens. At seeing this betrayal, it felt like her heart was being torn apart, and the woman choked back a cry at seeing them together. The man heard the small sound that escaped her and turned to look at the woman he loved very much. The woman could see the pain in his eyes as they stared at each other, but she could also see the warmth and excitement he had for this new woman. Then she saw the bite mark just below his ear, the mark she was going to give him when she claimed him as his mate. But this other woman had done it instead, and when she looked toward her, her entire world shifted as she saw he had placed his mark on her too."

"The man and the pregnant woman weren't mates?" Skylar asks from next to her mom, further down from where me and Sam are sitting.

"No." I shake my head at her. "The man and the pregnant woman were just very much in love with each other. They chose to be mates and wanted to complete the ritual after they ran away, but they were not bloodmates. But that all changed when the man came across his bloodmate. There was nothing either of them could do, a bloodmate cannot be ignored or resisted. When bloodmates bite their mates, it stays for all of time. It's a powerful and special connection not many find, and the man just happened to find his bloodmate the night they planned to start their new life."

"What happened next?" Sam whispers, curling up next to me even more.

"Devastated, the woman ran out into the castle gardens alone. The man stayed inside with his bloodmate, unable to go after his lover and the babe growing in her womb. The woman ran for days, away from the castle, away from her home, until she finally stopped in the center of a blooming, grassy clearing surrounded by lilk trees."

I see Darius lean back against the bench out of the corner of my eye, his barely touched food resting on his knee as he listens to the story of how the Canaric wolves came to be from my family, not history texts. I meet his eyes briefly, finding his rapt attention on me, before looking back into the fire.

I take a breath and continue. "The woman sobbed and sobbed on the ground of colorful flowers, crying her soul out until she couldn't shed a single tear anymore. Heartbroken and lost, she lay there for a long time, until she went into labor early. She was in labor for seven days and seven nights until her baby girl was finally brought into the world, but she didn't move. Alone and with no hope in sight, the woman screamed to the land and the below, begging Zahariss and Cazier to save her baby, ignoring the pool of blood dampening the ground beneath her.

"What felt like hours upon hours, the Gods finally heard her screams and came to her. Zahariss was light in color, and Cazier dark. They were bigger than any other wolves that roamed the lands. They could do nothing for the woman, nor her babe. The child was born too early, and the heartbroken woman had lost too much blood. They could only offer her comfort. Zahariss laid down and wrapped herself around her right side, allowing the mother with her still babe to press up against her, offering her warmth even though it coated her fur in blood. Cazier, the ever-fierce protector took her left side, watching over them as they waited for her last moments.

"The woman was slowly fading. She knew she was close to taking her last breaths, so she begged the Gods in a broken voice for her child to be reborn. For her child to have a chance at life again, for her to find her bloodmate and live the life her mother felt she should have had. The woman's eyes closed for the final time after her pleading words, cradling her still child to her chest as her life's blood soaked into the earth, causing the surrounding lilk trees to change in color. At that moment, her will for her child to be protected seeped into the ground and traveled to the lilk trees. It is said that it's still there to this day.

"Zahariss and Cazier watched as their bright essence twirled up into the sky as the babe rested on her chest, the woman's now stiff arms holding her in place. Zahariss stayed where she was, and looked toward Cazier with a question in her eyes. Cazier walked over to the babe and touched his nose to her for a long moment as Zahariss watched him, her eyes glowing. A blue and black essence rose up and shot out in different directions into the night sky, and both wolf Gods sat next to each other and watched on until light broke the dark."

"That's how the Canaric wolves were made," Sam says in a tiny whisper.

I look down at her and put my finger beneath her chin gently until I see her eyes. I smile when she looks at me. "When the king's mate had another child, she delivered a female pup, not a babe. The king and his mate didn't know what to do, it had never happened before in the history of wolves, but they loved her all the same. On her seventh birthday, she turned into a little girl, and they were stunned, but extremely happy. The little girl had markings on her face, among other places and her parents later found out it was a symbol of the Gods, the markings on her body meant she was the Heir to the Goddess Zahariss."

A scoff sounds, and my head turns to Maize, who looks at me with disgust. My eyes flash in warning, and I see a wariness creep into her own eyes before she looks away, folding her arms and crossing her legs. My gaze moves to Darius, who ignores her and keeps his focus on me, head tilted. I look back into the fire.

"Many months later, another pup was born to another family, a male. On his seventh birthday he changed into a little boy and had markings on his back that went to the top of his shoulders and neck. They were different in color, but similar to the female Heir's markings. He was Cazier's Heir. There were only ever two born with Heir markings at one time, one male and one female, and they could do incredible things. They were honored by all wolves and set the balance of Vrohkaria, just like Zahariss of the lands and Cazier of the below did. The only time a new Heir would be born is when the current Heir died, and we wolves live a very long time, so it didn't happen for hundreds of years. An Heir hasn't been born or seen in over three hundred years now. It is said that they went into hiding as they were ruthlessly hunted by those that thought their Heir power was too dangerous to be left alive. But the Gods still watch over us, even if some of us are a bit misguided at times. But that's how the Canaric wolf came to be. Through the heartbreak of a woman losing the love of her life, wanting her babe to be reborn and have a chance at life and happiness, and the Gods granting her wish in the only way that they could."

"But why did Cazier and Zahariss decide to have Heirs? They could have just reborn the babe," Sam says, blinking up at me slowly.

"No one really knows," I tell her as her eyes begin to droop. "Some say because they couldn't be together, they had hoped that their Heirs could live the life they never had like the woman wanted, but there is no record that any of the Heirs ever mated. Others say their power was fading, so they put the last of it into making the Canaric wolves. Having their legacy live on in this way while maintaining balance in the lands. Either way, the Gods are always with us, protecting us as best they can."

"If the Gods protect us," Sam murmurs half asleep, her eyes closing, "why didn't they protect Mom and me?" Her head falls to the side, and I maneuver her so her face is against my neck comfortably.

I clenched my jaw at her words and will the burning in my eyes to stop. I tighten my hold on her, wanting to take it all away from her and ease her pain. I hear her mom sniffle behind me, and I reach a hand up and link her fingers with mine, giving her a gentle squeeze in support

I feel, rather than see when Darius stilled at Sam's words, and my eyes flick toward him as he looks at the girl in my arms. I watch as he looks toward the other pack members around us who have their gazes to the floor, feeling Sam's pain just like I am, and probably feeling their own. Darius leans forward on his knees, hand clasped under his chin as he stares at the ground in thought. I'm sure he's wondering what she meant, but I won't be the one to tell their stories. If he wants to know, it has to come from them, and they don't trust any of the Elites.

They may go around protecting the lands from creatures, but some here have asked for their help before and a blind eye was turned to their suffering. Why would they trust them now?

And as Kade comes over to me, picking Sam up so gently in his arms so that he doesn't disturb her and rubbing his cheek against her head, I know they will never trust the Elites with their secrets. With their pain.

Not when some have been the cause of it.

TWENTY THREE

RHEA

"You did what!" The screeching words hit my ears, and I wince.

"Shhh," I hush her, grabbing her arm and dragging her away from listening ears and looking around to see if anyone is nearby. "Dammit, Josie, keep it down."

"You just told me you got all frisky with Darius and you want me to keep it down!" Her mouth opens and closes like she can't believe the words out of my mouth. To be honest, I can't either. "How did that happen?" she asks as we continue walking to collect water from the river.

"I don't know. I don't understand how, Josie, but it just happened. What's wrong with me?"

She grabs my arm roughly, bringing me to a stop as the bucket from my hand drops to the ground. I look at her and her dark-green eyes flash at me. "There is *nothing* wrong with you. Do you hear me? So you did a bit of a dry hump and grind and got off, so fucking what? It's about time you had some pleasure from somewhere else apart from your hand."

My cheeks heat. "I have got off before without using my hand," I mutter as I bend to pick up the bucket and continue walking.

"That was one time, and you just wanted to get it over with. This was different, wasn't it?"

Of course it was different. "Yeah," I sigh. "I don't know what came over me, but I've never felt so… alive when his hands were touching me." I shake my head. "He's the fucking enemy, but maybe I can use this to my advantage," I muse, glancing up at the sun peeking through the canopy of trees.

"How so?" she asks, swinging her bucket back and forth as we walk.

"Let me think about it," I tell her, and walk toward the river. I bend down and fill the bucket in my hand with water as Josie does the same.

Darius obviously has some attraction to me, even if he said I was just there at the time. But maybe I can use that to sway his mind and see that my pack is good here, and that they need to stay here and be safe. If I can get him to see them in a different light to how he sees me, it could work.

"Just be careful, Rhea, but don't shy away from exploring that man meat if he's up for it."

I splutter a laugh. "Man meat?"

She smirks. "Oh, he's definitely a whole ass snack."

I bump her shoulder with mine as we head back to the gathering. "Don't let Danny hear you say that."

"Why would I do that? He'll get jealous and carry me off to our cabin and have his wicked way with me." She's not wrong.

"Devious girl," I tease.

"I prefer smart." She winks.

We arrive at the gathering and pour our last bucket of water into the pot at the center. It took us a few trips to the river, but thankfully the pot is now filled to the brim and ready to boil. Josie sets the fire beneath to prepare for dinner tonight. I watch out of the corner of my eye how the Elites wander around, but take extra care not to get too close to my pack members. Some have been brave and started sparring with them, but a lot still keep away from them. Understandably.

"I'm going to head off and find Danny." Josie smiles, mischief dancing in her eyes.

I laugh and touch her cheek to mine before she skips off, excited to make her mate jealous. I shake my head at her antics. That girl is about to have trouble sitting down for a few days after Danny is done with her.

I add a few more logs beneath the fire when a small head of dark hair catches my attention. I stand and move unhurriedly, walking between the scarcely placed trees around the gathering. I follow the little boy, keeping him in my sight as I look around for his mom. Not seeing her, I pick up the pace, but then come to a sudden halt.

I place my palm against the tree next to me as Jerrod, the big, red-haired Elite, stands still as Oscar runs to him and clings to his leg outside of one of the cabins. Shit. I step forward, about to open my mouth, when something grabs my arm, and I'm pulled back against a hard chest.

His scent hits me, making my tense body relax slightly as his breath tickles my ear. "Watch," is all Darius says, his hands on my hips gripping me firmly. He's not hurting me, he just wants me to stay put.

Curious and a little worried, I watch as Oscar babbles up to Jerrod, holding his little arms up to him as the Elite looks down. After a moment, Jerrod tentatively reaches down and gently picks Oscar up, his arms going under him to keep him steady. Oscar picks up Jerrod's long braid from where it was resting over his shoulder and looks it over before tickling himself with it on his nose.

A chuckle leaves me as he continues to play with Jerrod's braid, but I'm also a little shocked by the big redhead letting him do it. Every time I've seen Jerrod, which is not often, he's always careful with his words. But seeing how happy Oscar is warms my insides, and I'm grateful the Elite is letting him have his fun.

Darius's grip tightens on me as he rests his chin on the top of my head and I just let him, not understanding why. Hearing Oscar's name suddenly being called, I look toward the sound and see Katy running from between the cabin, her face full of panic. I go to step forward, but Darius holds me back as Katy finally spots her son.

She freezes at seeing her son in the arms of an Elite, and the distress on her face makes me wrench out of Darius's grip. He grabs me again by my ponytail and turns me toward him, our faces close together as he leans down, and I let out a low growl of warning that he immediately returns.

"Watch them," he murmurs against my lips. He reaches a hand up and grips my chin, turning my head in their direction.

Oscar still happily plays with Jerrod's hair, oblivious to his mom's presence, but Jerrod's eyes are locked with hers. I see Katy straighten her shoulders before skittishly walking toward them. Her posture screams fear, but with an Elite holding her son in his arms, she's being brave. She stops a few feet away from them and holds out her shaky arms. Her lips are moving, but we aren't close enough to hear what she's saying.

Her hands tremble as she holds them out for Oscar, and the big Elite slowly takes his braid from Oscar's hands, smiling softly at him and then lifts him from his embrace. He places him gently into Katy's awaiting arms and says something that has Katy ducking her head and cradling her son close. He reaches out slowly, and Katy tenses as her eyes scrunch shut. Jerrod pauses, hand still held out, before he ruffles Oscar's hair, and he turns and leaves.

Katy waits until he's a few steps away from them before she lifts her head again with eyes open, watching him go. Rubbing her head against her sons, she waits until Jerrod is out of sight before she walks off. Pride fills me from her actions. She was brave, put her fears aside and went up to an Elite. To a male. To get her son.

Being a mother can make you do things you never thought you were able to. It makes you more than the skin that holds and binds you together, makes you powerful enough to overcome your own mind.

"None of my Elites would hurt anyone, Rhea," Darius says suddenly, and I jolt, turning my head to look back up at him. He squeezes my chin gently, the action so at odds with the words he left me with the day before. "We don't harm our own unless there is a cause to. We hunt creatures, not people."

"I have no idea what you guys are capable of, Darius," I tell him honestly, my eyes bouncing between his. "But I know what my pack is and isn't capable of, and that was a big deal for Katy."

"He wouldn't have hurt her or the pup," he stresses, his eyes turning hard at the thought of it. "I won't allow it."

I shake my head as much as I can with his hand still gipping my chin. "I don't know that. I don't trust any of you." It's why the pack is never on their own, always with someone, and why me and the guys are watching the Elites closely. "But I'm glad you stopped me from intervening, that was good for her. Hopefully it gives her a little more confidence and a little less fear."

He studies me for a moment, probably wondering if any of my words are true, before he ducks his head, his lips a touch away from mine. I take in a small breath when his eyes drop to my mouth before coming back up to mine. I swallow at the heat in them, and he moves his hand from my chin, gliding it across my jaw and down until he reaches the back of my neck. Goosebumps appear all over my body and his eyes track those that are visible.

"A little fear is good, Rhea, depending on the circumstances," he rumbles, and the sound makes my stomach clench.

His gaze travels down to my now heaving breast straining

against my t-shirt, and a small sound escapes me that has his eyes snapping up to mine. He presses himself closer to me, that grip on my neck a solid force as he holds me still against him. He dips his head to the side of my throat and inhales deeply, a small, growling sound leaving his lips as I shiver. His tongue moves over my skin from the crook of my neck up to below my ear, and I damn near melt against him.

Runa comes close to the surface, a rumbling sound leaving her, and then I feel another wolf brushing up against me. Darius's wolf. Praise and contentment flow through me as his wolf rubs up against us through our touch. My eyes close at this strange and new feeling, relishing in it and the way my body feels like it's floating.

Darius kisses along my jaw, and I hum at the feel of his lips, enjoying his attention on me. Then suddenly he rips himself away. My eyes spring open, giving myself a few seconds for my brain to catch up as I stare at Darius's confused eyes. My eyes lower to the obvious erection pressing against his pants then back to his face as my brows furrow.

I open my mouth to ask him what the fuck that was, when another voice enters the gathering. "What's for dinner? I'm starving," Damian says as he walks between the benches and takes a seat near the fire. He ruffles his brown hair before holding his hands out, warming himself even though it's not cold.

I clear my throat and shuffle on my feet as he looks between me and Darius. "Stew," I say, running my hands down the tops of my thighs, not missing the way Darius tracks the movement. "It will be ready a little later. I'm just waiting for the water to boil first." I point to the pot.

"Uh-huh," Damian mumbles, giving Darius the stink eye.

"Right. Well, I'm just going to go and do some… stuff until then," I eventually get out, and turn to leave, my cheeks on fire.

Fucking Gods. Could that have been any more awkward? Damian must have seen us being so close, and Darius attacking my skin with his mouth.

Why am I drawn into Darius's aura? Why do I let him put his mouth on me? Again.

Gods, what is happening to me?

TWENTY FOUR

Rhea

"The females who are beginning their heat are all in the cabin and have taken their tonics to prevent any unwanted pregnancies," Josh tells me as I continue piling wood up in the storage shed.

It was time again for us to prepare to make sure those in heat are as safe and comfortable as possible. We have the routine running like clockwork after so many years of doing it, but I still get anxious. You really never know what can happen during this time.

"Good. I already sorted a change in jobs this morning to make up for the females and the few males that will be unavailable." Grabbing more wood from outside the shed, I haul more into my arms and take it inside. It's nearly summer, and we mostly use these months to stock up for the winter season. I know it's a long way off yet, but I want to be prepared early, especially if I'm not here. "Are you just going to stand and watch?" I ask Josh, coming back outside to stare at him leaning against the shed.

He scratches his chin, looking thoughtful for a moment. "I think I've done enough today. You know how females get when their heat is due. I've had my ear chewed off for hours this morning about what they need. I told them they had their hands." He shrugs, and my mouth drops open, barely managing to resist the grin that wants to break free. He's kidding, but I go with it anyway.

"Wow, Josh." I shake my head at him. "You really woke up and chose violence today." He opens his mouth, but I'm already lunging at him, tackling him to the dirt floor. The oomph that comes from him is satisfying to my ears. I move and straddle his waist to try and get to his nipples, but his hands grab mine.

"Oh, you think it's that easy, do you?" His light gray eyes laugh at me and then he shifts his hips. I'm on my back in a flash, and now he's the one over me. He grabs both my wrists in one of his and attacks my ribs, tickling me.

"Josh!" I squeal at him. "Don't you dare! Stop it!" I laugh, trying to wriggle away from his fingers. He ducks low and licks the side of my face, laughing at the disgusting sound that comes from me. "You little shit."

"Little?" he scoffs. "Who is little?" His tickling ramps up, and all I'm able to do is squeal through my laughter at him, gasping for breath. "Tap out, Rhea," he sings. "You know you want to."

"Never!" I say breathlessly, screaming as he goes to lick my face again. Dirty bastard. "I don't want your saliva on me, you overgrown dog."

He stops tickling me and slowly brings his head back to look down at me. Oops, he didn't like that. I bite my lip while he looks around for something. I work to release my hands and fail. He reaches past my head, and when I try to see what he's doing, cold liquid is poured over my face. I splutter, screeching while shaking my head at the coldness as Josh howls with laughter.

"I think you need to cool off, Rhea. Bringing dogs into it?" He tsks at me. "I think you woke up and chose to be too big for your boots."

"My boots fit me perfectly," I gasp as he rolls his eyes. "Don't you bring my boots into this." I glare at him through the wet strands of my hair. I love my boots. Then I see his fingers going for my ribs again. "Joshy," I warn, knowing the name will piss him off.

"Am I interrupting something?" a cold voice asks, and Josh's fingers freeze in their tracks. We both turn our heads and look toward the voice. Darius and Leo stand a little away from us, the former glaring at me and then at Josh.

Well, this is a tad awkward considering the position we are in. It's a normal occurrence for me and Josh with how many play fights we have, but the Elites don't know that. I can honestly say that if looks could kill, we may have been taking our last breaths.

Spoilsport.

Josh huffs as he gets off of me, reaching his hand out to help me up. I sigh and place my hand in his, letting him pull me off the ground before gathering my hair and putting it in a quick braid. I give a cheeky kick at Josh's shin as I turn my back on them all and continue grabbing wood and taking it into the shed.

"Such a child," I hear Josh mutter under his breath, causing me to smile. "What do you want?" he asks Darius and Leo sharply.

"Some of my Elites can sense that there are females going into heat," Darius says, and I pause. Still holding logs in my arms, I walk out of the storage shed and step up next to Josh, waiting for Darius to continue as he watches me. "Most are fine, but some of the trainees are struggling. They are already having difficulty controlling their dominance." He folds his arms and shrugs. "I couldn't care less about it, but the last thing I want to deal with is my trainees trying to fuck anything in sight while trying to get to your females. I need somewhere to put them for the time being, away from the females."

Hmm. I tilt my head and study his face. His mouth is set into a tense line, and I see the slightest bit of concern in his pretty green eyes. He says he doesn't care, but yet he's coming here to see if he can put those struggling somewhere away from the pack while tensions are high and they could potentially assault my females. My gaze roams over him subtly. From his boots, up his strong, muscular legs to the t-shirt that I secretly wished was tighter, to finally back up to his eyes. I control my startled reaction at seeing his already on mine, and I feel my cheeks heating. Dammit.

I turn away and go back into the shed before I speak. "They can just camp out in the forest, outside of the lilk trees."

"Is it safe?" Leo asks, and I roll my eyes.

"They have been in The Deadlands for how long? It's a lot safer in this forest than out there."

"I can show them where they can camp out," a new voice adds, and I quickly put the last logs onto the pile and walk out of the shed.

"You could," I say warily as I look from Kade to Darius, both of them sizing each other up. "I need you for a bit though, we have someone to go and see," I tell Kade, walking up to him and rubbing my cheek against his in greeting.

"We do?" he asks, his eyes coming to mine.

"Yup." I go back to the shed and shutting the door. "I'm sure Taylor wouldn't mind showing them somewhere if we're back late."

"He's out with some Elites searching The Deadlands," Josh says. "I'll show them where they can stay for a few days." I look over at him and smirk, knowing how much he would rather pick up wolf shit than do this, but the pack safety comes first. "Shut it," he grumbles at me while I flip him off.

"Where are you going?" Darius demands, and I look from him to Leo before I speak.

"To see someone I need to speak to," I say vaguely. "I'll catch up with you in a little while Josh. We might miss dinner." I squeeze his hand as I pass him, Kade following behind. I hear another set of footsteps, and I sigh in frustration before letting out a small growl. "Is there something else I can help you with, Darius?" I don't even bother turning around to ask him.

"I'm your shadow, little wolf. You should be used to it at this point." I hear no care in his voice as to whether I like it or not that he's following me. But he's right. I do know it. The asshole follows me everywhere. I can barely pee by myself without him lurking nearby.

I'm sure he knows that I've sensed him following me around Eridian since he's been here, he just doesn't give the slightest fuck. He's kept his distance, observing and studying as I've gone about my daily duties. It's been strange to feel him at my back, but I can't say I haven't got used to it. It's frustrating, but strangely, comforting to have his presence near.

Even Runa has been feeling more placid within me instead of her usual grumpiness. I don't think she fears him, but he has some sort of effect on her, and I'm not sure what to feel about that.

Kade lets out a growl besides me as the big man continues to follow us, and I tap him on the arm to knock it off.

"I don't think you want to try me again. It didn't end well for you last time," Darius warns him, and I tense up.

"Would you stop." I exhale, spinning around to look at him. I don't want to remember Kade bleeding out on the ground, and I don't want him to set Kade off. "Seeing as I can't get rid of you, the least you can do is be quiet." I huff and continue forward, grabbing Kade's hand and pulling him with me.

"You didn't want to get rid of me the other day," he taunts, and there is no hiding the blush in my cheeks now as I remember us against that tree. A tree that I will never look at the same again.

I glare at him over my shoulder, catching him checking out

my ass, and I try to ignore the thrill that goes through me from his attention. Runa wriggles inside me, and I give her a mental shove to stop that shit. I cannot go there again, no matter how much I want to feel him against me, or how much I want to lick a path up his neck and breathe in his scent. An involuntary shiver runs through me, and I swear I heard a low growl behind me.

No. Nope. Not doing it.

Kade gives me a strange look, but I just plow forward, ignoring him and hoping he can't somehow read my thoughts. "We're going to see Solvier, aren't we?" Kade grumbles next to me as we pass the lilk trees. I watch him press a hand to them, the same way I do every time we leave. I let out a small smile at the sight.

"Yes, we are, if we can find him." I still haven't seen him for quite a while. I have no idea where he goes or how he even manages to hide, but he does it somehow.

"Isn't this supposed to be, you know, private?" he hedges, looking at me out of the corner of his eye.

Yes, it is, but the overgrown oaf behind us will always follow me, so it can't be helped. This conversation needs to happen. I'm not sure what Darius's reaction will be to Solvier, or if even Solvier will show himself to Darius. He is picky about who he shows himself to.

"Unfortunately, I have acquired a full-time babysitter," I answer him. "Gods knows why, considering all I do is work around the settlement." I kick a rock on the floor and smirk at it, remembering throwing one at Darius.

"I can hear you," Darius gripes at my back, irritation leaking into his tone.

"Oh, shit, Kade," I whisper at him, grabbing his arm. "He can *hear* us! We're doomed," I put my hand on my head for added effect before flipping him off behind me. We both chuckle when we hear his sigh. The asshole shouldn't be on my ass then.

We continue walking, heading further south toward one of the lakes. It's quiet and peaceful. the slight breeze rustling the leaves on the trees as we pass. Sunlight flutters on the ground as it passes through gaps in the trees, creating pretty patterns along the forest floor. Being outside and smelling the earth beneath my feet with the scent of flowers in their air is a comfort I won't take for granted.

I didn't get to see the sky, feel the caress of the wind on my face or smell the scent of life embracing me for a long time. Until I left my old home.

I link my arm through Kade's as we walk, enjoying being with him, even with my babysitter at my back. It's the first time I've really spent any time with him since we got back from The Deadlands, and luckily his injuries are nearly healed. The thought of him dying on that dead forest floor makes me huddle closer to him, wanting to feel his warmth, and I feel Runa brushing up against him where my arm is linked with his, sharing the same feelings with his wolf.

I might not be his birth mother, but I brought him up. I taught him to hunt, how to build a fire and forage. I comforted him at night when he had nightmares, only for him to wake and have no idea it ever happened sometimes. I held him through his grief and guided him when his wolf came. He is mine in every way he is not *theirs*.

We're a few miles from the lake when the ground trembles beneath me, and I stop, taking my arm out of Kade's to bend down to put a hand on the grassy floor.

"What are you doing?" Darius asks from somewhere behind me, and Kade shushes him, getting an annoyed grunt in return.

I close my eyes and concentrate, feeling the gentle quake beneath my hand. I smile when I pinpoint which direction it came from. "Let's go!" I grab Kade's hand and pick up our pace to a jog. "Come on before he leaves again." I chuckle as I drag a reluctant Kade behind me, smiling wide.

We run along until I see a flash of light gray ahead through the trees. I let go of Kade, taking off with a laugh of giddiness washing over me. "Solvier!" There's a pause in the trees and then a huff-like sound reaches my ears. I sprint ahead, leaving Kade to catch me up with Darius not too far behind him.

I squeeze through the last trees between us into a little open clearing and see two light gold eyes looking down at me in amusement. I laugh as I launch myself off the ground and jump at him. He lowers his head when he sees me coming, and my arms wrap around his neck the best I can, gripping his fur tightly. I snuggle into him and breathe in his scent, grass and blossoms, before sliding down to the ground, grinning up at him.

"*Hello, Rhea,*" he says in my head, his voice a deep rumble as he brings his nose down to touch my cheek. I stroke his muzzle before scratching under his chin, giggling and bouncing on my feet.

He makes a chuffing sound, tapping his head against my forehead before rubbing his cheek against my hair. I've missed him.

"I've been wanting to talk to you," I tell him, taking a step back and looking up at his towering frame. "But you haven't been around. Is everything okay?" I ask. It's been over two months since I last saw him.

"All is as it should be," he tells me. *"I see you have brought young Kade with you. And another male,"* he says, his eyes peering over my head.

I follow his gaze and see Kade coming toward us, a smile on his face. Darius isn't far behind, his eyes looking around the area, his head tilted. Kade greets Solvier while I keep my eyes on Darius, watching for his reaction. I'm surprised the big wolf even let him see him.

Darius stops when he's a few feet away from us, his eyes peering into mine before looking to Kade, and then finally, to Solvier. He holds his arms at his sides, but I see the tension in his body as he looks up at Solvier.

Darius is tall, but Solvier is taller. His paws are as big as my head.

It's not every day you see a six-foot wolf. In fact, he's the biggest wolf I've seen. I thought I would get more of a reaction out of Darius, but he just keeps staring at Solvier, his eyes scanning him until he finally moves toward a tree to lean against it. He acts like seeing Solvier is just another occurrence in his daily life. Does nothing phase this guy?

"How are you, Rhea?" Solvier asks me, his golden eyes looking into mine.

"I'm okay," I mumble, peering over my shoulder at Darius before looking back at him.

"I see." See what? I want to ask, but he moves his attention to Kade. *"Are you still struggling with your wolf, young Kaden?"* he asks, maneuvering his body until he lays down in front of us, clearly not seeing Darius as a threat. Though nothing much is a threat to Solvier. His bite could tear you in half. At Kade's reluctant nod, Solvier tilts his head toward the ground in front of him. Kade sits. *"Come, tell me."*

I stand there awkwardly and look at them both, realizing I'm not going to be part of this conversation from the silence in my head. I move away from them and sit on the ground, pinching my lip with my fingers as I watch them for a while. I take out my knife and pick up a branch from the floor, idly nicking at the bark. I glance at them from time to time, crossing and uncrossing my legs. Kade nods at something Solvier says, and his head bows, playing with the laces of his boot. But I swear I see tears in his eyes. I look away, giving him his privacy, knowing what they must be talking about.

Cassie.

He barely talks about her unless it's with Solvier, and even then it's not often.

I hope Solvier can give him some advice on how to control his wolf and emotions. I know no one wiser. He is family to us, and we trust him and his words. I know he will do the best he can and to steer Kade in the right direction.

I sigh quietly and look out toward the trees. The only problem with that is that puts Darius in my line of sight. He's still leaning against the tree, looking around the area, his body alert and ready. I let my senses out and feel nothing, but Darius isn't used to the sounds of Eridian like I am. He turns his head and catches my eye, his head tilting in question. I watch as his hair lands just above his eyes, tickling his eyes brows. Then my gaze drops to the slope of his nose and down to his mouth, remembering the feel of it on mine. I look away, but not before I hear him release a satisfied sound.

It does strange things to me when that man's eyes are on mine.

I keep quiet, not wanting to disturb Kade and Solvier as they talk even though I can't hear what they are saying. He needs it. I'm at a loss at what to do to help him. He's grieving all over again now that he has his wolf. He's struggling to find balance, and if I dig too deep, he just pushes me away. I'm sick of seeing the sad look on his face when he thinks no one is looking. But I see it. I can feel his pain like it's my own.

A growl snaps both mine and Darius's heads toward them, and I stand, putting my knife in my boot. Kade hunches forward, and then all of a sudden his bones begin breaking before his dark gray wolf is there, standing proud. Solvier seems unbothered by the sudden change, but I panic. Solvier moves his head, looking past the trees to our left, but my eyes stay on

Kade.

"Kade?" I start toward him, my steps unsure before he suddenly turns, snarling at me viciously. I jolt, shocked at his aggression. "*Kade,"* I try again in a lower tone down the link, but he blocked me again. "Dammit, stop shutting me out!" Still snarling, he ignores me and stalks forward, teeth bared, head low. What the fuck? I growl, warning him to knock it off, but he keeps coming. I don't want to hurt him. I would never hurt him. "Carzan, think about what you're doing." He's not stopping, his pace set as his blue eyes darken, his focus entirely on me. I brace myself, hoping I can shove him off me and snap him out of it if he lunges.

"You don't want to do that, pup," Darius warns in a tone so low, even I pause. He comes and stands a little in front of me, head lowered, his piercing stare on Kade. My heart rate kicks up.

I'm not doing this again. No way.

"Kade, stop it. What is wrong with you?" I take a step forward, but Darius's hand shoots out, grabbing my arm none too gently and pulling me behind him. "Darius, don't." I can't see them go at each other again, I can't. Kade won't survive it. He's not even fully healed, and he shifted when he shouldn't have.

Kade charges forward, and I suck in a sharp breath. Teeth bared, his aim solely on me, I can't even move. I can't protect myself.

Darius steps fully in front of me and turns, pushing Kade at his shoulder with his other hand when he's near to get him away from me.

"Enough," Darius commands, his dominance flowing freely while I barely breathe.

Kade stops, his snarls softening, and my heart breaks at the whine that suddenly escapes him. I look around the side of

Darius and see Kade's eyes on the ground. He shakes his head, backing away from us, before he turns and runs off. "Carzan!" I go to follow, but Darius still has his hand tightly gripping my arm, not letting me go. I grab the hand holding me when I realize he's staring at Solvier, who is still laying down. I stop and look between them, and Darius's head shakes slightly at whatever Solvier has said to him.

Solvier makes a small growling sound that makes me jump before he stands. He shakes out his fur, the light reflecting on the strands making it look like he has gold threads flowing through it. I stay still as he comes over to us, and he shocks the shit out of me when nudges Darius's cheek before doing the same to mine.

"All will be well with Kade. Trust in him. He will always come back to you." He nods his head. *"Trust the dark one too,"* he says. *"All will be as it once was."*

With those last parting words, he wanders off, disappearing into the trees.

As it once was? What is that supposed to mean?

TWENTY FIVE

Rhea

I stand frozen, my heart hurting over Kade's sudden reaction and wondering what Solvier meant. Something is… off with the big wolf. His last words sounded somber and resigned. I don't like that at all. What did he say to Kade, and why did he react that way? In fact, what did he say to Darius?

"What did Solvier say to you?" I ask him, both of us still looking in the direction Solvier left. I feel a twitch beneath my palm and realize I'm still grabbing onto his hand with mine. I drop my hand quickly and step away from him, making him release me.

He turns toward me, his brows low. "Nothing important," he answers, looking me over curiously. "What was that language you used?"

I shake my head at the sudden question. "What?"

"You called the pup Carzan? What language is it?" His stare is intent on mine as he folds his arms over his chest, his eyes watching, waiting for something. I gulp.

I didn't mean to use the language my family used, it just slipped out. When I don't answer, he comes for me, and I stumble back, rough bark digging into my back when I hit a tree. What is it with me and trees lately? Darius doesn't stop until he's inches away, bringing his arms up on either side of my head, caging me in. Dropping his face so he's directly in front of mine, he asks me again.

"What language?" he demands, and my fingers grip the bark behind me as I try to think of a way to get around this. The use of that language has always been sacred, pure. I don't want him to taint it. He growls low when I don't answer, and I growl right back, unable to stop the reaction, baring my teeth. His hand comes up to my neck, squeezing gently in warning, and I swallow roughly under his palm. He feels it beneath his hand, his fingers twitching lightly before moving a finger over my pulse, rubbing back and forth slowly, as if he's savoring it under his touch.

"Why does it matter?" I whisper eventually, looking into his eyes and searching for those flecks of glass, needing to watch them float around in his eyes as they darken.

"I want to know. I haven't heard it before, and I have heard many languages. The writing of your tattoo is old. Is that the language you speak?" I grit my teeth and move to look away from his penetrating stare. He doesn't let me though, moving that hand from my throat to grip my jaw, leaving a trail of goosebumps in its wake. "You seem to think you have any say here. The least you can do is answer me after what you did in The Deadlands," he growls low, his fingers digging into my jaw to keep my eyes on him. "Tell me."

He releases more dominance, and it crashes into me at full force, drawing a whimper from me. It wraps around me, swirling around my legs, over my hips and eventually rests against my chest. The pressure builds, like a weight pressing into my skin. I know he won't let up until I tell him, and I don't think a lie, or a half truth is going to cut it.

"It's my family language. It's of the old Gods, or so I was taught," I say begrudgingly, answering him this while the guilt of The Deadlands hits me. His reminder that I killed some of his trainees deepening the stain in my soul.

"Your mother and father spoke it?" At my nod, he continues. "I thought you didn't have any family apart from the one you chose?"

"I *had* a family. They were stolen from me," I tell him. "Kade and Josh are my only family now. They have been for a long time." They are the closest thing to me, the closest anyone will ever get, and even then I still don't give them all of me.

The ugliness within me, the grime of black on my soul, of the things that I have done… They don't need that. They don't need that burden. And I don't need to make them uncomfortable in trying to comfort me when no one can.

The burden is mine to bear, mine to shoulder. I keep those vines of thorns squeezing my heart all to myself as I feel their damage day in and day out.

"Is the pup yours?" Darius questions, and it brings me out of my own head to see those flecks of silver beginning to float from the edges of his irises.

My gaze follows those flecks, captivated by them as I answer. "He is mine in every way that counts. I did not birth him, but that does not make him any less mine." I feel my pupils dilate, my protectiveness over Kade showing in my eyes. "You will not take him from me." I don't care what I have to do, he will not take him to the Highers.

We stare at each other, sharing the same air as it feels like the earth stills around us. I watch those flecks, and he watches the darkness that has undoubtedly creeped into my eyes before I manage to pull it back. He stares at me so deeply, so intensely with a look I can't place. But I'm not scared. It feels like a caress on my soul. My forearm begins to tingle, the sensation causing my body to tremble before his eyes turn hard once again, a layer of indifference coating them as he blinks away whatever emotion was just there.

"I won't take him from you," he agrees, and my shoulders

drop their tension. "But I will take you from him." I jolt at his unexpected words, glaring at him. "You will be coming back to Fenrikar with me where you will be put on trial and then your punishment will be passed over to me." He moves closer, our noses softly brushing against each other, and it's such a contrast to his harsh words. "What the punishment will be has yet to be decided. I may be inclined to change the type of punishment you receive if you're a good little wolf."

Heat fills his eyes, and I suck in a breath at the sight, the space between my thighs warming. He moves his hand from my jaw, picking up a piece of my hair that's fallen on my face before rubbing it between his fingers thoughtfully. He hums, watching his movements as he feels its softness, twirling it around one of his fingers.

"You don't need to remind me about going to the Highers." I swallow. "I already told you I accept that. But you can't tell them about Eridian."

Anger flashes through his eyes, the green losing their heat before he drops my hair and takes a step back. "Why should you and your pack have this safe haven all to yourself? Stop being a selfish bitch."

I stand straighter at the insult, looking him dead in the eyes and giving him some truth. "All I have ever done is protect my pack, my family. Anyone knowing about this place is bad, Darius. Really bad." I bring a hand up and rub the back of my neck. "We... *they...* cannot be taken to the Highers, and the Highers cannot come here. Why can't you understand that? Why can't you *see* that?" He's not stupid.

"I've seen your pack scared, yet I'm not entirely sure why," he grinds out in irritation. "I've been here for over a week, and I have gotten nothing out of you or them. If you want them to stay out of the Highers' eye, you'll need to give me a fucking good reason for it."

"Darius," I growl. "I will not tell you their stories, their lives. I will not betray their trust like that." I shake my head and put my hands on my hips. "Read between the lines, asshole. You know damn well why some of them are scared. You heard what Sam said at the gathering the other night. I know you did. I'm the one who wronged you, so punish me and leave everyone else out of it."

He moves so fast I don't see his hand reaching for me until he has my hair in his grip and my head tilts backward. "I will punish you, but on my own terms, little wolf. I have already told you that you have no say in it."

He glares down at me, and I've had enough of his manhandling for one day. I nudge Runa, and my knee shoots up, aiming for his balls. He moves to the side to avoid it, my knee hitting his thigh instead, but I'm already swinging my fist forward toward his face. He releases my hair and moves back, but not without me catching his jaw as he does.

He straightens to his full height, all six foot four inches of it, rubbing his jaw slightly. I preen at hitting him, feeling accomplished that after him shoving me around, I got a hit in. I ready myself for him to come at me, and he doesn't disappoint. I smack away the hand that tries to grab me and aim a kick at his shin. He takes the hit, grunting at the force of it, and grabs my arm. Leaning back slightly, he pulls me toward him forcefully and moves to the side to throw me forward with the momentum. He lets go of my arm, and I stumble over my steps before I right myself. Growling, I reach down for my small blade in my boot. Hearing him coming for me, I grab hold of the hilt and slash out as I spin around to face him. Metal on metal clashes as his blade halts mine, the hit vibrating up my arm. I growl at him and kick out, aiming for his stomach as he chuckles coldly, deflecting me easily. I move backward, holding my blade so it runs down my forearm while he twirls a similar sized black blade in his hand, tilting his head at me.

"If you wanted to play, little wolf, all you had to do was ask." He licks his lips, and his smirk is downright wicked before he lunges.

His blade comes at me, aiming to slice at my neck and I bring my forearm up, stopping his blade with my own. I jump up and pull my left fist back, aiming for a hit to his temple with our blades still connected. He moves his head back, avoiding it as I snarl in anger. He grips my left wrist with his free hand and brings it down between us as I land back on my feet. I slide my blade down his before he takes my legs out from under me and lets go of my wrist. I fall hard to the ground, a grunt quickly turning into a snarl when he follows me down and straddles me.

"We have been here before, haven't we?" he murmurs down at me. "It didn't end well for you then either." He drops his blade to the side and grabs my forearm, pinning it to the dirt beside my head so I can't use my blade, and then he does the same with the other.

"How do you know this won't end well for me this time?" I pant and twist beneath him, trying to dislodge the big fucker.

"Because if you don't stop wriggling, you will have another problem to deal with," he says in a low, gravelly voice.

"Fuck you." I squirm more against him, and he shifts down slightly, giving me more of his weight. I push my hips up, aiming to buck him off, when I find the problem he mentioned.

My eyes fly to his, widening when I feel his hardness between us. He raises an eyebrow at me, smirking, then he moves his knees between my legs and pushes them until he's resting between my thighs. His cock presses against my center and a ragged gasp leaves me. He runs his hands up my forearms, sending delicious shivers through me until he reaches my wrists and moves them to one big hand.

"What are you doing?" I whisper, and he just stares down at

me, confliction in his eyes.

He moves his hips forward, and a moan escapes me before I can stop it. His eyes light up at the sound and any doubt he had vanishes as he does it again, but I'm ready this time and only expel a heavy breath. He growls low and heat fills me at the sound, but I make no outward reaction.

He lowers his face to my neck, and I hear him taking in a deep breath before nipping my skin lightly. He leaves open mouthed kisses against my skin, his nose trailing up and down before his body tenses. "You're going into heat." He takes another deep breath, a rumbling sound coming from him as he rubs into the side of my neck. "You smell like you want to be fucked." He rocks into me again, and I whimper.

"You're wrong." I tell him breathlessly as he continues pressing into me at a leisurely pace. "My heat isn't for another few months." I can't be going into heat, I would know. I only have one heat a year, and it's during the winter months.

He chuckles deep and low into my neck as his free hand trails down the side of my body. His fingers caress over my shoulder, following down the side of my breast before stopping just above the waistline of my shorts. I hold my breath at his touch, feeling his wolf come to the surface. He moves his hand underneath the bottom of my t-shirt and circles my belly button with a light touch, the feel of his skin against mine making my head spin. I feel delirious. A tiny moan escapes me and I arch my back, wanting more, craving more. My body feels itchy and sweat beads at the back of my neck as heat fills in my stomach. Wetness soaks through my panties, and I whimper, knowing what these sudden signs are. What they mean. I shake my head in denial.

"I can't be," I growl, pissed and achy all at the same time. "It's not time yet."

"Your smell tells me differently," he murmurs, moving his

fingers down from my belly button to caressing just inside my waistband. I shift beneath him. "And you smell delicious," he mumbles against my skin, licking at my neck.

He pulls his face out of the crook of my shoulder and looks down at me, desire filling his eyes as his fingers tease the edge of my panties. I close my eyes and will myself to calm down, to ignore the sensations those fingers are creating and the closeness of his body to mine.

This isn't happening. No matter how much my body is begging me differently. I won't give in just for him to throw it in my face later. He already lashed out at my heart when we lost control against the tree. Why are we like this again?

I can't be.

I open my eyes and I feel Runa there, pinning him with our stare. "Get the fuck off me, Darius." He smirks, his fingers skimming under the edge of my panties before he removes them all together. Releasing my wrists, he gets to his feet in one fluid motion.

I sit up, breathing through my mouth to ignore his scent as he steps beside me and stops. He crouches down and grabs his blade, twirling it in his hand before I feel his breath in my ear. "I look forward to making you beg me sooner or later, little wolf." He nips at my earlobe, and my body trembles, my hands clenching at my sides to stop myself from reaching out to him to help with this need he just created. The only one who ever has.

I wait until he's out of hearing distance before I release a growl of frustration, my fingers digging into the dirt. My body aches from Darius's attention. How the fuck am I going into heat five months early? And why am I acting this way around him? Why him?

"I'm going crazy," I mutter to myself. "Fucking crazy. This isn't normal."

I stand, dusting my hands off and head off to do a perimeter check, my body cooling down the more I walk. That's what's important right now, not the thought of a male grinding on me. One particular male. I huff and swing my arms as I walk, shaking them out when a blur of black catches my eyes to my left.

I swing my head that way, the bushes there swaying with too much force for it to be the light breeze, and I swear I caught the back of someone's dark head moving further along. I let my senses go wide, but there is nothing out of the normal. I wonder if it's one of the Elites, shit, did they see us?

"Where did you place the Elites?" I ask Josh quickly.

He takes a second to answer me. *"I took them south. Why?"*

"I'm east at the moment. What are the chances of an Elite being out this way?" I creep forward with silent footsteps as I head in the direction of those bushes, keeping my eyes peeled.

"Small. They could just be exploring. A few others have done that."

"Yeah, I guess." I reach the bushes and inhale deeply, scenting nothing but the greenery and berries around me. I look ahead of me through the trees and spot nothing out of the ordinary. I don't sense anything. It was probably just an animal.

Shaking my head, I retrace my steps and continue on to the base of the cliffs to start my check. No signs of rogures still, which is a plus, but since Kade killed the few he saw a while back, I'm still cautious and have been checking the perimeter regularly on my own. Even when it's already been done. The guys usually shake their heads at me when I do, but they know how I can be sometimes.

I pull a tree branch out of the way and my tattoos catch my attention in the light. Looking down at my forearm where it tingled before, I run my fingers across the swirls and lines. Bringing my fingers to the free space in the center, I circle around the clear skin and sigh. I think it's time to let go of that tiny little bit of hope I have in the back of my mind of it ever being filled.

Part of me never wants it to be whole, but I would be lying to myself if I said the other part of me didn't want it to be. I'm a wolf, and wolves want certain things.

And even as I look in the direction where Darius went and lie to myself that it's all down to Runa thinking this way, the human in me wonders if it's possible.

TWENTY SIX

RHEA

I'm hot, too hot. I fan myself with the paperwork I was going over before leaning back in my chair, sighing at the brief relief it gives me. Runa has been acting strange for a couple of days since Darius mentioned my heat, rolling around restlessly within me. It's making my skin feel like it's crawling, like I want to rip it off me, and that is something new. Josh eyes me from across my desk, tilting his head in question, his eyes amused as he watches me.

"Do I smell different?" I blurt out, heat filling my cheeks instantly.

"What?" he laughs, his gray eyes popping wide. "Where did that come from?" he asks. I grumble under my breath.

"You're what?" he questions, not quite able to make out what I'm saying.

I growl before speaking up. "I'm going into heat." Sebastian's head whips around from where he stands next to my window, his tawny eyes brightening at my words.

Here we go.

He saunters toward me at his full height, a sexy grin spreading over his face as he leans down and shoves his face in my neck, taking a deep breath. I shove his face away, scowling at him. "I can smell it a little," Sebastian hums, his eyes lazily traveling over my body. "Are you finally going to let me see you through your heat?" His eyebrows wiggle suggestively as he speaks, and I don't even hesitate in my reply.

"Not a chance." He asks me every year. And every year, I turn him down.

"It's early," Josh says to himself, ignoring Seb's flirting. "Your heat is in winter. We are only just nearly hitting summer. Why is it so early?"

I've been racking my brain at the very same thing. Since my eighteenth birthday, my heat has always come the last week of winter like clockwork. Not once has it changed in all these years. So why now? The only thing that has changed is the Elites turning up. Darius turning up.

"I know it's early, Josh, but I can't think of a reason why."

"Maybe your heat is being brought on by the other females. They do all tend to sync up," he grumbles, running his hand through his hair that's not in a bun for once. In fact, he doesn't look put together at all. He looks as agitated as me.

"But why now? That's never happened before." I blow out a breath. Generally, females go into heat once every three months. I only have mine once a year, and that's never changed. "Well, either way it's early, so I'll be gone for a day, maybe two, when it hits. You guys will be okay handling the Elites, right?"

Hudson grunts from the seat to the left of me, with Colten on the floor by his leg, looking at some papers on the low table in front of him. "They're still looking for Sarah, you know," Hudson says, running a hand over his shaved head. "I heard some of the Elites talking about there being a time limit or something, but didn't catch enough of their conversation to know what they meant."

"Why do they have a time limit?" Colten wonders, pausing in his reading and looking up at Hudson who shrugs in response.

"Could they need to get back for something?" Taylor offers next to my office door, his bulky frame taking up space.

"Maybe, but what?" I ask them.

"Does it really matter?" Josh shrugs. "The sooner they're gone the better for us."

"Did you forget the part where they know about Eridian and that I'm going back with them? Darius won't have it any other way." I stare out my window, refusing to feel the fear that knowledge sends through me.

I never thought I would have to leave my home. I thought we were safe here. I thought I would live the rest of my days in our little corner of Vrohkaria.

Going back and seeing the Highers… seeing *him.*

I shiver.

It's for Eridian, for my family, I tell myself.

For Kade.

Taylor huffs before saying in a deadly voice, "Do you really think we'll just let him take you to the Highers?" His amber eyes turn hard at the thought, and I smile internally at his words. Unfortunately, it won't make a difference. We are way outnumbered.

"How have we known each other for so long and you don't know?" Josh says, shaking his head at me. "How could you think we'd just let you leave here to be taken to trial by the Highers… and then what? We just stay in Eridian and get on with our lives? What about Kade?"

"You have to. I'm asking this from all of you and Kade is my chosen Heir for Eridian. He will take over."

"He's unstable," Josh bites out.

"He's still the next Alpha of this pack," I snap back at him, feeling my eyes flash as Runa comes close to the surface. Kade will be fine, he must be. "He needs a bit of healing, and I know you all will guide him. Solvier will also help him."

"I don't think he will heal," Seb tells me in the most serious voice I have ever heard from him. "That's a wound that will never heal." I don't want to think it never will for Kade, but I know Seb is speaking from his own experiences.

The room is silent at his words, pain noticeably on Seb's face, and I want nothing more than to go over to him and offer him comfort. Seb will be Seb though and either flirt or joke it off like it's nothing. When it's everything.

I know I can't bring Kade's mate back. But that just can't be it. Surely the Gods wouldn't be so cruel to have those who lost their mate suffer until the end of their time. I won't accept Kade suffering for the rest of his days. There has to be something.

"Anyway." I shift in my seat, diverting the conversation back to the topic at hand. "Bottom line is, I will be going to the Highers if I can't convince Darius otherwise. Which, at this rate, is looking like there is no hope in it."

"The Highers will know as soon as they see you. *He* will know," Josh whispers, his face dropping at what that means.

"Maybe not if I don't reveal it," I say stiffly. "I haven't in all these years, and I don't intend to, okay?" He nods, but I can see he's not convinced, and neither am I. The silence in the room lets me know the others aren't either. "I will do my punishment and come home," I say with false confidence.

"Rhea," Colten starts, his voice hesitant. I hate that they don't want me to go and there is nothing I can do to ease it away.

"Look, we didn't even know if we would make it out alive in The Deadlands, but we did. Just let me go and all will be well. As long as they keep Eridian secret, that's all that matters to me, and that you are all safe." I look down at my hands and pick the side of my finger before looking back up at them. "I have loved being here with you all." I give them a small, sad smile as pain washes over their faces. "I will aim to come home if I can and it's safe to do so. If I cannot return, then I accept that, and you all should too."

"Is this your final decision?" Josh asks, knowing he won't be able to talk me out of it.

I nod. "It's my choice. I will do what it takes to protect you all. I owe each of you so much," I tell them. "*I owe you my life,*"I say to Josh down the link, and his eyes shine with moisture before he looks away. "Let me do this, even if it's the last thing I might do. I have lived many more years than I thought I would in the first place." I blink my eyes, willing myself not to shed a single damn tear. "If I have to be punished for then so be it, I can handle it. I don't think Darius will kill me, it would be too quick for his liking." The male really has it out for me, but as long as it stays aimed at *just* me, I will deal with whatever comes my way. I have to. "So, once he's done with me, I can come home. The Highers won't bother with me by then." At least, I hope so.

"He's always staring at you, you know?" Colten informs me, referring to Darius with a grimace on his face.

"Yeah." I chuckle. "He's plotting all the ways to make my life a misery." I get up from my chair and throw down the papers. "I'm going to do my checks and finish this up later." I round my desk and touch my cheek briefly to Josh's before leaving my office. I need some space.

I head for the front door, put my boots on, and then make my way to the deck. I reach my arms up as I walk toward the gardens, stretching out my achy muscles and groaning in relief at the feel of it. I don't think it will be long until my heat fully kicks in now, and I'll need to make sure I'm away from here when it happens. I don't want to be around anyone and give in to temptation.

I never have, but I won't take that chance.

Following the trail behind our storage cabin, I step between the trees behind it and enter our gardens. We plant vegetables back here, harvesting them every season when they're ready. Most of the women spend a lot of time here. It's quiet and the work keeps them busy, as well as the pups who play in the small clearing in its center. I make my way toward the pups playing, smiling softly at their newfound freedom. It wasn't always like that for some, but they're still young enough to hopefully not have many lasting effects from their life before here.

"Alpha!" they call out when they spot me, their faces lighting up as they rush toward me. I bend down, not reminding them to not call me by my title, and open my arms as they launch themselves at me.

I laugh, falling on my ass as they climb on me. "Hey, what are you guys up to?"

"We were just deciding who's going to be the wolf and who's going to be the rabbit," Elijah tells me, bouncing on his feet as his light hair swishes on the top of his head.

"Hmm, is that so?" At their nod, I smile. I sit up, and they back away from me, getting ready. "Well, I'll count to ten, and if you little rabbits aren't hidden enough, I'll gobble you up!"

"Quick, let's go!" Leah squeals, her hair swirling around her as she grabs Oscar's little hand and runs. Elijah and Nathen take off in another direction while Lacy hobbles over to her mom deeper in the garden, her little legs taking her as fast as she can go. I'm about to start counting when I notice Samantha sitting on her own near one of the garden patches, looking ahead of her but seeing nothing. I wander over to her slowly, not wanting to frighten her and take a seat, unbothered about the dirt beneath me.

"Hey," I say softly to her. "You doing okay?" She nods, her head bobbing slowly before picking at the dirt in front of her, her hair shielding her face from me. "You know you can talk to me about anything, right? Even things you don't want your mom to know about." She stays silent, not answering me, and I lift my head to the sky, trying to think of a way to get her to open up.

I've noticed she's been withdrawn since the fire when I told her the story of the Canaric wolves. My only guess is memories are haunting her from the time before she and her mom came here with how she questions why the Gods didn't protect her. I feel at a loss as she continues to pick up dirt in her hands and then let it fall through her fingers. I don't know why she wasn't protected as she should have been, or her mother. It's the case for most of us here. We were let down by our own. We were in pain because of our own.

I breathe through my sudden rage, and Runa perks her ears up.

I move my hand and take one of hers in mine gently, dirt and all. She startles, and I bring an arm around her, drawing her closer to me, not letting her go. I hear her sniffle, and I squeeze her tighter, resting my head on top of hers. I hate seeing any of the pups upset, but I have an extra soft spot for Sam. She reminds me of myself sometimes. She deals with her pain on her own, silent in her hurt because she doesn't want to bother anyone else. Not knowing *how* to bother anyone else with it. Her mom might have been there and experienced what they both went through in their home, but Sam saw things through different eyes. She experienced things a kid should never have to have seen or heard or felt.

I hold her there for a while as her quiet sniffles become less and less, and I'm just grateful I can be something for her. To shield her from anyone else coming near her while she's vulnerable, while she lets out a little pain and shares it with me. I didn't have this at her age. The comfort or care of another. I just had four walls and a monster or five that came to visit.

Until Josh.

"Is she okay?" Kade's voice suddenly sounds in my head, and I turn and see him at the storage cabin watching us. He looks tired, his shoulders tense as he waits for my reply.

"Yeah, she just needed a moment." I smile softly at him, and he

relaxes a little.

I haven't seen him since he went off into the forest. It was only days ago, but it feels longer. We are drifting apart, and I have no idea how to stop it, how to keep him closer to me like he used to be. I miss the days he would run up to me smiling as he told me about his adventures in the forest that day, or how he caught his dinner and waved his hands around as he talked excitedly.

Those days feel like a lifetime ago.

He looks between me and Sam, a grin about to spread wide before he tenses up again. *"When we went and talked to Solvier..."* he trails off, rubbing the back of his neck, showing he's clearly uncomfortable.

"Don't mention it," I say when he doesn't continue. *"When you're ready to talk, I'm here. Always."* He nods his head at me before looking down.

We both know he won't talk to me.

"Tell her she can come for a walk with me if she wants," he mutters after a few moments when Sam's last sniffle reaches me.

"Really?" He likes being alone a lot, but then he and Sam have a different bond than he does with anyone else, so I shouldn't be surprised.

At his nod, I look down at Sam. I nudge her with my shoulder, and red puffy eyes meet mine. I smile at her and flick my head in Kade's direction. Her brows scrunch up before following my gaze. Her face instantly lights up when she sees him, quickly getting to her feet and running toward him.
I stand, dusting myself off and watch as she dives for him, hugging him close.

Kade has always been good with the kids around here, but seeing how gentle he is with her, even as he picks her up and puts her on his back melts my heart. My smile widens at them as I watch them go, their own smiles wide, and I laugh when Sam tells him to go faster.

I feel eyes on me, intense and devastating. I turn my head and lock eyes with Darius. He's leaning against one of the apple trees, muscles bulging where his arms are crossed. My smile slowly drops as his hair falls in front of his eyes when he tilts his head, looking like every bit of the animal he is. I lick my lips as I remember grabbing those dark strands in my hands as his tongue tangled with mine, his hips rocking against me, and I flush as the images pop up into my mind. His eyes heat as he notices my reaction, and he smirks, his eyes slowly roaming over my form. When I feel a wetness pool between my legs, I know it's time to go.

I turn and walk quickly in the opposite direction, aiming for one place and one place only, knowing the countdown has now begun.

My heat has started, and I need to get away before I do something really stupid.

And stupid has a name.

Darius.

TWENTY SEVEN

RHEA

I walk swiftly inside the tunnel hidden in the cliffside, my steps rushed as small cramps fill my belly. I enter the cave, breathing a sigh of relief even as sweat begins to coat my skin. I take a steady breath as another cramp hits, blowing it out slowly through the pain. It's only uncomfortable at the moment, but when my heat hits full force, it will sear through me as I'm seeing it through on my own.

Just like I do every year.

I head over to the furs I keep here at the back of the cave, walking around the pool and run my fingers through the water flowing down over the edges from the opening above. The cool water chills my clammy skin, and I bring my wet hand to the back of my neck, letting droplets of water run down my back.

Reaching my furs, I crouch down and arrange them to my liking, taking extra care in their placement before taking my boots off and placing them down next to my bed. Standing back up, I begin to undress. My t-shirt sticks to my skin as I draw it up over my head, my hair sticking to my neck in the process. I undo my pants next, my shaky fingers undoing the ties before shimmying them down my legs. Standing in just my bra and panties, I tie my hair in a knot on top of my head and walk toward the water.

My bare feet pad along the cold, rock floor until I reach

a smaller flow of water coming down from the top. I step into it, gasping at the sudden coolness and holding myself under it for a moment before taking my first steps into the pool. I wade toward the center slowly, my fingers running over the shimmering surface, until the water reaches just below my collarbone. I take deep breaths, the cramps coming stronger, and I tilt my head up to the now dark sky, the tiny specks of stars covering the darkness. Wisps come out from behind the lilk trees and greet me briefly, twirling in front of my eyes before floating upwards and out of the opening above me, until their green-blue glow is out of sight. I groan and clench my eyes shut as another wave of heat flows through me, my chest heaving through its strength.

I sink lower and dip my head back, letting the water soak my hair before lifting my legs to float, feeling the coolness encase me. I remain like this, running my fingers over the surface, creating ripple after ripple as my body burns to be touched, to stop this heat that's slowly overwhelming me. I stand upright suddenly, a disturbance in the air alerting me that someone has entered my cave. I stand still and take a deep breath, then unintentionally let out a groan at the scent that hits me. Cedarwood, damp earth after rain, and power, with a hint of something that is just *him*.

I don't turn around. I just keep looking straight ahead at the water cascading down and breathing through my mouth to avoid taking in more of his scent which is like an aphrodisiac. His presence makes me very aware of every droplet of water that runs over my heated flesh. Runa cocks her head at the smell of him, standing in his presence, knowing who is here. I mentally shove at her, telling her to pack that shit in.

I hear him moving around the space, his footsteps loud as if to let me know he's here. I already know. I can sense him. It's like my body has a direct link to his, to his every breath, and I *hate* it. I hate not being myself around him, I hate the way my body responds to him, and I hate that he has the audacity to show up in my space like this, knowing I can only control so much.

I growl. It's low and in warning that he better turn his ass around and get out of my space. All I get is a low chuckle in response, like I'm an insignificant threat to his balls. My fists clench beneath the surface, and I turn slowly, the water gently moving with me as I prepare to face him.

He stands between a parted section of flowing water at the edge of the pool, his eyes heating as he takes me in, seeing me nearly bare for the first time as his eyes pierce through the clear water. His gaze slowly roams up my body, and every caress of his eyes has my body burning. My stomach drops and my breathing picks up even as my deadly glare homes in on his face. When his gaze reaches my throat, black bleeds at the edges of his irises and flecks of silver float in his darkened green. He lowers his head, his fingers twitching at his sides.

Our eyes finally collide in heat and anger as my body flushes, my cheeks warming with the onslaught of desire coursing through my body. His nostrils flare, a small rumbling sound escaping him. My lips part at the noise, my chest heaving. I don't move a muscle, scared to make one single move as Runa tries pushing me forward, wanting me to go to him. I growl loud and viciously, a snarl at my lips at her and at him for entering my space. It's mine.

"Get the fuck out," I order him, trying to ignore the obvious erection I see straining against his pants. He cannot be here. He's not welcome here.

"Why would I do that, little wolf?" he murmurs, his voice laced with seduction. He moves a step back and begins to walk around the edge of the pool.

"You're not wanted. You're not invited here!" I snap, still

refusing to move as he's now walking at the side of me.

"Your heat has come," he states, and I hear him breathing deep as he walks. "You want to be fucked, need to be."

My core tightens at his words, and I release some of my dominance, letting it fill the space. I feel him still behind me, then a moment later he snarls, his dominance flowing through me, making my back start to arch before I can stop myself.

Another wave of heat hits me, and I moan, my eyes rolling as my head tilts back of its own accord. My hand runs a path from my neck to between my breasts, water dripping down as my body aches with need. Aches for relief.

Through my haze of desire, I hear him stop in front of me once again and my head snaps forward, my lips peeling back at him as he just watches me. The only sounds I hear are the pounding of my heart and my ragged breaths over the flow of water splashing into the pool. My hand drops, and I walk slowly toward him, our eyes locked in challenge as I stop a few feet away. His gaze lowers, resting at the apex of my thighs as water trickles down my skin, the pool's water now resting just below my knees. His jaw clenches and a sound echoes deep from within his chest as his dark hair falls forward at the tilt of his head. So animalistic. So Darius.

"I do not want you here, Darius. Leave." His eyes flash black, locking with mine as his lips tip up into a sinful smirk.

"Your body says otherwise, Rhea. What I don't understand though, is why are you out here on your own?" He tilts his head in the other direction. "Don't you have someone you've chosen to see you through your heat?"

"It's not your business," I breathe. "What I do with *anything* in my life is none of your business."

He chuckles low. "See, that is where you are wrong." He straightens and grabs his t-shirt, pulling it over his head and revealing inch after inch of tan, tattooed skin as I squeeze my thighs tightly together. The ache intensifies as I imagine what his bare skin would feel like on mine. "Since the moment I locked eyes on you, little wolf, you have been my business, my enemy, and mine in every way that I want." He drops his t-shirt to the floor, watching me rake my gaze over him, watching my face flush in desire for him.

I can't tear my eyes away as I lock on the dark tattoos swirling down from the sides of his neck to the top of his shoulders, reaching his collarbone. A mixture of script and harsh patterns flow down over his pecs and down the side of his ribs, caressing the edges of his abs before disappearing beneath the waistband of his pants. I bite my lip and wonder just how far down they go.

As if he could hear my thoughts, he bends and takes off his boots, kicking them aside before straightening. His hands are sure and steady as he undoes the ties of his pants, and I can't look away, my attention solely on him. Fixed on him. He shoves his pants down and steps out of them, completely unashamed of his nakedness as he stands before me, hard and thick. Only a few thoughts run through my mind at that moment.

Pure. Male. Alpha.

My mind goes hazy as I devour him with my eyes, a whine escaping my lips as more wetness comes out of me as my body prepares itself. My heated eyes stay locked on his cock straining against his stomach, pre-cum leaking from the tip, and my mouth fills with the urge to taste him, to lick him from base to tip and savor him. I want to swallow him down and scent mark him. I've never done that before. I've never wanted to.

Darius hurts me with his words and threats, but he also makes me feel things I have never felt before. A desire, a need, an unrelenting craving that won't leave me.

It makes me think of the moon and the night colliding in a beautiful disaster, before it all goes dark with no end in sight.

No matter how I tell myself I won't let this happen, it feels like I have no choice in the matter, that the situation is out of my hands and I know I'm going to fall. I can feel it, sense it, I just have to hope the landing will be soft and I survive it.

He growls a different sound. It's lighter, an approval of my reaction to him, and I echo him, finally moving my eyes up his muscular body and staring into his black ones. Chills run over me as he takes a step forward into the water, and I growl a warning at his approach. He growls back, just as fierce, and I snarl as he stops just two feet in front of me.

"Do you want me to fuck you, little wolf? Do you want my cock deep inside you?" he purrs, bringing his hand up and wrapping it around himself. My eyes lower as I watch him stroke a fist down. He holds himself briefly at the base before bringing his hand up and collecting his pre-cum on his fingers. "Do you want to taste me just as much as I want to taste you?" He lifts his fingers up to my lips, trailing over them and coating them with his essence. "I won't let anyone else touch you, so make a decision, you have two options." He moves closer, pressing his fingers harder into my lips until they part and my tongue peaks out, tasting him for the first time. I feel my eyes dilate as my pussy clenches, wanting his scent all over me. He dips his head, our noses touching, eyes locked. "We can fuck, or we can fight then fuck."

My legs tremble at his words, and with the scent of him invading me along with the taste of him, my stomach cramps once again. My body becomes an inferno, tingles erupting all over me, and I know I'm in full heat. I also know that with him being here, it's inevitable. I can't ignore him, just like he can't seem to ignore me. He followed me here, stalked me, hunted me. I think his words over in my head and come to a decision. He smirks at me like he knows what it is, and I do the only thing left to do.

I pounce.

TWENTY EIGHT

RHEA

Launching myself at him, we stagger back as I wrap my legs around his waist and grip his hair in my fists, wrenching his head back. He smirks up at me, eyes lighting up as he grabs my ass and draws me closer to him, his cock resting at my stomach. My nearly naked body connecting with his has tingles spreading through me, and I squirm, causing him to let out a soft groan as his cock rubs against me. He spins, taking us out of the water, and I squeeze his ribs hard with my thighs. He smacks my ass in response which causes me to growl down at him. I let go of his hair with one hand and bring my arm up, aiming my elbow down toward his nose, but a fist in my own hair has my upper body being pulled back away from him.

I unlock my legs from around his waist, and he releases my hair as I release his, landing on my feet. I fake a hit to his right side, which he dodges, but he doesn't dodge the hit I aim at his ribs on his left. He grunts, my punch well aimed as he glares at me. I smile. If he wants my body, he has to earn it.

We mirror each other as we circle, waiting to see who will make the next move. It's him. He moves quickly, landing a kick to my thigh that has me stumbling to the side, then a sudden push to my shoulder has me going backward as my fist shoots out, catching the top of his arm as we growl at each other. He stalks closer, aiming to grab me, and I drop to one knee, coming face to face with his delicious cock for a moment before I hit him at the back of his knee and roll forward past him. His knee gives way momentarily, and I kick him in the back when I hop back up, sending him staggering forward. He releases a dark chuckle when he spins around to face me, his tongue dragging along his front teeth as he takes me in, eyes heated, cock leaking more of that pre-cum that I want to have on my tongue.

I charge, fist ready as I aim for his jaw which he easily dodges, bringing a hand up to bat mine away. Runa comes to me, our speed increasing as we go after him, hit after hit and he deflects every single one. We don't slow down, we keep going, our dominance slowly increasing as he matches it. I aim a kick at his groin, my foot just missing him as he moves with confidence, easily avoiding it as he grabs my ankle and pulls me closer. I jolt forward and go to lift my other leg, using his hold to my advantage, when he yanks me to him. I collide with him, his warm skin touching mine as I scratch at his shoulders. His heat burrows its way under my skin as his free hand grabs my hair and yanks my head back.

We stare at each other, time suspended as our breaths mingle and another cramp hits me. A whine barely releases from my lips before he smirks, then his mouth slams onto mine. The kiss is angry, firm and invading as he devours me. The taste of him hits me and more wetness floods between my thighs. He groans as I bite his lower lip, his teeth coming to mine in reprimand before his tongue tangles with mine. He drops my ankle and starts walking me backward, his hand still in my hair, the other now on my throat, never breaking the kiss.

My bare feet hit something soft, and then I'm being lowered down, my back hitting soft fur as Darius settles between my thighs. His releases my throat and reaches behind me, unhooking my bra within seconds, and in the next, it's off me and thrown somewhere. His lips leave mine, trailing across my neck while I gasp for breath, my eyes closing at the feel of his mouth caressing me. His kisses leave a wet trail as he reaches my breast, his tongue swirling around my nipple and sucking slightly before he releases it and bites down next to it. His teeth sink lightly into the flesh, and I moan at the slight pain and his marking of me. No one has ever done this, given my body this attention. The one time when someone was this close to me, it was over quickly, just the way I wanted it to be. It never made me feel so alive like I do now.

I lift my hips, wanting more, needing more as his cock leaks on my stomach. Then my hands are back in his hair, gripping the strands and pulling him closer to me, as close as he can get. His free hand pays attention to my other breast, rolling my nipple between his fingers before his mouth is on me again, nipping, sucking, leaving marks all over my chest while he growls hungrily, and I hum in approval.

My head tilts back, my hips rolling with the need to be filled, for this ache to be soothed in a way I haven't felt before. I should be scared of the cock between his legs, wanting to get away from it instead of wanting it inside of me, but for some reason, I know he won't hurt me. Not in a way I didn't want.

His body heat disappears and I look down, watching as Darius holds either side of my panties before tearing them from my body, throwing the plain, white scraps of fabric aside. He stares at the most vulnerable part of me, but I don't feel shy or the need to hide from his view. A low rumbling escapes from his chest before his fingers hit my center. I jolt at the first touch as he moves them leisurely over me, gathering my wetness and rubbing it around me. Then he brings his hand to his mouth. My lips part as he licks my taste off his fingers, his eyes closing on a groan as his cock twitches.

Darius's eyes flash open, pinning me with his stare. His eyes still pure black, the silver flecks more prominent around the edges of his green irises as he takes his fingers out of his mouth and brings them back to my center. Giving my clit a light touch, he circles around it, making me moan. He does it again and again as I squirm beneath him, his other hand holding my thigh in a firm grip. His fingers tease my entrance before bringing them back up to circle my clit again, not giving me enough. I need more.

"Darius," I whimper, my hips lifting to try and get his fingers where I want them. Need them.

His fingers dip slightly inside of me, my pussy clenching around them, trying to get him to stay there. "Yes, little wolf?" he purrs, taking his fingers away before bringing them back and pushing in just a little further.

I move my hip down, taking his fingers a little deeper until his other hand moves from my thigh to grip my hip, stilling me. He looks over me, his hungry gaze lowering from my face, over my breasts to my navel, before finally stopping when he reaches my pussy. His fingers move inside me slowly, watching what he's doing to me, and the look in his eyes makes me tremble. My hands gripping the furs beside me as he keeps moving at a slow, punishing pace.

I whine, and he finally shoves his fingers forward all the way. My back arches as he begins to fuck me with them roughly, so deeply that my legs part wider. I claw at the furs, my head tilting back as he continues his assault, growls leaving him as he continues to watch. He curls his fingers inside me and brings a hand up to my throat, pinning me down and watching my every reaction. The move should cause me to panic, but it only heightens what he's doing to me. We stare at each other as he brings his thumb to my clit and I groan, my hips grinding, wanting it all. Pleasure rushes through me, and I can feel my orgasm building, my moans getting louder as I near my peak.

"Do you want to come?" he snarls, my movements speeding

up, and I can hear how wet I am, smell how wet I am, and it turns me on even more. My toes curl as my pussy tightens around him, and he removes his fingers suddenly, laughing coldly as I stare at him with wide eyes.

I claw at his hand around my neck, trying to bring my leg up to kick at him, but he lowers himself back on me, his weight pinning me down. I still. I can feel his cock between us, pre-cum leaking on my stomach, and I snap.

"What the fuck is wrong with you?! Can't please a female, Darius? Do you even know what you're doing?" I taunt.

"Is that what you think?" He laughs, and I ignore the jealousy I feel at the thought of him with others. "You really think I can't make you quiver in a mess of need and make you come again and again?"

"That's exactly what I think. If you're not up to it, I'll do it myself." I move my hands down my stomach, my fingers grazing his cock as my hands reach my pussy. He snarls, taking my wrists and slamming them down above my head.

"You don't get to give yourself an orgasm, little wolf," he rumbles. "Not unless it comes from me."

"Fuck you, asshole. You don't get to decide that." I buck beneath him, glaring at him when he doesn't move an inch.

"Oh, I fucking do," he mocks, watching my struggles with a smirk on his face.

"Can you even give someone an orgasm?" I taunt him some more after I slump down into the furs when I realize he isn't moving.

He squeezes my wrists in his hands. "Are you questioning my ability to please a female in bed?"

"Of course, I am," I laugh mockingly, earning a scowl from him. I start wriggling beneath him again to get him off of me. I ache. I need release, and this asshole is stopping me. "Get the fuck off of me!" I shout. "If you're not going to fuck me, then

I'll find someone else to–"

He pulls back and slams inside of me in one, brutal thrust. I scream, my back bowing as he fills me completely, my body tensing with the burn of it. His snarl is terrifying, his dominance powerful as he unleashes it on me at full force. My pussy squeezes him as he thrusts into me at a punishing pace. My moans are loud as my body is finally getting what it needs. He releases his hold on my wrists and my hands land on his shoulders, my nails digging into his skin as he pulls out nearly all the way before slamming into me again, laughing as I whimper from pain and pleasure.

"What's wrong, little wolf? Too much?" It is too much, but not enough at the same time. He leans back on his haunches and grabs hold of my hips in a tight grip. He smirks at me as he holds me still while he fucks me. Hard. A groan tears from me, and I wrap my legs around him as he picks up his pace. "So. Fucking. Tight," he growls the words out with each shove of his hips. My core clenches, and I can feel more wetness coating his cock, making it easy for him to push inside of me again and again. The sound of skin slapping on skin with my moans and his groans just takes me higher and higher. My world narrowing down to the feel of him moving inside of me, to the pleasure he's giving me.

He lets go of my hips suddenly and comes back over me, his forearms on either side of my head and we both groan at the feeling of him entering deeper inside of me. I claw at his back, my legs tightening around him as he bites at my neck. His thrusts become harder, my moans louder, and I sink my nails into him as my orgasm hits me fast and hard. My back arches, my toes curl and his mouth lands on mine, swallowing my scream, claiming it for himself as he fucks me through it before releasing my mouth.

"Your pussy is strangling my cock," he groans, his teeth

clamping down on my shoulder. I whimper in pain, digging my fingers in harder. He growls, his pace picking up before he slams into me one more time before stilling. "Fuck." Heat floods me as he comes, his essence coating my insides as his teeth dig further into me while his hips still move with small, shallow thrusts.

We still, breathing heavily and my body shakes with tremors. I release my hands from his shoulders and drop my legs from around his waist, letting them fall to the sides. He releases his teeth from my shoulder and slowly brings his head back to look at me. His eyes are now a light green, his features soft before he suddenly snarls. I frown, shoving at his shoulders, wanting him away from me as I realize what we just did. How could I be so fucking stupid?

He grips my throat, getting in my face, and my pussy floods with more need around him, causing his now soft cock to twitch inside of me. "We found one good thing about you," he says, a look of disgust crossing over his features. "Your pussy is worth something, at least."

My gaze hardens, my own hand moving to grip his throat, and I feel his fingers twitching. "It's a good thing you have a cock, Darius, because without it, all you would be is a walking, talking asshole."

"You think you can play with me and win?" he asks, his head tilting as I'm unable to stop the rock of my hips. He starts to harden inside me.

"I know I can." He brings me up into a sitting position, his cock moving inside me as he does. I moan, and he grunts before he pulls out of me and spins me around until I'm on my hands and knees. His warmth comes up behind me before his hand lands on the back of my neck, pinning my head into the furs. I growl as he parts my legs with his own, and I feel his cum leaking out of me, running down my thighs. He growls, gathering it with the head of his cock before he circles my entrance.

"Let's see how well you play, little wolf," he groans before slamming back inside me.

TWENTY NINE

RHEA

"Fuck," Darius groans, thrusting back into my already tender flesh.

He kneels behind me, his hand on my throat and an arm around my front to hold me against his chest as drives into me. I moan, rocking my hips to meet his thrusts, our sweaty skin sliding together as I bring my hands up to hold on to the sides of his neck. His hand moves across my chest, squeezing my breast and playing with my nipple, making my breath hitch. My orgasm builds, my pussy clenching around him as my movement speeds up. He leaves my breast and skims his hand down until he reaches my clit, rubbing circles over the sensitive bud that causes me to buck against him.

"Already there, little wolf?" he taunts, nipping at my shoulder. His fingers tighten around my throat as he tilts my head back to rest on his shoulder.

"Yes," I whimper, as he nuzzles my neck, his breathing heavy. Those far too skillful fingers of his speed up over my clit, his thrusts coming faster, and I can't hold it off. I shatter. My fingers dig into his neck, my back arching as my pussy spasms around him. He holds me in place, growling in satisfaction as the hand pressing against my pussy keeps me still as he fills me with his cum.

I slump back against him, moaning with little aftershocks

while his hand moves lazily down to my entrance, feeling where he's inside of me. He guides me forward by my throat until the side of my face hits the furs beneath us, and my exhausted body melts into them. He pulls out slowly, then gets up and walks toward the water. I watch him though half lidded eyes, feeling his cum drip out of me as he ducks his head under a flow of water. I follow that flow, watch it travel over his back where my scratches are along with his tattoos that mirror the ones on his torso, down and over his sculpted ass to the back of his thighs.

It really is unfair that he has a body like that, but I can't help preening at the marks I've left on his body. Something about them satisfies me in a way I haven't felt before.

"Your heat is nearly over," he states as he turns and walks back over to me. I hum and roll on my side away from him, too exhausted to hold a conversation.

We've been fucking and fighting for three days. The marks on my body show as much, just like mine on him. I have bite marks on my shoulders, chest and inner thighs. I also have no doubt his handprints are bruised on my throat and hips where he's gripped me as he drove into me. I squirm a little at the reminder. It's been a haze after the first time we fucked. The memories are blurry, but there is no doubt from the soreness of my pussy that we fucked. A lot.

Fingers trail up the back of my thighs before lifting the one on top slightly. He freezes, and I feel his stare on my center, on his cum staining my thighs. A low sound escapes him before he drops my leg abruptly. I groan as the sudden movement, pain shooting through me.

"Oww," I grumble.

"You can handle some pain, it's not like you don't deserve it," he growls.

"You're really doing this now?" I huff, snuggling into the furs more and closing my eyes. "Don't be an asshole, Darius. I'm tired." He can take his ass elsewhere. I need to sleep.

We have been in the same space constantly for three days, and he's not once brought up anything from outside the cave. No Elites, no laws, nothing. We have been too focused on each other, on him owning my body like it has never been before. I let him, my heat tearing down any willpower I had left. He and I both knew I wouldn't be able to resist.

He grabs me, my body moving like a rag doll as he pins me down with his weight on top of me. I growl, opening my eyes and giving him a deadly stare. "I will do what I want, when I want, Rhea." His fingers tighten around my throat, cutting off most of my air. "Stay still."

"You have to be kidding me?" I croak. What suddenly crawled up his ass? "I'm not in the mood for your shit, Darius." I dig my nails into his hand around my throat, drawing blood as Runa lends me some strength.

"I don't give a fuck." He slips between my thighs and shoves into me, his smirk cruel as he tears a small groan from me. "That's it, little wolf. Feel what I'm doing to you."

He rocks into me, his fingers tightening around my neck, and my eyes roll into the back of my head. He leans down, his breath at my ear as he slams into me, over and over again. With every slam of his hips, they become harder, angry. My vision starts to blur, both my hands digging into his wrist as he groans above me, enjoying me at his mercy. He lets his fingers up every now and again so I can get air in as he drives into me, before cutting it off all over again. He keeps his pace, only slowing when I'm nearing my orgasm to deny me of my release, and I shake my head in frustration, tears stinging my eyes.

His fingers suddenly tighten around my throat painfully, his other hand grabbing my hair and yanking my head back as he growls into my neck, his thrusts becoming jerky until I feel his essence filling me. His fingers loosen, and I take in gulp full of air, tears sliding down the side of my face at him getting his release and denying me of mine. Over the last few days, he's never left me without coming. In fact, he's pushed my limits demanding more, like he needed to see how many times he could make me come. And now he just decides not to give it to me?

When I can speak, I grab his hair, shoving him away from my neck as he laughs. "Get the fuck out of my cave, Darius." He slips out of my sore flesh, standing in one fluid motion as he looks down at me.

He takes me in, from my feet all the way up to my center, his eyes resting there, watching his cum leak out of me with furrowed brows. He then takes in his markings on my breasts, my shoulders and neck until he reaches my watery eyes. His voice is cold when he speaks, his lips curling as he looks at me like I'm a piece of shit, like what he sees disgusts him. I barely suppress a flinch.

"You weren't a bad fuck, Rhea." He shrugs, tilting his head at me. "I wonder how many males have slipped between your thighs beforehand though. Is that how you became Alpha of this pack? You fucked the old one, and he had an unfortunate accident?" I jolt at his words. "You say bad shit happened here, yet I don't see the cause of that bad shit. Only scared people and you opening your legs so easily to anyone willing to climb between them." He tilts his head the other way. "Or is that lying, bitch mouth of yours still spewing bullshit and manipulating her own pack?"

I'm frozen, wondering where this is coming from. What caused this change in him to make him so cruel? We have been at somewhat of a truce. I let him inside my body, and he wanted it. He came to me. Yet I let just anyone in? Why is he doing this now?

I get to my feet, my legs shaky with exhaustion as I face him.

I stand there, bare, trembling and feeling more vulnerable than I can ever remember while his cum drips down my thighs. But my voice is hard, no emotion shows in my tone as I tell him, "Careful of the words you throw around so carelessly, Darius. Be careful how far you dig, because you might not like what you find just below."

"You think I care what you think? All I want right now is to find this missing woman, get the fuck out of here, and drag you and the rest of your pack with me to the Highers. Don't get attached to my cock, Rhea. It's not yours. You're just a hole for me to use, and I will make that a part of your punishment." He flicks my hair over my shoulder before his fingers press into one of the many bite marks I have there. I grind my teeth, refusing to show him the pain he's causing me. "By the time I'm done with you, little wolf, you will be all used up, crying and begging for mercy." He gets lower, his face now directly in front of mine as our noses touch while I keep silent. "But you'll do well to remember, I have none."

He stands, picking up his discarded clothes as the space fills with tension, and without another word, he walks out of the cave. Walks away from me again. My legs collapse beneath me, unable to hold me up any longer, and I grip the furs, my head hanging low. I'm exhausted. Not just physically, but mentally, and his words hit harder, deeper than they ever should.

Having the Elites here has me on edge. I'm waiting for the moment they find Sarah and drag us all back to the Highers. Kade is acting differently, and that's making me question if I can even help him. I'm trying to find a way to get Darius to keep Eridian out of my punishment and let it remain a secret. I thought I could convince him to keep the pack out of it. I thought if he saw them and realized how strange their behavior is, he might consider that they needed to stay here. I thought with what we shared over the last few days I could speak to him, maybe even soften him a little toward me. But how fucking stupid am I? I have just given him another way to punish me, another way for him to slowly break me down. He's only the second person I have let into my body, and he treated it like it was nothing, accusing me of giving myself to many. When to me, it was so much more than that.

My skin feels like it's crawling. I feel dirty with his cum dried on my thighs and shame fills me with what I did here. In my space. I clench my eyes closed, biting my lip until I draw blood, until the pain brings me back to the now. It's for the pack, I remind myself. It's for Kade.

I'll do whatever it takes. This was my choice. This is my body. No big deal.

I repeat this over and over in my head as I stand. As I walk into the pool and wash his scent off of me, rubbing furiously at my skin even as Runa whines at me. As I get out and walk numbly toward my carvings, my bare feet slapping against the stone floor. I repeat it as I pick up the wolf I made years ago and examine its twin tails. I bring it with me and lay down in my furs.

Wisps float near me, the glow reaching past my closed eyes, and I pull furs over me to warm the chill in my bones. Fingers run through my hair. It's gentle, soothing.

If only they could sooth my soul instead as I drift off to sleep.

"Mommy?"

"Yes, sweetheart?"

"Are you and Daddy bloodmates?" I ask, picking the grass between my fingers.

She sits next to me in our garden, a sad smile on her face as she replies. "We are not, but we chose each other. Love is love, and me and your daddy are very much in love. It's how we made you."

"With love?" I wrinkle my nose at her.

"Yes." She laughs, and bops my nose. "Without our love, you wouldn't be here, and you are very precious to us." Her face turns serious as her eyes, the same as mine, look back at me. "Love when you can, sweetheart, and love hard. You don't know when it will be taken away from you. So keep it close. Hold it close and never let go."

"But I love you and Daddy and you're here. You are always here," I say with a frown.

"We won't always be with you, Milal," she tells me as her eyes tighten.

"What? Why?" I grab onto her as she pulls me closer, and I burrow into her side. She's scaring me. Mommy never scares me.

"Sometimes people don't understand where we come from, and they don't like it."

"They don't like us? But we're good, we're fun!" I cry.

"That may be true, but others don't believe it. It's why you can't show it, sweetheart. You must not reveal it." She cups my cheeks in her hands and wipes my tears away. Her forehead rests against mine as she whispers, "I pray to the Gods that you find your bloodmate, my darling girl. For he will protect you more than most." Tears spill over her eyes, and I don't like Mommy crying. Mommy never cries. "I pray he keeps you safe."

I jolt awake, gasping for breath as tears roll down my face. I clench the wolf carving to my chest, holding it close as I silently cry. I cry for my parents, for the lost time we should have had together because of another. I cry for my soul and the sins that stain it that can never be wiped clean. And I cry for my heart. The heart that is bound to get broken many more times than it already has by what I fear is to come.

THIRTY

RHEA

I walk slowly down the stairs, rubbing my tired eyes. My sleep was fleeting after yesterday in the cave, and I stayed up late to see if Kade came home. He never did. I wanted him close, needing to see him, but he's shut down the link yet again. Hearing voices coming from the dining area, I go across the hall and enter through the open doorway, seeing the Elites and some of mine eating their breakfast at the table. I blink slowly, taking them all in as they look back at me. I ignore them and head into the kitchen to make coffee, passing Zaide leaning against the wall, staring at Colten with curious eyes.

"Are there any other areas that you can think of where this woman and the one who was with her could have gone to?" I hear Damian ask the room.

"We have shown you all the places we can think of in The Deadlands without entering anywhere dangerous," Taylor replied gruffly. Coffee made, I hop up onto the counter and watch them while they talk. Making extra sure I keep my eyes off Darius while everyone looks me over, no doubt seeing the marks that Darius gave me during my heat. I'm only wearing shorts and a t-shirt, so they aren't hard to miss. My cheeks heat.

Leo speaks up next, shaking his blond head. "She's dead, as well as her companion." I remain silent, hoping they stick to that conclusion. They won't be going home soon though as his men still need to heal.

"We assume the same thing for them both." Josh takes a sip of his drink before continuing. "There is no way they survived, especially if they haven't entered The Deadlands before, and I'm assuming they hadn't."

"Morning, Rhea," Sebastian calls, looking over his shoulder at me from where he sits, eyes on my legs as they swing back and forth. I grunt in response and look out my window. It's still early morning, the sun barely up in the sky.

I really don't feel like talking much, my head still swimming with thoughts of what happened in the cave with Darius. His words cut me deep while I stood there naked and vulnerable, and I don't know why I'm letting him affect me so much. I suspect it's because I feel some sort of odd connection toward him. Though it may not be as odd as I think. Does he feel the same toward me? I doubt it with how he speaks to me. The problem is, if he is who I suspect he is, he's the Alpha of the Elite. He's close to the Highers, and that's even more worrying. Even more terrifying.

"Eat more," Hudson tells Colten, and I look over at him as he points to the food on Colten's plate.

Colten sighs, pushing his plate away. "I've eaten enough–"

"I know you," comes a deep voice, and all our heads snap to Zaide leaning against the wall with his eyes on Colten, who freezes at his words along with Hudson.

"What?" Colten asks, his brows low, the grip on his fork tightening.

"Your father is Alec Hallow. He was with the Elites for a long time. He said his son would be joining, but he didn't turn up for the rite of passage and shamed his whole family. Alec wanted him to join the Elites, find a mate, and have pups to continue the family line. He said his son was unworthy of their family name and disowned him after he didn't show up," Zaide informs us in a flat tone.

My mug is paused halfway to my mouth when his words hit me, and a slight tremor runs through my hands. I barely breathe as Hudson slowly stands from his seat next to Colten, whose brown eyes now vacant, staring into nothing. I put my mug down slowly on the counter and get down, walking toward Colten as Hudson takes measured steps toward Zaide. I hold my breath as Leo, Damian, and Jerrod stand, looking at us in confusion and no doubt prepared for anything as Darius just watches on, curious to see how this will pan out.

I position myself next to Colten, Josh standing at my side with Seb and Taylor close by. I put my hand on the back of his Colten's neck, rubbing circles there as I watch Hudson come to a stop in front of Zaide. There is no point trying to intervene, not when Zaide clearly knows who Colten is and Hudson's protectiveness over him. It would make things worse.

"Do not *ever* mention that family in front of Colten again." Hudson doesn't shout, he doesn't even raise his voice, but you can hear the deadly intent behind his spoken warning. A warning that he has every right to give.

Zaide tilts his head at Hudson, his eyes flicking to Colten's vacant ones briefly, looking him over before coming back to Hudson. He shrugs, nodding once, and I release the breath I was holding. Surprised, but thankful he agreed.

Hudson walks back over to Colten and grunts as he sees the look in his eyes. I move back, giving his neck one last gentle rub, and let Hudson deal with the situation. Crouching in front of him, Hudson lifts a hand and grabs his jaw gently, giving him a little shake. "Come on, pup. Let's go for a run," he murmurs. Colten's eyes go to Hudson's, and he nods woodenly before getting up and letting Hudson guide him out of the cabin.

I wait until I hear the door close before I speak, getting my words out before the questions start. "Sit down," I tell them all.

"I will explain."

"You better do just that, Rhea. What happened to you all living here from birth?" Leo demands, and I swing a hard glare his way, letting Runa come through my eyes.

"I said I will explain, and I will. So sit the fuck down before I put you down again, Leo," I spit, ignoring his growl. "And you." I point at Zaide. "Never mention that fucking piece of shit family around Colten again, like Hudson said. Or it won't be just him you will have to deal with." Without waiting for his response, I take a seat in the space Colten left as Josh sits down next to me, squeezing my hand where it rests on top of the table. A low rumble echoes through the room, and we all freeze. I peek at Darius through my lashes curiously as he glares at Josh's hand. I move it away.

Elites on one side, Eridian on the other, our lines divided. I can feel their anger at me for lying about us all being here since birth, but I don't care. It's not the only thing I lied about, and I didn't exactly expect Zaide to know Colten's family.

I link my hands in front of me. "Colten came here a few years ago. His… family were not happy with his life choices to say the least, and he had to get away." I pause, licking my dry lips before I continue. "He was lucky he came here. If he didn't, he would be dead, they would have killed him. They nearly did."

"No way," Leo scoffs, and I scowl at him. "I remember the Hallows. They're good people, and Alec was a damn good Elite."

"You saw what they wanted you to see. Wolves hide monsters beneath their fur, Leo." I shake my head at all of them. "You all need to open your fucking eyes, and see people for who they are, not be blinded by their false intentions."

"We're Elites, wolf. We're not blinded by anything," Damian chimes in, and I huff out an infuriated breath.

"Your arrogance will cost you," I assure him. "The Elites

have been around for hundreds of years, said to be made by the Highers council after the King of Vrohkaria died. Can you tell me why it was formed?" I ask him.

"The Elites were made to protect the lands against all threats. It's an honor to become an Elite, an even greater honor when you have proven yourself enough to become a Higher if that's what you want," Damian says.

I look out the window and try to reign my anger in. An honor? Yeah fucking right. Where is the honor in turning a blind eye to the suffering in packs? They protect the lands from creatures, but what about the monsters in our homes? Who protects us from them? Is it honorable to look someone in the eye and brush off their desperation as rambling nonsense like they did with Sybill and Samantha? What about Katy and Oscar, begging on a dirt path for help? What about me when people came to see me? My fingers clench around each other in front of me on the table at the thought of us begging for help yet receiving none from those that are meant to protect us. All Elites are the same. Memories bombard my mind, and I take in a ragged breath.

"When I see this honor you speak of, when I see the Elites truly protect Vrohkaria from the true threat, then I will honor you for what you are. Whether you believe what I said about Colten's family is up to you," I grind out to Damian, not looking at him in case I launch myself at him over the table. "But it is the truth."

"I don't know who you think you are." Leo stands, putting his hands on the table, and I look at him as he leans forward toward me. "But you are nothing but a little girl playing Alpha. You have been here all your life?" he mocks. "Then how the fuck do you know about honor? The Elites? Gods, even what goes on outside this fucking valley? No, you just stay here, hidden away and let everyone else fucking rot! You know what you are?" He leans even closer to me over the table, and Darius stills. "A pathetic, weak, selfish cunt who doesn't have an honorable bone in her fucking body."

"Weak little girl. Come on, stand for us! Don't you want to eat tonight? Do you not want little Kaden over here to eat?"

"Pathetic, can't even do as she's told. She's fucking useless! Throw her back inside her cage."

"Aww, are you crying again? I'll give you something to cry about, bitch."

I'm suddenly hauled back, hands dragging me away from the table while I blink the room back into focus. Sound enters my ears slowly, like I'm just coming up out of the water, and growls and grunts hit me. I shake my head and look over to see Josh on top of Leo, laying into him as blood stains his fist. Leo lifts his elbow and aims for Josh's face, the blow causing him to fall to the side. They both get to their feet, ready to go again, when Darius lets out a menacing growl so fierce it rattles the windows. The room stops, everyone barely breathing as my eyes are drawn to Darius as he gets to his feet with a snarl on his face.

"What the fuck was that?" he questions, and I look to Josh and Leo, waiting for their reply in a daze as Taylor keeps his hold on me.

When none comes, my eyes slide back to Darius. It's then I realize he wasn't talking to them, he was talking to me. His eyes hold mine as I waver on my feet a little, the memories making my stomach turn as he prowls around the table and comes to a stop in front of me. Taylor lets go of my arms, but stays behind me as Seb moves closer. Josh watches Darius warily as he takes a step toward me, concern etched onto his face.

"I said, what the fuck was that?" he repeats to me when I just stare up at him in confusion. I look around the room. My guys have worry in their eyes while the Elites are cautious and curious.

What the fuck?

My brows lower. "What was what?" I try to think what he's talking about and come up empty. "I didn't do anything."

"You blanked out. Your eyes went darker, and you were staring into nothing. I tried to talk to you, but you wouldn't answer," he growls as he looms over me. Is that…concern in his eyes?

"Did I do that?" I ask Josh through the link.

He replies instantly. *"Yeah, is it happening again? If it is–"*

Darius grabs my jaw, shaking it a little when he demands, "Stop talking through the link, little wolf." The link shuts down.

"How do you do that?" I rip my face from his fingers and take a step back.

"What the fuck happened after Leo spoke to you?" he counters, ignoring my question.

Neither one of us breaks our stare off, neither one of us backs down as his eyes roam my features. Josh clears his throat and comes to stand beside me, pulling my stare away from Darius. I look him over, his lip is split, and he has blood coming out of his nose.

"You good?" he asks me, reaching out and squeezing my hand, and I see Darius's jaw tick out the corner of my eye.

I nod at him and take a breath. "Let's finish our conversation, shall we?" I don't wait for them to answer. I just pick up my chair from the floor where it must have fallen over and take a seat, Josh in the seat next to me again and Taylor and Seb sit on my other side.

I hold my breath while I wait for Darius to take his seat, still not liking him at my back. As everyone picks up chairs and seats themselves, I calm my nerves from the memory of a time I wished I could forget. I wipe my sweaty palms on my shorts and shift in my seat. Taylor nudges my knee with his, and I look at him and give him a small smile.

Darius hasn't moved yet, his stare focused on the side of my face like he can pick me apart and see all of me. I feel he could if he really wanted too.

"What else have you lied about? We can't believe a word that comes out of your mouth," Darius says, his tone hard and demanding as he eventually takes his seat. "You won't answer questions, and you only tell us things when you have little choice to do so."

"I have told you again and again that I will not tell you about any of my pack members' lives. I have told you the basics of Colten's because Zaide recognized him. If you want the rest, ask him," I dare. "Hudson won't be happy with the attempt though, and neither will I."

"You don't scare me, little wolf," he states, and I shrug. Just because I don't scare him doesn't mean I can't slice his throat if I have to. He smirks like he can hear my thoughts, and my lips peel back at the asshole.

"Try me, asshole. See how far you get," I challenge, and Jerrod huffs out a laugh. The red head is clearly amused, but I'm deadly serious.

"I have tried you," he murmurs, licking his lips as his pupils dilate. "And I find I like playing with you." I shift in shift in my seat, the ache in my body a reminder at how he owned it. I was not expecting his words after the way he left last night, with the things he said to me… Is he playing me? Using me? It would make sense as we are using each other to try and get what we want, though he has no reason to touch me to take me to the Highers. He can just drag me there with the threat of Eridian over my head, he's already doing so.

A laugh comes from further down the table, and I see Sebastian looking between us at the bite marks and scratches the two of us have with a grin on his face. "You know," he chuckles and says. "The best fucks are the hate kind."

"Sebastian!" I snap, glaring at him even as my cheeks heat. He winks back, smiling like he knows something I don't.

"Come on, Alpha," he purrs, his voice silky smooth, and I feel rather than see Darius tense. "Releasing some tension is a good thing– Oww!" he whines as Josh slaps the back of his head.

"Thank you, Josh. It was either that or the knife." I pull out said knife from my boot and start chipping away at the table in front of me.

"And who taught you how to use a knife?" Sebastian lifts an eyebrow at me, putting his head in his hand as he leans an elbow on the table.

"You," I admit, pointing my blade at him. "The student surpasses the master." I grin, feeling some of the hazy darkness lift from my memories. I close an eye, pretending to throw my knife at him. The bastard doesn't even move.

"Fucking children," Damian mutters, while Zaide and Jerrod grunt in agreement.

"Smiling won't fucking kill you, you know?" I tell him, the miserable idiot.

"What is there to smile about?" Damian asks. "I've been stuck in The Deadlands for weeks and weeks, looking for a dead woman with a time limit over my head and staying in a place that has the bare minimum. Sure, I'm all smiles."

This little shit. "You know." I fake a smile. "If your stay in our subpar home is as awful as you say, you're *very* welcome to fuck off back where you came from." I bat my lashes at him. "I'll even help you pack."

"We have a few weeks left to fin–"

"Alpha!" A scream comes from my doorway, and I shoot to my feet in an instant, my chair slamming to the floor while I rush for the front door. I enter the hallway and see Sybill staggering inside, tears down her face. My heart instantly stops.

I run to her and grab her shoulders as she falls to the floor. I go down with her. "What's wrong?!" I panic, making my voice harsher than I intended it to be.

"S… Sam," she gasps. "I can't find Sam anywhere." I snap my head to Josh, but he's already aiming for my front door, Seb and Taylor following.

"What do you mean? Where did you last see her? Did she seem okay?"

Sybill shakes her head, a sob escaping her. "She was last at the river earlier today, but she doesn't go further than that. I went back and checked on her when she hadn't come back for a while, but she wasn't there. She's been quiet and jumpy the last few days, I thought she may have wanted a bit of time alone, but now she's gone." She grabs my hands and squeezes. Sam doesn't know the forest very well. She's only been out there a few times and only if she's with someone. "Please find her. Please." Sybill begs, lowering her head to my hands. "She wouldn't just run off, and she would tell me if she was with Kade."

I pull her to me, giving her a quick hug before pulling back. "Stay here and wait for me. It'll be okay." I help her stand and take her over to the seats in my living area. "I'll find her, I promise. Try not to worry."

THIRTY ONE

Rhea

I race for the door, grabbing my blades and holders and attaching them around my thighs. I waste no time running out the door, jumping the decking steps and heading for the gathering. I sprint, Runa helping me to reach the others as quickly as possible without question. I try to reach Kade through the link as I look around for any sign of Sam in the area, but he still has me shut out.

"No one has seen her," Josh tells me when I reach him, Taylor, Seb, and Hudson. Their postures tense.

"She's gone into the forest," I tell them, and start heading toward the river we use to get water. "She's only been out there a few times with her mom and Kade. She won't have a clue where she's going."

"Why would she stay out there on her own anyway?" Taylor asks, searching the floor for any sign of footprints.

"Sybill doesn't know. It's not like Sam to do something like this," I rush out. "She's not inside the barrier, we would know." Someone would have seen her if she was. "Fuck," I mutter when we pass the lilk trees and reach the river, my eyes glancing everywhere trying to see if she's here. She's not, and there is no scent of her either.

"I'll go right and see if I can see any tracks or pick up her scent," Taylor tells me, and he speeds off.

"Josh, go across the river and search that side. I'll follow it down. Seb, go further out to Josh. If you see Colten, tell him to go up the river and see if she went that way. I'm sure she's only been as far as this so we should find her soon. She couldn't have gotten far." I scan the river, the banks and the ground around it, trying to see *anything*.

"Where do you want us to search?" Darius's voice sounds behind me suddenly, making me jump. I didn't even know he was following us. I'm surprised by his question, but with more people searching, we can find her quicker.

"Split your Elites up with mine," I tell him, already moving down the side of the river. "If you see her, make sure one of mine goes to her. It will scare her off if an Elite does it."

I rush forward, letting my senses roam free while Darius joins me. All I hear is the water from the river and sticks crunching underneath our feet. Not a single sound of another person can be heard. The forest is quiet, too quiet. I stop when the river splits off into two different directions and look at the bank, seeing if I can see any signs of her. I walk into the river and wade through the water, ignoring cool liquid splashing against me. Reaching the other side, I stand on the edge and look down, no footprints, no disturbed earth. I look up and down along the grassy ground and see nothing to suggest another person was here apart from me and Darius.

What if she fell in and got swept down river?

My head snaps to the water at the thought and panic really starts to set in. "Shit." I jog alongside the river, checking the ground and the water for any signs of her. Darius stays on the other side, keeping pace with me. The longer we follow the river, the more I feel dread starting to set in. The river deepens and the water turns rapid down here, violent and deadly. It's like a vice grips around my heart, squeezing it until I wheeze out a breath. Where in the Gods is she?

"Anything?" I ask Josh, hoping he picked up something.

"Nothing yet," he replies through the link, his voice strained.

"Can she swim?" Darius asks from the other side of the river, looking at the water like I am.

"I don't know," I choke out, my throat tight at the thought of her not knowing how to swim. Why haven't we been teaching the kids how to swim?

"Surely you would know if she can swim. She's what, ten?"

"Thirteen, and I don't know, Darius!" I snap at him, then come to a sudden halt when I hear a snap to the left of me. "Sam!" I call out, rushing toward the sound through the trees.

The scent of Kade hits me just before dark gray fur appears. I go to him, not caring about the fact that the last time he was in wolf form he was about to attack me. His blue eyes look between me and Darius, and I grip his muzzle in my hands, making him focus on me. "Kade, Sam is missing. She was last seen at the part of the river we use to collect water. She's not been seen since. Have you seen her?"

"No." He shakes his head, his ears standing up and alert as panic shows in his eyes. *"Has she been caught up in the river?"* He moves around me, lowering his nose to the ground and takes deep breaths, trying to catch her scent.

"I don't know! Can you go on the other side of Darius and search that side of the forest? You're faster with your wolf, and then you can meet up with us after you have searched there." He nods, his eyes full of concern as he takes off, crossing the river and runs past Darius.

"Why aren't you in your wolf?" Darius questions as we continue moving down the river.

"Why aren't you?" I counter. If I could be in my wolf I would, but I can't. I don't need the fucking reminder of how useless I am.

"I'm keeping pace with you, and you told us not to approach

Sam if we find her."

"When," I growl, glaring over at him.

"What?" His brows scrunch as he looks at me over the river.

"When we find her," I tell him forcefully. "It's not if we find her. It's when."

There's no other option.

"How much further does the river go?" Darius asks. It's the first time either of us has spoken in hours, too busy searching for Sam. The sun is slowly setting, and we are quickly running out of daylight. We have to find her soon.

"Not far. We're nearly at the edge of the forest, coming up to the Unforgivable Sea."

Kade and Josh haven't found any sign of Sam in all the time we've been looking. Not a single trace. How could she have just disappeared? The only explanation, which is one I don't want to think about, is that she's got caught up in the river. But it's calm where we collect water. It doesn't become violent until you travel further down, sweeping you into its current and not letting you go.

"The edge of the forest?" Darius wonders, looking around to keep an eye out. I don't know why he's helping me, I would have thought he wouldn't care. But here he is, helping us look for her.

"Yeah. The river opens up more toward the end of the forest. Its current goes to the crest of a waterfall between an opening in the cliffs that goes over into the Unforgivable Sea. That's where the forest ends. It's the only way out of the valley apart from climbing up the cliffs that surround us."

"When I was on the top of the cliffs, I saw the Unforgivable Sea from where I stood, but I thought the valley would slope down into it. Not just stop abruptly."

I glance over at him as I answer, our pace now a walk since my energy is fading. He doesn't look the least bit out of breath, his movements still strong. I'm panting slightly, my walk is more pained with my whole body aching. "It just stops," I tell him, shrugging. "The only way to get to the sea is down by the waterfall, and no one survives it. The cliffs cage the sides of the water, so you can't walk near the waterfall and try to climb down that way. Before the cliffs cage on either side, there are two statues facing each other on opposite banks. Their hands reach out to one another across the water, their stone faces sad, pained, and desperate. Apparently two lovers died there, swept away by the rapids and into the Unforgivable Sea. The female fell in, and the male dove in to try to save her, but he was unable to get to her and they went over the edge. We call it Lovers Rest.

"The statues were built as tribute to them, but also as a warning for others to be careful. We have unfortunately had some who have used that warning as an invitation." I swallow hard at their memory, at my memory of standing there and ready for it all to end. "When life gets too much for so long, they come here and give themselves over to the waters, finding peace the only way they can, in death." I don't know why I told him that last bit. Maybe exhaustion, or maybe to make sure he understands that down here is dangerous. Deadly. I just hope Sam didn't come this way.

He's quiet after my words, his green eyes searching my face until I look away from him, feeling too raw and not wanting him to see the failure on my face at not saving the ones who chose the sea. I never know when people sneak around to go to the end of the forest. I saw no warning signs in the people we lost. No cause for me to be overly concerned. I should have looked more closely. I should have known they were hurting so badly they would choose death over life. I should have seen something.

I stop dead in my tracks.

Is this what Sam chose? She couldn't handle her memories anymore and came out here? She had been withdrawn, and Sybill said she's been quiet. Am I going to find her scent at the edge of the river as she enters the water to be swept away? I squeeze my eyes shut, feeling tears well.

"Rhea?" Darius asks, his voice low, a question in his tone. "What is it?" I snap my eyes open and pick up the pace again, not answering him. I need to know she hasn't been there. I need to know she hasn't chosen this.

The trees get thinner, the river opening up more and the current picks up speed, causing me and Darius to be further away from each other as we push forward. I clear the trees on my side of the river and my eyes instantly go toward the crest of the waterfall, seeing nothing. The statues in front of the base of the cliffs haunt me with the reminder of how many people have lost their lives here.

"Sam!" I shout, rushing forward into the open area and stopping at the edge of the water, turning in a circle looking for her. "Sam!" I stop spinning and stay still, my senses open to listen for any noises, anything that could be her. Nothing. Nothing apart from the rapids and the mess of emotions running through me. I'm happy she isn't here, but hurting because we still haven't found her.

Where are you, Samantha?

Wait. I tilt my head toward a sound and look over at Darius who is doing the same. His dark head turns forward until it stops, and I follow his gaze to the female statue on his side of the river.

He walks forward slowly before stopping ten feet away from

it. That's when I hear it, a whimper. My breath stalls in my lungs as I go toward the edge of the bank, walking along as far as possible to the water until I'm parallel with Darius.

"Sam," I call out gently, and a small cry reaches my ears. My breath whooshes out of me when I recognize it as Sam, and I move to the male statue on my side, my eyes never leaving the female one. *"Kade, we have her. She's at the female statue at Lovers Rest."* My eyes flick to Darius as he stays in his spot, watching me and not moving any closer.

"Sam, sweetheart. Are you alright?" Another cry. "I'm going to come round and get you, okay? I won't be long, just… just stay where you are. Please." I see a flicker of movement behind the statue, and her head peeks out from behind it. My heart breaks at the sight. Her eyes are red from crying, tears running down her face, and she's shaking, her body jolting with every tremor. When she sees me, her face crumples, and she starts to move out from behind the statue toward me. "Stop!" I shout, my voice a screech of panic when she doesn't realize how close she is to the water. It's splashing up against the edges a few feet from her, the current fast and deadly. She stops, her body jolting at my harsh tone before she moves back to behind the statue. I hold my hands up at her. "Sam, you need to stay there, okay? It's dangerous." I gulp and move my eyes to Darius, who's moved a little closer, slowly as if to not startle her. I look between him and Sam, wondering what's for the best when Kade's wolf breaks the tree line on Darius's side.

Thank the Gods.

Kade slows until he's standing beside Darius, who looks down at him briefly. Darius steps back and away from him, letting him go to her. Kade moves slowly toward the female statue, emitting a gentle growl as he pads toward it. Sam's eyes move from mine as she peaks her head around the female's legs at the sound, her tears coming in full force. She maneuvers herself on her knees and grips the side of the stone as she leans around it to see Kade coming. She suddenly stands on shaking legs, and I let out a cry of distress, my stomach dropping as my feet hit the edge of the bank, hand reaching out as if I can grab her and keep her safe from falling.

She doesn't fall though. She grips the stone and moves around the legs until she's running and heading straight for Kade, her eyes locked on him. Sam throws herself at him, her face burrowing into his neck. When I hear her sobs, I drop back on my ass. My breathing picks up, short, shallow pants coming from my tight chest. My fingers tremble as my vision waivers in and out, and I put my head in my hands, trying to calm down. She could have fucking fallen in. She could have been swept over the edge into the Unforgivable Sea, and I wouldn't have been able to grab her. I wouldn't have been able to reach her and keep her safe. She could have been lost to us.

I shake my head and squeeze my eyes shut, the vision of it happening replaying over and over again through my head. A soft touch on the back of my neck has more tears forming in my eyes with how gentle it is. How did he even get across? Hands reach for my waist, and then I'm being picked up, cradled against a solid chest as his scent starts to calm me. I breathe it in deep, and the sound of the river gets quieter, the thoughts of her falling in fading. I move my hands from my face and my gaze lands on Darius, his face so close to mine as he carries me away from the water's edge. My breathing slows, my body shakes less as I stare into his green eyes that are grounding me, not blinking for a single moment as I take in deep breaths and slowly exhale, copying his own.

He watches me, looking over my face until he stops when he notices the wetness in my eyes. He places me down onto my feet gently, keeping one hand on my waist as if to keep me steady, as he brings his other up to my face. I don't move as he runs a finger softly underneath my lower eyelash, collecting a tear there, and my breath catches. He examines my tear intently, his eyes squinting as it runs down the side of his finger before he brings those light-green eyes back to my ice-blue ones. The world stops at the look of determination etched on his face. When he speaks, it's soft, but with demand.

"The only tears I want to see in your eyes, little wolf, are the ones I put there from pleasure," he murmurs, a frown appearing on his face. "I don't like to see them otherwise, it makes me... angry."

"Angry?" I whisper, stunned and confused by his words.

He nods, looking at the wetness on his finger. "Yeah, angry, because something else caused you to shed tears, and I prefer to cause them as you scream for me and me alone." He puts his finger in his mouth, and I watch in rapt attention as he tastes my tear, his eyes capturing mine with a look I'm not sure I understand. "So don't shed a tear unless you are on my cock, Rhea."

I blink, and then eventually come out of my stupor. "Listen, asshole." I try to keep my voice hard, but it comes out choked as I bring a finger up and poke his chest, ignoring the smirk that spreads across his damn kissable lips. "None of my tears belong to you. They're mine and mine alone, and when they come, it will be of my choosing." With a huff I turn on my heel, clearing my throat and ignoring him as I make my way to a safer spot in the river where I can cross. His body heat caresses my back as he stays close, forever my shadow babysitter as he chuckles.

"Keep those eyes open, little wolf, and have them on me," he says, and I look over my shoulder at him. I have no idea what he means by that, but the seriousness of his tone sets me on edge.

I continue on, I need to get Sam back home, and we have a long walk ahead. I haven't got the energy or patience to deal with his ass right now, but at least I'm calmer now than I was before.

And that's all because of my enemy, who I won't thank.

Because then things may start to shift between us, and I will have no idea what to do about that.

THIRTY TWO

RHEA

We walk back slowly Sam on the back of Kade who's still in his wolf. Axis seemed to want her close and refused to move until Sam was safely on his back. She seemed to know what he wanted straight away, and she hopped onto him without question, without fear, which makes me think they have done this often. Sam kept staring at Darius, her face pale and hands shaky as she gripped the wolf's fur tightly, so we hung back from them to give her space. She's been sleeping for a little while now, exhaustion winning out over her fear of Darius being near her. Seeing her look so small and fragile cracks my heart open.

She's not the only one exhausted though. I haven't slept properly since the news of the Elites from Illium, and after my heat and today's emotional strain, I'm ready to fall flat on my face. I yawn, bringing a hand up to cover my mouth as I sway to the side before I right myself. *Just a little further, Runa. Not long now.* I feel her grumble inside me, her last reserves of energy running low as well.

We come to the part of the river where we collect water, and I see Josh up ahead, his gray eyes showing their relief before they quickly change to concern as he looks at me. He comes forward, running a hand over Kade's muzzle, careful not to disturb Sam, before he comes at me. Without warning, he scoops me up into his arms, and I go without protest, snuggling into his familiar chest and his comforting scent. I know Josh will get me home. I breathe a sigh of relief at the pressure being taken off my body. Again, without warning, I'm jostled and ripped out of Josh's arms and moved into another. My eyes spring open, and I glare at Darius. Josh's growl is ferocious at me being taken so roughly from his arms, and Darius growls back at him, unbothered.

Darius doesn't look at me as he walks toward my home. "Just what do you think you're doing?" I grind out, wriggling about and trying to get him to drop me. His hold tightens as he ignores me.

"You can't just grab at her when you want," Josh barks at him. "She's not a fucking toy to be passed around."

Darius stills, his head turning toward Josh with a move that is all animal. "I will do whatever I want, and she is to be whatever I want her to be." His tone is cold, his eyes sharp toward Josh, and my muscles tense at his sudden display of hostility.

I push out of Darius's hold while he's distracted by Josh, landing on my feet and stumbling a little. I rub my temples, just wanting the day to be done, but know it's not over yet. I open my mouth to cuss him out when Sam whimpers from Kade's back. My head swings her way, and I walk to her as Kade lets out a low growl. It's not for me this time, it's in displeasure that Sam is upset.

I reach their side and I grab Sam's hand, holding hers as she sleeps as we continue on. We leave Josh and Darius behind to size up each other's dicks, my focus on getting Sam home.

Josh has always been my protector since we left our old home. He's my brother in every way but blood. I don't think Darius sees it as that though. It's amusing and ridiculous that he seems to feel possessive of his *toy*.

When we hit the lilk trees, I try and guide a sleepy Sam off Kade's back, watching as she opens her sleepy eyes and snuggles closer to him, not letting go. "Come on," I tell her gently. "Kade will be back shortly. You know we can't go wolf inside Eridian."

She lets me take her off his back and I cradle her against me as Kade nuzzles her cheek. I hold Sam tightly as we walk, keeping silent as we pass a few people from the pack who visibly relax at seeing her. I give them a reassuring nod and continue.

I guide her past the gathering and up to the path that leads to my cabin, Taylor, Seb, Hudson, and Colten already there and waiting. They all let out a breath when they see us, and Taylor opens the door, letting us walk past as they stay outside. Padding down the hallway and through the open doorway of my sitting room, Sybill flies off her seat, rushing toward us and grabbing Sam in a tight hug as they both cry, holding one another close.

"Mom," Sam cries, burrowing her face in her shoulder.

"I'm here, I'm here," Sybill tells her over and over again.

I swallow the lump in my throat at seeing them embrace, at the look of sheer relief and love on Sybill's face to have her back in her arms. A mother holding her daughter so close, like she's afraid she will disappear. I give them a few moments together in peace as I turn to collect myself. That was me and my mom before it was stolen from us.

I take a seat across from them as they sit, huddled close together. I want to give Sam some time, but it's important I know what happened. I hear my door open, and Josh rounds the corner with Darius on his heels, their mouths both set in a tight line. Sam lets out a squeak, her body shaking as she sees Darius and hides her face from him.

I look to Darius and back to her, my brows scrunched in confusion. I know she's not great near males, but we and the Elites have been eating at the gathering for a while now, and she has been getting better in their presence. So what happened? "Sam?" I say gently. "What's wrong?" I stand and put myself between them, blocking Darius the best I can from her view. She doesn't answer me.

"Are you hurt?" Sybill asks her, moving her daughter back a little so her gaze can roam over her. Sam shakes her head, eyes to the floor as she gets as close to her mom as possible. She squeezes her eyes shut and opens her mouth to speak, but no sounds come from her.

She's petrified.

I kneel before her, looking at Josh and Darius before asking. "What are you scared of Sam? Nothing will hurt you here. I promise."

Her bottom lip trembles, and tears fall from her eyes. "There… there was a man in the forest," she whispers, her voice trembling.

I nod. "Yes, some of the Elites are camping in the forest while some of the females are in heat," I tell her gently.

She sniffles, shaking her head. "He was shocked to see me there at… at first, but then he told me to go with him," she whispers, and my blood turns cold, ice dripping into my veins as I still. The whole room stills. "I didn't want to, so I turned to come back home when he tried to grab me," she cries. "I was near the… the river so I ran across it when he tried to get me again. He started following me, and I heard strange noises, like whispers of voices all talking at once." She shivers, her breath hitching as more tears fall. "I ran," she sobs, her body curling in on herself. "I just ran and ran, and I didn't stop until I was at that statue."

Sybill pulls her closer as a deep, growl echoes throughout the space. I hold my hand out, waiting for him to come to me, knowing he needs to be close. *"Kade, calm. She's already scared,"* I urge him down the link. This time it isn't shut down.

I hear him take a deep breath before he puts his hand in mine, the warmth of his skin heating my own as I pull him down to the floor, his knees landing next to me. Sam's red rimmed eyes look up, and as soon as she sees Kade, she falls into his arms, burrowing into his neck. He pulls her close without question, and I see him swallow as her gut-wrenching sobs increase in volume, barely taking a breath between them.

The room is deathly quiet apart from Sam, and I lift my hand, rubbing soothing circles on her back while bringing my other hand to the back of Kade's nape, squeezing there lightly. He sighs, squeezing Sam closer, and we wait until her sobs calm down. I can feel Darius's eyes on us, watching everything we do, listening to what we're saying. His eyes are like a caress on my body as he stands at the back of the room, guarding yet imposing. I want him to hear this though, because I will rip apart whichever Elite attempted to grab her, and I will happily give them to Kade after I'm done with them. Because his eyes are deadly, dangerous and volatile.

"What did he look like, winglet?" Kade whispers against her hair.

"He was… was as tall as Josh, dark hair and his eyes were dark, but not. They changed color." Changed color? Was his wolf coming out? "They went to a lighter brown, then blue, darker I think. I don't really know. I just wanted to get away from him. I didn't like him or his smell."

"His smell?" Kade rumbles, pulling her back slightly to look down at her.

She nods. "He smelled bad. He smelled of iron, but bad iron and old." She shakes her head and looks at me as she shakes in Kade's arms. "I haven't smelled it before, I can't really tell you."

My brows furrow and I try to recall if I've smelled anything along the river like that, but I can't. I look at Josh who shakes his head, telling me he didn't smell anything either.

"Thank you for telling me." I drop my hands from Sam and Kade and stand, turning to Sybil. "You're both welcome to stay here if you like. Use the spare room at the back of the cabin."

"I'll think about it, Alpha. Thank you," Sybill murmurs, her eyes never leaving Sam's.

"Are you going to stay home?" I ask Kade, and he looks down at Sam, her eyes slowly shutting, her body snuggling against him. She's so tired.

"I'll stay until she is settled," he whispers, and I get up, touching my cheek to his before walking into the hallway with Darius and Josh on my tail.

"I want that Elite found," I whisper hiss at Darius as soon as we make our way outside of the cabin. Josh shuts the door behind us, standing beside me as Taylor, Seb, Hudson and Colten come closer, no doubt they listened to everything at the door.

"That's all well and good," Darius drawls. "But I don't have an Elite with me that matches the description of height, eye color, hair color, and smell." He shakes his head before folding his arms, looking down at me. "He wasn't one of my Elites."

"That's not possible," Taylor starts. "You guys are the only newcomers here. Who else could it have been? The only scents around here are the packs and Elites. We check the perimeter daily and no one has been in here." Taylor would know, he is responsible for this after all.

"It's not any of my Elites. I would know." Darius tilts his head. "You also didn't smell what she claims to have smelled by the river, and neither did I. Maybe she just got scared and imagined it."

"Are you fucking stupid!" I growl at him and he scowls. "That girl knows what is and what isn't scary to her, and a man scared her. She didn't just imagine it, she's thirteen." There is no way she did. I saw the fear in her eyes as she told me. There was someone here. Someone is in Eridian, and if Darius is right, it wasn't any of us.

Then who was it and how did they get in? I rub my arms, my body still feeling cold to my bones.

"Do you know what she meant by the smell?" Josh asks, scratching his chin in thought.

"I'm not sure," I reply, then look at Darius. "Have you?" I haven't been through all of Vrohkaria like he has. I've only been through a little portion of the lands and through The Deadlands to here. If anyone knows this smell, surely, he would.

His eyes turn unfocused for a second before he shakes his head. "No. Only old blood comes to mind when she mentioned bad iron, and you would find that on a rotting corpse, which is not something I'm assuming she came across." He pauses in thought before continuing. "I'll have my Elites that are not in The Deadlands search the forest and have Maize scry it as well if your adamant someone was really here."

I ignore his last words. "She won't be able to scry inside the lilk trees, but she could do the forest. Where is your witch anyway?" I ask Darius, looking around to see if I can spot her.

"Probably with my men in their cabin." His reply is blunt, and I can't help but look him over to see if he is affected by that. He isn't.

"I'll talk with whoever is searching the forest, I can help them look and we can speak to the ones camping out there too," Taylor tells Darius, and they walk down the deck steps.

"Wait," I call out and they both turn. To Darius I ask something that's been niggling at me. "Why are you helping?"

He thinks for a moment. "If someone was here, it might be the person who helped the missing woman in The Deadlands." His stare pins me to the spot, and I swallow, knowing that won't be the case. "We are on a time limit to find her, and my patience is running out. Rogures are slaughtering everything they can throughout Vrohkaria as we speak. We are needed out there, not wasting our time here."

So there is a time limit like Hudson said.

I fling my arms out. "Then why don't you just leave? Go

back?" He's the Alpha of the Elites, he can go back when he wants.

"I need to find this woman who has either been taken or is trying to escape her responsibilities," he grinds out, his jaw ticking.

Responsibilities? Like what? Being in a fucking hole on her back for how many years for sick fucks to rape?

I take a deep breath "She is most likely dead. I've told you neither she or the other person would not survive out in The Deadlands. The search for her is useless."

He looks at me curiously, his jaw ticking. "I have some time left, the Highers sent us here personally and their request needs to be fulfilled before we return home. Either she is found dead or alive, or we go back empty handed with no answers, which isn't an option." With that he turns and walks toward Leo, Damian, Jerrod, and Zaide, who are waiting further down the path. Taylor scowls at him before following them to organize a search in the forest. Seb, Hudson, and Colten lag behind them, making sure the healer's cabin is off limits discreetly when they return to Eridian and, no doubt, search here too.

"I have a bad feeling," I whisper to Josh. "Who is here and how did they find us? Why did they try to grab Sam?"

He squeezes my shoulder gently as we look over Eridian from my deck. "I don't know, but I don't like it. Will Solvier know?"

"I'm going to find out, he knows all who enter here." I chew the inside of my lower lip as I rack my brain for the smell Sam mentioned. I don't recall one exactly like it, but I may have smelled something similar before.

I pray to the Gods I'm not right. Because if I am, I don't want to think about what would happen.

What it would mean for Eridian.

THIRTY THREE

Rhea

"Solvier!" I call through the trees. I could really do with him being here right now.

I put my hand to the dirt ground, closing my eyes and opening my senses to feel for tremors. Nothing, not even a slight disturbance. I stand and sigh, rubbing the back of my neck as exhaustion hits me. *"How's the search going?"* I yawn down the link to Josh.

"Nearly done. No strange smells around, and we haven't seen anyone matching Sam's description of the man she saw," Josh tells me, and I slunk down on the ground with a grunt. How can someone just appear in Eridian and leave no trace? Better yet, what the fuck is anyone doing here in the first place?

This is really bad.

I rub my calves, groaning as I knead the muscle, trying to ease its soreness. They feel on fire and my feet are more than likely covered in blisters with how long I've been searching for Solvier. It's way into the night now, and after searching for Sam all day and now searching for Solvier, I don't want to move for a week after this. When is this shit going to stop?

I huff at myself. "A girl can wish."

"What do you wish for?" a drawled voice speaks behind me.

I jolt, my head whipping around with a hand on my chest as I spot Darius behind me, head tilted with a small smirk on his face.

"You scared the shit out of me! What is wrong with you?" I'm already on edge as it is, and I don't need my babysitter creeping up on me. I put my hands on the ground, heaving myself up. I hold my breath through the pain shooting through my body as I do and then start forward again.

"Hmm, there is nothing wrong with me. What is wrong with you?" he questions, striding beside me, those eyes of his roaming over me. I do the same with him. How does he look like he rolled out of bed on twelve hours sleep while I look like a shit mess?

His dark hair is messy, but in a way that looks natural to him, and those light-green eyes, though guarded, are full of life. No sign of exhaustion at all. I look over the thin white scar on his nose to a jaw I want to bite. My eyes lower to his neck, following the trail of tattoos until they disappear underneath the collar of his t-shirt. The sight of them makes me want to trace every one of those markings, find hidden treasure in them and translate the words he has hidden in the harsh lines and patterns. I hadn't been able to get a closer look at them when he was naked. I was in too much of a daze during my heat to examine them closely, and there is no way I would ask him about them now.

He catches me looking at him and tilts his head down and toward me. I wave him off, not bothering to answer the question in his eyes and head northeast. Maybe Solvier went to his spot. I've caught him there a few times so hopefully he is. We walk… Well, he walks, and I shuffle on in silence. The sound of the night animals reaching us in the cool night. He stays close to me, his eyes roaming around us and alert. Even if he doesn't believe Sam saw someone, his actions speak differently.

My foot gets caught on an exposed tree root, and I grunt, hands bracing for the fall, but it never comes. Darius's arm shoots out, hand gripping my wrist as he pulls me back, yanking me toward him. I hit his solid chest, his scent wrapping around me immediately and filling my lungs. I slowly lift my head, and his eyes capture mine, and it's all I can see. His eyes bounce back and forth, and black begins to spread slowly from the edges of his whites. I watch as Runa gets some energy and stirs inside me, and I feel my eyes start to change from his reaction. His brows lower in confusion, and I try to hold back so he doesn't see. Glass-like flecks enter his pupils, the opposite to mine, and I follow each one of them, entranced as they float in the green and know his wolf is looking at me, just like Runa is looking at him. They're unable to help themselves, just like us.

My soul glows as we watch each other, feeling a wash of… everything flow over me. It feels like his gaze traveling to the deepest part of me, examining every drop of my being, caressing every part of what is me. I suck in a sharp breath at this powerful, heady feeling, my forearm tingling as Darius's eyes lower to my lips. He dips his head closer to me, stopping just a whisper of a breath away from his lips touching mine. We're so close, our breaths intertwining, and I can't move. I'm frozen from the intensity of his gaze and his closeness to me. A branch cracks and his head snaps toward it as he drops my wrist and takes a step back, taking his warmth with him.

I blink, coming out of the trance and clearing my throat, knowing whatever moment we had just now is gone. He scans where the sound came from, and once he determines it's just an animal, we continue walking.

I cast glances at Darius out of the corner of my eye, wondering what he's even doing here. How does he even keep finding me for that matter? I'm deep in the forest in the dead of night and have been gone for hours. Yet here he is, appearing out of nowhere, not making a single sound. It's really beginning to annoy me. I've learned to home in on every little noise since

I was little, yet I can't hear him coming, and when he is around, all my focus is drawn to him without my control. I really don't like it, yet all I feel from Runa is contentment in his presence most of the time. It's the same feeling she gets when we are at the cave, and that worries and confuses me. I don't understand it.

"What are you doing here?" I grumble, unable to stop my curiosity.

"I've spoken with my Elites apart from the ones in The Deadlands, and as I said, there is no one matching the girl's description of this male. There is no scent, no trace, and no tracks of anyone ever being there either." He looks at me, brow lifting as we keep walking.

"Your point?" I grind out, looking through the trees ahead of me.

"My point," he drawls, "is that there is nothing there, and there was probably nothing there to begin with."

I stop, hands on hips and heave out a sigh at him. "Darius," I say, exhaustion showing in my voice. "I don't care what you *think* you know. I believe Sam. The whole thing feels… off. Like there is a disturbance in the air, and I don't like it."

"Off how?" he folds his arms as some of his dominance hits me, and I don't show just how that affects me. I don't show that I want to wrap it around me like a second skin.

I rub my temples. "Just, I don't know. It feels like something has shifted. Something has come into my territory and it's wrong." It's like a vapor of rot intertwining with the air. Invisible to the eye, but you feel it all the same.

"You're making no sense, you know that right?" He shakes his head, eyeing me like I'm crazy.

"I might not make sense to you, but I make sense to me. I need to find Solvier." I pick up the pace again, pushing myself and scanning the trees with the help of the moonlight to catch sight of him.

"Who is Solvier anyway?" he wonders aloud.

"You could say he's the guardian of the Eridian. He's been here for a very long time." Hundreds of years.

"How has he been here, and no one knew?" he questions, moving a branch out the way for me as I pass.

"How am I supposed to know? You're the Elites. You're supposed to know everything." I roll my eyes at that. You can't know everything. It's impossible.

"The Elites record everything, and it's combined with the Highers' knowledge of Vrohkaria in their library. We didn't know this place existed, so how would we know about a wolf guardian?" he says in a low tone. "Don't get cheeky, little wolf, I may just spank your ass raw," he warns, and I stumble over my feet.

"The fuck!" I splutter. "You wouldn't dare." My cheeks are blazing hot, and I look at him with wide eyes.

He drags me to him, my back to his chest as he rests his lips near my ear. "Are you playing with me again?" he murmurs in a low, husky voice, and goosebumps raise over my skin. A shiver runs through me as he inhales deeply at my neck, letting out a quiet grunt. He presses into my back more, and I feel his hardness beneath his pants. "It excites me when you do, you know that." He takes another deep breath and nips at my skin. "Maybe this time we can fight until I quieten that mouth of yours." He rocks into me, a whimper spilling from my lips.

Flashes of my heat run through my mind and wetness coats my panties at the memory of him moving inside me. His hands on my naked flesh, his teeth marking me, licking me, and a small sounding breath escapes me. A rumble comes from him, and he grabs my hips, pulling me further into him as he leaves a wet trail of kisses on my neck.

"Do you want to play?" he murmurs, his teeth scraping my

ear.

Do I? We fucked during my heat. I chose to allow it, and he was an asshole when he left. I'm not in heat now though, and the cruel words he left me with in the cave stung, they cut deep. If he wants to use me as just a hole for him to fill as punishment, then so be it. But now is not the time, and I'm not under punishment. Not yet.

Bringing my hands up and over his on my hips, I find the will power to peel them off me and continue on. "You can do what you want, right?" I call back, not bothering to stop. "But right now, Darius, I have some things to do. You may think Sam was just imagining things, but I know this forest and something is wrong. I need to keep my pack safe from whoever is here. I can't do that with your cock inside me."

He catches up to me, his gaze on the side of my face. "You are mine, I have a responsibility to protect you from any threat that isn't me. Your pack is an extension of you, so they will also be protected as long as you are." I turn my head toward him, stunned at his words. "I don't do well with sharing, little wolf, so if something is going to take your attention away from me, I will get rid of it."

With Darius's words running through my mind, we don't speak as we reach the most northeast edge of the forest, stopping at a waterfall coming out of the cliffside. It's one of the larger ones, and if you go through the water, there is a cave behind it where Solvier sometimes rests. He isn't here though, and there is no sign that he has been in a while.

My shoulders slump with that knowledge. He would be around if Eridian were in danger, right? This is his home, and he protects it, meaning he protects us. He's been distant, going away for much longer than usual. His behavior is odd, and I don't understand why he's not here if someone has entered

Eridian. Is it really just Sam's imagination and my paranoia?

At least everyone at home is okay. I spoke to Josh a little while ago, and he said all is fine, but they are keeping an eye on the Elites. Kade is still with Sam at the main cabin, not wanting to leave her as she's having nightmares. Every time he tried to get up, she would scream, only settling when she's curled up next to him. I'm glad she feels safe around him and that Kade's helping her, I know he won't leave her until she's okay.

I bend and pick up a few stones from the ground, throwing them into the pool of water at the bottom of the waterfall, watching the ripples. I feel Darius's stare on me as I continue throwing while he stands with his arms folded, the moonlight shining down on us.

"You said the rogures are causing havoc across the lands," I start, rolling a stone in my hand. "If you are trying to get rid of them, why have the Highers sent you here for one woman? Surely getting rid of the rogures is more important?" Rogures are lethal. I'm glad we haven't had more encounters with them, but I do feel for everyone in the rest of Vrohkaria having to suffer their wrath.

They are scary motherfuckers, and if I could help I would. But what could I do? Sure, I could open Eridian to refugees, giving them a safe place to live. The cost of that, however, is losing my family. My pack would have to return to where they escaped from and be put on trial. The pups would be taken, and the Highers? They would punish them all. Especially if they get their hands on me.

We are lucky to have Eridian to protect us, but there are more monsters in Vrohkaria than just rogures.

"The rogures are my main concern, but the Highers think this woman is more important right now."

"You don't think so?" I ask, curious of his answer.

He shakes his head, not even hesitating as he answers. "No."

I chew on my lip for a moment in thought. "I know you plan on taking me to the Highers, but what if I stay here and you bring people to me that need help? A safe place to come and stay. We could do it slowly, make room away from the center of Eridian and place them in new cabins, as long as the Highers don't know."

He shakes his head. "You are going to the Highers either way, and your punishment will be given to me. People will come to Eridian whether you like it or not."

I clench my jaw and stare at the water. "It will do more harm than good," I tell him. "I guarantee that. Just go home, Darius. Forget we exist," I sigh and he grunts. "No one is stopping you."

"If I could just go back empty handed, I would."

"I guess the Highers do have control over the Elites," I mutter.

"They don't without my say so. They just want me to do something I want to avoid at all costs. My goal right now is getting rid of the rogures, nothing else, and I won't let anything get in the way of that. Even if I have to take a detour doing this shit." I huff, and his next question catches me off guard. "How do you know anything about the Highers and Elites anyway? You're all the way out here, practically in your own world. So how do you know so much about Vrohkaria?"

"Well..." I trail off. When his hard stare is still on me, refusing to let it go, I continue. "You know Colten came from the lands. We sometimes have others come here. They tell us things about what's happening in Vrohkaria." I chew the inside of my lip and look away from him as his face calls bullshit on my words. "Don't ask questions I can't answer, Darius," I half plead and half warn him.

"So now it's not just Colten? It's others too?" He scoffs. "I know something isn't right here, Rhea. I will find out what. One thing I know for sure is that I can't trust a word out of your damn mouth. You're the cause of whatever is happening here with your pack. They're petrified more than not."

Everything is your fault, you stupid bitch. If you would have just done as you were told and stopped, I wouldn't have had to kill anyone. But you had to tell what you heard, didn't you? You had to go and open that fucking mouth of yours and cause all of this. Cause your mother's death!

I blink, willing myself out of the memory. Why am I having so many flashbacks? My hand shakes as I throw the next stone, watching as it sinks to the bottom of the pool, never to be found and forever stuck there, laying in eternal darkness.

Darius has moved closer now, watching me intently. Noticing my hands trembling, I shove them into my short's pockets, looking out over the water that feels like it's entered my lungs, drowning me in memories. "Some things may be my fault," I agree on a whisper. "But all I've ever tried to do is protect them as best that I can. I'm not the bad guy here, Darius. I never was. If I start believing that I am, then there is no hope for my pack. Or Kade." *Or me.*

We lock eyes, mine a little sad, his a lot curious. I start to feel that pull toward him again, locking us in the embrace of our stare.

"Who are you?" His question is genuine, wanting to know all the parts of me. I can see it in his eyes and the way he looks at me sometimes. The confusion, the curiosity, the need to yank out my soul and take a look for himself.

My reply is gentle, solemn and accepting.

"Someone you probably don't want me to be."

A gentle touch to my cheek has me leaning into it. It's soft, reassuring, and confusing all at the same time. It's familiar, yet new to me. I've felt these phantom touches over the years, a light pressure surrounding me at times, but it's gotten so much more frequent since the Elites appeared. Since *he* appeared. I watch as Darius's head turns to the side suddenly, his brows scrunched as his eyes move around the space, searching for something. I see a flash of pale against him before vanishing into thin air.

Wisps float from the trees and into the night sky above us, both of us watching as they dance with each other, twirling and swirling near the water flowing down the cliffside. A few float down to me, tickling my skin before going over to Darius. He watches them slowly move closer to him. When they are in arms' reach, he brings a hand up, holding it steady as a smaller wisp moves toward him. It hovers above his palm before jiggling playfully, its glowing body of essence moving gently from side to side.

Then the lands stop.

Everything stops.

My breath hitches as I take in his face. The lightness of his green eyes seems to glow, and the gentle smile on his face seems soft in the light of the wisps. He looks unnatural, peaceful. More. His face is gentle as he looks at them, and his lips move as he murmurs words to it. It's a quiet sound I've never heard from him before, and it causes my chest to warm. I bring my hand toward it, rubbing gently as that warmth spears over my body from the center of my chest. Runa rubs against me, experiencing the same thing that I am. A small smile graces my face as I watch him, unable to stop it. Right now, he's not the Alpha of the Elites, he's just a male content in watching as the wisps play around him. The small one hovering above his palm twirls around him before shooting into the sky to join the others above us, glowing softly against the dark.

As we stand there, watching them under the night sky, the only thought in my head is one I never thought I would have. One I'm not sure how I feel about and not entirely sure if it rings true. But as I look back over at Darius, the heat spreads a little stronger within my chest and tingles spread along my forearm, making me wonder.

I look down at the delicate swirls and writing there, following down to the symbol of the Gods at my wrist, feeling those tingles beneath my touch. I move my hand back up over my skin and run my fingers over the empty space in the middle, the space left bare for your Vihnarn. The place where the sensation is the strongest.

I breathe deep, taking in the scents surrounding me, and the scent that is just Darius as my eyes slowly move back to him. I watch the small smile slip from his face, his lightened eyes darken to a coldness that causes the heat in my chest to evaporate, the tingles abruptly stopping. The softness in him turns to anger as I drop my hand from my arm, my own smile vanishing as I remember who I'm standing with, remember that this isn't just a male, but the male who will be taking me to people I never wanted to see again in my lifetime.

"Under the moonlight, the darkest of nights shine the brightest," I whisper to myself.

"What?" he asks, his jaw tightening.

I don't reply as I silently pray to the Gods, staring at the man who may just be my downfall.

I pray that whatever they have in store for me, I can overcome it and come back home to my family. I pray that I can keep them safe and forget all about the male with light green eyes and a gentle smile that makes my soul scream in a way I have never experienced before.

And as I look back down at my forearm, I know that it will be an experience that I will never have with another, and I know most of my prayers will not be answered.

THIRTY FOUR

Rhea

I grab some extra furs for Darius, passing them to him as I move about the cave. It's awkward, and the tension is high, but I haven't got the energy to make the walk back home and be free from his presence. I could just make him stay outside, but I'm not an asshole like he would be. Eridian is safe, there are no signs of this man anywhere, and although the air still seems to be disturbed, there is no sense of anything wrong at the moment.

I ignore my cheeks heating as I bend, shuffling my furs around until I'm satisfied with them. I always make sure they are just right. I can still slightly smell Darius's scent on them from the last time we were both here, and I'm not sure if I'm comforted by that or not. Mostly not after the weird moment we had outside and the tingling in my arm. I try not to think about what that could mean, though it's not far from my mind.

He makes his temporary bed close to the entrance into the cave, taking a space against the dark rock wall. I move over to the tables I have here and rummage through a pack, taking out some dried meat and a water skin. I shuffle over to him and hand it over without a word after taking some for myself. We sit down and eat our bland meal in silence, him on his bed and me on mine, the cool night air flowing from the opening at the top.

Not a wisp is in sight as I grab some old wood off to the side before sitting more comfortably on my furs, pulling my blade out from my boot. The moonlight shining through gives me enough light to work. Darius watches me intently as I begin to carve, mindful of keeping the shavings on the ground rather than in my bed. I'm rounding the back of the carving when he speaks.

"Did you make all those as well?" I look over at him and see him nodding toward my many carvings in the crevasse of the rock wall. I nod and continue to scrape my blade against the wood, making indents the best I can. I hear him shuffle around before he gets up and walks toward my carvings, causing me to pause and watch him.

If he breaks them, I'll break his neck.

"There's a lot here," he muses, and I grunt in response, never taking my eyes off of him.

He reaches a muscular arm up and takes one I did of Josh years ago, and I bristle at him touching my things without asking. "I thought Josh was your mate when I first saw you both." He turns the carving over as he studies it. "You fucked him?"

I tilt my head at him, wondering why he's asking all of a sudden. "Why does it matter?" I shrug and place the wood and my blade down. Getting up, I walk toward him, taking the carving out of his hand before gently putting it back in its place.

"Just answer the question, Rhea," he says in a low, demanding tone, and I look at him. Why does he want to know this so badly when according to him I've spread my legs for anyone and everyone?

After a moment, I answer him truthfully. "I have been intimate with Josh,' I pause, my eyes widening in surprise as he growls. "He was my first and only. Until you." The words hang in the air between us, my eyes never leaving his as they flash to black, and then settle again.

He scoffs at me. "No way." When I continue to stare at him

and say nothing, he looks at me more closely. "Why be with me then, if he's the only man that has ever touched you?"

I sigh, looking back at my work I've done over the years, letting it ground me for my answer. "I wanted to see if that was a way to get you to be… considerate of keeping Eridian out of your mouth when you take me to the Highers." Also, because for some reason my body reacts to him in a way it hasn't for anyone before. I don't tell him that pesky bit of information though.

"You fucked me in the hope that I wouldn't tell the Highers about Eridian, but not to try and convince me to leave you here?" He shakes his head a little and folds his arms. "It was more than that, and we both know it."

I do. "You followed me here, you came to me."

"I did."

"Why?" I ask curiously.

"Because no one touches what's mine." He says it without any hesitation, without a hint of doubt that his words are not true.

Shaking my head at him, I look toward the wall. "I did want you at that moment," I admit. "But I also did it for that reason." I wave a hand at the carvings of my pack, mainly of Kade and Josh. He looks over them. "I know I'm going to be taken to the Highers either way, so I thought why not give in and also try and keep this place safe." I cock my head at him. "Which obviously hasn't worked. You're right about one thing, I do manipulate when there is a good reason to, well… try to." I laugh, but it's hollow, and his brows pull down. I pick up a carving of Kade, looking over his face and running my finger over the smile I carved there.

He moves a little closer, his eyes on me as I turn the figure over in my hands. His scent wraps around me and I want to keep it to myself, lather my skin with it so it's always with me.

"Have you ever loved someone so much, with all that you are? So much that you would do anything you could to protect them?" I ask, turning toward him. I watch him swallow, looking at the carving in my hand before his eyes come back to mine. "I don't mean just saying you would, I mean you *would.* You would sell your soul, stain it, abuse it and hurt it beyond repair. Just to keep those you love safe?" He watches me intently before finally looking away.

"I did at one time," he says quietly, shocking me that he told me something personal. Who was it? And why not anymore? Did he have a mate? I clear my throat over the jealous growl I want to release.

I give him a small smile, looking down at the carving of Kade before handing it to him. He takes it from me hesitantly, our fingers grazing as his eyes ask a question he doesn't voice aloud. I take a breath and prepare to ask him something I know he will probably deny. But I have to try, I see no other way.

"You have part of my world in your hands," I whisper, watching as his fingers squeeze tightly around the carving, looking it over. "I will do whatever it takes to protect it. I *have* done whatever it takes to protect it." I pause to swallow my pride. "Will you help me protect it?" I ask him, my enemy, and maybe the only one who can help. I know something is wrong, I can feel it in the air, and I don't know if I can keep everyone safe on my own from whatever is coming. He also has me in a chokehold. He can hold Eridian over my head, and I will do anything he demands to keep it safe. It's why I'm going to the Highers without question, we're outnumbered. We can't just keep them here as prisoners, I don't think we have the strength behind us to even consider it. They are Elites, trained and deadly. We are just average. I thought about every way I could to try and get them to listen, *him* to listen. This is my last resort… damn near begging.

"You want my help?" he asks, his eyes flicking up to mine. But surprisingly, there is no smugness there. I nod. "What do I get in return if I don't tell them?" My hands shake at his question, but I continue on.

"I will gladly accept more people into Eridian, without a fight, if you and I can assure that the original pack members are safe here. I will make sure it's a peaceful transition with the members already here. They can help build new homes and teach them the land, and we can make sure they live together peacefully. That is something only I can do smoothly. It will be a disaster if anyone else attempts it. They can be safe here, away from danger, away from the rogures. There is so much more room in the forest for them to create a life without damaging what's thriving inside of it." I take a breath before straightening my spine. "My problem is not sharing Eridian, Darius. It's sharing it with the wrong people. The kind of people who hide beneath their flesh of lies and strike behind closed doors, revealing who they really are to those that are in no position to get away from the monster beneath the surface."

He twists the carving of Kade over in his hands, feeling the smooth edges that took time and care to make. He tosses it in the air, and I hold my breath before releasing it when he catches it. He says nothing for so long that I feel he's just going to shrug off my suggestion. But then he speaks.

"Do you know these people? Hidden monsters?"

I look at him closely, wondering if I said so, he would feel something about that. The Elites are meant to be protectors of all of Vrohkaria, but I'm a speck on the map of life, my ability to breathe is no more important than others, we are all equal. We all end up in the dirt.

"Maybe," I whisper, not exactly telling him yes or no. I look away when his stare feels too close, too forceful in his search for the truth.

"I will take you to the Highers for trial to set your punishment for what you did in The Deadlands. That won't change."

My shoulders slump. He won't help me. "I know," I tell him, biting my lip as it trembles.

"However," he begins, and my eyes go back to him. "Those fucking eyes," he mumbles. "I will keep this place quiet if your pack will welcome others and help those that need sanctuary to live peacefully away from the rogures. It will helpful as I don't have time to fuck around here dealing with those issues. Instead, I can continue to look for a way to stop the rogures while protecting those that need it by bringing them here. I will make sure those that come here are not dangerous, but you will have no say in how many there will be." I blink a few times when his words register. "Make no mistake though, little wolf, I might have agreed to this, but you are still under my paw."

"You really won't tell the Highers about Eridian and take them to Fenrikar?" I breathe, my chest blooming with hope.

"No," he says gruffly.

"Why?" I ask.

"They couldn't give a shit about the victims of the rogures while they sent me here on this goose chase, and I can't help them and take care of the rogures. There are only so many of us." I search his eyes for any sign of deception, but all I see is truth.

I let out a shaky breath, looking down to avoid his eyes as I try to keep my body from dropping in sheer relief. He's actually going to keep them hidden, they will be safe. When my reaction is more controlled, I look back up and hold my arm out to him. He looks at it for a moment before lifting his own and clasping mine in his, forearm to forearm. He grunts, and I shiver as those tingles start up again.

"Do you vow it?" I ask him.

"I vow it."

"I agree to the conditions of the deal before Zahariss," I say in a rush, hardly believing this is happening.

"I agree to the conditions of the deal before Cazier," he vows, making me look at him curiously. I thought he would vow it on Vrohkaria, like everyone else does with the Highers vow, but it seems the Highers have pissed him off before he came here.

"It's a vow before your Gods, not mine." He shrugs, answering my unvoiced question. I nod and he gives my forearm a gently squeeze before releasing me. Ignoring the loss of that connection, I move toward my bed.

I lay down, finding a comfortable position facing the entrance and covering myself with the light furs. My body relaxes for the first time since I received the letter from Edward, exhaustion finally catching up with me as Runa curls up inside of me. My lids are just closing when I'm sure I still see Darius at my wall of carvings, looking intently at one of them before my eyes shut altogether and blissful sleep takes me away.

Running, running, running. My heart beats wildly in my chest as I head through the woods, my small legs moving as fast as they can to get back home. Tears drip from my face, and I choke back a sob, my hair flying around me as the small stones and sticks dig into my bare feet.

A twig snaps behind me, and I whimper. I push off a tree as I pass it, willing myself to go faster, to get away. A demented growl sounds behind me, and I begin to shake from the fear that they are going to get me. They're going to catch up to me, and they scare me. I didn't mean to hear anything. I didn't know they were in our woods.

"Get back here, now!"

I start crying harder when their shouts get louder. I want my mommy and daddy. I want to go home. I want–

A blur ahead of me and off to the side has me nearly tripping over my feet. A huge, dark wolf comes out of the trees. It has a strange tail, almost like there are two of them. It's the largest wolf I have ever seen, and its head turns toward me, its gaze focused on me before it turns toward the way I came. It starts prowling in that direction, ignoring me as it passes by and I let out a frightened squeal. It growls deeply from somewhere behind me, and I panic, not daring to look back.

Snarls and growls reach my ears and my heart feels like it will stop, a small cry escaping my lips. Keep going, keep going! I see a figure coming from the same place the wolf had, and I bit my lip to stop me from screaming. The dark shape moves closer and closer, and I don't stop. I just keep running so they don't get me.

Running back home to safety.

Running back home to tell my parents what I heard.

I just didn't know it would change everything.

My body jolts, and then I feel strong arms sliding around me, encasing me in warmth. I think I mumble something, my eyes still shut, and the arms around me squeeze tighter. "Shhh," a voice says from somewhere. "Settle, I got you." My body relaxes, sleep claiming me again as I feel a soft touch against my forehead.

My eyes slowly open, blinking away the morning light surrounding me as I shake off the dream, the nightmare that changed my life. I groan, my muscles sore as I lift my hands above me to stretch. I immediately freeze, arms up in the air as I try to make sense of the heat next to me.

Turning my head to the side, my eyes widen as I take in the half naked male laying down next to me, hands behind his head and eyes on me. I gape at him, wondering if I'm still half asleep. It isn't until he rumbles in a gravelly voice that I know that I am not, in fact, dreaming.

"You're finally awake."

I bolt up to a sitting position, glaring down at him, and a sinful smirk spreads across his mouth. "What are you doing in my bed?" I ask, ignoring his naked chest and sleep tousled hair.

"You were tossing and turning in your sleep, murmuring some shit." I blink, and then my eyes double in size. Shit. Did I say something to him? Anything about Sarah? Edward? "You wouldn't shut up, so here I am."

"Here you are," I say slowly. Darius climbed into my furs with me because I was having a nightmare, and wanted to… Comfort me? My brain is still trying to play catch up when he nods, bringing a hand to trail a finger down my bare arm, his eyes heating as he watches goosebumps appear.

I grab one of those skillful fingers, bending it back as I dig my nails into his wrist with my other hand. "Darius?" I purr. His eyes trail over my face as I lean toward him, my lips hovering over his. His pupils dilate at my closeness, and I internally smirk.

"Yes, little wolf," he murmurs, bringing his tongue out to lick along my lower lip. I suppress the flare of desire coursing through me because he needs to realize something. No matter how my body reacts to him, he needs to know one thing.

I lower my face further, my lips brushing against his as I speak. "Just because we made a vow last night, and just because we fucked before then, doesn't mean you can invite yourself into my bed and touch me like you think you have the right." I bend his finger back more, not stopping until it's close to breaking and he releases a small grunt. "Think twice before coming into my bed uninvited, Darius. I used you when we fucked, just like you used me. Don't think for one second you can come to me unless I allow it."

With a look that I'm sure would shrivel his balls if he was any other person, I jump to my feet before going into the pool. I ignore his deep, amused chuckle and let the water cool my skin up to my knees. I would bathe, but I'll do that when I reach home. When I'm alone, without temptation. Getting naked again in front of Darius is not a good idea.

"You're feisty this morning," he acknowledges, and I sigh in response. "Don't tempt me to tame that wildness, you know how I like to play with you, and playing with you has become a favorite pastime."

My body heats at the thought of him holding me down as he fucks me. Instead of giving in, I watch as wisps come out of the trees spread around the cave, floating around me in greeting before heading over to Darius. I look at them from beneath my lashes as he holds his hand out briefly to them, getting to his feet and showing me what the Gods gave him. It's really fucking unfair that the only attraction I have ever felt to someone is to him.

I heave out a breath, hands on hips and lifting my face to the morning light. Closing my eyes, I let my senses flow, making them go wide. I pause, noting a familiar feeling just outside the cave. I hop out the water quickly, not bothering putting my boots on as I make my way to the tunnel that will lead me outside.

"Solvier is here," I tell Darius in a rush, not waiting for him to catch up.

I quicken my steps through the tunnel, the only light coming from the veins of ulcalim ore running through it. We could mine it and use it for weapons, but with it being white and glowing, it's not a great color for camouflage. I round a narrow section of the tunnel and shield my eyes from the glare of the sun when I reach the end, my bare feet hitting the dirt beneath me. Solvier sits there, waiting patiently for me and I go to him, wrapping my arms around his neck as I always do before stepping back.

Golden eyes watch me as I ask, "Did you feel it?" Darius appears at my back, the heat of his body seeping into me as he barely leaves any space between us.

"I did. It won't be long now," he answers, tilting his large head, his ears flicking as if he hears something.

I look over my shoulder at Darius, seeing his eyebrows scrunched together, letting me know Solvier is speaking to the both of us. I look back at him, pinching my lip with my fingers before asking. "Won't be long for what?" I shuffle on my feet waiting for his reply, unsure why he seems so solemn.

"For everything to begin anew, and to right a wrong."

THIRTY FIVE

Rhea

I swirl a cloth around the pot, lowering it to let more water into it before cleaning it some more. Dinner went well, surprisingly so with the Elites there. The pack have definitely got used to them over the past two weeks and are slowly being less hesitant around them, especially the kids.

I should stop their interactions altogether, but seeing some of those towering males make them laugh… I just can't bring myself to tell them to stay away. Maybe if the Elites got close to them, they would become another protector for them. The Elites know some of the pack still shake in fear when they get too close, but they never cross boundaries with them. It's surprising they respect it, considering some are the cause of some members suffering.

I sigh and tip the pot forward, letting out the water into the river. "How are the injured Elites doing?" I ask Anna as she washes a mug beside me. It's only Anna, Josie, and I out here. I asked them earlier to help me so we could talk privately.

She wipes a strand of red hair from her freckled face. "They are healing well. A bit too well if we want to delay their trip back to the Highers."

"It's been what? Nearly three weeks now since they arrived. They are getting restless, especially Darius." He's itching to get back, the male won't leave me alone, especially after we made the vow that he would keep Eridian from the Highers. He doesn't even try to hide that he's always following me.

Anna has been slowing the injured Elites healing as much as possible so we had time to figure out how to handle the situation. I don't know whether Darius believed her when she told him she's limited in her healing abilities and lacks all the supplies she needs, it's all true, but we also needed time to keep Eridian safe.

"You mentioned they had some sort of timeline, right?" Anna asks, and I nod. "Do we know when that is?"

"No idea. We haven't heard them speak of it again since Hudson overheard them the first time." I put the pot to the side and grab a plate. "Not knowing isn't helpful either." I need to prepare for when I leave for the Highers.

I've barely slept since they've arrived, apart from the time in the cave with Darius, or really eat. The fact that Darius and Leo are staying in my cabin only raises my anxiety. I can't function like this. The fear that I'll wake up to them telling me it's time to go to Fenrikar is ever pressing in my mind, never letting up, never leaving me alone.

"It's not," Anna agrees. "We will have to deal with it when it comes to you leaving. None of us want you to go."

"Are you sure you will be back?" Josie asks, rinsing another pot out on the other side of me.

"I will have to help them bring new people here, so yeah, I'll be back," I tell them. I told them all about the vow I made with Darius a few days ago, it took a lot of persuading to reassure them that this is for the best.

"Can you trust him? They are the Highers' weapons after all," Josie grumbles, hefting another pot into the river to clean.

"He vowed before the old Gods, as they call them. I don't take that lightly, so I think we can trust him in this. For now, anyway." I sit back on the bank, shaking the water off my hands as I watch the river flow in a smooth rhythm. "I haven't come across someone like him before," I murmur. "Before I came here, Josh, Kade, and Cassie and I were just staying out in the woods or abandoned barns. We never interacted with anyone unless it was absolutely necessary when we went into a village to try and steal some food, or pay with coins we stole. Even then we kept our answers to a few short words. We weren't around a lot of people. Darius is so different from Josh or Taylor or Danny, or anyone here."

"In what way?" Josie follows my lead and sits back, waiting for my answer.

"He's just… more." I shake my head, tipping it up to the slowly darkening sky. "He has an aura around him I have never felt before."

"He's an Alpha," Anna says, squeezing out water from the rag.

"So are many others here too, and most of the Elites. Darius just feels like something I can't explain," I say, shaking my head, frustrated I can't put it into words.

I know what an Alpha feels like when they release their dominance, but Darius has an undertone of something I'm not sure anyone else realizes. It's subtle, but that something swirls around, entwining with his natural dominance and flows through it discreetly. Just not discreetly enough for me to not pick it up.

A howl pierces our silence, and I smile, bringing my head forward and looking into the trees on the other side of the river.

"Someone is calling you," Josie chuckles, and Anna gives a matching smile.

"So it seems." I get to my feet and begin piling up the pots and cutlery I've washed when Josie bumps my hip with hers.

"Go, I'm sure you miss them." I look around, unsure. "We will be fine, we have been on high alert for days, and nothing has been reported as unusual. We will take the pots back. Go, relax a little." I look at Anna, who nods and rolls her eyes at the next howl demanding my attention. "Quickly, before you're hunted," she laughs, and I chuckle, knowing how right she is.

I touch my cheek to both of theirs in goodbye before I roll my loose pants up to my knees and take off my boots. Once in hand, I walk across the stony bottom of the river, hop up, and put my boots back on. Thankfully, it's shallow where we are and I can cross easily.

I turn and give one last wave before heading into the tree line, opening my senses and heading for that howl. I nudge Runa for a burst of speed, my heart pumping as I get closer and closer to the sound. It isn't long until a branch snapping to my left has my head whipping that way, and a grin spreads across my face as the sight of fur. The wolf follows alongside me through the trees, keeping pace as another joins me on my right, gliding through the bushes.

A chuckle falls from my lips, and I lift my face to the branches above, releasing my own human howl as they echo it. The feeling of being free as I run sends air into my lungs, even as I exert myself. I feel like the coating of Rhea, Alpha of Eridian, falls away, and underneath it is just Rhea, a woman with no responsibility, no fear or anxiety. No thoughts of Solvier's strange words to me the last time I saw him, or thoughts of being in front of the Highers.

I'm just me, free for a little while.

The two wolves burst through the trees on either side of me as we approach a hollowed tree. They stroll toward me as I slow down to a walk, and then I stop and wait. I look at the wolf to my left, our eyes connecting, before I look down at the one on my right, its stare already on me.

We still.

We wait.

Then, we pounce.

I dive for one while the other comes at me. I tackle one to the ground as the others jump on my back, nipping my shoulder as I laugh and roll. A sloppy tongue comes on my cheek next, and I chuckle as I push the muzzle away as the other flops itself down on top of me.

"Stop, stop." I laugh, shoving them both to get them off of me. Runa comes closer to the surface, taking in their touches against my skin before lying down, happy to be close as we play.

Tiny yips and cries reach my ears, and the wolves instantly jump off of me and sit on their haunches, heads tilted to the side as their eyes go to the hollowed tree. I sit up, grinning as the cries get louder and louder. I wait, keeping quiet until a tiny black nose pops itself out of a large root, and then two tiny paws come next. The little gray furball, the one I named Leif, comes blundering out as soon as he notices me. His two brothers and sister come out after him as he lands on my legs and climbs up my chest, licking my face.

"Hey, little man," I say, lifting him up to my face so I can nuzzle him, his little tongue covering me in saliva. More yips and the other three get bundled in my arms as I lay on my back, getting attacked by the little fur balls.

I move my eyes to the large tree, seeing their mama sat there, her head tilted as she watches her pups play with me. She's always with them, but she keeps her distance, trusting me not to hurt them. Her mate, however, can be a bit trickier in assuring his pups are fine.

The two older wolves I was playing with come back to me, licking and nuzzling us before we continue to play on the forest floor, chasing each other and hiding from the pups as they hunt us down. I grab one of the pups, tickling its back as it spins and yips, its front paws to the floor, bum in the air as he gets ready to come for me. Leif darts between my legs and tackles his brother, the other pups joining in their wrestling match. I bend down and bat at their paws, tickling their noses. I bring my hand back before they can nip me and run away as they chase me.

I eventually collapse when the moon is high, panting on the floor with the dirt and twigs making a home on my body. One wolf curls up next to me as the other trots off to its mama, who watches her pups lay on my chest, their little eyes closing after their long playtime.

"It's okay, mama," I tell her, and she tilts her head as I bring a hand up and stroke the nearest fluff ball on my chest. "A couple more minutes, and I'll bring them to you. They aren't the only ones who need sleep."

She makes a huffing sound before nudging her head against the other wolf next to her. Then she stills, her lips peeling back and hackles on end as she stands and growls in the direction across from me. I move in an instant, rolling over and bracing my forearms over the pups that fell off my body and are now beneath me, hovering over them protectively. Mama and the two younger wolves move to my side instantly as I look through the trees as a figure appears.

"I didn't know you'd find wild wolves a good talking companion," a deep voice murmurs, and I blow out a breath. I get to my feet, making sure I don't stand on one of the pups, and face Darius as he emerges from the trees and into the moonlight. He looks toward the wolves, holding eye contact with mama for a beat as she growls, before he nods his head. "You know I won't harm them," he says to her, and my brows raise to my hairline.

Mama's growls become quieter, and I watch her out of the corner of my eye until she eventually relaxes. She doesn't take her eyes off Darius though. A yip has my head turning to the ground and Leif, ever the curious pup, gets on his little feet and runs toward Darius at full pelt. I take a step forward, wanting to… what? Protect him? But mama doesn't make a move to, and it's not my pup. So, I stay back and hold my damn breath.

I don't know what I thought would happen, but it wasn't Darius smiling wide and picking the pup up gently in his large hands, bringing Leif to his face and rubbing his nose against him. That was the last thing I expected.

I watch on, stunned with how careful he is and my chest swirls uncomfortably, so uncomfortably that I bring my hand up and rub the spot as I watch Leif try and nip his nose.

And then…

Then Darius releases a sound I haven't heard from him before, and I swear the earth beneath me shifts and breaks before aligning into something new. The sound is deep and hearty, and I can't take my eyes off the grin on his face as he laughs at the pup. His eyes light up even more as he puts him down and picks up a stick, waving it in front of him until Leif latches on to it with the most adorable, tiny growl. My heart just melts.

Darius sits down and does a small, gentle growl back, as if not to scare him. He grips the stick and moves it back and forth, Leif's little front paws coming off the ground as he tries to hold on and take it from him. His brothers and sister get brave and run toward them, their own little growls coming from them as they jump on Leif and try and get the stick for themselves. Darius laughs again, picking up another stick to share while I stand there stunned.

Wordless.

And utterly captivated at the sight of Darius, Alpha of the Elites, playing with wild wolf pups and *enjoying* it. He has the same look on his face as he did in the forest with the wisps, and once again, that heat hits my chest.

I let out a breathless chuckle and plonk down on my ass, crossing my legs as I sit and watch them. Mama comes next to me, bumping my cheek, and I reach a hand up to scratch behind her ear. She makes a small sound, and the pups stop attacking the stick and look up at mama before trotting over to her, their tails high. Mama bends her head and nudges them toward the hollowed tree, and I keep my eyes on a reluctant Leif who stays with Darius.

I get to my feet and walk over to them, not raising my eyes to his curious stare and still ignoring the heat within my chest. Bending down to stroke Leif's head, I give him a good scratch on the back of the neck. "Come on, fluff ball," I whisper as I place my hand under his belly and lift him up. "Time to go." A dark shadow comes out of the trees, and I turn, meeting the gaze of a larger wolf. He stops short at the sight of me with his pup until his gaze turns to Darius. "Daddy's home," I mumble.

They stare at each other, and I don't move, too nervous as I don't know how this will go. I usually leave when he turns up. He's not much of a fan of mine, but with Darius here, I'm not sure what will happen. I tense up, waiting for the male wolf to snarl and lunge. Only he doesn't. He cocks his head to the side before he walks over to me, his paws silent on the ground. He stills when he's in front of me, looking from me to his pup, and I have no idea whether I should hold on to Leif or put him on the floor.

"Give the pup to him, Rhea," Darius says, his breath at my ear as his arms come around. I didn't even hear him, in fact, I didn't hear him coming here in the first place. He followed me didn't he? Did he hear what Josie, Anna, and I were talking about?

I swallow. If he knows she's been slowing his Elites healing, everything could fall apart.

His large hands engulf mine, and my head turns toward him. My mouth touches his jaw, and he releases a little sound that has my insides fluttering. Squeezing my hands gently, he guides them out, making sure we both have a firm hold on the wiggling pup as we bring our hands down toward Leif's dad. I watch as the wolf opens his mouth, and my fingers dig into Leif's fur, not wanting to let him go. Darius's nose nudges behind my ear, not taunting, but more letting me know it's okay. I release a small breath.

Darius moves our hands to just inside the wolf's mouth, then his own fingers slip between mine as we slowly let go. Leif wriggles, but his dad gently presses down onto Leif, his hold secure, but not hurting him as he turns to where mama waits for them. Mama licks her mate's face as he passes with their pup, and she wastes no time heading into the den herself with the others, disappearing out of sight.

I breathe a sigh of relief, thankful daddy wolf didn't attack Darius, then I jolt at the squeeze of a hand against mine. I look down at our threaded fingers. His are much larger than mine, and I can't help but think how good we fit despite the size difference. I have never just held someone's hand, not like this, and I've never felt the need to keep it there. His chin lands on my head as we stay silent, listening to the odd sound of critters nearby, not wanting to disturb the bubble of peace that has descended between us. I relax back into him, wanting his warmth to seep into me as he brings his arm around me, pulling me closer.

I don't feel threatened in his arms. I don't feel scared or like my lungs will give out from not getting enough air at being held against him. I never have felt truly threatened by his touch. Some part of me instinctively knowing he won't hurt me in that way. Not physically.

I just feel peaceful, and that isn't something I should feel. Especially with him. My enemy.

"Let's go, little wolf. It's late." I nod my head beneath his chin, and he releases his arm around me before turning me with my hand still in one of his. He pulls me along as we walk in the direction of Eridian, the moon our only witness as he keeps hold of my hand and doesn't let go. It feels like a secret, something only known between us and the night.

I don't try to release my hand from his, wanting to keep the connection thrumming between us at the small contact, our wolves pressing up against each other. After making the vow in the cave, we have a truce, no matter how tentative it may be. I just hope when the time comes and I am brought to the Highers, I can eventually return home to my safe haven and go back to some sort of normalcy.

But as we walk back while holding hands, silently taking in the night air, it feels like something has changed. Something that neither one of us is willing to admit. We can't stay away from each other. I feel his eyes on me all the time, watching, protecting, and I always search for that feel of him watching me. Deep down, I don't want that to go away, it's become so familiar to me since he came here. It feels like something that is just… mine.

He suddenly stops, bringing me to a halt and tips my chin up with a hand. We hold ourselves captive to the pull, our eyes bouncing between each other. Darius blinks, a small hum coming from him before placing a surprised, gentle kiss to my lips. I give in to the feeling that courses through me at his touch. I open my mouth and let him taste me as I taste him, breathing in each other's scent. He growls low in the back of his throat at my submission when I let him take control, his tongue tangling with mine as he brings a hand up to the back of my head and threads it through my hair, bringing me as close to him as he can. All the while still holding my hand.

There, under the moonlight, I feel like it's possible to have the impossible for just a moment. I'm not the Alpha of Eridian, and he isn't the Alpha of the Elites. We are not enemies, just a man and a woman with no responsibilities until the sun rises and the day begins anew.

And as he softens the kiss and rubs his nose against mine, I know I will remember this moment as one of those precious ones. Where he let himself indulge, and I let myself be selfish until we go back to reality.

THIRTY SIX

RHEA

I trudge up the steps to the healer's cabin in the dark of night the next day, the air warming with summer approaching. Anna opens the door for me silently, looking around for signs of anyone else before letting me in.

I've been doing checks around Eridian all day since talking to Solvier last week, making sure all is well, which it is. There have been no signs of anything wrong and The Deadlands atop the cliffs are quiet. A bit too quiet after having such high activity recently. The Elite search party has been coming back empty handed and frustrated every so often, finding nothing in their search for Sarah. Darius was furious this morning with them, his face murderous as he spoke harshly to his men. It seemed that Leo was trying to talk him down, but Darius just shook his head and walked off with Maize, their heads bent together talking. Leo, Damian, Jerrod, and Zaide held back, choosing not to follow after Darius. They watched me and the guys closely as we passed them, and I didn't like the look in their eyes. They were hard and cold, far more so than usual, and it makes me wonder just what was said because I hadn't seen Darius since. Since the vow was made, all Elites have been more laid back, so seeing them like that has rattled me a little.

I wonder if their deadline is approaching.

"She's awake," Anna whispers, bringing me back to her, and

she nods her head for me to go through the door to Sarah's room. She hasn't left this room since she's been here, over three months now, making this space her own. Not that she could leave the cabin if she wanted to with the Elites turning up.

I enter her space with Anna behind me, closing the door softly. Sarah sits on the bed, looking at something in her hands before she notices us. She quickly puts the item beneath her covers on the bed before getting herself comfortable. She's looking better with the weight she has gained and with her healing increasing now that the dassil flower's effects are fully out of her system now.

She's made the room her own. Scattered papers with drawings litter the room's surfaces, paints and dried flowers haphazardly collected together on a table in the corner. I see several different varieties of them. Who's been bringing her flowers? I give her a smile as I bring a chair from the side of the room, dragging it toward the bed and taking a seat.

"Hey." She smiles, her toffee eyes lighter than they have ever been. "I saw you just last week, I didn't think you would be back so soon." Neither did I, but I said I would keep her updated, and I will. I've been sneaking into the cabin when I can in the night, making sure no one is around to notice. Apart from the couple nights I've seen her, Josh has been keeping her company when he can, but we have been busy for the last week.

"It's just a quick update," I tell her, and then steel myself for what I'm about to tell her, unsure how she will react. I wanted to be the one to tell her myself. "There was a man in the forest last week. He tried to grab one of our girls, Sam." She tenses at my words, and her worried eyes lock with mine.

"Is she okay?" Her voice trembles as she asks, but my heart warms that even though she doesn't know this girl, she's still worried for her.

"She's shaken up, but Kade is with her." He hasn't left her

side since. She won't let him, and he can't refuse her. "We don't know who this man was as there is no sign of him now. Sam said he was as tall as Josh with dark hair and his eyes were brown, possibly lighter, but then maybe blue. She also said he smelled like bad iron. Do you possibly know of anyone like that?" The thought crossed my mind that it could be someone else looking for Sarah, and even though I doubt it, I have to ask her.

She thinks for a moment before eventually shaking her head. "No, not that I know of. Though I don't know for sure because my memory is still blurry from them giving me the drug," she whispers. I nod, assuming as much. "Do you think it's someone from my pack?"

"I honestly don't know," I tell her. "We haven't had anyone come to Eridian unless we brought them here. Now the Elites are here and a male suddenly appears only to disappear again."

"Are the Elites still looking for me?" She picks at her fingernails, waiting for my answer.

"They are. Their search party came back from The Deadlands today and found nothing. I don't think they have long left on their time limit and should be going soon. It seems tensions are running high. The Elites that are using the spare cabin are slowly healing, but Anna can speed that up when we need her too. There is not much that can still keep them here."

"Those Elites are nearly healed," Anna says from her position by the door. "They should be ready to go in a few days if I let them. Their witch, Maize, has been helping. She is a very curious one, so I've had to be careful with what I do. She's not a healer, though she knows the basics, so I try to occupy her with other things when she's around them."

"What do you mean curious?" I question her.

"She always watches me closely when I tend to the Elites, and I've also seen her watching the pack when she thinks no one notices. She stays hidden and far back unless she eats dinner with us at the gathering. I don't like it, Rhea." She moves to lean against the table beside Sarah's bed, her brows scrunched in worry.

Now that I think about it, I haven't seen her around all that much. A few times at dinner at the gathering, but that's it, and she didn't go with the search party into The Deadlands. So what has she been doing?

"What level witch is she?" I ask Anna.

"High, if I were to take a guess."

"That's worrisome," I mutter, and sit back in my seat in thought. "If she was up to something that she shouldn't be, we would know about it by now, right?"

Anna sighs, a curtain of red curls flowing around her face as she looks down toward her feet. "I don't know if she is up to something or just curious, but it's just strange how she observes us so closely, especially me when I'm healing. I know this place is new to her, but she takes that curiosity to another level. I've seen her try to talk to a few members, but she gets nothing from them. She tries to talk to Kade a lot when she sees him, but he just straight up ignores her," she huffs. "We're loyal, we won't tell her shit. But she never seems overly frustrated when she gets shut down and then stomps off into the forest."

"I will keep an eye on her and ask around. No one has come to me about her yet, so maybe her curiosity is innocent, but it's worth asking them anyway. If the Elites are ready to be fully healed, a few more days and they will be leaving if their time limit is up. We will have to see." Anna's eyes turn sad at the thought, and I give her a small smile.

"You will still be going with them then?" Sarah asks, already knowing about me going to the Highers. Josh updated her on that.

I nod. "Yeah. I committed a crime against the Elites, and with the vow I made with Darius, you will all be safe."

Sarah looks down at her hands before tucking some of her dark hair behind her ear. "It's my fault the Elites are here in the first place," she whispers. "You shouldn't be punished when it's my fault.

I reach forward slowly and take her hand in mine. I wait for her eyes to come to me before telling her. "It was my choice to go into The Deadlands, and it was my choice to do what I did to try and stop them from finding Eridian, even if it didn't end up the way I wanted," I laugh sadly, shaking my head. "But it was my choice to do what I did, just like it was your choice in choosing to live and come here." Tears fill her eyes, and she squeezes my hand tightly in her grip. "Never feel bad for making that choice. The situation isn't the best right now, but we will make do. We always make do with what we have. The pack will be in good hands with Kade with many guiding him, especially Josh while I'm gone." At the mention of him, a smile spreads across her face, and my own genuine smile appears.

Josh thinks I haven't noticed him sneaking in here for more than check ups, but I have. I won't push him though. He will tell me when he's ready if something is going on with them. I'm just glad Sarah seems to have someone close to her, especially a male with what she's been through. I know Josh won't hurt her, and I guess she knows that too.

I stand from my seat, giving Sarah's shoulder a squeeze. "I'll see myself out," I tell them both, moving for the door. I go into the hallway of the cabin and pause to take a breath.

I don't think it will be long before I'll be leaving Eridian for who knows how long, I don't even know when I'll be back. I don't know what my punishment will be either, but I'll take it to keep everyone safe here. Edward told me about the trials that happen at the Wolvorn Castle, but he never went into details on what kind of punishments are given. Darius wants my punishment to be passed over to him, but will that be the outcome? Does he have the power to be granted that request by the Highers?

I guess time will tell what's in store for me.

I walk to the front door, pressing my ear to it and listening for any signs of movement on the other side. When I hear nothing, I silently open it and close it behind me. I scan the area, seeing no sign of anyone before I make my way toward the gathering in the center.

I press my hands to the trees in greeting as I pass them until I reach my seat. I slump into it, stretching my feet out in front of me. The fire pit in the center is just a glow of embers at this time of night, the slight warmth from it reaching me. I take my knife from my boot, looking over the hilt and running my fingers over the familiar writing there. *Arbiel Canna.* We bleed wolf. It's a vow to love and protect. A statement to be true to who we are, what we are.

My father gave me this knife as an early birthday present, he couldn't wait to give it to me. I smile as I remember how mad Mom was at him, telling him he should have waited until my birthday later on in the week. She didn't stay mad for long though. Dad and I went to pick her favorite lesia flowers, and she couldn't keep the smile off her face when we gave them to her. I still remember how they smelled, how their pale blue petals darkened at the edges. I loved rolling around in them when I was a child. Mom would take me to the blooming meadow in our woods that was full of them, and tell me stories of the Gods while Dad was busy being Alpha of our pack. The pack that betrayed us, betrayed their Alpha.

The smile fades from my face as I remember what happened the day after Dad gave me that gift, after Mom sang me to sleep that night. If I had just stayed home instead of wandering into the woods behind our house… If I hadn't overheard a conversation I shouldn't have, would things be different now?

Would Mom and Dad still be alive? Would I have been free?

My fingers grip the hilt of the knife tighter, remembering my mom's screams as they came for us during the night. My dad hadn't returned home, and I wanted him to come back and help. There were too many of them and they were too strong. I tried to get them off Mom with my knife, cutting one of them before I was grabbed from behind and hit in the head. When I woke up, I was alone in a room, a cage surrounding me. It was a little later after I had woken up that they came. They would taunt me with my parents' deaths, saying it was all my fault, that I was to blame. And I should accept my punishment and do what they want.

I remember my own screams echoing in my ears at the pain they inflicted, my ankles and wrists raw from trying to get the chains off. My stomach felt like it was eating itself in hunger, my throat so dry that only cracked sounds escaping from me. Then came my fourteenth birthday, when Runa came to me. They were prepared for the day that my wolf would come, though they just didn't think it would happen so soon. I didn't either. I managed to bite and claw two of them, injuring them greatly, but I was restrained again quickly. I spent days in agony from then on, forced to stay in wolf form to see how much I could take, how much I could heal, if I showed anything out of the ordinary.

They finally let me shift back, but then Runa refused to come back out after all we had endured and knowing how much pain would come again. But then we were dealt more pain for not doing as we were told. It was a lose-lose situation, and both options were us suffering.

Runa growls at the thought within me, at the thought of them and the pain we endured for so many years. I don't hate her for not coming back out, she was protecting us in the way she thought best. Being in human form was the lesser of two evils, they couldn't do as much as they wanted to do to us in human form because I couldn't heal as quickly. But it was still torture. Runa has been frightened to come back out ever since, fearing that what happened before would happen again. She knows we're safe here in Eridian, that no one would hurt us here. But having just come to me for the first time when I was fourteen and then immediately experiencing that trauma, I wouldn't want to come out again either. Innocents shouldn't suffer at the hands of monsters.

I inhale sharply as the blade cuts my fingers, blood welling to the surface. I bring my hand up to my face, watching as the red liquid trails down my hand. Who knew something could hold so much power, yet also be an invisible burden?

I'm always at war with myself about if I did the right thing being in Eridian. Did I make the right choice hiding away from the whole of Vrohkaria, helping those who need it in secret when I can instead of the lands as a whole. But then when I look at the smiling faces of my pack and watch the pups play, smiles so wide on their faces as they laugh, I can't say I regret it.

I shuffle forward in my seat before lowering myself to the ground and crossing my legs under me. I take my bloodied hand and press it to the earth, closing my eyes and murmuring a prayer. *"Ir mal terria, dah vek et ce."* My blood pools on the ground, the soil gently letting it seep into the earth as my hand warms against it, the land saying its thanks. I open my eyes when the warmth leaves me, and bring my hand back up to look at it. There's not a cut in sight, just the stain of my blood, and I let out a small smile.

Then the air changes around me, and I don't move as I tense. I don't even look in any other direction as the words come from me with a snarl on my face.

They're low, deadly and vicious. A warning.

A threat.

"Who the fuck are you, and what do you want?"

THIRTY SEVEN

RHEA

How did this person get through the barrier around Eridian, and how did they just turn up here unnoticed?

"Someone is here, an outsider. Make sure Axel, Finn, and Eliza stay close to the cabins. Those that were in heat came back to the main area this morning. Tell anyone who is able to, to go to the pups' houses and protect them. Tell Kade to stay at home with Sam and Sybill, but you guys need to come down here," I order Josh, knowing he'll do what I say without a second thought. "*Notify the Elites.*"

I get up slowly from the ground and turn and face the intruder. My insides twisting at someone being here uninvited, it hasn't happened before. The pack needs to be safe, and I don't think this person is here to talk. The figure stands in between the trees, shadowed in all black with the hood of his cloak pulled low over their face. I can only make out the bottom of their chin as I face him. I suspect this is the man who tried to grab Sam. What are the chances that person that entered the forest a week ago, and this person inside the barrier are two different people? The chances are slim. The figure doesn't speak, but I feel eyes boring into me, making my skin crawl. As I twirl the knife in my hand as anger takes over, causing me to growl low and deep from my chest.

"Who are you?" I repeat, walking forward until I'm at the end of the seats, making sure nothing is in my way. Still, they don't speak, and it unnerves me.

I hear the crunch of twigs behind me, but I don't look at the guys as they settle in around me. Josh stands to my left side, blade in hand as Hudson and Colten stand at my back. Taylor takes my right with Seb. The air is tense and full of violence directed toward the intruder.

Their gloved hand comes up and we all tense at the movement, but all they do is slip it inside their cloak. They pull out a small, dark crystal, holding it in their palm as they tilt their head to face us. As their body turns, I see Darius and his men entering the gathering, their postures as tense as mine.

Darius's expression is hard, muscles straining against the fabric of his dark t-shirt, and his black blade rests in his right hand against his thigh. Leo has a bow aimed at the intruder, Zaide has his twin blades out and Damian and Jerrod have their weapons at the ready. I watch as Darius gets closer to the intruder, scanning them from head to toe before stopping a few feet away from them. Darius looks my way briefly, his eyes roaming over me, seemingly to check me over before turning back to the cloaked person. I watch as they silently stare at each other when I see movement to the right, a blur of long, dark hair between the trees surrounding the gathering.

"Who sent you?" Darius demands with a growl, and my head whips his way. What does he mean who sent him? Does he know who this is? My hand tightens around my knife at the thought.

The cloaked figure shrugs, before tossing him the dark crystal. Darius catches it with his free hand, never taking his eyes off the hooded figure who nods his head at it. Damian and Zaide walk closer to Darius, keeping his sides protected as Darius looks down at the crystal.

"Where did you find this?" he asks, confusion evident in his tone as he turns the crystal over in his hands. The figure waves his hand around us, indicating it came from Eridian and my brows furrow. Darius looks over at me. Our eyes connect as tension rises between us, a frown on his face. before he runs a hand over the top of the crystal, and small, yellow sparks ignite from it before his eyes turn unfocused.

My eyes widen at the sight, and I take a step closer toward him without thought. I sense magic in the air coming from that crystal, magic. How is that even working inside the barrier? I stop moving again when more small sparks fly out of the object he holds, becoming brighter as Darius just stands there, his men protecting him. My heart thunders in my chest, feeling a sense of wrongness coming off that crystal. Something isn't right.

We all stand motionless for a time, some staring at the figure, some staring at Darius. My eyes flick to the intruder when the deepest growl I have ever heard suddenly rips from Darius. My heart drops to my stomach, my blood instantly running cold. The crystal stops producing sparks, the glow from them fading, and Darius's head slowly turns toward me. His eyes are now clear and aimed directly at me filled with pure, uncontained fury. His eyes bleed black at the edges of the whites and I swallow over the lump in my throat. I look around subtly at everyone to see if I'm missing something, but my guys look just as confused as I am at this sudden hostility. The Elites look between the two of us trying to make out what's going on.

A dark chuckle sounds from Darius, and every single hair on my body stands to attention at the violence in it. At the pure darkness vibrating from it. Runa flattens her ears, teeth bared to the sudden rage pouring off of him. It feels like it's wrapping itself around me, suffocating me with every breath I take and leaking into every fiber of my being. My heart rate picks up, and my hands tremble.

"Your sins keep coming, little wolf." He moves toward me, a deadness to his eyes I have never seen before. They're so different from the lightness I saw in them with the wisps and the wolf pups. So different from when he kissed me under the moonlight. "You are the cause of everything. Yet you stay here, thinking you can live out the rest of your life in peace while the rest of the lands suffers because of you?" he roars, and I recoil from him, my eyes going wide at his words. At his outburst.

Because of me? What? I shake my head quickly, my voice hesitant when I ask, "Darius, what do you—"

"You think you can get away with what you've done?" He cuts me off, and my mouth slams shut as I swallow hard. "You think you will not pay for the deaths you have caused!?" He snarls, teeth bared as he looks over my body in so much disgust that I feel my soul aching from it, hiding from it. "You're not even worth spreading your legs for the lowest of the low, and you thought you could keep peace by having an Elite in your bed!" The guys start shouting at him, telling him not to speak to me this way while I'm stood frozen. "I will make you wish you never met me by the time I'm done with you. I will carve you up, chew you out, and make you suffer in your own filth for the rest of your days," he spits at me, and I suck in a wheezing breath as tears sting my eyes at the absolute carnage of his words.

Confusion and flight or fight war inside me as I watch him in shock, in disbelief. Darkness starts to seep around the edges of his body, dominance leaking out until it hits me hard and fast, feeling like it's tearing through my flesh and hitting my lungs. I inhale sharply at the pure power radiating off of him, and everyone around us struggles to stay on their feet as the ground trembles beneath us. Beneath him.

What the fuck is happening?

The cloaked figure lets out a low, menacing laugh. Their voice is mixed, sounding like more than one person is talking as they speak. "It seems we have found the answers we have been looking for, Alpha Darius," the intruder croons, letting me know that he is in fact a male. I look at him as he steps up beside Darius. He brings his gloved hand up and clicks his fingers once. The snap is so loud in the all but silent air, like a whip cracking against bark. "I'll let you take care of retrieving the traitor and all who aided her." With those words, they nod at each other before he vanishes into nothing, making me look around the space for him. He's nowhere to be seen. Did he port without a stone? Who's a traitor? Who aided the traitor?

"What the fuck is going on?" Josh growls next to me as we stare at the spot where the male vanished.

A lone, long howl pierces the air, and my whole being locks up, pain radiating through me as I look toward the night sky. The glitter of stars spreads across it before ripples of dark pink and orange appear on Eridian's now visible barrier. Small at first, until they become bigger and spread across the surface.

My heart stops.

"Josh." My voice trembles as I speak, at what I'm witnessing happen before my eyes. That lone howl still echoes around us, haunting me until another one is released. "Solvier," I breathe, my body shaking. "It's Solvier." The barrier starts to blink, appearing and disappearing, and I look away from it, locking eyes with Darius who smirks at me. "What have you done?" I whisper, not believing what I'm seeing.

"In a matter of moments, my Elites and the Highers' guards will be porting just outside the barrier to take you all back to the Fenrikar," he says coldly. "They will all pay for aiding the traitor of Vrohkaria, especially the pup."

"Traitor?" I shake my head, waiver on my feet. They will all pay… the pup? What is he talking about? "I don't understand, what is going on?" My breathing increases, my palms start to sweat. "Who is the traitor, Darius?" I ask, my voice high as panic sets in.

"You are."

Time stops. The breath leaving my lungs as shouting reaches my ears, screams along with howls soon joining until it slowly fades away. I look at Josh, my movements sluggish and slow. His face is enraged as he points at Darius, his mouth moving, but no sound reaches me. I look to my other side and see Taylor, his blade up as he stands half in front of me, as if he's trying to shield me. I look toward the Elites, their faces enraged and weapons held tightly. I don't understand. How am I a traitor to Vrohkaria?

What was that crystal?

What did it tell him?

How do his Elites know the location of Eridian?

Who was that man?

My mind bombards itself with questions as my eyes slowly come back to Darius, his light-green ones locking with my ice-blue ones. Darkness floats around the edges of him, like he has two shadows at his back. The power radiating off of him is just waiting to be released, unleashed. My eyes roam over his face, the tense set of his jaw, the way his hair falls against his forehead, the flatness in his eyes. I realize now more than ever why he is to be feared.

A buzzing reaches me until I hear someone talking. Quiet at first until it finally reaches me. *"Rhea! What's happening? The barrier is coming down."* A panicked voice reaches me in my mind. Who's talking to me? *"Rhea, please! Answer me!"* It's Kade.

Kade. The pup is Kade. Fuck.

"Kade, run! You need to go. Now!" I scream back at him down the link.

"My head hurts, I don't know what's wrong with me, what's going—"

"Kade?" I call. *"Kade!"* He doesn't reply, the link shutting down.

"You're not fucking touching her. Do you hear me!" Josh roars, and the world finally starts moving around me again. Sounds coming from all directions.

My body finally moves and I turn and run, nudging Runa harshly to give me strength as I head toward my cabin. Toward Kade. Shouts sound behind me. They're shouting at me, but I ignore it, just like I ignore the dark, low laugh Darius lets out that sends my body trembling with the danger in it. I bite into my left arm, blood flowing into my mouth with the deep wound, and I bring my opposite hand up, gathering the blood there on the palm of my hand. I press it to any trees I pass, gathering more blood from my wound as I go and repeating the process.

When no trees are left for me to place my hand on, I gather the last of the blood welling on my arm and paint my right hand with it. With enough blood there, I quickly press it to the ground, whispering under my breath as I continue to run home. "Zahariss, hear me. Grant me protection against those who have ill intentions. Against those that bring injustice upon us. *Va ka reidu, lec fa dienn,*" I plead. I beg and I pray and scream and shout inside of me that I can reach Kade before it's too late.

THIRTY EIGHT

RHEA

People suddenly appear out of nowhere twenty steps away from my home, coming from in between the cabins all clad in dark leather armor. Some have green straps across their chest, others black. I spin in a circle, looking at all who surround me with their weapons out, aimed at me. I bend slowly with my heart in my throat and take my knife out from my boot, growling at them. Visions of light illuminate gently across the ground, like a flowing misty river, causing some of the armored males to grunt in pain when it reaches them while others fall to their knees. Zahariss answered my call. I head for two that have slumped to the floor, aiming to jump over them to get to Kade. The glint of a blade to my side catches my attention.

I lean back on myself, the male's short sword an inch from my chest as I spin and aim a kick at him. I hit his stomach, and he grunts, folding over on himself. I grab the back of his head and bring my knee up, smashing it into his nose. Pain radiates through my kneecap as it threatens to buckle, but I hold steady. Slashing out with my knife and then kicking the male over, I move toward an opening in the circle. Darius suddenly steps into the gap I was aiming for, and I snarl at him, coming to a halt. He now wears the same armor as the men around us, but he has two leather straps across his torso, one red, one gold. Making it known he's the Alpha of the Elites.

"Rhea!" Josh shouts, and I turn, seeing him running toward me with the guys, but men stop them, engaging them in a fight. The sound of clashing metal hits my ears over the racing of my heart.

Colten jumps on Damian, blade in hand. Hudson tackles Jerrod to the floor while Taylor goes blow for blow with Zaide. Seb grabs a guard off of Finn and aims for his temple, while I spot Axel tackling another. I look around, seeing Elites and the Highers' guards grabbing my pack, the cries of the kids for their moms piercing my soul. My breathing picks up as I look toward my own cabin, seeing no lights on inside and screams flood my ears from all around me. I look back at Darius as he grunts and looks toward the ground where light is shimmering along the surface. His brows dip until he bends down and places a hand atop of it. He mutters something I can't make out and the light stops, sinking into the ground and disappearing all together. Zahariss's small protection ending. The sighs of relief come from the men surrounding me as they stand to attention with the Alpha of Elites in their presence, glaring at me.

"Arhhh." A pained shout comes from ahead, and my eyes widen when I turn and see Kade staggering out of our front door, Maize at his side.

An Elite grabs a hold of him, dragging him roughly toward us, and I growl. No. No, no, no, no. I step forward to go toward him, but the Elite that has a hold on him brings his blade up to Kade's throat, the threat clear. Maize smirks beside them, her posture relaxed as her eyes scan the chaos before her. Kade holds his head between his hands as I'm unable to move, his face scrunched in pain. The circle of men creates a space for him as they reach us, and he's thrown forward. He stumbles and then falls to his knees. I rush over to him as quickly as possible.

"Carzan," I whisper to Kade as he grunts in pain, gripping his head tightly between his hands, his fingers pulling the blond strands. What is wrong with him?

My body trembles as I raise my knife, kneeling protectively next to him. Grabbing the hilt, I go to slice my palm, ready to ask Zahariss for more help, when an arrow whizzes past me and grazes my cheek. I stop short as I hiss, the scratch stinging as blood trickles down and drips from my jaw. I turn my face to Leo, bow in hand, arrow notched as he moves his aim to Kade who's still holding his head before me.

"Be careful of your actions, Rhea." Leo warns, pulling the string of his bow back, ready to fire at Kade. I know he won't hesitate to do it, the look in his eyes says as much. I lower my knife slowly and place it in my boot as he watches my every move.

I need to get Kade out of here. I need to get him somewhere safe.

A commotion has me looking toward my cabin, and I see Sam run out, Sybill on her heels. Sam stops short at the mayhem around Eridian, looking around wildly until she spots Kade at my feet. Her face crumples, tears flowing, and she makes a move toward us. Sybill grabs her and holds her close as she tries to get to him, shouting his name with so much terror in it. She has never shouted before. Maize steps up next to them, a look of disgust on her face and blade in hand. Sybill drags Sam behind her, shaking her head wildly at the threat, backing up to protect her daughter as another a male joins them. My hands shake as I watch my home being overrun by Elites and guards, my pack dragged around and tied up. *How did this happen?*

The barrier around Eridian flickers aggressively, and as another pained howl echoes around us, my body trembles with awareness. I turn my head and see Josie and Danny are trying to get to each other, screaming for one another with desperation. Taylor is still fighting with Zaide while Hudson has managed to get near Colten. They stand back-to-back as they deflect

Damian and Jerrod's attempts to subdue them. Seb is on the floor, two Elites trying to wrap rope around him. Another cry reaches my ears, and I see Katy at her cabin door, holding little Oscar close to her chest as they try to take him off of her. A sob bubbles up in my throat. I go to stand on shaky legs to try and do anything to help, but one look at Leo with his aim still on Kade has me frozen.

"Josh!" A scream comes from the left of me. A scream so full of desperation my blood turns cold, so very cold as I slowly move my head to look at the healer's cabin, tears stinging my eyes.

Oh, Gods.

An Elite has Sarah in his grasp, pulling her down the steps as Anna follows, her face bloody as she lifts her palms. Red tendrils flow from her hands, twisting strands ready to strike when a guard backhands her, her head twisting to the side as she crumples to the floor. The male is on her instantly, winding rope around her wrists until it glows. I watch as she struggles until she finally slumps into the ground, subdued.

I look back at Sarah as she claws at the male Elite dragging her, screaming and kicking with everything she has for him to release her. Josh aims a punch at a male's temple, not even waiting until the guard collapses to the ground before he makes a run for Sarah, his growl deadly. He dodges Elites, pushing one out of the way, and slicing another as he makes his way toward her. He's so close to reaching her when a body hits the side of him, and they both go down in a tangle of limbs.

"Get off her," he shouts at the man holding Sarah as he tries to get the guard off of him. "Don't you fucking touch her!"

The Elite holding Sarah tightens his grip on her, one arm around her torso, the other around the front of her throat as he drags her over to us. I stand slowly on trembling limbs as a tear escapes my eye. I keep close to Kade, making no move to attack as Leo keeps a watchful eye on me. I watch on as if I'm in someone else's body as Darius looks at Sarah curiously. I watch on as he steps closer to her and grabs her chin, moving her face side to side, and I watch as his eyes light up in recognition as they come to mine before looking back at her.

Josh is still shouting. Taylor, Seb, Hudson, and Colten are still fighting a losing battle. Anna is still slumped on the floor, and Danny and Josie are tied up beside her as they huddle together. An Elite and Maize have Sam and Sybill backed into a corner and someone has finally taken Oscar from Katy. The Elites and guards are taking my screaming pack members out of their cabins, the kids petrified and crying, mothers begging. Kade is whimpering in pain on the ground next to me as I look around me at the sheer number of people, and the position we are in. Then I finally look at Darius, and I know it's all over.

"You said you would protect them. We made a vow," I whisper at him. I know Darius hears me, but he's still looking over Sarah's face, whose eyes are wide with horror, looking up at him as his tall frame towers over her.

"We did," he agrees coldly. "But no more. Time to go home, isn't it, Sarah?"

And there it is, he knows exactly who she is, the woman he has been searching weeks on end for. The reason he entered The Deadlands. The reason he hasn't been able to go home and continue his search to stop the rogures. I was hiding her from him all this time and now he finally knows.

My vision blurs around the edges at the look in Sarah's eyes. They're lifeless now, it's like she doesn't even breathe anymore. Darius releases her chin without another look and steps into the circle of men as the barrier that was rippling around us finally breaks. Tiny specks of light fall down around Eridian, dark pink and orange dropping like small droplets of rain. I look up as another tear falls from my eye, my world imploding around me. The haunting last painful howl of Solvier burrows in my heart as it reaches me. Wisps come out of the trees, the cabins, and the ground, floating in between the specks of the barrier before coming toward me. I hold out a shaking hand, reaching toward them as a sob rips from my chest, the force of it nearly bringing me to my knees. The wisp's warmth touches me, their glow slowly dimming as the smallest one makes contact with my cheek. I close my eyes as more tears fall, feeling the connection between us and their familiar presence for what feels like the last time. The warmth slowly lessens, causing me to open my eyes. I look up with blurry vision, watching them fly into the night sky, their glow fading as the last speckles of the barrier sink into the ground, disappearing.

The blood from my cheek mixes with my tears, dripping onto the dirt below me, and it's like I can feel the earth beneath my feet weeping at the loss with me. The slight breeze caressing me is the land's cry, the swaying branches of the trees reaching out to each other in comfort are the wisps' heartbreak as Solvier's presence graces us no more.

Runa whimpers inside me, curling up against the pain in our soul, a lone howl leaving her. I encountered Solvier within my first moon cycle at Eridian, and he's been by my side for eleven years, helping and guiding me. He has been someone I can go to for words of wisdom. I don't have that anymore, Eridian doesn't have its guardian anymore and the land has lost a being that was worthy.

And now all is lost.

The screams of my pack still surround me, the gut-wrenching cries of the kids calling for their mothers as the Elites and guards drag them away, separating them. Just like I feared they would. I watch with detachedness. A numbness I'm all too familiar with but haven't felt in a very long time. I didn't know I could feel this way anymore. I didn't think I would ever feel the clutches of frozen shards surrounding my heart, piercing it with every breath I take, squeezing it with every scream I hear, bleeding it as every cry lodges itself deep inside.

Darius enters my blurry vision. He steps in front of me, looking down at Kade briefly before his cold, green eyes meet mine. He watches my tears fall with indifference, tracking them down my face then back up to the cut on my cheek until finally, his eyes meet mine.

They bounce between my dull ones before addressing everyone. "The laws of Vrohkaria have been broken. You are all to be taken to Wolvorn Castle in Fenrikar to be held there and put on trial. The traitor and her closest will be chained for aiding her, her pack will be questioned," he states, and a drowsiness suddenly starts to take over me. I look down sluggishly and see some sort of dark mist appearing around my ankles, seeping into me as I fall to my knees before him. My last remaining strength leaves me, and Kade slumps forward, his hands limply falling from his head as I reach out to him. Trying to keep him close and out of reach of anyone that can hurt him. My eyes go hazy and dark spots enter my vision as I lay on the ground, my hand touching the side of Kade's face. Everything goes quiet as I slip further into unconsciousness, my limbs struggling to respond as Runa tries to help me, pawing at me to get up, to move, but I'm too weak.

My eyes flutter as Darius crouches down beside me, his eyes still cold as they hold my rapidly closing ones. "Darius… don't, vallier… please…" I murmur to him as my eyes finally close, unable to keep them open.

The last thing I feel is coldness against both of my wrists as darkness overtakes me.

THIRTY NINE

RHEA

A wheezing sound releases from me, a steady flow of pain running through my body as the fog slowly begins to lift from my mind. My fingers twitch first, and I feel hard ground beneath me, my body laying on its side. A groan escapes me next as the coolness of the ground seeps into me despite the sheen of sweat coating my body. I blink my eyes open slowly, my hazy vision gradually coming into focus as I see dark-gray stone in front of me. I cough, my chest rattling, but I inhale deeper on the next intake of air to calm myself. The scent of damp hits me along with distant smells of other people, musk and old blood, causing me to shiver.

I moan softly as the pain fades to a deep ache, and I slowly stretch out my limbs, bringing my arms out in front of me. The sound of clanking brings my attention down to my wrists, and my heart drops like stone. I stare. Stare and stare and stare unblinkingly at the harsh metal surrounding my wrists. I follow the chains that are attached to each wrist in a trance, examining each loop until they end, welded into the hard stone ground.

I maneuver myself into a sitting position, still staring at the cuffs and chains attached to me, as ragged breaths leave me, providing the only sound I can hear in the empty space. I grab hold of the chains with both hands with my heart in my throat, and yank on it, trying to get it to come free as a whimper leaves me. I get to my shaky legs, looking around to see if there is something that can help me, but I'm surrounded by stone with bars on one side of the room. I'm in a cell. The only light I can see is coming from the hallway on the other side of the bars.

I pull on the chain more, backing up as far as the chain allows me and pull with my whole body, the cuffs digging into my flesh. I ignore the pain and the blood welling there, and just keep pulling and pulling, trying to get them off. Oh, Gods. Get it off, get it off, get it off. A cry escapes me, my body trembling, but I yank harder, a gritted scream coming from me when they don't move. I collapse to the ground, my fingertips digging into the stone.

"No, no, no," I whimper, moving over to where the chains are attached to the floor. I grab the metal in my hands, yanking, pulling, wrenching to get it to break open until I exhaust myself.

I thought I had escaped this.

I fall on my back, taking painful breaths of air as I squeeze my eyes shut until I have my breathing under control. I don't have my blade, my boots have been taken. I'm barefoot, only having my t-shirt and shorts. I don't know where Josh or Kade are. The link is shut, closed off to me. Runa's curled up inside of me, exhausted from trying to fight off whatever sent us into unconsciousness, and I don't even know where the fuck I am.

A scream comes from somewhere, and I jolt, my heart racing as I look toward the bars with wide eyes and into the cell across from me. Nothing moves in there, and when the scream stops there is only silence. Only a few drops of water leaking through small crevices above me can be heard. There is no sign of anything.

I move until I sit cross legged on the ground, the chains not long enough for me to reach any of the walls to lean against. I face the bars and try to ignore the metal around my wrists and the memories that try to invade my mind of the last time I was chained. I breathe deep and get a hold of myself. I can't think if I panic. I need to get out of here and find my pack. Then I need to find somewhere safe for us. *Eridian isn't that place anymore.* I swallow roughly over the thought of Solvier. He was connected to the barrier, had his essence intertwined with it, and now the barrier is gone.

I close my eyes and block out the pain. I need rest to gather my strength, but I suspect it won't be possible because it's not just iron in these chains that encase my wrists. I need to try though, because while I don't know what's coming, I know it won't be good. How did this even happen? Why did Darius break our vow and bring everyone to Fenrikar… That's where I am, where he said he was taking us. I must be in Wolvorn Castle, in the dungeons.

The reminder of Darius and the way he looked at me with lifeless eyes sends a shiver down my spine. He's looked at me coldly, in fury and disgust before, but never in the way he looked at me after holding that crystal.

I rest my head on my knees and wrap my arms around myself. I need to rest. I need to prepare for anything, everything. Whatever knocked me out has drained me. If I could just talk to Darius… He will see reason, he has to. I'm not a traitor, I don't understand where he's got that from. I've done nothing but protect people and give them safety and a home.

Both of which we don't have anymore.

Tears leak from my closed eyes, and I give in to the urge to shut down for a little while, to let my body try and recover from exhaustion and my bleeding wrists and cheek. I lay down, curl in on myself and pretend I'm not chained to the floor, but back home in Eridian, where we lived our simple life.

Six days. It's been six days since I've been down here. I've been doing my best to track time with the light coming and going from the hallway on the other side of the bars. The only time anyone comes near me is when the guards come to give me water and small pieces of bread at random times. I take it without a word, not wanting to receive anything from them, but knowing I need any source of energy I can get.

I sit in the center of my cell as footsteps sound far away from the left. Fast paced and hard. I lift my eyes to the bars, waiting. This isn't a guard that's coming. A figure rounds the corner, and when his all too familiar green eyes meet mine, my heart kicks up a notch. He looks over me, from the wound on my cheek from Leo's arrow to my frame that has lost a little weight. Then he notices the blood on my wrists. He stares at them for longer than I thought he would care to before he puts his hand to the bars. Some of the bars disappear, just enough that he can pass through and step into my cell, still clad in his armor.

"Where's Kade?" I ask him, my voice scratchy. I stand on my feet, wavering slightly but pushing through, not wanting to be at a disadvantage. Not wanting him to see me weaker than I already am.

"He has been seen by a healer and is waiting in the great hall to be put on trial." His voice holds no emotion as he closes the distance between us and grabs hold of my cuffed wrists, running his fingers over where the chains are attached. A glow escapes from them, runes appearing on the cuffs quickly before disappearing again. The chains drop to the floor at my feet, the sound echoing in the space with a loud clang. A thick chain appears between my cuffed wrists, connecting to each other as he grabs hold of it and turns, dragging me behind him roughly.

"What do you mean healer? Is he okay?" I stumble over my feet, still weak from whatever that mist was, and the metal infused within the iron cuffs that is making me heal slowly. He ignores me as we walk down the stone hallway, and I look into the cells on either side of me, trying to see if any of my pack is inside, but there is no movement. "Where are we going?" He ignores me.

Darius opens a wooden door at the end and begins to climb the steps leading upwards as I nervously look around. Torches light the way, my bare feet scraping against the jagged stone steps until we reach the top and another door. Pulling me through it, we enter a courtyard of sorts. Smooth stone slabs guide us along a path with sand circles dotted around the area that look like fighting rings, dried blood mixing in with the lightness of the sand.

"Darius, listen to me, you have to help us get out of here." I try to pull back, to get him to stop, but it's useless. "I don't know what happened in Eridian. I…I don't understand how I'm a traitor or—"

Darius whirls around on me and grabs a hold of my chin, his fingers digging into the wound on my cheek. I hiss in pain. "Shut the fuck up, Rhea. I don't have to help you with anything, I *won't* help you with anything." His fingers dig harder into my skin, and I wince. "I'll happily break your jaw to keep your mouth shut after what you have done." A breath leaves me as we stare at each other for a beat. I never thought he would physically hurt me. I have always felt strangely safe with him, but now, fear rattles through me at the look in his eyes, and I know he could be capable of it.

Please believe me that I'm not a traitor, that I don't even know what's going on, I plead with my eyes.

He turns and continues to drag me with him.

My stomach swirls with nausea as I look further in the direction he's taking me and notice we're inside the castle walls. They're tall, a dark imposing form that sends dread through me. The darker stone gleams off the sunlight and I recognize the flags of the Highers that float from the top of the battlements from the books Edward has given me. A green and black symbol of the moon cycle above a howling wolf, twin daggers resting on either side of it. It's the emblem of Wolvorn Castle, and a mockery of everything that the Highers are supposed to be.

I see guards around the area. Their armor is black with green straps compared to Darius's red and gold. They stand to attention, weapons at the ready as they watch Darius pull me along behind him. One of them spits at my feet as he opens a side door to the castle, leading me down a cold, narrow hallway. The sun shines through the high arched windows as we pass them. He takes me down more hallways and up another set of stairs before we finally reach another door.

This door has two guards standing on either side of it. They nod to Darius, opening the door so we can step through. The slam of the door behind us echoes around the large space. Tapestries of battles line the walls of the large torch-filled, domed space. Intricate patterns embedded into the marble floor along with the Highers insignia as we walk forward to two huge, dark oak doors at the opposite end. Darius nods to the guards beside it, and my heartbeat pulses in my ears as they open them. The creak of the hinges rattles against my skull as they push the wood, opening up to what must be the great hall.

People fill the space. The scent of wolves, witches, and others hitting me strongly after days of smelling the few same things in my cell. Even though my senses are weakened, the hall is so full of beings their scents assault me almost painfully. They turn when they see Darius and I enter, sneers on their faces as they make way for Darius to pass as I stumble along behind him, curling in on myself. The people surrounding us take their seats on the dark tiered benches that go at least fifteen stacks above me. Darius continues dragging me forward and then comes to a sudden stop. I collide with his back. I want nothing more than for him to shield me right now, enemy or not, but he pays no mind as he tugs the chain linking my hands and drags me forward forcefully until I'm in front of him.

A ragged breath leaves me at the sight of the chairs raised on a dais in a semicircle across from me. The chairs are elegant with green and black stitching against the pale seating pillows, with the largest one in the center curving high at the top with the Highers emblem hovering above it. Four hooded figures are lined below the dais steps facing us, their robes reaching the floor as their hands are clasped in front of them. A sound comes from a lower sunken level of the room before me, and my gaze lowers, following the few steps down with my eyes until I see Kade in the center to the right, and then Josh to the left. Their wrists are bound in chains that are connected to the floor between their feet, and I hold back the tears that want to escape. Josh turns his head to look over his shoulder, his gray eyes widening at the sight of me, full of worry.

One side of his face is covered in dried blood. He has a cut on his lip and temple with bruising on his jaw. His clothes from the day we were taken are filthy, mine faring no better. Kade on the other hand has clean pants and a t-shirt on, his hair clean from what I can see from the back of him as he hasn't turned his head toward me like Josh has.

A hard shove at my back sends me down a couple of steps before a hand on the back of my neck grips me tightly, guiding me to the center to stand in between Kade and Josh. I look down at the chain attached to the floor beneath me and Darius picks it up, attaching it to the chain connecting my two wrists. I feel his eyes on me, but I don't take mine off Kade. He's looking straight ahead, looking to be deep within his own thoughts. A tug at my chain has my eyes snapping to Darius, his green eyes hard.

"Dar—" I cut my self off with the snarl on his face. It's cruel, twisted. He turns and walks toward the steps that lead toward the hooded figures and then stands to the side of the dais. He turns and looks down at us as the people in the room finish taking their seats around the hall. They stop around the edges of the sunken floor we are standing in. The cloaked figures shuffle to the side as Leo, Damian, Zaide, and Jarrod come forward and stand at the edge of the dais with Darius, who looks toward them briefly before he folds his arms, watching the three of us.

My eyes go to Josh, looking at his bruised and bloodied face as his now dull eyes nod off to the side, the tightening in his face showing his unease. I follow the direction and the breath whooshes from my lungs as I see the people I never, in my life, wanted to see again. Oh, Gods. Brown hair, brown eyes. Blond hair, blue eyes. My heart rate picks up as my eyes swing to Kade, panic rushing through me. I go to step toward him, trying to reach him, only for me to jolt back when the short chain restricts me from going any further.

"Kade," I whisper, my voice trembling as I see him shake, his own fist clenching as he scrunches his eyes closed. "Kade, look at me. Just stay here with me. I'll get you out of this okay," I assure him, looking back over the people that haunt my memories and see their smug smiles and hostile glares.

I pause as I look them over, my own body beginning to tremble as I face some of my own monsters for the first time in eleven years. My Aunt Selena looks at Kade then back to me, her blue eyes lighting up as she folds her arms, a sadistic smile upon her lips. Uncle Paul stands next to her, the same tall and imposing figure I remember. His dark brown eyes flick to me before he turns his head to the side and starts talking. When my gaze moves to the male beside him, I stop breathing. Blue eyes so full of cruelty meet mine, and I can't hold back the shiver wracking my body as I'm locked in the stare of my cousin, Patrick.

Runa whimpers inside of me, retreating into a corner as she sees who I'm seeing. The people that were supposed to protect me, but instead helped have me tormented and tortured for years, never allowing me to leave the room that I thought I would die in. *Wanted to die in.* They didn't care that I was their blood, didn't care that my screams of pain radiated through that room. Some even joined in, one in particular, wanting to be in good favor of those in power.

I eventually break his stare, looking over at my other cousins, Richard, Alister, and Sophia, before my eyes land back on Aunt Selena. The way she's looking at Kade, the way her eyes light up in delight and with a knowledge that I don't know of threatens to cave my chest in.

"Darius." I look up at him in panic, ignoring his warning to keep my mouth shut and shake my head. "Don't do this, you're making a mistake." The room goes silent as I speak, but I don't care who listens. I just keep my eyes on him. "We made a vow with the Gods as our witness," I breathe, ignoring the scoff of people around the room at the mention of our Gods that they think have abandoned. My pulse pounds at Kade being in this room with these people. He can't be here. "Don't go back on it. You can't, please."

He stands there, unmoving, his bored stare leaving mine to look around the room. He ignores me, pretending I'm not even here, like I'm not right in front of him. His men grunt and scoff at my words, looking at the three of us with sneers upon their lips. They won't hear me, none of them will.

"Kade, listen to me," I rush out, as I turn to walk as close as the chain will allow me toward him, stretching as much as I can to be near him.

"You lied," he says in a tone I have never heard from him before, and my body tenses. "You lied about *everything*. I don't have to listen to anything you say. I won't." He finally looks at me, betrayal and anger shining in his eyes as I shake my head at him. "You stole me. You stole me from my family, from a life I could have had with my pack, but you kept me in Eridian." No, no, no, I try to tell him, but my throat has seized up, my mouth unable to make a sound. He remembers I took him from our old home? "You messed with my memories, hiding them from me, but I have them all back now. The ones you tried so hard to block out. My life would have been so much different if you hadn't taken me away. I could have been with my mate, happily living the way I was supposed to, but instead, I was trapped in Eridian, my mate died, and I had my memories fucked with. You did that, and I will never forgive you for it. Never," he spits so vehemently at me that I jolt.

I back up a step at his words, pain slicing through my soul and cracking me open. I blocked his memories because he was suffering from nightmares from when he was in their hands. I didn't know what else to do. If he had his memories back, he would know what they did, what they all did. I look toward my blood family and see their heads lowered to hide their smiles at the words Kade just said. And it's then I know… I know they've done something to him. They must have.

"Kaden," Josh calls to him, but he just scoffs, looking around me to see him.

"You're no better than her. You both took me away, and for what? To make sure my family suffered because you couldn't handle my father becoming Alpha? I was just collateral damage for your fucking twisted minds. And then you help her unleash a curse on Vrohkaria? You're both sick."

"What?" I gasp. That's not true. "What curse? No, Kade, that's not—"

Circular barriers suddenly appear around each of us separately, and I tense. The shimmering pale violet floats in waves around me before disappearing, but the barrier is still there confining us inside. A door to the right of the dais opens and more cloaked figures enter the hall, but instead of joining the other cloaked people, they walk up the steps of the dais. Maize follows behind them, her black hair elegantly up on the top of her head in a bun, smiling down at us before joining the Elites as the figures each take their seats. Darius still stands before the dais, his men near him, as new arrivals sit themselves in the empty seats.

The people around the room all bow their heads in respect, all but the Elites, whose stares mainly bore into mine. The cloaked figure in the center of the chairs then clears his throat and pulls down his hood. Dizziness overtakes me, and I sway on my feet, my fist gripping the chains attached to my wrists as hard as I can to keep me standing. My eyes freeze on the man in the center as he looks directly at me, the air disappearing, a bolder on my chest cracking me open. His eyes light up slightly before they roam over my body in satisfaction, making me want to peel the skin from my bones so he could never look at it again. *He knows who I am.* I swallow roughly, trying not to throw up as I hear his voice for the first time in so many years.

"Let's begin the trial."

FORTY

Rhea

Lord.

Higher.

Charles.

His voice echoes throughout the hall. That deep sound is so ingrained in my mind that I squeeze my eyes shut to gather myself, to stop my racing heart from bursting and stopping all together. I haven't heard it in so long, but I remember it well. I remember it laughing as I cried, mocking me as I screamed, taunting me about my mom and dad dying, giving me false comfort only to take it away in an instant, I remember it making me always wonder when he visited me which side of him I would get, until it was only ever pain.

Memory after memory rushes through my mind, causing my knees to weaken, and I'm unable to stand the force of them. My hand reaches out to the barrier to steady myself, warning sparks of pain come from it that shoot through my palms. I slowly peel my eyes open, keeping them on the ground and the chain there as I breathe. *Just breathe, Rhea.* I look to my left, seeing Josh's glare at him, knowing everything that he had done. He moves to the edge of his barrier closest to me, eyes full of hate and anger and concern on my behalf. I shake my head subtly when he glances at me, then turn my head to the right to look at Kade.

His spine is straight, fists still clenched at his sides as he looks in front of him, ignoring Josh and I entirely.

Kade might know these seated males are Highers, but he doesn't truly know who they are. It's the same with his parents and siblings. It's the same with fucking everyone. I've told him all his life to keep away from them if there was ever a time he was near them. It looks like that's been completely ignored by the smiles on our blood family's faces. What the fuck did they say to him and does he really have his memories? Because if he did, he wouldn't be acting like this. He wouldn't have said the things he did to me. He would be tearing them all apart.

I breathe deep and manage to straighten myself, I have to get him away from them. He can't go back to his family, and he can't be in the clutches of the Highers. With that thought, I raise my eyes and look forward, determination running through me.

"Alpha Darius, present why these three wolves are on trial. You have spoken to me briefly, but let the rest of the room know," Lord Higher Charles says, waving a hand toward the seated people in the hall and relaxing back in his seat, but I feel his eyes on me. It's like fire licking at my feet until it burns me alive.

I look across the dais and see the other Highers removing their hoods, expressions neutral on their faces. I look at each one, looking for a familiar face, but Edward is nowhere to be seen. Where is he? Does he know I'm here? He has to. I look further across the five Highers. Two seats are empty, but the five seated can still cast their votes when it's time.

"These wolves have been found traitors to Vrohkaria, some more than others. Kaden," Darius begins, nodding in his direction, and I tense. "He may be innocent, but he may have also aided Rhea in her treason, which I will get to last. I spoke with Kaden's family who are currently guests here. They saw him being taken to the healer's wing, and his mother was in hysterics as soon as she saw him. His mother, Selena, informed me he was taken as a pup, and he was never seen again. They searched and searched for him, but he was never found. It was around the same time their niece and an orphaned male went missing from the Aragnis pack. It turns out, Rhea and Joshua are the ones who had stolen him in the night." He points to us, loathing in his eyes, and I swallow. "Joshua aided them in leaving, making sure they were undetected with Kaden, but two of the Aragnis pack guards saw them." I gulp at the memory of killing one of them that tried to stop us, the other guard retreating as a blade went through their friend's heart, running back to announce us escaping. "All three were thought to be dead after they murdered a guard on their way out of pack territory, and they weren't seen again." The Highers all shake their heads at Josh and I, noises of disgust coming from them as the crowd murmurs.

"Alpha Paul, can you confirm for the room that what Alpha Darius has said is in truth?" Lord Higher Charles asks, turning his head toward my uncle.

I refuse to look at him.

"It is true. My niece caused great harm to us as a family when she was taken in by us when her mother and father went missing." I grind my teeth, that's not fucking true. "We gave her a home, and she repaid us by giving us nothing but trouble when she lived with us. But we never thought she would steal our son." His voice rings across the hall, strong and sure of his words. "Please go easy on my son. I'm sure my niece has filled him with nonsense over the years. The healer confirmed she had blocked his memories. They have only now been restored to him. He has lost so much time with us already."

"Did you know that your cousin had blocked your memories, Kaden?" Lord Higher Charles asks him, and I look over at the boy I raised since he was seven years old.

"No, I didn't know anything until the healer unblocked them. All she and Josh ever told me was to stay away from our old pack and that it wasn't safe." He turns his head, looking me dead in the eye. "She never let me leave where we lived, never let me go into other parts of Vrohkaria. I thought she was just being protective, but now I know how wrong it was. She was keeping me from my family as some sort of sick punishment for them."

"Carzan," I whisper, shaking my head at him, pleading. "That's not true, don't listen to them. You *know* me."

"My niece is clearly trying to manipulate him, even now, Lord Higher," my uncle interjects. "She brings great shame to the Aragnis pack, and the Kazari family—"

"Keep *my* family name out of your piece of shit mouth you… Arghhh!" I scream, caught off guard by a sudden pain shooting through my whole body. I press both hands against the barrier, panting as the pain fades away just as quickly as it came, listening as the crowd shouts in outrage at my words.

He doesn't deserve to have my mom's name. None of them do.

"You will act civilized in my hall!" Lord Higher Charles booms at me, and I let out a growled breath. Hating him, hating them, hating what they did. Hating them all so deep in my bones I would snap their necks in an instant if I could. Lord Higher Charles waits for the hall to calm again before he speaks. "That's enough from you at the moment, Kaden. Thank you. Joshua, did you or did you not take this woman and Kaden away from your pack territory without first applying to change packs, and then waiting for confirmation to that proposal."

"It's not that fucking simple! Unghh!" The barrier around Josh glows briefly as he falls to one knee in pain, and I realize he just got hit with whatever I did just moments before.

"It is a simple question to answer, Joshua." Charles snarls. "Yes or no."

Josh looks up at me, still on one knee, and I see in his eyes what he's about to do. The resignation and determination in his eyes. He opens his mouth to speak, but I beat him to it. "I forced him," I cut in, ignoring Josh's shocked eyes. "I made him believe that we could go to another pack and start a life together. With him being orphaned and my family line, he knew it would be impossible for us to be mated in the Aragnis pack as the current Alpha would deny it. He had a soft spot for me since we were kids. So I told him that for us to have a life together, we would need to leave with Kaden. We couldn't tell anyone we were leaving as with the pack being of my family line, it was forbidden for me to do so." I feel all eyes on me as I finish, but I hold Josh's eye, pleading with him to stay quiet. He swallows hard before dropping his head forward, his chest rises and falls as he takes deep breaths before slowly getting back to his feet.

"Is that correct, Joshua?" Lord Higher Charles demands, and at Josh's slow nod, he hums to himself. "Seems you are quite the manipulator. You still, however, have committed more crimes," he tells Josh, and I look over at Darius, his eyes boring into Josh's before looking me over with distaste. "Let's move on. I've heard enough on this particular crime, and I will take into consideration what has been said."

He waves a hand to someone off to the side, and I hear the creak of a door opening. A murmur spreads across the hall as a tall, blond male approaches the front of the dais, dragging a lifeless Sarah behind him. I hold in my reaction to seeing her. The tall male stops at the first step, guiding Sarah to stand next to him.

Lord Higher Charles takes in Sarah's disheveled appearance and shaky frame before looking to the male beside her. "Alpha Christopher, your daughter was taken from her home over three months ago. Has she told you where she has been?"

Shock courses through me. She's this Alpha's daughter? Fuck.

"Yes, Lord Higher." Alpha Christopher bows his head respectfully. "My daughter has told me she was taken and brought to a place she had never been before and couldn't leave. She was kept prisoner. She had extensive injuries from trying to fight off those who took her, and she was unable to get out of bed from those injuries, practically bedridden." Josh growls deep and low beside me, and I shoot him a warning look to stay quiet.

He's lying through his teeth, we know that. We don't know how this will play out though, and if Josh shows a reaction to her, I don't know what will happen.

"Is that true, dear?" Lord Higher Charles addresses Sarah, who stays looking at her feet, fingers twisting around each other. She eventually nods her head once, and my heart cracks even more.

I know she's scared, and that's my fault. I said I would protect her and keep her safe. Now she's in the hands of those that hurt her. She's petrified. Did he beat her before she walked into this room? Threaten her? I don't know, but whatever he did made her just lie to everyone in this room and confirmed what Alpha Christopher just said. I glance at Josh and see his face drop before he smooths it out into a neutral expression. But I know her words caused him pain.

"We are glad you have returned, Sarah. You are safe now. You can have all the time you need to recover and proceed with your arranged mating with Patrick Kazari." Lord Higher Charles smiles down at her, and I swear I stop breathing as a stillness comes over Josh.

I look over at my scum of a family, watching as a convincing, gentle smile spreads across my cousin Patrick's face as he looks at Sarah. It slips as she is taken from the room again, being rushed out a door and out of sight. That's when his blue eyes come to mine. Malice gleaming in them, and I bare my teeth. He grins, licking his lips, and I shiver.

"Alpha Darius, please continue," Lord Higher Charles commands, and it brings my attention to him.

"Rhea caused the deaths of six Elite trainees when we were in The Deadlands searching for Sarah. She admits to their murder, but she also had Sarah hidden in her home where we went to get our injured Elites healed. We asked her and showed a sketch of Sarah. She and others stated she had no idea who she was and told us she was probably dead if she ventured into The Deadlands. They clearly lied as we found her healing from injuries in a room in a cabin. Her pack also didn't tell the truth when we went around and asked them about her. They are all guilty of that crime, and hiding that they had created a pack."

"More lies and manipulations," Lord Higher Charles murmurs as the rest of the Highers mumble their agreements.

Darius walks closer to the steps at the bottom of the dais, and I watch his every move as he pulls out the crystal he held in Eridian. "This crystal was given to me by Higher Aldus."

That has to be the man that was in Eridian, that caused all of this with that crystal. How did a Higher get there? I scan the Highers in their seats, but none of them speak.

"Yes, you said as much when we briefly spoke. Unfortunately, Higher Aldus had to attend an urgent meeting that cannot be missed so he had to be absent today. He did confirm he handed the memory crystal to you after he traveled to meet with Maize to check on the progress of your search for Sarah," Lord Higher Charles states. Maize informed a Higher where we were living? Fury runs through me. "He also confirmed he found it in the place where these traitors were living."

A memory crystal? Found where we were living?

"The memory crystal showed me Rhea performing some sort

of ritual," Darius continues, his eyes coming to mine as I shake my head. "That ritual cursed Vrohkaria and brought the rogures to cause havoc across the lands, slaughtering and tearing villages and towns apart," he tells the room, turning the crystal over in his hands.

Shouts echo around me as my wide eyes look from Darius to the crystal, and then back again. "That's impossible. It's not true," I shout at him, my chest heaving at the thought. My words are ignored as people curse at me, letting me hear their words of how I should pay for my treason. Hanged, stoned and whipped over something I didn't do. My panicked eyes turn to Josh, his mouth moving, but no sound reaches me. They've blocked sound from escaping the barriers, not letting us be heard until they want us to be.

Darius passes the crystal to Lord Higher whose eyes go dull as he holds it, sparks coming from the object. "What Darius has stated is the truth. This is a grave crime you have committed against Vrohkaria. You have committed treason against us all, against your own kind." Charles passes the crystal to the other Highers, waiting until they have all seen this apparent memory of me bring the rogures upon us as I shake my head. "You are a disgrace to our kind. Tell me." He leans forward in his seat, dark eyes penetrating mine. "Why did you cause the lands to be plagued?"

"I didn't," I grind out, and Darius scoffs at me, his anger penetrating through the barrier.

"The evidence is damning," Lord Higher Charles barks, the sound sharp enough to rattle my bones, making me feel like a little girl again. Defenseless. Weak. "You cannot deny what we have seen with our very own eyes!"

"Can you deny what I've seen with *my* own eyes? What had been done to me?!" I scream back at him, my chains rattling as I bring them up and bang on the barrier. His eyes turn hard as pain rattles through me again, a warning to not say any more. I grit my teeth as he keeps a neutral expression on his face. A perfected facade.

"Why would the Highers and I take anything that you say as true? Why would anyone?" he says, and I grind my teeth. "You have lied and manipulated. You ran away from your pack, *stole* a child and blocked his memories. You killed Elite trainees and took a person of interest, kept them hidden whilst also failing to inform us that you had formed a pack. On top of all that, you have performed a ritual and brought savage creatures to Vrohkaria that slaughter and kill anyone they come across," he spits. The Highers murmur in agreement as more shouts from the people around the hall lash out at me while the Elites growl, glaring down at me.

"I didn't perform any fucking ritual. I have no idea what you are talking about!" I glare at Darius. "What you saw is wrong. What you all saw is wrong."

"Memory crystals cannot be changed," Darius tells me. "They cannot be tampered with."

"That is a lie because it obviously has been," I grind out, my body shaking at the implication of what they are saying, but I didn't do it. "I didn't do it."

I would never do such a thing, even if I knew how.

"You're lying again, Rhea," Darius snarls. "Your sins are put out before you, and you don't even have the decency to tell the truth."

"I am telling the truth," I shout. "I know nothing of a ritual. Know nothing about how the rogures came to be! They kill everything and anything. What reason would I have to do that when we are all in danger from them?!"

"That's what you're going to tell us," Lord Higher Charles says, and I scream. My body feels like it's being hit with raw electricity as my back arches from the pain coursing through me. I fall to my knees, chained hands on the floor as I feel blood trickle out of my nose. "Tell us why you cursed the lands and how we can stop it." I stay quiet, panting through the lingering pain when it hits me again.

I fall on to my side, my whole body shaking, and I bite my lip on a cry as my blurry eyes find Kade. He's finally looking at me again, finally giving me his blue eyes that I have seen every emotion in. Except hate. That's how he's looking at me right now. His eyes are full of hate, and a strangled sob escapes me at the sight, but I quickly quiet as the violet glow fades from the barrier and the pain slowly subsides.

"Thirty lashes, maybe that will loosen her tongue," a different Higher says, and the crowd all cheers and shouts their approval. I stumble to my feet, my hands clenching as I glare at them all while my body aches.

I bring my hands up and wipe the blood from under my nose when the chain attached to the one linking my wrists together suddenly pulls me downward. I'm thrown to the ground, my knees hitting the floor, and I hiss. I pull at my hands, but they are locked in place on the floor, I'm immobile. I can't stand, I can only stay on my knees as the barrier around me blinks out.

I lift my head, watching as Maize approaches the Highers with a whip in her hands. She bends at the waist, presenting it to them. Lord Higher Charles tilts his head, looking over at me before he turns, his gaze landing on Darius with a sadistic smile on his face. "As Alpha of the Elites and with Rhea extending your search, therefore keeping you from protecting our lands, I think you should do the honors."

FORTY ONE

RHEA

He wouldn't, would he?

Darius looks at Charles while the other Elites look around the room in silence. Charles continues to stare at Darius, his smirk never wavering. "I'm sure this will quell the rage within you at her deceit for a little while. This can be my gift to you, for all that you have done for Vrohkaria and all that you will continue to do," he tells him. When Darius doesn't move, Charles tilts his head at him.

Darius reaches a hand out toward Maize and grabs the whip by its black, worn handle. I swallow roughly. He pulls back slowly, letting the leather strips of the whip fall, the pieces nearly touching the floor. I swallow, looking it over from where I'm restrained, hands clenching. I pant through my nose, and I see Josh beside me, banging on his barrier the best he can, veins straining against his neck as he shouts, but I hear nothing. I just see the panic in his eyes. I look over at Kade, seeing his eyes widen slightly at what Darius holds, but he quickly clears his expression and looks down.

Is he still in there? Does he feel anything for what's about to happen to me? Does he not care anymore?

"Let's get the rest of her deplorable followers in," Lord Higher says, making my head snap in his direction.

Moments later, Taylor, Sebastian, Hudson, and Colten are

brought down the steps. Anna, Josie, and Danny follow behind them, all struggling as they are shoved forward and down the steps to where we are.

Their wrists are chained together, muffled sounds coming from behind the cloths tied around their mouths as they look over at us with wide eyes. Leo, Damian, Zaide, and Jerrod each take a place behind them, replacing the cloaked figures who brought them in. The Elites push them to their knees in front of me, their features pained when they hit the hard floor. Their clothes are as dirty as mine and Josh's, their faces also showing bruising where they have obviously been beaten.

How is this allowed? They did nothing wrong.

"They have all been questioned, as well as everyone else that was in your settlement. They refuse to talk. The blood witch is especially hard to crack. Maybe they will after we have given you some lashes," a Higher says, his bald head gleaming under the torchlight.

"That is yet to be seen, Higher Frederick," Lord Higher Charles tells him. "I'm sure they will talk eventually. If not, the traitor will." His confidence speaks loudly throughout the hall, so sure in himself.

"Will Joshua receive lashes as well for the start of his punishment for aiding a traitor," the Higher with dark brown hair asks Charles.

"I think that will be appropriate, Higher Mathew," he hums. "Higher Berthold, Higher Aiden?" The Highers both nod their head in agreement, their faces unkind.

"I will take his lashes," I croak, and my pack stills. Even Darius pauses at my words. I clear my throat, spitting out the blood dribbling down from my nose. "The law allows a replacement to receive punishment from those on trial. I will take it."

"You speak of the law, yet you break it so easily," Lord Higher Charles sneers.

"Law is still law." I lift my eyes, my resolve clear in them.

He sighs. "Although I disagree with this particular law under these circumstances, it is indeed the law, which I abide by." Bullshit. "Something you do not. Add twenty lashes to the current thirty." My pack renew their efforts of getting to their feet, their muffled cries getting louder behind the cloth on their mouths, but the Elites subdue them, keeping them kneeling easily in their weakened state. "Kaden, you will receive fifteen lashes. But as you are somewhat innocent in the crimes committed. I will allow you to pass your punishment on to the traitor. Do you agree?"

Kade looks down at me on my knees for a moment, eyes blank as he answers the Lord Higher. "I agree." My heart bleeds, but I'm thankful he doesn't have to endure the pain that's about to come.

My head turns as Darius walks down the steps slowly, the whip trailing along the floor. I look up at him. Silver specks float in his eyes, and I wince at the sight of them now instead of feeling captivated. Runa whimpers inside me, and I mentally stroke along her head, hoping to soothe her with the calmness I send to her. *It's okay. Everything will be okay.* I'm not sure if that's true, but I have to believe that.

Darius stops in front of me, his boots at my chained hands, and I look down at them. They're clean, laces tied tightly. I breathe in his scent, wrapping it around me as deeply as I can to prepare myself as I'm sure the air will soon be filled with the scent of my blood instead.

"Will your pack speak up and save you? Or will you finally tell the truth?" he muses, bringing the whip up and running his free hands through the strips of leather.

"I have told the truth. I didn't perform any ritual. I don't know what you think you saw, but you're wrong, Darius. You are so wrong," I whisper, my voice cracking on the last word.

He crouches low with a grunt, and I lift my head so his face is close to mine as I speak. "Think about what you have seen with your own eyes back at Eridian. Think clearly. I admitted to killing and harming your Elites, I never shied away from that. I made a vow with you to *protect* my pack. My world. Why in all that I am, would I ever do anything that would put my world in danger? Why would I do something like bringing the rogures here?"

"You lied about Sarah, right to my face, and hid her right under our noses. Many have died from rogures. I couldn't protect them because I was searching for her, because you kept her from me," he growls. "All you do when you open your fucking mouth is lie!" I look into his speckled eyes as I sigh.

"Darius, please, you have to believe me. I thought… I thought we got to a point where we were beginning to understand each other. I though…" The only reaction I get is the tightening around his eyes. My shoulders slump when he says nothing. He's not going to believe me. I did lie to him in Eridian, but I did it from a place of protection. I did what I had to do to keep us all safe, and it was all for nothing anyway.

We lock gazes, his eyes once again looking over my features as I wonder once again if he would really hurt me or if this is his anger speaking. After everything that happened between us in Eridian and the look of barely restrained fury in his eyes, I think he would really hurt me now.

The knowledge of that sends another unwanted crack through my already bleeding heart. I really thought after the few moments we had of this… connection between us, this pull of our bodies coming together regardless of the circumstances, that maybe he would be lenient with me when he brought me here. He would see me in some way other than this person he claims me to be.

I now know I was wrong to think that. I was wrong in that

moment in the forest, with wisps dancing around him. I was wrong about the warmth I felt in my chest when we played with the pups as he smiled and laughed. I was wrong when he kissed me under the moonlight, holding hands with me because he wanted to. He was wrong when he told me that I was his to protect, because he's not protecting me now.

"Do it," I tell him, and I feel my eyes hardening with what's to come.

"What?" he asks, confusion plain to see on his face. I see his knuckles whiten around the handle of the whip, his eyes darkening.

"I said. Do. It." I nod at the whip in his hand and shuffle on my knees, trying to get as comfortable as possible. "This should be easy right? Whipping a traitor. So get on with it."

He pauses, searching my face with his mouth in a tight line. "You're not going to try and lie your way out of it with that mouth of yours? Not going to plead for mercy?" he asks.

I look him dead in the eyes and whisper him a truth I know too well. "There is no mercy in Vrohkaria, Darius. You should know that with the Highers sitting on their self-appointed throne of lies, and the rogures roaming the lands at their feet." He blinks, his teeth grinding together as those silver specks get a little larger.

"Are we ready to proceed, Alpha Darius?" drawls Lord Higher Charles, and Darius holds my eyes a moment longer as he tenses, his eyes flashing black before he stands. His hand clenches around the handle of the whip, the leather creaking from the force as he moves behind me and out of sight.

I breathe deep through my mouth, slowly expelling my breaths as the fabric of my t-shirt tears at my back, exposing my skin to him, and I flinch as the cool air hits me. Runa whines inside of me, curling up to my back. I look over at Josh, giving him a sad smile as his eyes shine with unshed tears, still screaming and banging against the barrier, but nothing can be heard. I try to reassure him with my eyes before I turn my head forward, looking at my pack members one by one, my closest. Tears stream down Anna and Josie's faces, and they're all struggling against the Elites holding them, but they stop when I shake my head, my eyes telling them that it's okay.

Lastly my eyes go to Kade, my sad smile still in place as I look him over until our blue eyes meet. "I forgive you, Carzan." I don't know if he can hear me in his barrier, but even if he doesn't think he needs to hear it, I need him to know he has nothing for me to forgive him for. One day, it will all become clear, he will see, and he will hate himself for this moment. I know he will, but I won't let him. I see him swallow hard, emotion leaking into his eyes before he faces forward, not wanting to see what's about to happen.

I look up at the Highers, at Charles, seeing the sadistic grin he tries to hide behind the hand covering his mouth as he leans on the arm of the chair. I see it in his eyes though. I have seen it many times before when he told me he killed my mom and dad. When he taunted me until I cried for them, sobbing for them to save me. When he would try to use Kade against me to get me to do what he wanted. He loved how he could see the war within me as I tried to decide whether I should or shouldn't bend to what he asked of me. I've seen it over many years from when I was nearly seven years old to just weeks before my eighteenth birthday. I've seen it thousands of times in the basement below my mother's and father's home that he and others, including my blood, turned into my own living nightmare.

"Alpha Darius, proceed," Charles orders, waving a hand in our direction. No movement comes behind me. "We haven't got all night, I would hate for another punishment to be added."

My brows furrow at his words, but then a barely there growl comes from behind me before Darius finally moves. I hear the whip slicing through the air. I hear it glide with precision until it connects with my back, making my body arch from the sharp, burning pain. I try to hold it in, but a strangled scream escapes me as the second hit comes fast and quick. Then a third and a fourth, again and again.

No hesitation. No mercy.

Just like he said he had none.

Blood runs down my sides from my skin splitting, and I breathe through my nose, looking at a single spot on the floor as tears roll down my face as I wait for the next strike. A sob-like breath of air escapes me, and I grit my teeth and growl when it comes. Red paints the floor, the splatters making its own pattern before it becomes too much and pools around me. Agony fills me as another hit lands right on top of my already torn flesh. My body shakes from the intense pain. Runa whines inside of me as she presses as close to the surface as she can, trying to soothe me, but it's no use. I choke on my next breath.

Another strike.

I bite my lip, my teeth punching through it.

Another crack.

Just accept it. It's not forever, Rhea. You've had worse.

Another slash.

Breathe. Concentrate on the ground beneath you. Just stay looking at that one spot. Ignore that this is Darius doing this to you, your—

Another hit.

More tears pour from my eyes. *Hold it in. Don't you dare make another sound. Not one fucking sound.*

Another lash.

Do.

And another.

Not.

And another.

Break.

FORTY TWO

Rhea

My vision is hazy, my breathing labored as I'm being moved, lifted harshly on to something, but I still don't make a sound. My clothes are wet, the smell of blood all around me, soaked into my clothing and my skin. Voices sounding like they're underwater reach me as my head lulls to the side. Fingers are on my neck next, a growl, voices getting louder and then cold air hits me. I'm jostled as we move, blood rushing to my head as a shoulder digs into my stomach, my arms hanging loosely below me. I feel liquid trickle off my fingertips, and I imagine a trail of red splashes following us as we start going down steps. My eyes open slightly, seeing the stone before me before they blur again.

A pained breath comes from me when my body hits the cold ground, my head bouncing off the hard surface. Pain shoots through my skull. A whimper comes from me at the rattle of chains jangling, then my body is being moved again and my wrists are being pulled and then dropped. A sharp kick in my ribs follows, knocking me over onto my torn back, a scream catching in my throat until the air stills around me.

No sounds. No movement. I'm alone.

I blink my eyes open slowly, not moving as sobs wrack my body. The taste of copper comes next as it fills my mouth, and I hold back a gag at the taste. I inhale shallow breaths, feeling the pains in my body. Wrists, ribs, back. Definitely my fucking back. I stay still for a long time, not daring to move as I stare at the ceiling. Drops of water slip through the cracks of the stone, and I watch them in fascination as they drop down, escaping from being trapped within. Eventually I realize that being on my back is just causing me more pain, and I squeeze my eyes shut to gather some strength.

I roll slowly onto my stomach, silently screaming into my arm as I feel the skin split more as it's stretched, fresh blood trickling from the wounds. Gods, that fucking hurts. I pant heavy breaths, fingers digging into the ground as I ready myself to get to my knees, sweat beading on the back of my neck. Another wheezing breath, and I get my chained hands under my face before I push off the ground, moving myself back until I have my knees under me. Bile rises in my throat from the pain, and I can't help it. I throw up what little I had in me as I gasp through it.

When there is nothing left, I bring my shaking hands to my mouth and wipe, getting ready to move my abused body again. More breaths and more silent screams later, I'm finally on my haunches, my vision coming and going, and I grip my thighs to steady myself, scrunching my eyes shut until it passes.

Opening my eyes and seeing the stone stained red beneath me, I follow all streaks of it to the bars of my cell. I definitely got dragged in here then. I sigh, then grimace at the burning pain from my back as I shuffle on my knees, moving to the center of the room and away from where I've just gotten rid of the contents of my stomach. I carefully peel my torn t-shirt from the front of my body, whimpering in pain. The blood soaked material sticks to my skin, and I slowly drag it down my arms. I throw it off to the side the best I can, the wet slap against the floor telling just how much blood it has absorbed. Streaks of red decorate me, my white bra now a bright red as I look myself over. I can see bruising on my ribs appearing through the lighter streaks, and I know whoever kicked me had decent sized feet.

I don't remember much after the thirty-eighth lash against my back. My vision was blacking out so I must have passed out from the pain or blood loss. I remember it felt like a whip of fire searing at my back, but I didn't make a sound again, just like I promised myself. They didn't deserve to hear my pain, and the fact that Darius is the cause of that pain made my resolve harden further.

The connection I thought I had with him was wrong. All the times we were locked in each other's gazes, seeing more than we thought possible of each other every single time.

We were both wrong in what we saw.

I thought I saw good in him that I could claw out, he only saw the bad in me.

I wonder where they took Kade? Is he with his mom and dad? Is Josh with the rest of my pack back in a cell somewhere like I am? I look across from me and see no movement again. Where are they if they aren't down here?

I gently rest my hands on my thighs, my skin feeling hot as I try to relax my body the best I can with the feeling of lava racing up and down my back. I close my eyes and check on Runa. She's sleeping, just as exhausted as I am. I rest along with her, try to take my mind elsewhere and find some sort of peace.

I don't think I will ever have it permanently, only snippets here and there. In the last twenty-one years, I could count the number of times I felt true peace on my hands. It's depressing to think how little I have felt that way.

Have the Gods really abandoned us? I think this is the first time I truly feel like they have, even if everything within me recoils at the thought.

It feels like hours before I hear a scuffle sound from in front of me, and when I open my eyes again and toward the bars, a face I haven't seen in a very long time is looking back with distraught eyes. He's aged slowly over the years, but he still looks very much like the man I met all those years ago. His midnight eyes look over at me, concern written on his face as he grips the bars in front of him tightly.

"Rhea," he breathes, and I hold back a sob at the sorrow in it. "I'm so sorry I wasn't here. I didn't know there was even a trial until it was too late." He shakes his blond head, bowing it as he speaks low. "This should have never happened."

"It's not your fault, Edward," I assure him, because it isn't. He's done nothing but protect me. "This was always going to happen at some point. We both knew that." It was inevitable.

"Are you okay?" he asks, sighing as he looks over at the state of me.

A hollow laugh leaves me. "I've been better." I rub a hand down my face, trying to ignore the flakes of dried blood coming off it. "Have you seen anyone else?" He shakes his head. "I need you to get Kade and my pack out of here. Can you do that?"

"I'm not sure, Rhea. The other Highers have been having meetings without me, excluding me from important business and sending me on useless trips to other towns and villages. I don't know what's going on lately, but I sense nothing good from it."

"You have to try. They said they saw me perform a ritual to bring the rogures to Vrohkaria. How is that possible?" I don't even know of any rituals that would bring chaos to the lands.

"I don't know. Memory stones cannot be altered, but it must be possible. I haven't heard of it ever happening before, I will have to search in the library, see if I can find anything in the old tomes."

"Do you believe I did it?" I whisper, my voice shaky.

Edwards goes to his knees, uncaring that his smart black pants will be dirty as his hands still grip the bars, his eyes hold mine.

"Gods no, Rhea. You would never do such a thing."

My lip trembles at his unwavering faith in me, and I want nothing more than to go to him and seek the comfort that I know he would offer me. Just to have someone hold me for a second.

"Kade said his memories returned, but I think they have also altered them, Edward. He wasn't making any sense." I sniffle and wipe under my nose, pretending I don't hear the chains rattle. "Who is powerful enough to do that? It took you years to produce the memory stone that blocked Kade's memories from what happened with the Aragnis pack. How do they have enough power to bring them back, but also to change them?"

"Lord Higher Charles holds the most power. He could do something like that with a high-level witch. All of our powerful witches haven't been at the castle for a few weeks though. Lord Higher Charles sent them off to collect something for him. He didn't tell me what." His face holds frustration as his hands squeeze against the bars.

"So, Charles got to him then, but why? What does he benefit from messing with Kade's memories?"

"Seeing you suffer," he murmurs, his eyes dropping at his own words. "He thought you were dead for a long time, Rhea. He's going to make you suffer for escaping him in any way he can." His hands release the bars, and he runs them through his hair, sighing.

"How powerful is he, really?" I know his dominance is strong. I know what he can do with his hands and some magic. But how does he hold the position of Lord Higher.

"He is a wolf and more," Edward says, and I tilt my head. "He has power that no one has seen and can use it as he sees fit. I was told of the barrier you were surrounded by in the great hall. That is part of his power." I swallow, memories flashing through my mind of the pain it caused me from touching it.

"He can do more than that, and no one knows why. Some say he's the new God, after the old ones abandoned the lands, their names and Heirs are ash in the mouths of anyone whispering about them, and never in kindness." He looks up at me quickly before looking away again.

"What is it?" There's something on his mind but he won't tell me.

"Rhea…" he trails off.

"If I need to know, Edward, then I need to know. No matter how much you don't want to tell me."

He sits down, crossing his legs as he leans his forehead against the bars, a look of defeat spreading across his face. "Charles has been searching for someone like you since you left and couldn't be found." I blink, my brows furrowing. "He's been going from pack to pack, trying to find others that might be… suitable."

"What do you mean," I whisper, dreading his answer.

"He's been training up young pups until they are old enough to see if they show any similar signs," he tells me regretfully, and I choke on a sound, shaking my head at what he's telling me. "I can't prove it, he covers his tracks well, but I know he's been doing it. I can't stop it."

"Why haven't you told me this before, I thought it was just me he did that to," I wheeze.

"What would it change? We are powerless. There is only you and I, and that is not enough. He keeps an eye on packs, looking for pups soon to be born and then goes to them when they have arrived under the facade that he's blessing them. Welcoming them into Vrohkaria. When really he's looking for anything that resembles you. With you being thought dead and no others found, he thought he could find a way." He swallows roughly. "He takes the ones he has a liking to from their homes and trains them. Prepares them for their new life," he whispers, voice shaking as he speaks.

My eyes are wide as I open and close my mouth, shock rendering me speechless for a moment. "I've been hidden in Eridian all this time, hiding from the Highers and my family, and all this time." I gag. "All this time he's been doing that to others." I hunch over at his nod, ignoring the pain in my back as I choke on nothing. "He's been taking *children* because I wasn't around. Training them. Oh, Gods. No."

My palms hit the wet floor, tears dripping down my face as my stomach turns. What has he put children through? How many have died because of me? Children. He's been taking fucking children when I was playing happy families in Eridian.

What have I done?

"It's not your fault, Rhea." He tries to placate me, but he's wrong. So fucking wrong. "You had to stay hidden from him. We couldn't let him have you."

"Children, Edward," I cry. "He's doing what he did to me. I thought with me gone, he would stop. That he would just give up trying to be more than he should be."

"I know," he says sadly. Nothing more to add because what can he say? Either way you look at it, Gods knows how many children have been put in my place because I was hidden away.

Is my life worth all of theirs?

"I will try and get Kade and your pack out of here, though I'm afraid it's not looking good. Just hang tight, we will figure it out. You can't be left in their grasp. Charles and the other Highers are determining your sentencing soon and many demand it be public, so he can't do anything right now. That gives us time to come up with something. I can't stay, or they will notice my absence. I will try and be back before they come and get you."

I shake my head, so utterly defeated before lifting it to look at him with my blurry vision. "Just get them out, vallier, Edward."

Please.

He nods, his eyes solemn. "Don't lose hope," he pleads with me. "I will find a way." He gives me one more small smile before leaving me alone in my new prison.

But all I feel is my soul crippling inside me. Sorrow at how much innocent blood has been spilled in my absence from so many young pups.

There is no hope for the essence that's being tainted by the Highers.

No Gods.

No justice.

Only destruction and blood. That's all that's left.

FORTY THREE

DARIUS

We sit in a dining hall within the castle, all seated around a light wood table as way too much food is set down before us. Leo sits to my right, followed by Damian, Zaide, Jerrod. Maize sits next to Charles who's at the head of the table, the other Highers seated across from us as they discuss the trial. Though Higher Warden and Higher Aldus are not here.

"What do you think should be done with the boy?" Higher Frederick asks around a mouthful of food.

"He will return to his family of course," Charles says. "Poor boy has been traumatized. I've ordered Maize to be involved personally with his recovery, and he can leave once he is better." I look toward Maize as she gives him a smile.

"I never agreed to that," I interrupt, leaning back in my seat.

Charles's eyes swing to mine, food halfway to his mouth. "I don't need to get your permission. She is skilled and will help the boy. You're not going to deny his recovery, are you?"

All eyes are now on me, waiting for my answer. "I need to get back to hunting the rogures. We found what caused them to be here, but haven't found how to stop it. So in the meantime, we all need to be out there protecting Vrohkaria." Until Rhea tells us how to reverse the ritual, if it can even be done, there is nothing else we can do until then apart from cutting them down.

"I will be seeing to it personally that we get the information needed out of the woman to stop the rogures," Charles says. "We will be close to peace throughout Vrohkaria again after the trial, and those who are rebelling against us will disband. Many have spoken of my capabilities of handling the traitor so far and put faith in me to put an end to the rogures. I will not fail the people."

"What if it can't be undone?" asks Higher Aiden, his dark curls swaying as he shakes his head. "Can we even trust what she says with what the Elites have told us? She may have us do another curse unknowingly if we take her word for things and have her perform another ritual, if that is needed."

"That is a concern," Charles agrees, rubbing his chin. "We have to have some form of leverage over her so that she has no other option than to tell us the truth."

"Like what?" Higher Frederick asks. "She's a traitorous cunt who has caused so much death. What could we possibly hold over her when she cares so little for the world she lives in?"

"That is true," Higher Mathew chimes in. "The bitch couldn't care about anything."

"What about Kaden?" Maize muses. "I watched her in the pack. She was always with him if he was around, and she protected him from Darius in The Deadlands." She looks at me, teeth showing with her laugh. "Well, as best she could. She was crying on the floor, scared to death that Darius would slice the kid's neck. She obviously cares about him even though he hates her now."

You have part of my world in your hands. Will you help me protect it? I shake my head as Rhea's words echo within me, and Drax growls. With him being so close to the surface, I have to forcefully shove him back for control, taking his anger and holding it at bay. He's been unstable since we watched Rhea being carted off out of the great hall unconscious, bleeding from her wounds.

Wounds I inflicted on her flawless back.

Everything revolted inside of me as soon as I stood, whip in hand and staring down at her. But she lied about everything. Despite all of that, I nearly refused Charles's order, even though it was an order with an undertone of a threat. Then I nearly lost control of Drax during it.

"Hmm," Charles hums thoughtfully. "It could definitely work then along with other suggestions, if her feelings are true," he says to Maize, a glint in his eyes. "Which we don't know for sure since she's a manipulative woman. With the trouble she had caused the Aragnis pack over the years after her parents' death, Kaden's family may agree." He shakes his head, seemingly lost for words. Which I know is bullshit.

"How did her parents die?" Leo asks, taking a drink.

"A terrible accident. It's a shame. Her father was a great Alpha and a very dear friend of mine. It was a sad day when the news of his death reached me, and it saddens me what his daughter has turned out to be."

"You knew them?" My brows furrow at him. Why hasn't he mentioned this before now? We have sat here for hours, and we talked before he ordered a trial.

He nods. "I did, I was even there for the birth of Lasandrhea." He sighs. Lasandrhea? That's her real name? "I was her chosen guardian of sorts, along with Higher Warden. I'm ashamed of what has become of her. I wonder if she had stayed in her pack if I could have guided her. I visited often over the years, but she was volatile. I thought it was the death of her parents that had caused it, but clearly the girl is unstable." He glances at the drink in his hand, a look of sadness crossing his face.

"You seem to be taking it in well," Zaide states, not looking at him as he cleans one of his blades. I have to wonder why he's asking, the guy rarely talks to him unless he has to. But that's why he's the best at what he does. Observing. "Considering you were close to her parents and there when she was born, I would have thought you would be more conflicted over this."

"Yes… well." Charles clears his throat. "I am Lord Higher, and my personal feelings cannot get in the way of a wrong that has been done." He takes a drink before continuing among the Highers about Rhea's sentence, and how they can get Kade to help the process of her undoing the curse.

I tune them out, wondering why Rhea never mentioned her guardians were Highers. She was adamant not to let them know about Eridian, well mainly her pack. Was it because she knew they would know she was alive with Kade and Josh, and punish her for stealing Kade and having Josh help? She was going to be punished anyway. She said she had no family, and yet she has an aunt and uncle, who are the Alpha of the Aragnis pack and many cousins. That pack has been around for hundreds of years, even before I was born, and is well respected and in alliance with the Highers. So why did Rhea leave? She said her parents were stolen from her, but they were killed in an accident. It doesn't make sense, yet does it matter?

She caused the rogures to come to the Vrohkaria, performed the ritual to make it happen. I saw it with my own eyes. It's her fault my parents and little sister died, mauled to death by them. I was away hunting rogures in a nearby village when they attacked the town we lived in. Isabell was three years old, a whole life ahead of her, and it was ripped away along with my mother trying to protect her. I found their mutilated bodies huddled together at the side of our home next to our garden they spent many hours in. My dad survived a week from his injuries from the rogures until he couldn't hold on any longer. He made me promise on his dying breath to aid the Highers in what they need to do and become Alpha of the Elites. I keep that promise to this day.

Rhea has murdered thousands with what she did. Living away in Eridian without a care and letting Vrohkaria rot around her. She will undo the curse and pay for what she has done for the rest of her miserable life. The only question I want answered now is why.

***

I walk down the steps toward the cells, the smell of death hitting me as I open the door. It slams shut behind me, and I walk down the stone hallway toward the end. I can smell her blood in the air mixed in with her usual scent, and I lock down Drax before he can react. He growls inside me at her smell, the smell of her blood. Reaching her cell on silent footsteps, I walk to the bars and lean up against them.

Rhea is on her knees facing the bars, but her head is turned toward the wall, just staring at it, unaware of my presence. Or ignoring it. My eyes track down her body, looking her over with precision. Dried blood covers her in splotches, darker in places, especially around the sides of her ribs. Bruising is appearing on her left side, and I tilt my head at it, studying it intently and wondering where that came from. Her chained hands rest on her thighs, not even a twitch coming from them as the silence continues. Not even her breaths can be heard. More dried blood covers the ground to the side of her, and I see the t-shirt I ripped to expose her back has been thrown off to the side. I refuse to acknowledge the feeling bubbling up inside of me at the sight of her.

I look down at the streaks of red from where she's sat to the cell's bars, and fury rises within me at the knowledge that she was dragged into her cell instead of placed down. "Why did you do it?" My tone is neutral, almost bored. I'm only greeted by silence, not even a twitch. She knew I was here. I tsk, waving a hand and making an opening in the bars before entering. I walk until I'm a few feet away from her before crouching, resting my arms on my knees. "Can you undo the curse?" I move a finger, and her chains pull at her wrists in warning, jolting her, and she finally turns her head to me.

Dull eyes collide with mine, and I hold back my reaction at seeing that look in her once lively ice-blue orbs that sometimes look like glass. No fire, no light, no flecks… just nothing. Not even tears, though I can see she has been crying, her eyes puffy. But the look in them is so much different than what I have seen over the weeks since I have been her shadow. Since the moment our eyes caught and collided in The Deadlands.

Why don't I like that look?

Everything within me feels restless, and Drax growls low and deadly, hackles standing high. That I react at all to her is starting to piss me off. From the very first moment, it's like I'm attuned to everything about her. I want it gone. I want it to stop. This need I have to be around her, on her, in her all the time. I want to scent her, bite her, mark her so I can see them on her skin for myself, just like I did after we fucked. It's a constant need, never wavering. That's why I was following her around for weeks. Sometimes she noticed, when I let her, other times she didn't. Especially when I followed her into the forest and watched her play with wild wolves like she belonged there. I stood there, watching from a distance, and nothing could have taken my eyes away from the way she laughed and smiled so freely. Playing with pups and their mother just watching on with trust in her gaze, letting me know that wasn't the first time she had done so. I suspect she went to see them often.

Yet she fucking caused a plague of rogures to wreak destruction across the lands, caused my family to die painful deaths for no reason that she has given, so my reaction to her can get fucked. She deserves a lot more than the whipping she received for what she as done. I will just have to contain my fury and instinct in the process.

Drax moves within me, tries to come to my eyes, and I remember how hard I restrained Drax when I let the whip glide through the air to split her skin on her back. I ended up having to shut myself down to punish her for the crimes she committed, because everything in me told me to get her out of there to stop that from happening. I didn't even want to whip her, but I couldn't back down from Charles. He had a challenge in his eye when he said I should be the one to do it, and to refuse would make me weak. Expose a weakness I don't have. So, I held that whip and gave her the lashes until she passed out, listening to Drax snarling inside of me with every strike. Every tear. Every drop of fucking blood.

She didn't grow up in Eridian. She was born in the south in Zakith, at the Aragnis pack, stole a kid, and manipulated another male. How did the other pack members get in Eridian? How did she make them stay? She must have stolen them too, like Sarah. Though I have no idea how that even happened. That girl is terrified of everything that moves, even her father.

"Do you know we have a graveyard in the forest?" Rhea says suddenly. Her voice rough from the lack of water, and my hands ball into fists at the thought. "We made headstones after a few years of being there. I made one for my mom and dad, and others made them for the ones they lost too. We have a celebration of their life every year at the end of winter and then to welcome the new life that appears in the spring."

"Why are you telling me this? I don't fucking care," I growl. Where is she going with this?

"I doubt I will see it again, to add more graves there for the ones that have been taken from us. I would have liked to celebrate Solvier's life with my parents and some of the members we have lost over the years. He protected Eridian, you know? He had done so for so long. Remember the story I told at the gathering? I told the story of the Canaric wolves. He was the male in that story, finding his bloodmate when he was about to run away with his pregnant chosen mate. Years later, that male's bloodmate died and he went searching for his daughter and the woman. He eventually arrived in Eridian, and the Gods spoke to him, told him what had happened. He was distraught, unable to believe it and full of many regrets. But how can you go against what the Gods had chosen for you? He made a pact with the Gods that very day that he would protect the last place his chosen mate and daughter were, connecting his essence to the lilk trees that surround our home, which made the barrier. The Gods granted him a longer life than what he would have had, ensuring he could protect Eridian for a long time, but that didn't make him immortal. When the barrier broke, so did he."

"What's your point, Rhea?" I sigh. The barrier had to break to get the Elites and guards inside. Aldus made sure it was done.

Solvier, the so-called guardian that he was, knew things he shouldn't have. I could tell Rhea was close to him, he told me as much when he spoke to me. But she doesn't know the things he told me, she probably never will.

"Solvier was chosen to protect Eridian and all who entered there that were worthy, with the barrier by the Gods. I was chosen to protect all life. Just like you were chosen to destroy it."

"What the fuck are you talking about?" I look her over closely, wondering where she is going with this.

"I wonder who will be in the graveyard when this is over."

"I don't care about your graveyard. Just tell me how to stop the curse," I growl at her. She needs to give me something.

She shakes her head slowly from side to side. Her hair sticks to the blood on her face and body as it sways. "I do not know, Darius. I didn't cause it, so how would I?"

"You're lying, I saw it from the memory crystal. You can't deny it." She was in the middle of a stone circle, writing glowing around the edges, her arms stretched out at her sides as she chanted her curse and darkness flooded into her. Rogures came from the dirt around her, clawing and snarling their way to the surface.

"What you saw wasn't real because I didn't do it." She hisses in pain as she shuffles on her knees, and my body jolts forward before I still myself, Drax pushing me toward her to ease her pain.

I lock him down.

"You will tell us eventually how to stop it, more blood will be spilled until then," I snarl at her and stand in frustration. Turning and flicking a finger at the bars behind to reappear, I ignore the sigh I hear come from her. It's weighted, resigned. I need to get out of here before Drax takes over.

"You have to believe me, Darius. I need to get out of here." Rhea's voice echoes after me. "You'll end up regretting this if you don't."

We both regret a lot of things, and meeting each other is one of them.

FORTY FOUR

RHEA

I'm dragged harshly from my cell by two guards. I don't know how long I've been in here since Darius came to see me, but it feels like days. I hated him coming to see me after what he did, after he tore the flesh from my back.

He's standing beside monsters, and he is none the wiser. To blind in his anger to see how impossible it is for me to have caused the rogures. Whatever he saw in this memory stone has made him convinced I'm the enemy, and who would believe a 'traitor'?

I'm jostled and shoved by one of the guards, a sneer on his scarred face, and I hiss through the pain. The cuffs around my wrists, that I now realize are infused with terbium, have slowed my healing process down. That particular metal is rare, and there is only one person I know who has access to it. My skin has barely begun to close from the lashes and every sudden movement splits the skin more, letting fresh blood flow down my back.

I'm taken in the same direction as the last time I went to the great hall until we arrive at its doors. The guards stop in front of them for a moment, righting their armor, before we enter. People fill the room again, looking at me with distaste and anger as they spit at my feet, curses falling from their lips. The guards shove me forward down the steps to the middle of the sunken area, Josh and Kade once again next to me. Kade doesn't even twitch at my appearance when he looks at me briefly as I'm once again chained to the floor. Josh has more injuries over his face, blood coming from the side of his head, his eyes are tired and full of pain.

"Are you okay?" he asks me quietly, and I nod, staying silent. He looks me over, his eyes tightening as he takes me in, but what else can I say?

My heart is bleeding more than the wounds on my back. Letting him know that I'm not okay won't help anything.

Footsteps come from my right, and I turn and see my cousin, Patrick, coming down the steps toward me, and my muscles lock up. His blue eyes bore into mine when he stops too close in front of me, and I hold my breath. My hands shake but I lift my chin, waiting for him to speak.

"Hello, cousin." He smirks, eyes lingering on my chest that's only covered by my bra. I bare my teeth at him, wanting to rip his throat out no matter how much fear I have of him. "No need to be so cranky. You're the one who has been naughty."

"Get the fuck away from her," Josh snarls, moving as close to me as the chains will allow him.

Patrick ignores him. "Are you happy that you took our little brother from us?" he says to me, referring to Kade. "You stole a child from his family and brainwashed him. I can't wait to see you punished." His eyes gleam. "I'm sure Lord Higher will agree to let me give you some of my own punishments as I am Heir to the Aragnis pack."

"I saved Kade from—"

His hand flies out, backhanding me and my head snaps to the side before he grabs and squeezes my throat, cutting off any more words. His touch on me has my skin crawling, my body trembling. I bring my hands up, trying to get him off me, but he's stronger than me at the moment. He squeezes harder with desire in his eyes. A choked sound comes from me as he brings his face closer, until I feel his breath on my ear. The Elites walk in at that moment, moving around the sunken area to stop in front of the dais. Darius's eyes bore into mine, taking in my now reddened cheek and Patrick's hold on me as my cousin murmurs quietly in my ear so only I can hear him.

"I'm going to finally have you." I swallow beneath his hand, my scared eyes on Darius's curious ones as he tilts his head at us. "I never wanted to wait before, but the Highers demanded it. It's different now. All that time we spent playing together when I came to visit you will be nothing like what I will do to you now." My eyes sting with tears, and Darius's eyes darken. "Do you know where Sarah is?" he taunts, and I dig my fingers into his wrist harder. "She's on her way to the pack, to be strapped down, ready and waiting for me. Don't worry, there is enough of me to go around though." He nips my ear, his lips on me making my stomach turn, and I whimper.

"Get off me—" He squeezes my throat harder, and I thrash, desperate to get him off me.

"That's enough," Darius orders from his place in front of the dais, looking between us.

"I just wanted a word with my cousin before she is sentenced." Patrick shrugs. "I'm sure I will be able to talk to her later on I suppose." He looks down at my body, heat filling his eyes as I move my gaze to the floor, wanting to escape him.

I suppress a shiver thinking of what would happen if he's allowed time with me. I have no doubt he will ask for it. But Sarah. Gods, Sarah is going to his home. I look down at my bare feet, sucking in breaths as I look over at Josh out of the corner of my eye. If looks could kill, Patrick would be dead as he walks back over to the family. When Josh finds out that Sarah is on her way to our old home, he's going to lose it, but I need him to stay calm right now. I need to get him out of a sentence so he can go and get her. I have to try.

"What did he say?" Josh whispers through gritted teeth. I shake my head, not wanting him to know yet.

"You need to agree that I'm the one who caused all of what they are assuming," I murmur, looking around to see if anyone can hear us. "You need to get out of here with the others. Blame it all on me. I'll figure something out." He starts shaking his head. "Please, Josh," I plead with my eyes, nodding my head in Kade's direction. "He needs you. They all do."

"Rhea, they could do anything to you." I nod, knowing I will probably be trapped in here for however long they want. Edward never came back, so he hasn't found a way to get them out. If I take the full blame. They have a chance.

The door at the back opens and Taylor, Sebastian, Hudson, Colten, and Anna are brought in again and put in front of us. Then Josie and Danny are dragged into the room. Attachments appear on the floor beneath them, and the hooded figures behind them attach the chains around their wrists to them, bringing them to their knees so they can't stand. Their mouths are still covered in cloth, not able to speak, but their eyes say it all. Taylor looks at Kade, disappointment in his eyes as he shakes his head at him. Hudson keeps looking toward Colten whose head is bowed, fiddling with the cuffs on his wrists like he could get out of them. My eyes come to Sebastian's sad eyes, and I already miss the lightness they had from him being his flirty self. Josie and Danny are put in front of them, Josie's eyes rimmed red while Danny tries to get as close to her as possible. They're chained to the floor like the others, all looking tired, shoulders slumping with exhaustion. I dread to think what they have been through with the bruises and blood covering them.

How did we even get here? Everything happened so fast. How did this Higher Aldus get a memory crystal, and how does it show me performing some sort of ritual? Nothing makes sense.

But whether it makes sense or not, my pack is in danger. Sarah is on her way to my old home, and my closest friends are with me for punishment. Kade hates me and his memories are all wrong. I don't know where my other pack members are either. Are the pups safe and with their moms again or are they still separated? And Eridian… Gods know what our home is like now.

It's not our home anymore though, is it? With Solvier gone, Eridian is probably overrun, and we are no longer a secret.

I look down at the tattoo on my forearm and then to my wrist through my own blood, silently asking for strength at what I may have to do. What I hope I don't have to do. I made a promise, but what choice do I have? Will I be strong enough to get everyone out of here? I have to try, but I'm scared, and I don't know how to make it happen. Is it even possible?

I've only done it once in my life, and Mom told me never to do it again. She made me promise. She told me under no circumstances am I to show anyone, and I haven't. My closest, apart from Kade, know what I am, but they have never seen it. Can I really do this? Show myself and him? He deserves nothing from me, not a single kindness, but he's hiding himself for a reason just like I am. I'm not sure if he knows or not, but I've seen his markings. He tried to hide them within his tattoos, but I recognize them. I knew as soon as I saw them that they looked familiar, but that day in the forest with the wisps confirmed it. There is no more denying it after what I felt.

I look over at Darius talking with Leo, his stare going to someone standing around the side before moving his hands rapidly while he talks. I follow his line of sight as he looks over Leo's shoulder again, and I see my family. My uncle stands imposing, his blond hair styled to sweep back off his face. My aunt stands next to him, her dark brown hair tied up in an intricate style. Patrick looks smug as he folds his arms across his chest, his blue eyes roaming over us below. My other cousins

Alister, Richard, and Sophia are standing next to him, looking bored as we all wait for the verdict.

These people were meant to protect me, protect our family. Instead, they helped destroy it. And for what? To be in the good graces of the Lord Higher. For power and titles. They just didn't expect me to escape before my eighteenth birthday, or to take Kade with me. What have they been doing all this time? Have they been helping Charles?

I didn't expect the Lord Higher to have gone on to take other children to see if they were like me. To train them like me. Charles rules over Vrohkaria like a king would his kingdom with the exception of a few lands that have refused to pledge their loyalty. So why does he want more so badly that after I escaped? He needs to be stopped. He needs to be taken down with the other Highers and my family for what they have done, what they are still doing. They all have to die for the blood they have spilled, or more will continue to soak the lands and taint it.

It was one thing doing it with me. I thought they had stopped. I understand that it is different now. They will never stop until they get what they want.

I'm not strong enough to do it on my own. The Lord Highers's power is strong, a force that is unmatched, especially aided by the other Highers and their witches. Over the years, I tried to find a way to get my revenge on him, tried to figure out a plan with Edward. Nothing came of it, nothing that would make us successful, and I had to learn to accept it. Accept what they all did to me and my mom and dad, knowing they were all still living and breathing, I had to let it go.

But I can't let go of them bringing innocent children into their power play for years. If I had known, I would have revealed myself. I would have gone to him, done what he wanted and accepted it. I would never have put myself before children, and

I unknowingly had by staying hidden in Eridian. Living my life, being safe, while others have been suffering.

This is another failure.

Another sin.

Another stain against my soul because of everything I am.

FORTY FIVE

RHEA

The doors open and the Highers enter the hall, walking up the dais and taking their seats. Once again, two chairs are still left empty and there is no sign of Edward. They all remove their hooded cloaks as the murmurs around the room go silent in their presence.

"It is time to sentence the traitor of Vrohkaria and her followers." Charles speaks clear and commanding, his voice filling the great hall easily. "We have spoken throughout the night on the best outcome of this rare situation. "The crimes against Joshua Satori are helping a traitor leave her pack and aiding in the kidnapping of a child, kidnapping others to be taken to Eridian to be kept there, failing to inform the Highers of a pack being established, and not handing over the traitor of the lands."

I turn my head to the side, begging Josh to do what I asked of him. "She made me do it," he blurts out, and I lose some tension in my body. He can't be sentenced like this, he just can't. "She threatened my life and others, therefore I couldn't leave or tell anyone as I would have been killing those that she said she would."

"Do you say this in truth, Joshua?" Lord Higher Charles demands, looking between us curiously.

"It is, but I worry she will kill those I care about. I'm trying to protect them, the kids especially." My spine is straight as I look directly into their eyes as he speaks. No fear. No tremble. "They are all scared she will kill those they love. That's why they haven't spoken, all except Kade." I glance at him, but again, he's not looking at either of us.

Darius scoffs, and the Highers murmur amongst themselves. "Why would we believe you in what you say? You are basically telling me that you had no choice but to aid her. Yet reports say you are her closest, like a brother to her."

"I had to be close to her to make sure we all stayed in line so she wouldn't hurt anyone. Or if someone did something wrong, I could let them know and they could pacify her." Josh swallows roughly, hating the words that are coming out of his own mouth. Damning me. "I thought we were in love. I was wrong, she just used me."

Charles hums and leans on his hand, elbow to the chair's armrest. "What was in it for you, taking people and keeping them in Eridian?" Charles asks me.

I shrug. "I wanted a pack, so I created one and kept them in line. Isn't that how we do things?"

"Her pack was scared," Darius adds, green eyes looking directly at me. "She wouldn't tell me why, but they always cowered in fear from us. Probably in fear of consequences if they spoke something that could kill their loved ones." The Elites growl around him, eyes locked on me with looks that could have me dead in an instant if it were possible.

"Hmmm." Charles taps his chin, dark eyes looking between the three of us as I briefly look at my pack members.

Their eyes are hard on Josh's, but when they come to mine, I hope they see in my own eyes that this is what I want, what has to happen. Josie shakes her head, eyes still red, and I blink slowly at her as Danny's knee presses against hers.

"Joshua, speak clearly. Did Rhea make threats in any way, to keep you and others in line?" Higher Frederick asks.

I feel Josh's gray eyes on me. I feel his hesitation at answering when he knows it's downhill for me, but there is no stopping it with or without his words. I turn my head, my eyes speaking for me. This is the way it has to be. The only way I could get them out of here is if I take the blame for it all.

He swallows, his voice rough when he finally speaks. "It's true. Everything I said and Alpha Darius has said is true."

More murmurs and looks of disgust head my way. "You really are a vile woman," a Higher says, waving a hand toward me as his scraggy, dark hair falls to his chin.

A barrier is put around me again, and I see it glow before pain wracks my body. My wrists strain against the cuffs as I try to move away from the burning within me. I grit my teeth, leaning against the barrier at my back as I growl through the current and the pain lashing up my torn flesh. I feel blood trickle from my ears, adding to my already bloodied body. Sweat gathers at the back of my neck as I hold in a scream that wants to be released, turning to look toward Josh for strength. His eyes hold mine through it, the anguish in them worse than the lightning racking my body. I know it kills him seeing me like this, but it will kill him more if he doesn't get to Sarah.

The current fades to a low buzz, and I breathe out shakily, wiggling my fingers to stop the tingles there. I stand straight from the barrier as it feels like tiny needles stabbing into me and take a step to the middle, ready for what's next. I have to be. I don't look at Kade or at my pack again as my eyes find Charles, that fucking grin on his face at seeing me hurt before he drops it, sitting up straighter in his seat.

"It's unfathomable how this female is of our kind. She is no wolf, no race of ours," Charles spits, and the crowd shouts their agreement, calling for my death. "I will accept what Joshua has said as truth. I believe this woman has done unspeakable things to her pack to keep them from leaving and reaching out to any sort of authority. Through no fault of their own, they have been taken and abused by this woman. Sarah Woodly has confirmed that, as have the wounds on her body." I don't move, I just keep my eyes on him as he throws out false statements. "A strong, lengthy punishment is to be served, as well as removing the curse on Vrohkaria to rid us of the rogures. Are you now going to tell us how to remove it?"

I stay silent, breathing evenly. They don't believe I'm not to blame for the curse, I can't persuade the room otherwise. I'm the bad guy, the person they are going to use to blame for all the suffering the rogures have dealt out throughout the land, when instead they should still be looking for a way to stop them.

I can't win in this situation. They won't listen to me, and I haven't helped myself with lying to Darius. All my words are just lies and manipulations according to them all. All I can do now is just endure. The barrier glows again, and my eyes connect to Darius as I'm brought to my knees, the current more intense this time, rattling my teeth as a whimpered breath comes from me.

His green eyes bore into mine, and I see them tighten around the edges, his shoulders tensing as he watches.

"Tell us how to stop the rogures!" Charles's voice booms inside the barrier as blood spills from my nose and over my lips as I cough. I squeeze my eyes shut, breathing through it as Runa whimpers inside of me, too exhausted to help share some pain. All she can do is feel it through me.

Charles knows I didn't cause the curse, so why is he going along with this? I was locked inside a cage and tormented by them. How could I have performed a ritual at seven years old? If for one second, one person would think clearly, they would know the time frame doesn't add up. The people are too blinded in their anger to see it, the Elites too blinded by what this crystal showed them. They all have fucking wool over their eyes, and they refuse to clear the fog.

The pain eases, and I rest my cuffed hands on the barrier in front of me, blood still dripping from my nose and ears, dribbling down my chin. My body aches, my muscles sore from tensing up so much and my back feels like lava. My eyes open and they lock with Darius's once again. Through the haze of my vision, I watch as his head tilts, his eyes roaming over my body and watching fresh blood flow from me. His hand twitches at his side before he crosses his arms, looking toward the Highers with a clenched jaw as they speak, breaking our connection.

"She will not tell us, Lord Higher," Higher Frederick tsks. "She cares none for Vrohkaria or our people getting slaughtered by the rogures."

"It seems she will not," Charles muses. "Kaden, say what you have to say to the traitor. Maybe you can persuade her."

I look over at Kade as he speaks, his voice cold and without any emotion as my breathing becomes labored. "I've had my memories blocked, you stole me from my home, and I lost many years with my family. That can never be given back to me. I unknowingly helped you bring people to Eridian under the guise that we were helping them, when you were really just stealing them and making them work in fear around us. I was blind to it all, but no more. The highest punishment should be given, even though I will never get any justice for what you have done to me. I will never get back the time I have lost," he growls, eyes full of animosity. "Nothing I say will make you tell the truth. You're sick and twisted, and I'm ashamed I spent so many years looking up to you as a mother when you stole me from mine." he spits at the barrier. "I want no connection to you. You mean nothing to me."

If you could see my heart, it would be bleeding from the wounds he had just caused. It would be on the floor beneath his foot as he stomped on it repeatedly, slowly fading into ash. I suck in a shaky breath as I try to remember that his memories are not what he thinks they are. Try to remember that something had been done to him to make him act like this. If he knew, he would be the first in line to remove their heads, I know he would. This is not my Kade standing in front of me.

It's probably for the best he doesn't know. It will keep him somewhat safe for now. But that didn't stop the pain in my chest that he thought I was capable of doing this. That I could steal someone from their home when all I have done is try to help those that need it after mine was tainted. I've been there through so many milestones in Kade's life, been there through nightmares and heartbreak. I've been there through his achievements and creations, through our sacred ritual of getting his tattoo and getting his wolf. It's me that has given him a life, gave him his laughter, taught him to read and write, and taught him how to be kind.

Not them. Me.

"Can I have a blade?" Kade asks suddenly, and my body stills, my bruised heart pounding against my chest.

"What are you doing?" I rush out, watching as Darius lifts a small blade and holds it out to him. Kade walks up the steps as his chains are taken away, and I track him until he's standing beside Darius.

"Undoing something I should have never let happen in the first place," Kade says as he grips the hilt of the blade tightly in his grasp.

I watch everything in slow motion as he brings the blade up to his marked forearm, and he presses the tip to his skin just below the inside of his elbow. Blood wells to the surface. Then in one quick move he slices down his skin, effectively slicing through the design Josh and I lovingly put there and severing our blood link. Destroying what we etched there in the name of the Gods. In the name of our bond, our family.

I fall as my knees give out, and I hit the floor hard, a whimper leaving me as I watch blood drip from his forearm, splashing against the floor. Then, a sharp, stabbing pain slices through my head.

I scream.

Scream and scream and scream as it feels like I'm being ripped in two as the link between us pulls taut. The strand of his link intertwining with mine stretches, pulling as far as it can until it starts to fray. I grip my head, still screaming in pain as tears stream down my face. "Carzan," I whimper. Then, the strands snap, his link disappearing into the darkness, and all that's left is a void where his link once was. An endless pit of black as I try to search for his link. Try to reach out and grab a hold of it and never let go, but it's not there. It's gone.

Sobs escape me, my body trembling at the loss. I don't want to feel it, I want it to stop. All of it to stop. It's too much. I can't take it. Kade falls to the floor beside Darius, screaming as he holds his head in his hands. Feeling what I'm feeling. They're going to destroy him. They're going to destroy everything he is to get to me. Breaking a blood link takes time to gently unravel the strings that connect us together. Shattering it like that is dangerous. A link is sacred, and he's just destroyed it because of what they have done to him. Broken the vows he made. What else would they make him do in the name of getting to me? He will be a shell of a person when they are through with him.

"Now tell us how to break the curse!" Charles demands of me as again as I sob on the floor, my body shaking with tremors as pain flares up at the sudden loss of Kade's blood link. I drag my blurry vision to Josh, who is on his knees holding his head in his hands, feeling the same effects of the broken link like Kade and I. "I think it's time to show her more consequences of refusing us."

I get to my hands and knees, coughing, barely taking in any air through my cries. I lift my head and see Darius looking at Kade on the floor, his brows scrunched up as he bends and picks up his blade. He looks at me, and the look in his eyes almost seems remorseful, but that can't possibly be true.

I see two cloaked figures appearing behind Josie and Danny, and my eyes go wide. The cloaked figures bring a knife up to their throats, and I scramble to my feet, my body slamming against the barrier as I bang on it, ignoring the needle-like stabs I get for touching it. My guys behind them start shouting behind the cloths covering their mouths as they try to get to them.

"No, don't, please. I don't know how to break the curse," I cry, still banging my chained hands on the shimmering violet barrier as the guys behind them try to get to them. I look at Darius. "I'm telling the truth. Please, believe me!" He puts his blade back in a holder and takes a step toward me from the top of the steps.

"Just tell us!" Charles shouts, standing and pointing at me.

"I can't!" I shake my head, looking at the cloaked figures behind Josie and Danny. "I was too youn—" The barrier glows again and I cry out in pain. "I didn't do it. Please, believe me. Vallier," I whimper as I watch those blades start to slice through their necks slowly, blood spurting out from them as my eyes meet Josie's.

Her dark green eyes are kind, telling me without words that it's okay as a tear slips from her eye. Her head turns toward Danny, blood coloring her lips, and they look at each other in so much pain, and love and heartache until her body falls to the side, her eyes closing for the final time. Danny lands next to her, his chained hands touching her like he always has done, wanting to be as close to her as possible. Even in death their bodies are close, always with each other, and as I watch their essence coming from their body, I let it all out in an anguished scream.

All the pain, all the hurt, all the heartbreak comes from me as Runa stands and lets out a mournful howl within me. Cracks form on the barrier before it flashes, and I'm flung back, my body hitting against it as my chains pull, and then I'm yanked to the floor.

I see black boots appear through my blurry vision in front of me, laces tied neatly but now covered in specks of blood. I lift my head, sobs still wracking my body, guttural sounds coming from me as Darius crouches on the other side of the barrier. He looks at Kade behind him, still gripping his head in his hands, to Anna, Taylor, Sebastian, Hudson, and Colten who are trying to get up, pulling on their chains. Then to Josie and Danny, their essence floating up and into the air. Then finally to Josh on his knees to the left of me, his head hanging low, before his eyes come back to mine, flashing black quickly before returning to green.

He clenches his jaw. "This is only the beginning for you if you don't—"

"Remember what I told you in the cave," I cry, cutting him off as my eyes lock with his. Darius's dark brows lower in confusion as I continue. "About someone you love, protecting it." My eyes flash, and my face begins to tingle. "I'm too late for them," I sob as I look at Danny and Josie's bodies behind him. "But I can't let anymore be taken from me."

"What the fuck are you on about?" he demands, voice harsh. He looks behind him, at Lord Higher Charles who still stands, looking toward us before his gaze meets mine again.

"I can't let it happen, but if I must reveal myself, so will you," I choke out. "But you are not worthy of being hidden, of being Vihnarn." His eyes widen at my words, shock spreading across his face as he looks over my features.

"Don't," he growls low, so low that a shiver goes through me as I hiccup through my sobs.

"We are all falling, and so will you."

I feel whispers of fingers stroking my face, palms cupping my cheeks, and I look deep into green eyes speckled with silver before I close them. Feeling a warmth spread all over my body, a warmth that's familiar.

Safe.

Home.

"It's okay, sweetheart. Let go. This is your path. You have done so well to stay hidden. I didn't want this burden to fall on your shoulders. I never did, Milal, but it has. I know you are frightened, but the lands needs you to right the wrong. It's time."

"Mom," I whimper, feeling the warmth become hotter, centering at my chest and traveling up to my neck and face.

"Yes, sweetheart, I'm here. I've always been here, within you. I made sure of it. It's time for me to go now, though. It's time for me to give you the last part of me that has been waiting for you."

"Don't go, Mom, please. I need you." I reach out in the darkness, but feel no one there.

"Hush now. It's alright. All you need to do is let go. You are not going to break the promise you made to me. I release you from it." Lips touch my forehead, tiny pinpricks of pain caressing there before it becomes hot, and I see flashes of light behind my closed lids.

Memory after memory rushes through my mind. Playing with Mom and Dad in the woods behind our house. Gathering the lesia flowers and giving them to Mom. Dad giving me my knife and the proud smile on his face. Mom and Dad dancing to their own music on our porch. Then pain and confinement. Hiding away from the opening of my cage when I heard footsteps. Sneers and mocking laughter taunting me as I cried. Them touching me. Josh hugging me and panicking about the amount of blood when he got me out of the basement. Josh holding me through the nights and promising me would always be with me.

Getting Kade and cuddling him as he cried after a nightmare and soothing him when he fell. Burying his mate, getting his wolf, and the smile on his face after he changed the first time. Getting our tattoos and creating the blood link. Josie helping me with her hugs and gentle touches, helping me with Kade when he would sometimes stop eating. The way her eyes lit up when they landed on Danny, and Danny twirling her around and laughing as they spoke in hushed whispers to each other. Meeting Solvier for the first time when I had tears rolling down my face in the forest, feeling so lost and having too much pressure from Eridian. Solvier curling up next to me, and me laying against him and sleeping. And him guiding and offering advice as we walked along the lakes and told me stories.

And Darius.

Darius's eyes landing on me in The Deadlands. Darius with the wisps. Darius with the wolf pups. Darius with his tattoos. Darius helping me find Sam. Darius as he held me in the cave when I had a nightmare. Kissing me under the moonlight, and looking at me with speckled silver flecks in his eyes, seeing deep into every fiber of my being.

Heat rushes through me, and I welcome it. I welcome it all with open arms as I let go.

"That's it. I'm so proud of you, sweetheart. You are strong, my girl. Show them."

"I'm scared."

"I know, Lasandrhea, but have courage and show them. Show them you will not break, that you will not surrender. Show them all exactly who. You. Are."

The heat leaves my body in a rush, the lingering touch on my forehead disappearing as my eyes spring open. My hair floats around me like I'm underwater, and I rise from the ground, barely feeling any physical pain. My legs are steady, my spine straight, and I feel power coursing through me, lighting me up from within. I keep my eyes on Darius as he follows me to standing, and I see his markings mixed into the tattoos on his neck pulse, reacting to mine on my face, neck, and torso.

He looks over my own markings, tracing them everywhere he can see them with light green eyes full of shock and awe. He follows the one in the center of my chest, traveling in delicate lines to spread along my collar bones to the top of my shoulders, then thinly up my neck. His eyes move to my face next, following my markings from my cheekbones to up and around my temples before stopping in the center of my forehead.

"So that's who you are," he whispers, reminding me of all the times he's asked as the great hall becomes silent. The last time he asked me who I was, I told him that I was someone he wouldn't want me to be.

"I'm Lasandrhea Zaphina Kazari, Canaric wolf, Heir to Zahariss, protector of the lands. You, Darius Rikoth…" I pause, watching as his eyes flash black and his markings crawl further up his neck to just below his jaw. "You are Canaric wolf, Heir to Cazier, destroyer of the below."

And then I let loose a blast of power, shattering the barrier around me and knocking him back as everyone screams.

To Be Continued…

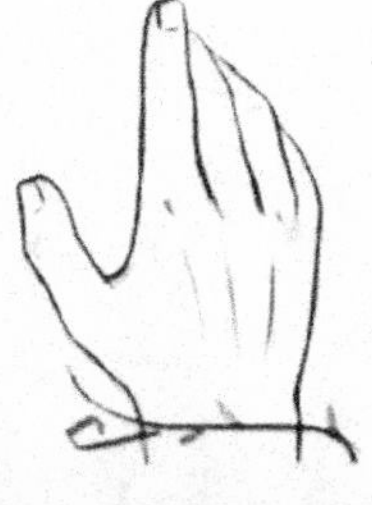

LANGUAGE

Arbiel canna – We bleed wolf
Vallier – Please
Milal - Female term of endearment
Carzan - Male term of endearment
Vihnarn – Unknown

AFTERWORD

Want an alternative POV from Darius? Keep reading to find out how.

On a scale of one to eleven, how much do you want to throw a rock at me? I mean, it's not too bad of a cliffhanger right? *nervous laughter*

Rhea was going through it at the end there wasn't she? And when I tell you I could barely write from the tears in my eyes as Danny and Josie died, gah! I felt everything in those last chapters, especially when Rhea was speaking to her mom.

I hope my words conveyed that emotion and made you feel it all too.

And Darius, oh boy, you are in for it!

I was super nervous with what Darius ended up doing to Rhea. I tried to change it, swap it, re-work it, and honestly? Their story just wouldn't let me, and I have to listen to them, their journey.

This book is so very close to my soul.

I poured everything I had into it for two years, and I can't believe it is out into the world.

This series was completely different and was meant to be a standalone, until Rhea and Darius went feral and took over completely.

It's scary and exciting and I'm so proud of my book baby.
Thank you so much for reading book one of The Hidden of Vrohkaria.
If you're interested, keep reading if you want to find out more about book two!
Much loves and reading.
-Kelly x

ACKNOWLEDGMENTS

My family.

There is simply not a word strong enough to say how much I love you. I wouldn't have clicked publish without your unwavering belief in me that I could do this. I love you to the moon and back.

Incognito

Without you, I honestly would be lost. Thank you so so much for your support.

My Alpha and Beta readers.

The feedback you gave me is invaluable, thank you so much for taking the time to help make this book what it is today.

K

With your edits, you polished it and gave it that oomph. Thank you so much.

Masochists

You know who you are, your support means the world to me. Let's always escape to other worlds together.

Reader.

You decided to take a chance and read something with your precious time.

Thank you so much. I hope you enjoyed Rhea and Darius as much as I did.

COME STALK ME

Book two in The Hidden Of Vrohkaria series is now out! Come and join my readers group for updates, teasers, giveaways and more here at – The Cove Author Kelly Cove on Facebook. **Want an alternative POV from Darius?** Scan below to see how you can grab it or visit authorkellycove.com

Made in United States
North Haven, CT
26 April 2024

51800079R00264